# OURS

Young, Dumb,
and Full of Bad Decisions

# OURS

## Dominic N. Ashen

4 Horsemen
Publications, Inc.

Published By: 4 Horsemen Publications, Inc.

4 Horsemen Publications, Inc.
PO Box 417
Sylva, NC 28779
4horsemenpublications.com
info@4horsemenpublications.com

Cover Illustration by Oxford
Cover Typography and Typesetting by Autumn Skye
Edited by Tilda M. Cooke



*Library of Congress Control Number: 2023946761*

*Paperback ISBN-13: 979-8-8232-0344-9*
*Hardcover ISBN-13: 979-8-8232-0489-7*
*Audiobook ISBN-13: 979-8-8232-0343-2*
*Ebook ISBN-13: 979-8-8232-0345-6*

# CONTENTS

# CHAPTER 1

"**N**ic, dude, you suck. Just give up and go get me a drink."

"No, Derek, *you* suck. *I'm* about to stomp Cory into the ground."

"Are you high? I've been kicking *both* of your asses all night."

It was a typical Friday night, and Derek, Nic, and Cory were spending the weekend alone at Derek's family's cabin the same way they had for the past three years. They'd been coming out here a lot longer than that, but it was only after their first year of high school that Derek's parents started letting them use it alone.

The three of them had been friends for almost ten years, meeting in the third grade and quickly bonding over a mutual love of cartoons, video games, and superhero movies. Over the years, their interests began to differ when things like girls and sports entered the picture, but through it all, they remained close. Now in their last year of school at Hartford Heights High School, though the boys seemed to run in different social groups, they still found time to spend together.

Derek Rothfield was the oldest, though only by a few months. Not *quite* a jock but still athletic, at 5'10" with dark brown hair, he had his pick of girls at school. Nic Herrera was even taller at 6'0", and being on the football team meant he also rarely had to look far for a date. His Latino background gifted him with tan olive skin and jet-black hair—hair that went *everywhere*. People often expected a much louder and brash personality, but he largely preferred keeping his emotions in check and to himself. Finally, the youngest of the group was Cory Davis. Just a little chubby, any interest he had in sports went out the window as soon as his mom got him his first computer. Now he spent most of his afternoons indoors, his curly brown hair growing shaggy and the lack of sun not doing his pale skin any favors.

All three of them were eighteen, with Cory's birthday only a month prior. For the last three years, they'd spent a couple of weekends a month in this cabin together, talking, watching TV, playing video games, and on the rare occasion, even studying. Whenever one of them was having a rough time with something, they'd all head out here together, and everything just seemed better.

"Aaaaanndd done," Cory announced to the room as the sound of an explosion and a spoken "Game!" came from the TV. Cory stood, ready to go to the kitchen. "Still want a soda, D?"

"Actually, I brought something special this time," Derek called behind him as he walked into the kitchen's pantry himself, exiting with a case of beer. He set it down on the kitchen counter and opened it, handing cans to Cory and Nic. "A gift from Tommy for starting senior year."

"Man, I wish I had a cool older brother instead of two annoying little sisters," Nic whined before taking a swig.

"Gabby caught me sneaking a beer last Christmas, and she turned *right* around and told mom."

Cory chuckled and popped open his own can, taking a sip. *Blech.* He never quite got used to the taste, but he liked the warm feeling of getting tipsy.

"Ready for another round?" Derek asked.

"Gimme a sec. Gotta pee." Cory set his drink down and walked to the bathroom.

Nic watched, waiting for the bathroom door to close. "You sure you still wanna do this, D?"

"Yeah. Why? You having second thoughts?" Derek asked in response.

"No, no, I'm still totally in but ... once we do this, there's no turning back." Nic was warning himself as much as he was Derek.

"That's the idea. We've been talking about this almost every day since we found out, and that was weeks ago. Things might change, but they're changes everyone wants," Derek reassured him.

Three weeks ago, Derek and Nic were having a very different conversation. They were at Derek's house, where Cory was helping the two of them with a history presentation they were due to give. He brought his laptop, which they used to type up their notes and put together a slide presentation. By the end of the night, Nic and Derek were almost done, but it was getting late.

"I gotta get home before my mom kills me, guys." Cory started packing up his bag. "You're almost done though, right?"

"Yeah, just need to run through it a couple of times, I think," Derek answered.

"Then you can hang onto my laptop and bring it to school tomorrow." Cory zipped up his backpack and headed toward the door. "I'll get it from you in the morning. I *really* gotta go!"

"Thanks, Cor. We'll see you tomorrow," Derek told him as he walked to the front door, watching as Cory mounted his bike and rode away. When he returned to his room, he saw Nic on his bed hunched over the laptop. He had a weird look on his face.

"Dude. You need to see this," he said without ever taking his eyes off the laptop.

"What is it? I swear if it's another one of those stupid jump scare videos, I'm gonna punch..." Derek trailed off as he stared at the screen. Staring back at him were a pair of men. A pair of men in leather gear and little else. "What the hell are you looking at?"

"I'm not looking at anything!" Derek cast Nic a withering look at his response. "I swear! I was trying to find a few more pictures for the presentation, closed the window by accident, and when I went to reopen it ... that came up." He gestured to the laptop screen.

Derek took the laptop from Nic and set it on his desk where they could both see. "So ... that means that Cory was ... looking at this stuff."

"Cory's gay?"

"Or bi. And into some pretty kinky stuff, apparently," Derek reasoned. He clicked through a few of the other tabs. "*Really* kinky."

There were a lot of open tabs, all of them carrying a similar theme: domination. Videos of guys being tied up, spanked, or fucked. Online sex shops selling things like cock cages and collars. Stories about guys being overpowered and used by their friends, bosses, teachers, cops—anyone with authority. It was like they had a full roadmap to all of Cory's desires.

"We shouldn't be looking at this," Derek decided even though his hand was still moving the mouse to the next tab.

"I just can't believe Cory ... I mean, I guess the gay thing isn't that big of a leap, but shit." Nic pointed at an image of a guy strapped to some sort of bench. There were two other men with him, one at either end, cock inserted. "*This* is the kind of stuff he's into?"

Even though they knew they shouldn't, the two boys spent the next few hours scouring Cory's laptop, curiosity urging them to learn more about their friend's proclivities. They didn't know it then, but something had been awakened in them both, something they never knew existed. New doors were being opened, whether they wanted them to or not.

Many, many hours later and far further into the night than either of them intended, Derek made the call. "Okay, that's it. We gotta stop. We need to finish the project and go to bed." He paused. "We *cannot* tell Cory about this."

"Yeah, man. I don't even know what to do with this info." Nic was more than a little confused, and the half-boner he was trying to hide in his shorts wasn't helping.

"Nothing. He's still Cory, still our bro. He just likes dick. Rough, kinky dick." Derek half-laughed. "We pretend this never happened."

Nic returned Cory's laptop the next day after making sure to scrub any evidence of their snooping or discoveries. As the days went on, neither Nic nor Derek could get the images from that night out of their heads. The more they thought about it, the more the idea of having someone on hand to sexually service them appealed to them. Not that they told each other.

At the same time, this led to more than a few weird interactions with Cory, who was becoming increasingly concerned about his friends' mental wellbeing. The normally eloquent Derek started stumbling over his words when a girl brought up *Fifty Shades of Grey* at lunch, and Nic nearly spat out his milk when Cory taunted his friend Stephanie with a "Why, gonna spank me?" Finally, after a week full of this, both boys were pushed to the edge—and Nic was the first one to break.

[Nic: Dude, are you up? I need to talk to you.]

The text notification chirped from Derek's phone, who was still awake and lying in bed, preoccupied with his own thoughts of bondage and domination.

[Derek: Yeah what's up?]

[Nic: Nah, in person. Can I come over?]

It was late but Derek's parents were out of town, so they would be none the wiser.

[Derek: Sure man, text me when you get here.]

He grabbed a pair of shorts and waited for his friend's arrival.

About fifteen minutes later, they were both back in Derek's room, speaking in hushed tones despite the house being empty.

"It's Cory. Or the stuff about Cory," Nic started. "I can't stop thinking about it."

"Me neither, man," Derek reassured his panicky friend. "I can barely even look at him sometimes, not without imagining him in those … situations."

"Are we gay?! Am I gay?!" Nic's voice nearly cracked, puberty be damned.

"Calm down, dude, seriously. I don't think it's a gay or straight thing. In like half those stories, the guys doing the dominating were straight." Derek knew this, of course, because he had gone back to reread some of them on his own. "It was about control, power. Replace any of those guys with a girl, and we'd still be into it." Not that he had tested that theory out yet.

"So what do we do?" Nic sat next to Derek on his bed. "I just want things to get back to the way they were before."

"I'm not sure they can ever get back to that, bro." Derek wrapped his arm around Nic's shoulder. "But maybe there's something else we can do..."

The flush of a toilet preceded Cory's return.

"Just follow my lead like we talked. I've got a plan," Derek reassured Nic.

Cory rejoined them on the couch in front of the TV, taking the center spot. "Alright, what are we doing?" Cory asked, taking another sip of beer.

"We do another round of Smash Bros., but this time we make it a little more interesting—we make it a drinking game," Derek responded.

"I dunno..." Cory started, sounding worried before smirking. "I wouldn't wanna give you guys alcohol poisoning."

"Nah, that's way too easy. Instead of the loser drinking, the winner does," Derek explained. "Every time you win a round, you take a drink. Think of it like a handicap to help the losers catch up." They had played drinking games before, mostly when watching bad movies together, but never against each other like this.

"You guys saying the only way you can beat me is if you get me drunk?" Cory challenged.

"Why? You not good enough to do it a little tipsy?" Nic taunted from Cory's other side.

Cory narrowed his eyes at Derek. "Let's go."

By the end of the third match, Cory was halfway through his can while Nic and Derek had barely started on their first. By the end of the *eighth* match, Cory had started on his third beer, and Nic and Derek had only just opened their *second*.

"You guys suuuuuuuuuck," Cory jeered, the alcohol causing him to draw out his words just a little too much. Then he stood suddenly. "Dammit, I have to pee again."

Nic waited until the door closed before turning to Derek. "I don't think we should let him drink much more. He's gonna get sick."

"Yeah, I know. Don't worry. This is going better than I hoped. Time to cinch this," Derek reassured him once more before Cory rejoined them.

After losing the next round in a rather spectacular display of inebriated coordination, Derek put forward the next step of his plan. "Alright, wow. I think we can say the playing field has been sufficiently leveled." Cory narrowed his eyes as he took a non-mandated sip of his beer. "No more drinking game for you. Let's switch to something else."

"Like what?"

"Strip poker. Or Strip Smash Bros., I guess." Nic spat out his drink at hearing Derek's suggestion. After giving his choking friend a strange look, Derek continued, "Since you're sufficiently drunk now, 'normal' rules: You lose a match, you lose a piece of clothing."

Nic had moved to the kitchen to finish his beer induced coughing fit, though it wasn't him that Derek was worried about accepting. He watched as Cory pondered the suggestion for a moment, the alcohol-lubricated gears turning in his head.

"I'm in." As Derek suspected, it didn't take much.

"You finished choking so we can get back to playing? Are you scared of someone seeing your dick?" Derek shouted toward the kitchen, Nic shooting him a glare as he walked back to the sofa, tossing the beer-soaked shirt at his face. "Well crap. If you were gonna take it off for free, I wouldn't have gotten the beer."

"Just shut up and play," Nic grumbled as he grabbed his controller.

As the night wore on and the beer cans were emptied, the clothing started coming off. A few rounds in and Cory was only in his jeans and underwear while Derek had only lost his socks, and Nic was still only missing his shirt.

"Nooooo, not again," Cory groaned as he lost his 4th match in a row. "Guys, come on. You don't want to see me in my underwear, do you?"

"Drop 'em, bud," Derek ordered, arms crossed over his chest. Nic looked at him expectedly.

With a dramatic sigh, Cory undid the fly on his jeans. Shoving them down to his ankles, he stood in front of his best friends, arms stretched out in classic, sarcastic "ta-da!" fashion.

"Happy? Weird-ooohhhshit!" Cory tripped over the jeans bunched up at his ankles, toppling unceremoniously to the floor. He angrily kicked off his jeans from around his feet as Nic and Derek laughed from the couch.

"You doing okay there, Cor?" Nic asked.

"Just shut up and play," Cory grumbled.

Luck was still not with Cory as he proceeded to lose yet another match, this time to Nic. Derek removed his shirt and looked at Cory for his turn.

"But I'll be naked," he protested.

"Yeah. That's what the 'strip' stands for. Lose 'em!" Derek ordered.

Cory stood still for a moment, clearly considering whether to grab his jeans and make a run for it. Then he remembered he was currently only in a pair of white briefs, stuck in the middle of the forest. Eventually and reluctantly, Cory quickly shucked off his underwear, dropping to sit on the floor and cover his cock and balls with his hands.

"There. You win. Can I put my clothes back on now?" he asked.

Derek smiled and took another swig of beer. "Who said we were done?"

"But I don't have anything else to take off," Cory reasoned.

"Guess me and Derek will have to think of something for you to do when you lose again," Nic chimed in, finally catching on to the plan.

"Like what?"

"I dunno. What about some of the things those leather daddies you like watching so much have their boys do?" Derek deadpanned, looking Cory right in the face.

Cory was sure he didn't hear that correctly. "Wha-What are you talking about, dude?" *Fuck. How did they find out? They didn't find out. Did they? Fuck.*

"That *was* your laptop you left at my place, right? The one with all the videos of guys in bondage and leather, the one with all the stories about boys like you being tied up and spanked? Pretty kinky stuff, man," Derek continued.

"I..."

"Cory." Nic put his hand on Cory's shoulder. "He's just fucking with you. It's okay, man. We don't care, really."

"Kinda the opposite. We actually think this could be a great thing. For all of us." Derek put his hand on the opposite shoulder.

"What... What are you guys talking about?" Between the alcohol and having his best friends reveal one of his deepest secrets, Cory's head was spinning. "How did you even..."

"Reopened a few too many browser windows when we were working on that history project. Sorry about that," Derek explained. "But as I was saying, there's nothing to worry about. You're still our friend, our brother. If anything, this opens up new stuff for us."

"What do you mean 'new stuff'?" Cory, red-faced and on the floor, still didn't understand what was going on.

"I think you know exactly what we mean, Cory. Nic and I have been talking about it since that night. Let's just say what this is: you're not just gay; you like the idea of a guy telling you what to do, throwing you around, right?" Derek and Nic were circling their prey, and Derek was going in for the kill.

"I-I don't know... I've ever done anything with a-anyone. It started with looking at porn, then I read a few stories..." Cory was unable to meet either of their gazes, trying to burn a hole in the cabin's rug with his mind. "I don't know what I like."

"Then why don't you let us help you figure it out?" Nic offered.

"W-What the hell are you talking about?" Cory's head shot up.

"Well... you're gay, and as far as you know, you like being ordered around to do sexual stuff to other guys." Now it was Derek's turn. "Last time I checked, Nic here and I both really liked blowjobs, and it's not like we'd get to try any of this stuff with our girlfriends. You get to lose your virginity and get in some practice before college, and we get our dicks sucked. Everybody wins."

"Isn't that kinda ... *gay* though?" Cory reasoned.

"If you think either of us are gonna return the favor, you've had more beer than I realized," Nic answered, stone-faced.

"But I think we all know that's how you want it," Derek added. "So what's it gonna be, Cory? You in?"

Cory sat in silence on the floor, contemplating his situation. He was feeling about a million things at once. The alcohol was making his head fuzzy, and he was starting to sweat. He was scared that his secret was out, but at the same time, he was relieved to not have to hide it from his best friends anymore. He was angry at them for having gone through his computer but also at himself for stupidly lending out his laptop without thinking to clear his history first. But even more than any of those things, he was horny.

Neither of them could tell, but half the reason he was still hiding his cock with his hands was because his erection had been steadily growing since he first got naked. How many times had he imagined something like this happening? Maybe not with his best friends (that he would admit to), but Cory had jerked off while imagining this exact scenario countless times. A strong, hot, guy dominating him and taking what he wanted. And now he had not just one, but two guys willing to do that. Maybe it was the beer talking, maybe he would regret it later, but right then, Cory could only say one thing.

"Okay. Yes. I'll do it."

"Yes, *sir*," Derek's correction surprised him for a moment.

"Yes, sir," Cory tried again.

"Good boy." Derek smiled as he turned to Nic. "So who gets the first blowjob?"

"Rock, paper, scissors?" Nic suggested.

"Let's go."

Cory couldn't believe his two friends were deciding which dick he would suck first with rock-paper-scissors like he wasn't sitting on the floor naked in front of them... Actually, it seemed exactly like something they'd do.

His cock was hard as a rock.

"Ha! I win!" Derek exclaimed gleefully. He spread his legs wide on the couch and patted the space between his thighs, smirking cockily. "Why don't you get comfortable down there, boy?"

Hesitating for a moment, Cory walked on his knees toward Derek, hands still attempting to conceal his very obvious erection. Once he was seated, he looked up for instruction. Even with all the porn he'd watched, he had no idea how this was supposed to go.

"Unzip me" was the first order.

Reluctantly revealing his crotch, Cory reached slowly toward Derek's zipper. He was so nervous his hand was shaking. Any moment now, he was sure they were both gonna jump up and say this whole thing was a prank.

"Well, looks like you were right that he'd be into this, D." Nic chuckled at Cory's hard cock.

Cory's face—and body—burned red with embarrassment at Nic's joke, and he hesitated while reaching for Derek's zipper.

"Hey." Derek was gently holding his wrist, not allowing him to pull it away. "It's okay, Cor. He's just messing with you, like always. We know you like this stuff. That's why we're doing this."

With a gentle smile on his face and Cory's wrist still in his hand, he drew Cory's hand up his thigh until it rested on the half-hard cock bulging through his jeans. Cory was breathing heavily, eyes glued to the mound under his hand. He gave a tentative squeeze, feeling Derek flex involuntarily. Growing bolder, he gripped it a little more confidently, stroking his hand up and down the length through the fabric as Derek continued to smile down at him.

"Good boy. Now, unzip me," he repeated his earlier instruction.

With a bit more confidence, Cory released Derek's cock and moved to his fly. After a little fumbling with the button, he managed to open the fly and get the zipper down. Derek was wearing a pair of green boxer briefs, his cock producing a sizeable bulge in the center. Cory once again grabbed and stroked it through the fabric, seeing a small wet spot form as it leaked precum.

"Now, pull my cock out of my boxers," Derek continued his instructions.

"Yes, sir." The words were out of Cory's mouth without thinking.

Swallowing his nervousness, Cory reached for the waistband of the boxers with one hand and pulled them down. With his free hand, he reached in and grabbed the first cock he'd ever touched aside from his own. It was warm. Like, *really* warm. And fuck, it was big too. Cory figured he was average sized himself, nothing to be upset about, but holy crap, this was bigger than he was for sure. He tucked the waistband underneath Derek's big, hairy balls before giving them a grope and squeeze too, causing Derek to inhale sharply.

"Shit, careful. My nuts are sensitive as hell," he warned. "Ball play always gets me going. Don't worry, boy. We are gonna teach you exactly what we like."

Cory could only nod, transfixed by the cock in his hands. Derek was content to let him play with it for now, slowly stroking it up and down. He *definitely* owed his brother for that beer after this. After enough stroking, another bead of precum gathered on his cockhead, and Derek saw an opportunity to move the training along.

"Now, Cor," he started, "I want you to put my cock in your mouth. Just the head." He made sure his tone was gentle. He'd been imagining what it would be like to train Cory to suck his cock all week.

Cory's mouth had never felt drier, but he was still so fucking horny. Grabbing the cock firmly in his hand, he pointed it toward his face and lowered his mouth, making Derek hiss as the warm mouth enveloped his cockhead.

"Good boy." He rubbed Cory's head like a pet. "Now, move your tongue around. Get a real feel and a taste of me." He leaned his head back and enjoyed the sensations of a tongue on his cock. It had been a while since he had gotten a girl to do this.

Cory was having as much fun as Derek. As the first bit of precum hit his tongue, he moaned around the cock in his mouth. The taste was unexpected, but knowing what it was just drove him to want more. He sucked gently as he swirled his tongue around Derek's head, hearing the words of encouragement coming from above him. Inhaling through his nose, Cory let Derek's musk fill his senses. *Holy fuck, this smells amazing. Why didn't I do this sooner?* He moaned again, feeling Derek's hands move to his head as he sucked.

"Okay, now try to take more, as much as you can before you start to gag." This was more instruction than Derek had ever given to any of the girls he'd fucked, but they were also pretty bad at it, so maybe he should start. "Then pull back and do it again."

Cory complied as best as he could, managing to take about half of Derek's cock in before he pulled off, suddenly coughing.

"Heh, gotta go slower than that at first." Derek pet his head again. "Don't worry. We'll get that gag reflex trained right out of you."

"Starting to feel a little left out over here," Nic said impatiently from his spot on the couch.

"He's only got one mouth, Nic," Derek pointed out.

"Yeah, but he's got two hands, D," Nic fired back.

"Dude, fine, whatever. Just quit ruining my blowjob."

With a gleeful snicker, Nic quickly undid his own pants before scooting down the couch to sit right next to Derek, their thighs touching. Derek sent him another withering look before turning his attention back to Cory.

With one of his hands, Cory fumbled along Derek's thigh until he found Nic's. Not one for patience, Nic moved the hand directly to his cock, already pulled out of his underwear. Cory groaned a little as he felt the heat in his hand.

Cory continued to practice swallowing down Derek's cock while simultaneously attempting to stroke Nic's. Luckily for him, neither of these boys had all that much experience and seemed pretty happy with the job he was doing so far. He was still gagging on occasion but was now able to take much more dick than when he started. Derek's hand hadn't left his hair, never quite pushing him down but letting him feel its presence. Unable to see past the crotch in his face, he could only assume that Nic was alright with what he was doing from the lack of complaints.

"Alright, time to switch. My dick is starting to chafe," Nic said with perfect timing as always.

"Fiiiiiiine. Just stop whining," Derek said with a groan. He looked down at Cory, who looked back with a dick in his mouth. "Boy, now move over to him, and keep using your hand on me."

"Yeththir." Cory spoke with his mouth still full before releasing Derek's cock and shuffling over to Nic, looking up at him expectantly. His cock was just as large as Derek's, maybe even a little longer. And it was uncut.

"Get to it, boy." Nic nodded toward his dick wearing a cocky smile, leaning back with his hands behind his head.

"Yessir" was Cory's reply before taking the second cock of the night—and his life—into his mouth.

Now that he knew some of what he was doing, it was easier this time around. He bobbed up and down on the first few inches, wrapping his hand around the part of the shaft that he couldn't reach without gagging yet. The foreskin was different, and when Cory ran his tongue along it, a burst of precum shot into his mouth. Without needing to be told again, he took his remaining free hand and moved toward Derek's crotch with some assistance.

Still buzzed from the beer, Cory seemed to almost zone out as he sucked and jerked his friends. If they were talking to him, he wasn't hearing it. The scents surrounding him only served to intoxicate him further, pushing any other thoughts and the rest of the world away. Nic smelled and tasted different than Derek. With both being athletic teenage boys, there were some similarities, but Nic tasted just a little saltier, or at least not as sweet as Derek. *Maybe it's their diets.*

"Wow, he's really into this," Derek mused, watching Cory swallow down Nic. "He's a natural."

"Ehn, he's doing alright." Nic, ever the impatient one, was ready to move things along. "Time to really kick start his training, don't you think?"

Derek gave a puzzled look as Nic placed one hand on the back of Cory's head and pushed down. Not expecting the sudden manual guidance, Cory gagged as the cock hit the back of his throat and pulled off coughing. Nic chuckled as he regained his composure.

"Sorry about that. Just trying to help." Cory shot Nic a glare. "Hey, watch it, boy. Back on your knees." His tone was almost daring him to say no.

"Yes, sir. Sorry," Cory apologized and moved back to his spot between Nic's legs. He didn't want this to stop either.

"Okay. I want you to try to take as much of my cock as you can and then hold it." As Nic spoke, he placed his hand back on Cory's head. "We start with just a few seconds and then have you work up to going longer and longer. We'll have you swallowing our cocks in no time."

Cory looked at Nic, annoyed, cock still lodged in his mouth.

"Let's go, boy." With a push, his head was lowered further. Cory went as far as he could go before stopping, feeling the head of Nic's cock tickling the back of his throat.

"Alright, Cor, I've trained *tons* of girls to deep throat my cock. I gotchu," Nic lied a little. It was *maybe* two, but that was still more experience than Cory had. "Breathe through your nose and try to keep your throat relaxed."

*Easy for you to say.* That was Cory's final thought before having his throat stretched around a dick for the first time. It started out so fine, Cory almost hadn't realized anything had happened. He felt the cock in his throat alright; it was just more pressure really.

Then he tried to swallow.

"I told you not to swallow." As Cory coughed and hacked his lungs up on the floor, Nic could only look down on him and sigh.

"No, you didn't!" Cory choked out between coughs.

"Oh. Well, I meant to. Don't swallow. You're not at that skill level yet." Nic spoke as though this was very obvious information that Cory should have known.

With another glare, Cory resumed his position in front of Nic. Nic was very tempted to point out he did so without being asked, but he bit his tongue. Instead, he put his hand back on Cory's head and guided him back to the now spit-slick cock.

Cory fared better this time around. Soon, he was able to take just over half of Nic's dick without gagging. He learned to time his breathing, zoning out as he methodically bobbed up and down, the smells and tastes once again clouding his senses.

"Fuck, see? He *is* a natural," Derek said from his spot on the couch, transfixed by the scene next to him.

"Oh yeah, you definitely pegged him for this," Nic agreed with a sigh. Cory seemed to not hear them, content to continue swallowing down more dick.

The longer Cory sucked, the more attuned to the tastes of his friend he became. Nic was steadily leaking precum directly onto his tongue every time his dick passed over it, and the thought was causing Cory to subconsciously salivate even more, some escaping around his lips and down Nic's cock as he would pull back. Cory either didn't notice or didn't care, content to continue doing this all night...

Which is why the second hand on his head, suddenly forcing him all the way down was more than a little surprising. As was the way Nic's cock seemed to grow thicker for a moment before it began shooting his load directly into Cory's throat. After only two spurts, Cory pulled back, once again violently hacking and coughing onto the floor. A single shot landed on Cory's face as he fell on his ass, Nic's remaining load spilling out onto his thigh.

Cory again glared up at Nic, who was cracking up on the couch at his reaction, dick still in hand. Derek attempted to maintain his composure but was unable to stop a few snorts escaping over Cory's predicament.

"Sorry, Cor! Shoulda warned you I was about to shoot, but I didn't want you chickening out and pulling back!" Nic explained through laughs. "A good cocksucker is supposed to swallow, especially the loads of hot straight studs like me." He flashed his teeth in a cocky smile.

Cory continued to glare, looking for his discarded shirt to wipe his face. He coughed a few more times, each time tasting a little more of Nic's load as it exited his airway, swallowing it back down without thinking about it. Now that he wasn't choking to death, he didn't mind the taste. But Nic didn't have to be such a dick about it.

"Come here, boy." Derek patted his thigh. "I'll treat you better than that dumb asshole." He wiggled his hard cock with his other hand.

With one final glare, Cory moved back over to Derek. He liked him better, he decided. And to prove that, he lowered his mouth to Derek's cock without being told and began repeating the skills he had just finished practicing on Nic.

Derek was thicker than Nic, so finding the right rhythm took a second. Cory could feel his throat being stretched even further than before as he made a few experimental test bobs. Once he had it set though, he felt confident in his skills.

Partly because he wanted to show Derek thanks for his relative kindness, largely because he wanted to stick it to Nic, and entirely because of the alcohol, Cory decided to try a few things. Just with his hands, for now. He started by gently running them up and down Derek's thighs. Then he brushed one hand against his balls in time with the bobbing of his head, eliciting a gentle sigh from Derek's mouth. He gripped onto the warm sack a little more firmly and allowed his remaining free hand to roam higher, against Derek's stomach and chest.

"Shit, I didn't get that kind of treatment," Nic whined.

"Well, I'm not a dick," Derek replied without ever looking up. Cory's eyes were closed, either in concentration or because he had once again zoned out, but either way, he looked almost peaceful. Happy, even. Derek could feel his own load building up, nearly ready to rise to the surface.

Not wanting to repeat Nic's behavior, Derek spoke up as he got closer. "I'm getting close, Cor. I want you to swallow my load, okay?" Cory opened his eyes and looked up as he continued to suck. "I'm gonna pull back so most of it lands in your mouth, but you're gonna need to swallow fast—I cum a lot."

Cory nodded as he continued to suck, now determined to see this through to the finish. He could feel the weighty sack in his hand as it started to tighten and draw up. Cory could easily believe that Derek shot massive loads, and he was about to find out first-hand—no, first-mouth.

"Fuuuuck, boy, here it comes." Derek gripped his cock as it slid most of the way out of Cory's mouth, whose lips were still clamped tightly around his head. Grabbing his cock, he jerked himself steadily, unloading directly into Cory's mouth.

Cory felt the first few spurts land on his tongue, his mouth immediately filled with the salty and musty taste of cum for the second time that evening. It wasn't as salty as Nic's, maybe even a little sweeter if he could call it that. He didn't exactly have a lot to compare to. He did have a mouth that was filling up quickly though, so he swallowed down what he could as Derek continued to squeeze out every last drop with his hand.

"Suck out anything left and then swallow, Cor," Derek ordered, taking a deep breath and letting his hand fall to his side

"Yes, sir." Cory did as he was asked, and after emptying his mouth, looked up at his friends. "Thank you, sir?" That last part came out like a question.

"Fast learner," Nic announced.

"Told you. A natural. Practically born for this," Derek said, looking down at Cory with a hungry gaze. Cory looked back, a little afraid and *very* turned on. "And the weekend is just getting started."

# CHAPTER 2

Cory awoke groggily the next morning. At least, he thought it was morning. Peeking his eyes open, he saw that the sun was up and probably had been for some time. He was on the pull-out couch with Derek while Nic slept on the other couch in the cabin's common area. His head was still fuzzy and his mouth was dry, but at least he wasn't hungover. He pulled his blanket over his head, trying to force himself back asleep, the sounds of Nic's light snoring coming from the other couch. Slowly, the previous night's events began to creep back into his head.

*Okay. So your friends know you're gay. That … That's fine. You were going to tell them, eventually… You were just waiting until you were far, far away in college. This wasn't how you planned to do this, but you also didn't plan on sucking their dicks. Oh my god, you sucked their dicks. You sucked both their dicks, next to each other. They wanted you to suck their dicks.*

*They wanted you to do more than just suck their dicks. It was like they planned the whole night out! …Shit, they planned the whole night out. How long have they been waiting to do this? We still have like a day and a half before we have to go back to school on Monday. What else did they plan? I mean, they definitely had fun last night. We all did. Right?*

Cory's mind reeled, the stream of consciousness in his head never slowing down. *What does this mean? Are we still friends? Are we still going to hang out how we used to? Are they going to tell anyone else?* He lay there for nearly an hour, brain never slowing enough to allow him to fall back to sleep. Just as he was about to get up, he heard Nic stirring and he stilled, not ready to face ... whatever this was yet. Maybe another hour would help. Or a year. Or ten.

From his sleeping spot, Cory listened as Nic got up, eventually walking to the bathroom to pee. Then he heard some rustling and the sound of keys being grabbed before the door was opened, closed, and locked. Cory released his breath and relaxed.

*That was dumb. It's not like I can avoid this forever. Or even that much longer. Maybe I should just go home. If I get dressed and start walking now, I can have Mom meet me at the gas station down the road in like thirty minutes.*

Just as Cory was gathering enough courage to put his own plan in motion, Derek shifted on the bed, rolling over, his arm falling over Cory's waist. After waiting a moment, Cory attempted to slip Derek's arm off him when the sleeping boy moved again. Cory's eyes went wide as he felt Derek's arm tighten and pull him back, pressing him against his chest.

Cory's voice caught in his throat. This was even weirder than whatever last night ended up being. What was Derek doing trying to cuddle him? *Isn't he straight?*

The sound of incoherent mumbling gave him his answer: Derek was still asleep.

Slowly, Cory's panic abated. Things were confusing enough as they were. Besides, it felt nice being held like this.

He could see doing this with a boyfriend or something in the future. Derek shifted again, this time grinding his crotch forward against Cory's ass, making the smaller boy's breath hitch. He had been ignoring his own morning wood this entire time, traitorously betraying any protests about his feelings regarding the prior evening.

This ... This, Cory could definitely see doing again. Fuck, that cock was big. It was a miracle his jaw wasn't still sore this morning. As Derek continued to periodically grind his cock against Cory, Cory began to subconsciously grind his ass back to meet him. The arm around his waist remained tight, but there was no indication that Derek was waking up. Mentally exhausted from all of the emotional hoops he'd been jumping through this morning, Cory managed to stop thinking and let himself enjoy this.

Cory was not new to having his butt played with. It was just that prior to today, he was the only one who had ever played with it. It wasn't like Derek was hitting the "target" anyway, but they were both in only their underwear—he could feel *everything*. Cory continued to grind his ass back onto Derek's cock, feeling every time it pulsed against him. He started angling his hips more and more, as much as he could with Derek's grip on his waist. If he could just move this way a little bit...

"WAKE UP! IT'S TIME FOR BREAKFAST!!!!" Nic's shout echoed through the room as he burst through the front door. Cory hadn't even heard the lock.

Cory couldn't hear anything over the sounds of his ears ringing and his heart pounding. His face was currently buried in the mattress, having barely fought the urge to scream in surprise at Nic's sudden return to the cabin. Derek was also startled awake, pulling away from him suddenly. As they both attempted to calm down, Nic dropped two McDonald's bags on the table before moving into the kitchen, all the while singing "Oh, What a Beautiful Mornin'" at an obnoxiously loud volume. Once he had caught his breath, Cory turned over, looking at Derek who met his gaze. He gave Cory a strange look for a second, a half-smile, like he couldn't remember something, before turning and standing from the bed.

"Thanks, and you're an asshole," he announced as Nic walked back into the room, both of them homing in on the bags of food.

Cory looked on in near disbelief before he heard his stomach growl. Fuck, he was hungry. After willing most of his erection away, he got off the bed and joined them, grabbing one of the sandwiches and tucking in.

"Fanks," he said around the sausage, egg, and biscuit in his mouth.

"Figured you would have learned last night not to talk with your mouth full," Nic teased from across the table, making Cory blush.

As the trio ate their breakfast together, Cory began to relax. Things felt like they always had, the three of them hanging out, having fun, being friends. Other than the full mouth comment, neither friend had made any attempt to push things in the direction they went last night. Cory felt somewhat relieved but also confused. What else were they plotting?

The rest of the day was pretty much the same. After eating, the three lounged around the cabin for a bit. Not like they had anything to do. They headed into town in the afternoon to grab some lunch, bringing it back to the cabin to eat. As the sun was setting, the boys were once again around the TV, this time watching a movie.

"This is somehow both the best and worst thing we've ever watched here," Cory said to no one in particular. The killer clowns were going on a rampage through town, though for what none of the three viewers could tell you.

"I dunno. *The Room* was pretty fantastically terrible," Nic called back.

"Hey, Cor, toss this in the sink and grab us some beers." Derek held out his empty glass and continued watching the TV, not waiting for a response.

"Uh, sure, D." Cory accepted the glass (and order) and moved toward the kitchen.

As he grabbed some of the remaining beers from the fridge, a feeling grew in the pit of his stomach. Something was coming. He walked back into the room and handed the cans to Derek and Nic, keeping one for himself.

"Good boy," Derek said, entirely sincere, and returned to watching the movie.

Cory then realized that the two of them had moved onto the couch, and he no longer had a seat of his own. He gave them both an annoyed look before sitting on the floor between them, nursing his beer. He was gonna need it.

Nic was next to ask for something: a bag of chips. Cory received another "good boy" for his troubles. Was this their plan after last night's blowjob training? Seriously?

After being given a few more minor tasks—another beer, Derek's phone, turning off a lamp—Cory had resigned himself to it being a boring night. He was sadder about that fact than he wanted to admit to himself. So Derek's next order caught him off guard.

"Cory, boy, why don't you move over here?" Derek spoke as he pointed to the floor between his legs. "My feet are killing me. Could use a foot rub."

"Uh." Cory looked to where Derek was pointing before looking at the two of them on the couch. Nic was smirking, wanting to see what was going to happen next, but Derek was simply smiling gently. Expectantly. "O-okay, sir. I mean, yes, sir."

Cory moved into position, back now turned to the TV. He could still hear it, but he wasn't paying attention anymore. Right now, Derek had all his attention. As he took Derek's right foot into his hands, he looked up and met Derek's eyes, his friend smiling down at him before returning to the movie. Well, Derek had his attention, but he wasn't giving it back to Cory. Something about that made it even hotter.

Cory got to work. He was by no means an expert at giving foot massages, but he did his best with what knowledge he had. He rubbed his hands over it gently at first before tightening his grip and starting to press in on the muscle.

"Mmm, that's good," Derek said with a groan above him.

Cory smiled, growing more confident with his hands. Every noise of pleasure from Derek was like fuel on the fire. Once he had finished with the right foot, he moved onto the left. Starting off gently as he had done before, Cory watched Derek's face this time as he worked. He did that. He was responsible for making Derek feel good.

"Fuck, boy. That was great." Derek was practically melted into the couch, a puddle. "Definitely going to have you do that again."

"Alright, my turn." Nic stuck both his feet out like a child. "Let's see if you're really that good."

"Yes, sir." Cory rolled his eyes and moved over to Nic.

He began his work again, having a routine worked out now. Nic was much, much more expressive than Derek had been with a near-constant litany of under-the-breath moans and barely muttered "holy fucks." He was also more ticklish than Derek, and Cory had a hard time holding onto his foot at times. Still, he once again enjoyed watching the face of his friend as he worked, knowing what a good job he was doing.

Eventually, he was done. The movie was still playing, but Cory had no interest in turning around to finish watching now. He remained in his spot on the floor in front of Nic, waiting to see what they might want next.

"Fuck, that was good. Good job, boy." Nic tousled his hair as he praised him. It actually felt sincere this time, too. "And since you're already down there..."

Nic began rubbing his cock through his shorts. Cory's eyes were drawn to Nic's hand and what it was doing, and he subconsciously licked his lips. He wanted more.

"Yes, sir." He shifted onto his knees, moving closer to the couch.

Feeling confident after the foot rubs, Cory didn't wait for Nic to pull his cock out and began to grope it through the fabric himself. He could feel it pulse as it grew under his hand. He then reached up toward Nic's waistband and pulled it down.

Nic raised himself up slightly, allowing Cory to pull his shorts and underwear all the way off. Cory kneeled between Nic's naked thighs staring at the exposed, pulsing cock. He reached forward to take it in his hand and began to gently stroke it, pulling the hood back over the head.

*Here we are again, old friend*, he told the dick in his hand. Laughing to himself, he aimed the dick toward his mouth and lowered his head, wrapping his lips around the head.

Nic let out a gentle sigh as Cory began bobbing up and down his cock.

"Shit, that took a lot less work than last night," Derek said from his seat, watching the show in front of him. "See, boy? Everyone is getting something they want. Don't overthink it."

Cory took note of Derek's words as he continued to work, trying to swallow down more cock without gagging. It wasn't easy, and memories of last night began filling Cory's head. He managed to swallow nearly three-quarters of Nic's dick before his gag reflex kicked in. So he soldiered on, figuring out just how much gagging he could take, drool escaping around the cock in his mouth.

After he found a good rhythm, Cory lost himself in what he was doing for a few minutes until he was brought out of his haze by someone grabbing his wrist. To his left, Derek's pants were already off, and he had clearly been jerking himself. Now he was closer and expected Cory to start multitasking. They were training him, after all.

Cory gripped Derek's cock and gently stroked his hand up and down. It took a little practice at first, but he was soon able to stroke Derek's dick with the same rhythm he was sucking Nic's. Neither boy made any attempt to slow down or change what he was doing. It seemed to be a pleasant surprise how easily and eagerly Cory was servicing them.

For his part, Cory simply wasn't letting himself think too much about it. He knew he would probably regret doing that later, but he also knew that he would have regretted not doing this when he had the chance. Derek was right. Everyone was getting something they wanted, so why fight it?

Without being told, Cory switched over to Derek. With his own saliva slicking the way, Cory stroked his hand up and down Nic's cock as he swallowed down Derek's. Already warmed up, he began to work the cock into his throat right away.

"Holy... Damn, boy!" Derek was happily surprised by the eager mouth. "Slow down. There's plenty of dick to go around."

Cory looked up at Derek, smiling with his eyes as he continued to work his mouth. He was enjoying the small amount of power this gave him over these two. Derek narrowed his eyes but smiled back. *Uh-oh. That's his "I've got a bad idea" face.*

Cory once again threw himself into his work, finding a good rhythm, and again lost track of everything except the now two cocks in his mouth and hands. He continued to swap between the two of them, spending a few minutes on one cock while stroking the other, and then switching. All the while, he kept trying to push himself further, to take them deeper, to hold his breath longer. The boy was well on his way to becoming a grade-A cocksucker.

The movie had long since ended, and no one currently on the couch could tell you how. In fact, as soon as Cory started groping Nic's crotch, any thoughts they had of watching the movie flew out the window too. Content to allow Cory to work, both boys could only lay back and watch. With Cory switching between them every few minutes, neither boy was particularly close to finishing. Cory had just moved back over to Derek from Nic when Nic got up from the couch. Cory paused, cock halfway in his mouth, and looked over.

"Keep going, boy. I'll be right back. Just gonna find something..." He trailed off as he headed toward the kitchen.

Cory resumed his blowjob, giving no more thought to whatever Nic might be up to. With only one person to worry about now, Cory could focus entirely on what he was doing to Derek. Cory became so focused on Derek that he was startled when he felt Nic touch his hip from behind, causing Derek to stifle a laugh.

"It's just me, Cor." Nic spoke to him gently. "Keep going. Just figured this was a good time to start the next part of your training." Cory felt his underwear being tugged down and heard the sound of a plastic cap being popped open. "This is gonna feel a little cold."

*What is he talking abou—AAAHHH!* Cory let out a yelp of surprise as he felt the cold, presumably lube-covered finger touch his ass, pulling off Derek's cock quickly. Little was an understatement. He turned and quickly pressed his back against the couch, protecting his backside from further prodding.

"What are you doing?!" Cory asked, as though he didn't already know.

Which was exactly the look Nic gave him.

"I think you know what I'm doing, Cory," Nic responded calmly. "We all know this wasn't going to stop at blowjobs. You know you wouldn't *want* to stop at blowjobs."

"But can't we ... talk about it first?" Cory fretted, almost whining.

"Okay. Let's talk about it," Nic continued in his calm demeanor. "You've enjoyed everything we've done so far, haven't you?"

Cory nodded. It may not have been how he would have liked for some of this to go down, but he couldn't deny how turned on he had been by everything. Not even just the sex but the domination—the parts where Cory had no say, where Nic and Derek had just taken and ordered.

"And you want to keep going, right?" Nic continued.

Cory nodded again, hesitantly. He thought he did. He was just a little nervous about everything that entailed.

And from his internet search history, he knew exactly what was at stake.

"So then, this is the next step, Cory: You getting fucked." Nic looked him directly in the eye as he spoke, tone still calm. "Here. Now. By me."

"Ye-yes, sir." Cory swallowed the lump in his throat, nodding his head in acquiescence.

Cory felt a hand begin stroking his hair. *Derek.*

"Hey. It's gonna be okay, Cor." His gentle tone helped calm Cory's nerves. "It's the same as last night. Who better for your first time than your two best friends?"

Cory took a deep breath and closed his eyes. He did want this. How many times had he played with his ass? Sure, it had mostly been with his fingers so far, and sure, maybe he bought a toy he kept really well hidden, but getting fucked was something he fantasized about all the time. And here he was with the chance to get fucked by not just one but *two* incredibly hot guys, his closest friends in the world. He focused on his earlier mantra: *Stop overthinking it and just do it.*

"Okay, sir." He peeked one eye open at Nic. "How do you want me?"

"Strip." Nic smiled in reply and winked. "Then get just how you were before, boy. A dick in your mouth should help distract you."

"Watch your teeth on my cock, Cor," Derek warned from the couch.

Cory laughed, tension leaving his body a little.

"Noted, sir." He settled back on his knees, face in Derek's crotch, and took him back into his mouth.

He felt Nic's hand on his hip before he felt cool fingers once again reach his ass. Shuddering at the temperature, he stopped himself from bolting again like last time. He tried to focus on Derek in his mouth as Nic's fingers prodded at his hole. Finding his target, Nic began to press his first finger in. Cory inhaled sharply and went still as he felt the finger breach him. He continued to take deep breaths as he felt Nic push farther in before stopping.

"Breathe, Cory," Nic instructed, trying to get him to relax.

Cory was doing his best. He had done this before, alone in his room, and it wasn't as though Nic had fingers massively bigger than his own. But it was so different having someone else do it. He couldn't control it, didn't know what was going to happen next. And he loved it. The stretch in his hole may have burned a little, but his cock was throbbing between his legs.

Cory resumed sucking on Derek as his breathing leveled out. Once he felt relaxed enough, Nic pulled his finger back before pushing it back in, a little deeper than before. Cory tensed up again, though not as much as the first time, and he tried to focus on the breathing and cocksucking he was also trying to do at the same time. This continued as Nic picked up the pace, eventually fucking his index finger in and out of Cory's ass up to the second knuckle with relative ease. Then, Nic found his prostate.

"MmmMMMmmm" was the noise that came from Cory, still attached by mouth to Derek. He pressed his ass back without even thinking about it.

"Haha, alright." Nic slowly removed his finger entirely causing Cory to whine at its loss. "Time for finger number two." He squeezed out a little more lube, applying it generously to both fingers.

"Ready?" Nic didn't wait for an answer as he pressed both his fingers into Cory's hole.

Another sharp intake of breath was all Cory can manage, Derek's cock falling out of his mouth entirely. Letting out a low whine of pain, he buried his face into Derek's thigh. Fuck, maybe his fingers *were* massive compared to Cory's?

"Hey, you alright?" Derek's hand was on his head as he spoke. "Your hand is kinda digging into my leg."

Lifting his head up, Cory saw that his hands were currently white-knuckling Derek's thighs.

"Sorry, sir." He released them hurriedly before lowering his head again.

"It's alright, boy. You seem pretty distracted." Cory could hear the smirk in his tone. *Asshole. Hot asshole. With a big dick.*

Nic cleared his throat before wiggling his fingers a little, getting Cory's attention before he pressed them farther in.

"Fuck…" Cory said under his breath before pointing Derek's now half-hard cock back toward his mouth. He just needed to breathe and focus on doing this.

Nic followed the same pattern as he had previously, pulling his fingers back and then pushing them back in, each time a little deeper and faster than before. Sooner than before, he once again found Cory's prostate. Cory again moaned around the cock in his mouth and began to push back onto Nic's fingers. Nic took his time, playing with his two fingers and seeing just what made Cory react the most.

Cory was in heaven. Eyes closed, he methodically bobbed up and down on Derek's dick while at the same time rocking his ass backward, thighs spread as much as he could manage. This felt great, better than any time he had played with himself. Every time Nic pressed against that gland, his knees would buckle, and he just wanted more.

Things couldn't end there, though. Nic extracted both his fingers, eliciting another whine from Cory. Chuckling, he quickly lubed a third finger and rested all three against Cory's hole. The still-virgin took a deep breath and tried to relax, knowing what was coming next as Nic pushed in.

*Fuuuuuuuck, that burns. I'm so full. Stretched wide. Seriously, what kind of monster fingers does Nic have?! Fuck!* He tried once again to focus on sucking on Derek. Releasing Derek's cock, he pushed his face into his balls, licking and sucking on the skin, anything to distract him. As Nic began pumping his fingers in and out, the burn lessened but the feeling of fullness never abated. He'd never tried this many fingers before by himself. What was a dick going to feel like?

He wouldn't have to wait long to find out.

"Alright, boy." Nic extracted his fingers for the final time. "I think you're ready." He punctuated his statement with a light spank.

Cory released Derek from his mouth and turned his head, waiting for his next instruction. Nic provided it. "Over to the bed. On your back. Might as well be comfortable for your first time, right?"

"Yes, sir," Cory agreed, standing and carefully walking over to the bed. Even though it was only three fingers, he still felt like he just got reamed out—and now it was time for the real thing.

"Since you got the first crack at his mouth," Nic spoke to Derek as he followed Cory, "I get first dibs on his ass. Cool?"

"Sounds fair to me." Nic sometimes made a big deal about going second, but Derek didn't mind.

Cory watched as his friends discussed his virginity like it was something to be traded for or sold. It made his cock throb again. Nic noticed as he stood over Cory and smirked.

"Glad to see you're enjoying yourself. Gonna need to do something about keeping that," he pointed to Cory's hard and leaking cock, "out of the way." He tossed some underwear to Cory. It was a jockstrap. "Put it on."

He did. It fit him well enough, maybe a little snug around the waist. His cock, still hard, was trapped in the front pouch, but his ass was still out in the open. Perfect for two straight guys who want to take advantage of their gay friend's holes without any unwanted penises getting in the way. Nic climbed onto the pullout bed, walking on his knees toward Cory, settling between his legs.

"Hey, hand me the lube?" Nic asked Derek, who was headed over for a front row seat. He tossed it to Nic as he walked over, standing behind the couch over Cory. "Thanks."

The bottle was old, dating back a few years to when the boys got their hands on one of Derek's dad's old porn DVDs, and they engaged in a little group masturbation. It would happen a few times their freshman year—and then was never brought up again. Cory watched as Nic opened the cap and applied it generously to his cock. He was entranced as the hand stroked up and down the slick cock, each passing stroke making him hornier and more anxious. When Nic was satisfied, he closed the bottle, moving closer to Cory and lifting his legs in his hands.

"Ready to have your cherry popped, boy?" Nic asked as he looked down at him. His tone was gentle, despite the crudeness of his words.

"Yes, sir," Cory answered. Not that he really thought he had any other choice at this point anyway.

Still smiling, Nic lifted his legs farther, resting Cory's feet on his shoulders. Then, aiming with one hand and holding one of Cory's thighs back with the other, Nic pushed his cock toward Cory's ass, seeking out his hole. Cory could feel the cockhead resting against his ass and tensed up.

"Relax, boy. Breathe," Nic spoke to him calmly as he pressed forward. "Think about how much you've wanted this."

Cory yelped when the head of Nic's cock breached the ring of his ass, quickly clamping his hand over his mouth to try and block the offending sound. Nic held still, allowing the boy to get used to the new stretch in his hole. Once he felt him relax enough, he began to push forward farther, getting Cory past the first few inches.

*Goddammit, that's a big cock. This was a terrible idea. He's going to destroy my poor hole by the time the night is over.* Cory's thoughts ran wild as he felt his ass being split open.

"Breathe, boy," Nic reminded him with an order.

Cory let out a breath he hadn't realized he was holding. He focused on his breathing and leveled it out, relaxing his ass in spite of the pain. As he relaxed, Nic pushed more until he was almost five inches inside of Cory.

"More than halfway there, boy." Nic spoke to Cory with almost a sense of pride in his voice. "That's deeper than my fingers went. Just a few more inches. You're doing great."

Cory gave what could best be described as a Charlie Brown smile, happy to receive the praise but unable to ignore the fact that his ass was on fire. Nic went still again as he waited for Cory to relax, watching his face for emotion. He could be patient when he wanted.

Now that he was most of the way inside, Nic was able to start thrusting. Pulling back by only an inch at first, Nic began to very slowly fuck Cory. Just like with his mouth, each time Nic pushed in, he would go a little faster and deeper. The more Cory relaxed, the easier it was to angle his thrusts.

As Cory relaxed, he started to feel things other than just the pain and burn of the stretch in his ass. The main thing he was feeling was full, but eventually Nic's cock began to hit the right spots inside of him. As Nic made longer and longer thrusts, his cock would scrape over his prostate, causing Cory to groan, and as Nic got faster, Cory's moans became more frequent.

"Fuck, dude," Derek said as he watched the scene from behind the couch. "He's fucking loving it."

Cory's eyes were closed, his hands grabbing wildly at the sheets on the mattress, a constant litany of moans and groans spilling from his mouth. The faster Nic moved, the harder it was to concentrate on anything else. Good thing that was all he needed to do.

"And I'm not even all the way inside him yet. I told you this was a great fucking idea!" Nic happily exclaimed as he continued to fuck most of his cock in and out of his best friend. Seeing the state Cory was in, Nic was done with the warm up and ready to really get this fuck started. On his next few thrusts, he closed the gap between his hips and Cory's ass, finally bottoming out inside of him. "That's it, boy. That's everything."

Cory could feel the scrape of Nic's pubic hair against his ass and thighs. He felt so full, which made sense seeing as he had a solid seven inches of cock in his ass. His hole still burned slightly as it stretched around Nic. He kept opening his mouth to talk, but whenever he did, he had no idea what he was trying to say. His foot twitched on Nic's shoulder, a reflex from some muscle he didn't know was being stretched.

"Nnngghh..." Cory whined as he looked up to Nic, unsure of what he was trying to ask for.

Nic watched the storm of emotions cross Cory's face. It was one of the only things distracting him from just how tight the boy was. Fuck, it was way tighter than any of the girls he'd been with. Well, except maybe Molly Paterson. She let him try anal—and taught him how to stretch her out first. This was at least as tight as that, if not a little tighter. Cory's hole was twitching wildly around his cock, squeezing him almost rhythmically as the boy was trying to simultaneously relax and expel the thick intruder. He didn't have a hair trigger, but still, he wasn't taking any chances.

Nic waited until Cory's breath was calm, his hands and feet no longer scrabbling and twitching, before he returned to moving his cock in and out of the boy's ass. Most of his hole was nicely relaxed by now, but Nic still only pulled back a couple of inches at a time, slowly, before pushing back in. As his hips met Cory's ass, a very low, half-whine/half-moan escaped from Cory's mouth. Seemingly involuntary, the moans only grew as Nic's thrusts became longer and faster.

"Fuck," Derek said from his spot behind the couch, "he's really getting into it."

"Yeah..." Nic trailed off, only half-listening.

He was far more interested in what was happening underneath him, what he was doing. He could see what Cory was feeling with every stroke of his cock. As he pulled his cock back, he could see, could feel Cory relax, until he was left with barely a few inches inside, almost gasping as he inhaled. That same breath would then be expelled as Nic drove his cock back inside in the form of a moan, punctuated with a slap as their skin met.

Nic watched the process repeat like clockwork, only changing the speed of his thrusts as he watched Cory's eyes. At times they were hazy and unfocused, looking up at the ceiling like it wasn't there, overwhelmed. At other times, his eyes were locked on Nic's, a silent plea to continue making him feel the amazing things he was feeling. And Nic had no intention of stopping.

He did want to change positions though. His thighs were getting tired from being spread the way they were, and it wasn't great for picking up speed either. Grabbing Cory by the backs of his knees, he pressed his thighs back, his athletic body easily bending Cory's into the position he wanted.

Moving his knees together, he knelt over his friend as he held his thighs spread wide. Looking down, he could see where his cock met Cory's hole, just below the pouch of the jockstrap.

"Get ready, boy." His eyes flashed darkly. "This is what it's like to really get fucked." *Slap.*

"Aaahh!" The first thrust already drew an increased reaction from Cory.

Nic wasted no time as he pounded his friend's ass for the first of many times. He was still watching Cory for what he was feeling but was moving far too fast now to pick out any one emotion from the storm that raged on the boy's face. He was moaning and whining, making unintelligible noises and pleas, half-aborted "mores" and "stops."

"Holy fuck, Nic." Derek was in awe. They'd seen each other fuck before (no homo); neither of them was a slouch in bed, but no girl had ever reacted the way Cory was. "Fucking wreck him."

*I don't think he had any intention of stopping, Derek.* Cory looked up at the thing closest to him—Nic. Using gravity to his advantage, Nic was continuously driving his hips down and forward into Cory. He was starting to sweat, holding his pace and speed as steady as he was. Cory watched as the sweat began to pool, rolling down his neck and chest. Without thinking he reached out, drawing his hand across Nic's muscular chest and stomach.

They watched each other as Cory continued to feel up Nic's front as he fucked him. While Cory looked up in awe, Nic's look was one of hunger and possession. He would remember later that this was exactly how he and Derek had planned for this to happen, that it was their goal to fuck Cory so hard, so good, that it would cement in Cory's mind the desire to serve and worship them. But for the time being,

Nic wasn't thinking about anything except his need to fuck. He needed more.

He let go of Cory's thighs, allowing his legs to fall back against Nic's chest and shoulders. Letting them drop to his elbows, Nic bent Cory almost in two, lifting his ass off the mattress as he positioned himself over Cory. Cock never leaving his ass for more than a few inches, Nic began to powerfuck down into Cory, fucking him missionary as he had so many of his exes. Their faces only inches apart, Cory couldn't hold back anything he was feeling even if he tried.

Every time Nic's cock scraped over his prostate, Cory saw stars. It was like every muscle in his body was having a spasm, and he couldn't decide if he wanted more or for it to stop. Each time he felt Nic slap against his ass, more sounds would come out. The groans and moans growing louder and closer drove Nic to fuck him harder and faster. Cory could only lay there and take it, a never-ending litany of "fucks" and "sirs" spilling out of his mouth alongside his noises of pleasure.

"Fucking take it," Nic growled in Cory's face. "Take that fucking cock, bitch."

Nic was pretty sure he heard a "yes sir" somewhere in there. He was getting closer to cumming, to filling his best friend with his load. His thrusts became more frantic and erratic, and he dropped his bodyweight almost entirely onto Cory. Releasing his legs, Cory struggled to wrap them around his waist as Nic covered his body. Nic's skin pressed to his, he could feel the scrape of the weekend's stubble against his neck.

"I'm loading you up, Cor," he growled into Cory's ear. "I just took your fucking cherry."

Nic saw white when he finally came, cock rooted as deep inside Cory as it could possibly be. An animalistic roar accompanied the first shot, the first person to coat the walls of Cory's hole. In this state of mind, he could only try and drive his hips farther into Cory with each additional shot. It was so hot, so tight.

Cory could feel the heat from Nic's cum as it exploded inside of him. Pushed even deeper than Nic's cock had been, the heat radiated in his gut. His arms and legs were tightly wrapped around Nic's body, toes curled and twitching at every slight movement of Nic's cock. The both of them were still breathing hard as the last dregs of Nic's load exited his cock, still buried to the hilt inside Cory. Slowly, their minds cleared as they came back to themselves.

"You always remember your first, Cor," Nic whispered in his ear before lifting himself up and off Cory. "I'm going to pull out. Squeeze tight—I don't want you losing any of my load."

Cory did his best, sucking in a breath of pain as he worked to tighten his hole. In addition to feeling sticky, it stung. He was going to be so sore in the morning.

"Alright, guess it's your turn, bro," Nic said to Derek as he slowly pulled his cock from Cory's hole. *Oh fuck, that's right. There's no way Derek wasn't going to want to fuck me, too.*

"Dude, I almost jerked off twice while you guys were fucking." Derek's cock was sticking out in front of him, rock hard. "Slide on over and let me in that ass."

Nic looked down at Cory, taking some pity on the boy in his fucked-out state. "Flip onto your stomach. It'll be easier on you now that you've been opened up."

Cory mumbled an unintelligible answer, still exhausted, but managed to roll over with some help from Nic. He felt the pullout bed shift as Derek climbed on behind him, knees brushing against his legs. His asshole twitched uncontrollably, already anxious about what was about to happen. He was so fucking sore. He gripped the bed sheets tightly, eyes closed as Derek climbed over him.

"Barely need lube, dude," Derek commented as he spread Cory's ass in his hands. Cory's hole was red and puffy, even winking at him on occasion. He pointed his slick cock down at it and pushed in.

Cory whined into the mattress, the burn in his ass returning almost immediately. Derek wasn't having any issues getting inside him, but that didn't mean Cory wasn't still feeling every inch. Bottoming out, Cory could feel all of Derek's weight on top of him. Derek held position for a moment, letting Cory get used to his slightly thicker cock.

Once Derek felt he was relaxed enough, he got right to work pumping his cock in and out of Cory. Continuing to whine into the mattress, Cory finally understood where the term "pillow biter" came from. Slowly, the burn of Derek's cock sliding in and out of him was outweighed by the pleasure of his prostate being pounded into again. From his spot above Cory, Derek was driving his cock almost straight down, directly into the small gland and drawing out louder and louder groans.

Derek saw the moment Cory fell back into the same headspace from earlier, felt his muscles relax underneath him as he allowed Derek to use and move his body however he wanted. Nic had completely wrecked the boy, damn near ruined him for anyone else. They would both have to work extra hard if they ever expected to top his first time. For now, Derek was happy to breed their new boy quickly and efficiently.

It wasn't long before Derek was ready to add his load to Nic's inside Cory. As he got closer, he dropped his body weight, laying on Cory's back but still lifting his hips up and down atop Cory's ass. As his cock began to shoot, he ground his hips down into Cory as hard as he could. His hands instinctively shot out, grabbing onto Cory's wrists as though he needed to be restrained, holding him down as he came.

"Fuuuuuuuck. This is the best weekend at the cabin ever," Derek said, still draped over Cory as he came down from his endorphin high. As he pushed himself up and made to extract himself, he tapped Cory sharply on the ass. "Tighten up!"

Cory did so without a complaint, the small amount of training he had already sinking into his malleable mind. He was riding his own afterglow. He may not have cum, but he still felt amazing. And as horny as he still was, he was also completely fucked out. He mumbled his agreement about the weekend, already fading into sleep.

Derek pulled himself out with a light pop and stood next to the bed. After a quick trip to the bathroom to clean up, he returned to find Nic had already shut off the TV and cleaned up what they needed to. Cory was already passed out on the pullout.

"Sleep?" Derek nodded toward the couch.

"Sleep," Nic agreed, turning out the last light and wordlessly climbing onto the pullout mattress.

Derek climbed onto the other side, leaving an already asleep Cory sandwiched between them, still in his jock. If the lights were still on, they might have noticed the small amount of cum leaking from his hole. Pulling the sheet up, the two friends drifted off to sleep wordlessly, unconsciously shifting to huddle together in the middle. The three of them had to head home tomorrow, and they would deal with exactly what that meant then.

# CHAPTER 3

"Oww."

The whine came from Cory in the center of the bed. Cory, who had been on the receiving end of two very rough fuckings last night. Who had lost his virginity last night.

"Heh, pretty sore, huh, boy?" Derek was already awake.

So was Nic, but neither had quite felt up to actually getting out of bed just yet. Getting up meant having to pack. All of their parents were expecting them home before dinner. They had school tomorrow.

"Yes, sir" was mumbled into a pillow.

It was still the morning, earlier than when they had gotten up yesterday. They probably had a couple of hours to putter around before they needed to get on the road. Derek stretched his legs from his spot behind Cory, making sure to give his ass a good grind with his morning wood before swinging his legs to the floor. He walked over to the kitchen.

"Come on. I bought bacon and eggs *just* for today," he said as he pulled out a couple of pans for the stove.

"Duuuuuuuude, you're the best" was Nic's reaction, also mumbled into a pillow.

Eventually the smell of cooking bacon was too much, and both boys migrated from the bed to the small table, eyes still heavy. Neither boy was really a morning person, but somehow Derek was always able to wake up easily. Cory winced slightly as he sat, his sore ass a thorough reminder of the previous night's activities. Once he finished cooking, Derek brought over two large plates, one filled with bacon and the other scrambled eggs. Nic and Cory reached automatically for a piece of bacon before even grabbing a plate.

"Fuck," Cory whined again as his butt moved on his seat, bacon in hand. "My ass is so fucking sore."

"Yeah… Sorry about that. Wish I had something to tell ya, but you're just gonna feel sore for a couple of days," Derek informed him. "Probably want to avoid eating anything spicy for the next few meals." He smirked, biting into his own piece of bacon.

"So," he continued, "we should probably talk about what things are going to be like once we get back home."

Cory looked between his two friends.

"Like I said before, things won't really change all that much," Derek started. "We're still gonna come over and hang out, do all the stuff we used to do. To everyone else, nothing will seem different." The three of them were close, that was no secret, so Derek and Nic knew it wouldn't be difficult to add any of their new "bonding activities" to their routine without arousing suspicion.

"When we are around other people, you act like you always have with us, but when we're alone, you call us both sir," Nic chimed in.

"Any questions?" Derek asked, piling some scrambled eggs onto his plate.

Cory thought for a minute. The only questions he had were along the lines of "What are we going to do next?" and he had a feeling he wasn't going to get any answers to that.

"No, sir," Cory said around the bacon in his mouth.

"Good boy." Nic pushed his chair away from the table. "Now, why don't you get over here? I got some extra protein for breakfast for ya."

Derek rolled his eyes as he ate his eggs, fully intending on taking his own turn *after* they ate.

Cory eyed Nic's crotch as he finished off his bacon. Nic was rubbing the growing bulge beneath his thin shorts, making Cory's mouth water. Or maybe that was the bacon. Cory swallowed it down, dropping to his knees and shuffling over to Nic.

As Cory pulled the waistband of his shorts down, Nic's cock sprung up, nearly smacking Cory in the face. With his slightly greasy hand, he guided the cock toward his mouth. Any indignities Cory felt were quickly forgotten when he remembered just how much he enjoyed doing this. Though the twinge in his backside had him hoping that his ass was off limits for the time being.

As he felt the warm mouth envelop him, Nic leaned back and closed his eyes. *This is the life.* Opening one eye, he looked over at Derek, who was chuckling at the sight. Nic smiled, content to enjoy his blowjob and breakfast.

Having just woken up, Cory's mouth was a little dry, but with his mouth being stretched open, Nic's cock was spit-slick in no time. Cory was soon quickly bobbing up and down on the first four or five inches of dick. His breakfast long gone, all he could taste—all he could smell—was Nic. Fuck, he loved this smell more and more every time he got near it.

The hand in his hair got his attention, urging him to speed up without actually pushing. As Cory worked his mouth faster, he started taking it deeper as well, just touching the back of his throat, letting him know it was there but without making him gag. He was going to be an old pro at this in no time.

A few minutes later and the hand on his head became significantly more forceful. Nic was breathing heavier, and his hips were rising just slightly to buck up into Cory's mouth as his hand pushed it down. Cory still managed to suppress his gag reflex, though he wasn't sure for how much longer. But from the erratic way Nic's hips were moving, he wouldn't have to worry too much longer.

"Fuck..." Nic muttered through gritted teeth. "Take it..."

Cory felt Nic's cock expand right before the first salty shot hit the back of his throat. Somehow managing to avoid a cough, he grabbed it with his hand, pulling back some and allowing the remaining shots to hit the roof of his mouth instead. He swallowed down the salty mouthful, leaving the cock in his mouth to catch any remnants.

Nic caught his breath, body flush and a smile on his face. Cory eventually pulled back with a smack of his lips that he was *definitely* going to feel self-conscious about later. He eyed the slowly softening cock before looking up at its owner.

"Good job, boy," Nic praised in his general direction. "Help yourself to some bacon, on me."

"Thanks, sir." Cory rolled his eyes while Nic's were closed. Then something caught his nose and he leaned closer. "Your dick smells like bacon."

Derek *howled* with laughter at that. Nic and Cory soon followed.

"*Dude.* That's what you get for not having him brush his teeth first. Bacon dick."

"Hey, *everybody* loves bacon. If anything, this is only going to get me laid *more.*"

"*Bacon dick*, new nickname!" Cory chimed in.

"*New nickname*," Derek agreed, cementing Nic's torment for at least the next couple of weeks.

"Fuck you guys," Nic groaned. "It's your fault my dick smells like bacon anyway."

"I only do what I'm told, sir." Maybe things really wouldn't be that different after all...

A few hours later and the boys were on the road, bags loaded into Derek's trunk as they headed home. Cory sat in the back seat, which was more often than not his regular spot. Not that he really cared about where he sat all that much. He stared out the window, watching the trees speed past as they entered the city. The car ride was quiet other than the occasional bad joke or bacon-scented burp as each of the boys contemplated the weekend in his own way.

Since he lived the closest, Derek turned into Cory's apartment complex first, driving around the buildings until he reached Cory's door. As Cory stepped out and got his stuff from the trunk, Derek and Nic followed him.

"Alright, we'll pick you up in the morning for school like usual," Derek said as he closed the trunk for Cory.

"Remember to follow all the rules we talked about," Nic added.

"Yes ... sirs." Cory nodded.

"Oh yeah, one more rule I almost forgot about," Derek started again. "No jerking off."

"What!?" Cory was indignant (and a little turned on).

"You heard him, boy." Nic looked cocky. "Personally, I don't really care what you do with your dick, but the way Derek explained it, this way we can keep you horny and ready to go for when we want."

"Yes, sir," Cory agreed reluctantly. "Anything else?"

"Nope! See ya in the morning." Derek gave his hair a ruffle before both he and Nic turned to get back in the car.

Cory sighed as he watched his friends pull away and then turned and walked toward his front door. This had been such a weird weekend. But, like, *good* weird. He tried to ignore his cock, but the more he thought about how he couldn't jerk off, the more he wanted to, while at the same time wanting to follow his orders. It was a very confusing and erection-inducing catch-22. Shaking his head, he unlocked the door.

"Mom, I'm home!" Cory called out as he walked in, relocking the door behind him.

"Cory! In here, prepping some meatballs for dinner later," Cory's mother Julia called back from the kitchen.

Cory tossed his bag over the couch and walked into the kitchen, kissing his mom on the cheek as her hands were currently full of meat. It had been just Cory and his mom for as long as he could remember. His dad checked out when he was really young, and Cory hadn't spoken to him in over a decade. His mom raised him herself, always working full-time to make sure they had a roof over their heads and food in their stomachs. Cory tried to do anything he could to help out around the house, but his mom wouldn't even let him get a part-time job. She wanted him to focus on school—and Cory knew that without a scholarship, he'd never be able to afford college. Not unless he wanted to be paying back student loans for the rest of his life.

"How was the cabin? How are Derek and Nic?" Julia inquired as she continued to mold meatballs, placing them in a glass casserole dish for later. "You guys get up to much trouble?"

"Uh, good." Cory was glad she couldn't see him blush as he remembered all the "trouble" they got into. "Same as always. Nothing special. Just hung out, watched movies, played video games."

"It's so nice of Linda and Rob to let you boys use that place so much," Julia continued, speaking about Derek's mother and father. "I should do something to say thank you. There's this cake recipe I saw on Facebook that I've been meaning to try..." Cory's mom loved finding excuses to bake.

"I'm sure they'll love it, Mom." Cory wasn't sure how his mom had the energy sometimes. "I'm gonna go unpack and stuff. Love you!" Cory called behind him, grabbing his bag from the couch and heading to his room.

"Love you, too! Dinner at 7!" After hearing his mom's response, Cory closed his door and threw his bag on his bed. He then flopped down on his mattress next to it. He had a million thoughts running through his head and didn't know where to begin.

"I told you to stop stealing my clothes!"

"You don't even wear this shirt anymore! I'm putting it to good use!"

"By going in my closet and *stealing my clothes!*"

Nic hung his keys by the door as he walked into the middle of yet another of his sisters' fights. This was a fairly regular occurrence, so he ignored them and walked back to his room, dropping off his stuff.

"*Carajo,* why are you screaming in my living room *again*?" That was Nic's father, Raphael. "What is it this time?"

"Dani keeps going into my closet and stealing my clothes!" Nic's eldest sister Gabriela complained.

"She doesn't even wear them anymore! *Papa,* I am just trying to make sure the clothes *you paid for* are being worn!" Daniela tried to appeal to her father's more practical side.

"How can I wear them *if they are never in my own closet*?" Gabby screeched back.

Nic reentered the living room and saw his father was pinching the bridge of his nose, a typical response to his teenage daughters' frequent clashes.

"*Daniela,* do I not buy you enough of your own clothes?" Raphael spoke with his eyes closed.

"Yes, but—"

"Stop taking your sister's things without asking. And *both of you* stop screaming in my home, or I will *give you* something to scream about."

"But *Papa*—!"

"*Enough.* Go see if your mother needs help in the kitchen. *Now.*"

That was the end of that. Daniela and Gabriela both marched out of the room, expressions still sour but mouths shut. Their dad had a talent for shutting down their ever-escalating screaming matches.

"*Puta madre...* Nic!" His father turned, seeing him standing in the hall. "When did you get home?"

"Just now, Dad."

"Must have been nice to come home to that." Raphael sighed and shook his head. "I swear they fight more every week..."

"Yeah... You know I try to stay out of it." Nic knew that was an exaggeration, but his sisters *had* been fighting more lately. He just figured it was them being girls in high school.

"You got a game coming up this week, don't you?" There it was. Football was probably the only thing he and his dad seemed to talk about anymore.

It wasn't that Nic didn't like football—quite the opposite, he loved it. It just seemed like the only time his dad wanted to talk to him was when it had something to do with football. The times he seemed most proud were after winning a game, and the longer time went on, the less they had to talk about.

Nic's parents, Raphael and Luciana, married young but waited a few years to have any children. Raphael was a successful trial lawyer and his mother a proud homemaker. Raphael worked hard to make sure he provided well for his family but as a result was rarely home to connect with his children. He was just as clueless about how to interact with his kids as they were him.

"Yeah, home game on Friday." Coach had been riding them pretty hard as the season went on. "We're 5-1 so far."

Raphael smiled. "Your mother and I will see you in action on Friday." Nic did like that—his family tried to never miss a game if they could help it. "All that hard work is paying off. Keep it up and you'll have your pick of colleges next year."

"Heh, yeah." Nic wasn't even sure if he wanted to play football in college yet. "That would be ... pretty great."

"Alright, I've got some work to finish now that I can concentrate." *And there's the exit.* "Tell your mother she might have to come get me for dinner."

"Okay, Dad," Nic said to an already empty room. He sighed.

Nic walked into the home's large kitchen, his mother over the stove tending to a number of boiling pots. The smell of cumin and coriander was thick in the air. Goddamn, Nic loved his mother's cooking. She had learned everything from her mother, Nic's *abuelita*, and had done her best to pass her skills on to her own children, Nic included.

"*Mama*, I'm home!" Nic walked over to his mother, who immediately turned to embrace him.

"Nicolas, *mijo*." She kissed him on the cheek as she squeezed him before turning back to the stove. "How was your weekend?"

"Good. Dad says to get him from his office when dinner's ready," Nic passed along his father's message.

"That man never stops working, I swear..." Luciana shook her head. "Going to work himself to death one day."

"Where are Gabby and Dani?" Nic looked around for his sisters. "Dad sent them in here to help you."

"Oh, I sent them to the store. When they're fighting, they only end up getting in my way." Nic's mom tended to be more practical about these things. "After spending all that time together in the store and car, by the time they are home, they will either have made up or not be speaking to each other at all. Either way, less headache for Mama."

Nic snorted. "You should teach Dad your tricks. He never knows what to do so he sends them to you."

"That man doesn't even remember to *eat* unless I remind him." He usually didn't.

"Dinner smells good, Mom." Nic kissed his mother on the cheek as he made his exit. "I gotta go unpack!"

"Okay, mijo, I'll call you when dinner's ready!" she called up the stairs behind him.

"I'm hooooooooome!" Derek shouted to a house he knew was empty.

His parents had been traveling on business the past four days. His mother was a management consultant and his father an event planner, so they traveled a lot. With his older brother Craig in college, it was a fairly regular occurrence that he would have the place to himself.

Walking through the halls, past all the empty rooms, he reached his and tossed his bag to the side before flopping down on the bed. He was bored, as he often was when he was home. There was plenty to do, but none of it really interested him all that much, not by himself—which was why he would usually find any reason he could to get out of the house.

His parents loved him, and he loved them, but as he got older and their respective businesses took off, they spent less and less time at home. By the time his brother had left for school, Derek was used to spending *weeks* alone at a time. He had his own car. His parents made sure he had food and that the house was taken care of. But fuck, he was lonely.

He had been thinking about asking his parents if he could get a dog, but he knew he'd just have to leave it here when he went to college next year. Then that fateful night with Cory's laptop had happened, and suddenly Derek had something to help occupy all that free time. Since then, he had spent many a night on all sorts of websites, looking at and reading about all kinds of kinks—all in the name of research, of course.

That reminded him: He needed to text Cory.

[Derek: Hey, boy. Being good?]

[Cory: Hello sir. Yes sir]

Derek smiled. He hadn't had to correct Cory on much so far. He was a natural.

[Derek: Unpack yet?]

[Cory: Not yet sir, just about to]

[Derek: Go check the front pouch of your backpack]

Derek had left Cory a surprise that, judging by his internet history, Cory would love—a jockstrap. Derek had made a point of wearing one a few times last week. Derek saw that a lot of what Cory had been jerking it to was sweaty, musky guys, often in a jockstrap and occasionally stuffing that jockstrap in the mouth of the boy that was about to get fucked. Derek was willing to bet Cory would still be sniffing that jock long after his scent was gone. It was a few moments before Cory responded.

[Cory: Wow uh thank you sir I think]

[Derek: What, don't like it?]

[Cory: Oh no its very hot sir I just don't know what to do with it]

[Derek: Well you were good this weekend considering it was your first time for everything, so that's your reward. You have permission to jerk off tonight while you sniff that jock]

[Cory: Thank you sir! Any other rules?]

[Derek: Nah, you can jerk it once and then you can do whatever else you want with that jock. I'll let you know when I want it back]

[Cory: Thank you sir]

    *Yeah*, Derek thought, *this is gonna be fun.*

"Derek and Nic are here. Bye, Mom!" Cory shouted as he closed the door, heading for Nic's car. Ever since Derek and then Nic got a car, it had become a routine: Nic and Derek taking turns driving to school. With Cory's house on the way, it was never an issue to pick him up too. Cory opened the backseat door and tossed his bag in.

"Morning."

"Mornin'."

"Goooooood morning, sirs," Cory practically chirped. Morning car rides were usually pretty quiet, the boys still pretty groggy from sleep, but Cory woke up today feeling *great*. He happily smiled out the window as the houses passed until Nic turned into the school's parking lot. Once parked, all three boys grabbed their bags and got out, scattering in different directions for their first classes.

"See ya at lunch!" Nic shouted behind him.

"Yeah, later." Derek turned toward the science building and took off himself.

"See ya!" Cory responded and headed to his first class—pre-calculus.

"Hey, Cory." That was Stephanie Jones, Cory's best friend after Nic and Derek.

"Hey, Steph." Cory took his seat and pulled out his stuff for class.

"You have a good weekend?" Stephanie asked.

"Uh, yeah. What about you?"

"Eh, it was okay. My aunt was in town, so on the one hand, I got to go to some nice dinners with the family. On the other hand, I had to spend dinners with my family," Stephanie deadpanned. "What about you? Do anything fun?"

"Nope, nothing really." Cory hoped his blush wasn't visible. "You know, hung with the guys, played video games…"

"That's cool." Luckily, Steph was too busy looking through her notebook to notice anything. "Sometimes doing nothing is the best thing."

"Yeah … nothing exciting at all…" Cory trailed off into his thoughts.

Truth be told, Cory knew that if there was anybody he could tell about this weekend, it was Steph. But Cory hadn't come out to even her yet. He thought that telling her that he spent the weekend sucking off and getting fucked by his best friends might be a bit too much right now. Lucky for him, the bell rang.

"Alright class, open to page 124," Mrs. Anderson, the teacher, instructed. "Today, we are going over vectors."

The rest of Cory's morning all went the same way—boring. His second class of the day was physics, which he had with Derek. They took their usual seats next to each other and had their usual banter, nothing out of the ordinary. The same thing happened in his third class, economics, which he had with Nic. They took their seats and talked like normal. Cory was beginning to think that things really wouldn't be that different.

Then, just as class was getting out, he felt his phone vibrate. It was Nic.

[Nic: Meet me by the bathrooms before we go to lunch]

Cory looked up to find Nic, who gave him a look before indicating with his head that Cory should follow him. Walking slower than the other students and letting them pass, Nic and Cory turned down a different hall that lead to the nearest bathroom. Once inside, Nic checked the stalls to make sure they were alone, then once he knew they were, he locked the door behind him.

"Finally, I've been waiting all damn morning for a blowjob." Nic was already reaching into his jeans and pulling out his cock. He sat up on the low counter between sinks, cock in hand. "Come on. We don't have a lot of time if you still wanna make it to lunch."

It took a Cory a moment to process what was going on, but once he saw Nic's hard cock, that was all he could focus on.

"Yes, sir." He swallowed nervously, kneeling between Nic's spread legs, looking around somewhat nervously. "Sir, what if—"

"The door's locked, and this bathroom barely gets used anyway," Nic pointed out. "Quit whining and get my dick in your mouth. The longer you complain, the longer we're gonna be here."

Cory moved to the floor between Nic's legs, the cold tile digging into his knees. He swallowed his nerves and then Nic's cock. Or at least as much of it as he could. He tried to focus on what he was doing, but everything around him kept distracting him. The way the fluorescent lights were buzzing overhead, the low hum of the air conditioner. Even the way the—

"Hey." A light cuff to his head got his attention. "The hell are you doing, boy? Let's go. I'm hungry and only one of us is getting fed here."

"Thorry thir," Cory apologized, resuming his work immediately, this time focusing on Nic: the way he tasted in his mouth, the musky smell of his crotch that grew strong each time his head bobbed down, the small pants of pleasure that came from his mouth when Cory would swallow down just a *little* more cock that usual. The rest of the world faded into the background.

Cory had his left hand wrapped around the base of Nic's cock to help cover the areas his mouth couldn't. It didn't take long for Cory to once again figure out how much cock he could take before gagging. As he worked, he ran his tongue along the underside of Nic's cock, mapping more of it with each pass of his mouth. As he felt Nic's cockhead tickle the back of his throat, he started to experiment by swallowing just a little too much, nearly triggering his gag reflex. It was never going to go away if he didn't start practicing, after all.

"Fuck..." Nic cursed to himself. "*There* we go." He moved one of his hands instinctively to the back of Cory's head.

Though Nic couldn't see it, Cory warmed at the praise. By now he had figured out that the hand in his hair didn't mean he was doing poorly. If anything, it meant the opposite—Cory was sucking dick well enough for Nic to need something to hold onto. Using his spit, Cory started to jerk Nic's dick in time with his mouth—he was going to make Nic cum, goddammit.

"Fuck, boy. I'm getting close," Nic warned. It was like music to Cory's ears. He nearly redoubled his efforts, concentrating on being as consistent as possible and then—

Two hands were suddenly forcing his head all the way down, Nic's cock practically punching its way into his throat as he started to blow his first load of the day. Cory struggled futilely as another load was blasted into his throat before realizing the best thing for him to do right then was to *swallow*. As the third and fourth shots hit his throat, he did his best to swallow it down but was still fighting against his gag reflex in vain.

Cory's hair was released as soon as Nic was done cumming. He immediately fell back in a coughing fit, his lungs too eager for the air and sucking some of Nic's unswallowed semen down the wrong pipe. As he hacked his lungs up, Cory looked up at Nic, eyes still closed and catching his breath. He had a red mark on his lip from where he had been biting it. Cory watched as his hairy muscular stomach heaved and his heart rate lowered, his cock still half hard and pointing at Cory. A small amount of cum was still hanging from the tip, and without thinking, Cory moved forward to clean it with his mouth.

"I didn't even have to tell you to do that." Nic sounded proud.

Cory finished cleaning off Nic's cock and then released it. Nic tucked himself back in his shorts and hopped off the counter to fix the rest of his clothes. Cory moved to the mirror to make sure he wasn't looking out of the ordinary as well.

"Oh my god." There was cum leaking from his nostril. Cum *actually* came out of his nose. He turned to glare at Nic, who could only chuckle.

"Sorry about that." Nic zipped up his jeans. "I thought I was helping. Making sure you swallowed everything!"

"Well, I don't think it ended up being all that helpful, *sir*." He also thought that was a load of bullshit—Nic knew exactly what he was doing.

"Woah." Nic's face scrunched up as Cory spoke. "You're gonna want to invest in some gum or breath mints, boy. Your breath smells like... Well, like cum. Now come on. I'm hungry."

Cory gave him a "no shit" look and then quickly made to wash his face and rinse his mouth out. There were vending machines on the way to the lunch quad that had gum. He'd make Nic buy him a pack.

A couple of hours later, Cory was chewing his second piece of gum in his last period of the day, English. Technically there was another period after this one, but since he was a senior, Cory didn't have to have a full schedule and was allowed to leave campus an hour early. Derek had the same schedule, but because of football practice, Nic did not.

Speaking of Derek, Cory had no idea where he was. When he and Nic had made it to lunch earlier, Derek was nowhere to be seen, and he should actually be in this class right now with Cory, but his desk remained empty. Their teacher was up at the front, talking about Chaucer, but Cory was only half paying attention. Just as he was debating sneaking his phone out to fire off a text, the classroom door opened and in walked Derek. He didn't look happy. He handed a note to the teacher and took his seat in silence.

Cory looked over to him, trying to see what was wrong, but Derek merely shook his head. They'd talk after class. Cory tried to pay attention the rest of the period, but his mind kept going back to whatever was wrong with Derek. It was about twenty-five more minutes before the bell finally rang, the students spilling into the halls to make their way to their last classes of the day. A few like Cory and Derek instead headed toward the front of the school to leave campus. Nic didn't have practice today, so as far as Cory knew, they were all driving home together.

Cory figured he was right when Derek instead began walking toward the auditorium, a favorite of theirs for hanging out after class. As long as the drama club wasn't working on a show, the building was almost always completely empty—and air conditioned, the perfect place for hormonal teens to be left alone for hours at a time.

Derek held the door open for Cory, making sure it shut behind them. They walked through the lobby to the main theatre, the lights on but very dim. It seemed they were alone, and Derek hopped up to peak backstage just to be sure.

"Good because I seriously do not feel like dealing with anyone else." Derek lowered himself to the stage. "On your knees, boy. I need your mouth. Now."

Cory shook of the shock of the order as quickly as he could, getting in position before his sir.

"Don't worry. I'm not angry with you, but just..." Derek didn't finish his sentence, fishing his cock out of his fly and pushing into Cory's mouth. "Guess who surprised me this morning after first period?"

Cory looked up at him questioningly.

"My parents!" Derek didn't look happy about this development. He fed more of his cock into Cory's mouth.

Derek's parents were gone a lot, usually for work. Derek didn't really like talking about it, but over the years, Cory had figured it out. He was good at hiding it, usually, but Cory started noticing that whenever his parents were gone, Derek would seemingly find whatever excuse he could to hang out at his or Nic's place. It must be lonely in that house on his own. So as Cory began to suck on Derek's cock, he wondered what exactly had him so upset.

"They're going to be in Australia for three months."

Cory's eyes opened wide at that. Three months? It was already October now.

"Mom got a consulting job she can't pass up, and Dad found some other work in the same area himself so he can stay with her." Both of Derek's hands were on the back of his head, and he began to move his hips forward rather than letting Cory's head move.

"They told me I could go with them," Derek continued speaking to his captive audience, "but I don't exactly feel like spending almost half of my senior year being the new kid at a new school in a foreign country." That was a fair point.

Derek was moving his hips faster now, and Cory was starting to have a hard time keeping up with it. On top of that, Derek was starting to push in far enough that Cory was starting to get worried about his gag reflex. Again.

"And of-fucking-course, they're *surprised* that I'm pissed off about this." Derek punctuated his curses with a series of quick, long thrusts. "What teenager doesn't want to be left alone for three months? It's not like a kid would ever want their parents around, right?" Derek's grip suddenly tightened. "Not like the one thing he wants is for them to *Just. Fucking. Be there.*" Derek again punctuated his words with his hips, this time holding Cory's head nearly all the way down after the last one.

Derek didn't say anything more, not with his mouth. After pulling his cock back out and letting Cory catch his breath for a moment, he drove it right back in, right down to the balls. After that, Derek's cock was never more than three-quarters out of Cory's mouth. He quickly began thrusting and was giving Cory no choice but to try and keep up.

With his head being steadily held in place, Cory was doing his best. He could feel the drool starting to escape the corners of his mouth as it was pushed out by Derek's cock. He had completely given up on suppressing his gag reflex and was now just trying to focus on not scraping anything with his teeth or spitting anything up.

If it wasn't in his mouth right now, he would have trouble believing just how much of it he was taking. With each thrust forward, he could feel the tickle of Derek's pubic hair on the tip of his nose. His throat was stretched to capacity and his eyes were watering. And yet despite all the discomforts, he was rock hard inside his pants.

Desperate for something to hold onto, Cory's hands scrambled until they found Derek's thighs, holding on tightly. Above him, he could only hear the heavy grunting as Derek continued to fuck his face, hard and deep. Cory couldn't even move his head enough to look up so he had no idea what might have been going through his mind. But that was the idea, wasn't it? Cory was just here to provide a service, a hole. Twice today, his friends had taken him aside and made him suck their cocks. And this was only the first day. The thought that this could happen more ... *would* happen more... Cory moaned around the cock in his mouth and throat. Unsure if it was his moan that triggered it, Cory felt as Derek's thrusting slowed slightly but maintained its movement nonetheless. Cory knew what was coming: Derek.

"Fuck... Here it comes..." As his jerking hips lost their rhythm, Cory felt his head being pulled forward to meet them. "Fucking ... take it..."

Cory could feel Derek's cock get even thicker in his mouth as he began to shoot. His face was mashed down as far as it could go. As he felt Derek's cum shoot down his gullet, he wasn't even sure he could spit it back up if he wanted to. It was being deposited directly into his stomach. Cory moaned again, weakly. Despite the abuse, he was still just *so* turned on.

Once the grip on his head relented, Cory pulled back, drawing in large amounts of air but thankfully not coughing. He leaned against Derek's legs as he caught his breath. He felt a hand on his cheek.

"Shit. Sorry, boy." Derek stroked his cheek again. "Didn't mean to be that rough ... but thank you. I needed that."

"You're welcome, sir." Cory smiled. His throat was sore, his face a mess, and his cock was so hard it almost hurt. "That's what I'm here for," he croaked out.

He was happy.

# CHAPTER 4

Things seemed to fall in place easy enough over the next few weeks. The boys resumed their normal routine— school together in the mornings, hanging out together and studying in the evenings. The only difference now was that sometimes, Cory would find himself either on his knees or his back when Derek or Nic required his "services."

Blowjobs at school were not uncommon, one of the boys hustling Cory into a bathroom or other spot where they could get some privacy. Cory's oral skills had improved greatly after so much practice, and he now felt fairly adept in his ability to swallow down cock. His gag reflex was still a bit of a problem, but it really only affected him these days when Nic or Derek really wanted to fuck his face, and he found that he didn't mind it that much anyway.

Cory's other hole had gotten its own fair share of training as well. It hadn't happened at school yet, and Cory hoped it would stay that way. As hot as it was to think about, he had learned multiple times over the previous week just how ... *involved* getting fucked could be. He wasn't sure how it had happened, but that night at the cabin was a total fluke.

Between the lube, the stretching, figuring out positions, finding places to even *do* it, and *oh god the mess*, it almost wasn't worth it.

(It was definitely worth it.)

That last problem though... Derek had sat him down and had a borderline traumatic discussion with Cory last week that *still* made him shudder.

"What's this?" Cory looked at the box Derek had pulled from his bag and tossed to him.

"That," Derek began what was sure to be a *fun* talk, "is an enema kit."

"*What?*" Cory's face felt like it was on fire.

"Hey, I don't wanna talk about this anymore than you do, but we gotta." Derek switched to a softer tone. "So let's not make this worse than it has to be, okay, boy?"

"...Yes, sir."

"Okay, well, the last few times you've gotten fucked we've had to stop to..." *Awkward pause.* "...clean up, and we can all agree that's not something any of us wants to deal with, right?"

Cory nodded, tight-lipped. Derek was right. He already felt completely mortified at the memories. It didn't just kill the mood; it made even hanging out the rest of the night feel weird. Last time, Nic hadn't even waited until he got out of the shower to leave.

"Well, if you use one of these beforehand, we can hope-fully prevent that." Derek nodded to the box in Cory's hands.

"...Do I have to?" Cory already knew the answer.

"You already know the answer."

"Yes, sir..."

"So, I think you should practice with that one," Derek instructed. "After I leave. Read the box and follow the instructions. Then when you're done, take your ass for a test run."

"*Seriously?*" Cory nearly squawked at that. "What? You want me to use my dildo or something?"

"I didn't know you actually *had* a dildo until just now." Derek raised an eyebrow at his response. "But yeah, that'll work."

"Please just go, sir, and leave me here to die of embarrassment." Cory buried his face in his hands.

"You'll be fine, boy." Derek laughed and ruffled his hair. "Text me later and let me know how it went, okay?"

Cory got up and walked Derek out before returning to his room. He briefly thought about just crawling into bed and going to sleep early. But he knew Derek was expecting a text later, and he didn't want to disappoint...

With a sigh, he grabbed the enema box and walked to the bathroom. He opened the box and read the instructions as he pulled out its contents. It all seemed pretty self-explanatory, but when sticking things in your ass, better to be safe than sorry. He still had a couple of hours before his mom would be home, and the last thing he needed was her asking questions about why he was on the toilet all night.

Still, no matter how many times he read through the box, nothing would adequately prepare him for bending over on the floor of his bathroom while he emptied this thing up his ass. Oh god, it felt so weird. And even weirder when he had to stand up and move onto the toilet after a few minutes.

It took a few tries before Cory really felt like he got the hang of it, whatever the hell that meant. Then he found out he was *still* wrong about that when he tried to use his toy the first time. By the time his mom was walking through the door, Cory barely had time to return his freshly cleaned dildo to its normal hiding space after finally having successful test run per Derek's instruction.

He left out a *lot* of details when he texted later that night. "Traumatic" was probably a strong word, but the event had certainly left an impression on Cory. But once he started including cleaning out as a part of his hygiene routine when seeing the boys, everyone saw the benefits. Nic and Derek were certainly taking advantage, making sure to give Cory a heads up if they were planning on using his ass that day.

Tonight was just such a night. Cory wasn't sure what they were going to be doing, but Derek had told him earlier at school to "prepare" for things and to plan on being busy most of the night. Neither he nor Nic would give him any more info when pressed. Normally, that would make him nervous, but lately, Cory had been learning to let things go and trust his friends-turned-owners. Things had been working out well so far, right?

Nic said they'd be there around 7 p.m. to pick him up, which gave Cory plenty of time to take care of some school work before hopping in the shower to clean himself, inside and out. Derek had said they'd be out late, though nothing crazy, so Cory let his mom know when she got home. By the time Nic was knocking on his door a couple of hours later, Cory had just thrown on a t-shirt and was ready to go.

"Cool, let's head out." Nic was pleased to see Cory was ready. "Hi Ms. S." He waved to Cory's mom. "We'll have him back at a reasonable hour."

Cory rolled his eyes as they walked to Derek's waiting car. Like staying out late was the thing to be worried about. Derek got in the passenger seat while Cory took his usual seat in the back.

"So... Where are we headed, sir?" Cory posed his question to either boy as Derek pulled out of the parking lot.

"Told you it's a surprise, boy." Derek met his eyes in the rearview mirror. "Just be patient."

"Yeah, you're gonna *love* it," added Nic.

Cory figured he wasn't going to be getting any more questions answered and resigned himself to staring out the window. Derek pulled the car onto the highway; it seemed they were headed out of town for the night.

The boys fell into a comfortable silence, the music playing softly as they pointed out the occasional weird billboard. They didn't go far, just one town over to Lakefield. It was only about an hour drive from their home in Hartford, Florida, but Cory texted his mom that he might be out late just in case.

Cory had been to Lakefield a few times over the years. It was a little quieter than home but not by much. It wasn't unheard of for Derek or Nic to hear of a good house party and drag Cory along. Cory didn't know the place well enough to know where they were going, but it became apparent when Derek rolled his car into the parking space in front of a particular storefront.

"Good Vibrations" proclaimed the sign. A little on the nose, but it served its purpose.

"We're going to a sex toy shop?" Cory asked aloud.

"Surprise," Nic answered. "We figured if we wanted to get any 'training implements,' it would be better to do it here instead of Hartford. No one here knows us."

That was smart reasoning. Cory remembered buying his toy online... The anxiety of having to check the mail before his mom got home, just in case the packaging gave anything away or she got nosy and opened it herself. Just the thought made Cory shudder.

"You coming, boy?" Derek and Nic were waiting for him on the sidewalk.

Cory shook off the thoughts of his mother and opened the car door to join them. Derek led the way into the shop. Rock music played softly over the store's speakers, and the faint scent of leather was in the air.

"Can I please see your IDs, boys?" a girl seated behind a counter by the door called them over.

Her hair was dyed red and black, and she wore a very revealing low-cut top. As they presented their IDs, Nic couldn't stop staring at her tits. If she noticed, she didn't seem to mind.

"Oooooo, fresh meat," she giggled before handing back the cards. "Daddy Carl's gonna like you. Have fun, boys!"

The boys pocketed their IDs and moved through a doorway onto the main floor of the store. It was sparsely populated, which was probably normal for a Tuesday night. The room was big—there was even a staircase leading to a second floor—and there were racks of clothing from wall to wall. Well, clothing was a strong word... These were more like costumes. Derek walked over and began looking through them, pointing out the stereotypical "sexy nurse" costume he found.

"Who the hell is Daddy Carl?" Nic asked no one in particular.

Cory tapped him on the shoulder and then pointed to an upstairs balcony where a large bear of a man was talking to a couple of women who looked very excited about purchasing whatever it was they were holding. He looked tall, taller than any of the boys, and he had a large barrel of a chest underneath a t-shirt and leather vest he had on. A full beard, shaved head, and leather gloves rounded out the rest of his outfit.

"I'm guessing it's him," Cory reasoned. "He looks like a daddy if I ever saw one."

"And you would know, right?" Nic teased but was still staring at Daddy Carl. The older man must have felt the eyes on him because a second later, he turned and met Nic's gaze. Nic looked away quickly, blushing, though he wasn't sure why. Luckily a side room with wall-to-wall porn DVDs caught his eye next. He headed inside wordlessly.

That left Cory with Derek, who was still perusing the racks. Most of the costumes seemed to be for women—there were even some that were nothing but lingerie—but there were a few things for men, like a cop or Tarzan. Nothing Cory would want to wear though.

"So, sir," Cory asked as he looked through the racks with Derek, "why a sex store?"

"Well, your little revelation the other night about your toy got me thinking." Derek smirked without looking up. "A place like this would have *all kinds* of useful stuff to help with your 'training.'"

Cory wanted to roll his eyes at the word "training," as if this wasn't just as much about the two of them getting all the blowjobs they wanted, but he managed to restrain himself. "Useful stuff like what, sir?"

"Well, for starters," Derek led Cory to a rack with men's underwear—notably, a lot of jockstraps—and thumbed through a few, "we should probably get you up a few more of these. I think we *all* enjoy having your ass easily accessible. Pick out a few you like. This whole shopping trip is on my parents. I'm gonna go find out whatever it is Nic is doing so I can make fun of him for it later." He patted Cory on the back and made his way to the side room.

*He must still be really pissed off at his parents*, Cory thought as he perused the hanging jockstraps. *Not gonna complain though. Free jockstraps!*

Cory had a thing for jockstraps. He always thought they looked so hot on the guys in the porn he watched. Like when some daddy would shove a boy's face right into his musky jock before pulling his dick out or the way they would frame a bottom's ass as he was getting pounded by that same daddy... Cory felt himself getting hard and tried to focus on the underwear.

"And who might you be?" A deep voice from behind startled him, making him drop the jockstrap in his hands to the floor. "Shit. Sorry, boy, didn't mean to scare you."

Cory bent down to grab it before turning around. "It's okay, just an accident..." Cory trailed off as he looked up, now face to face with Daddy Carl himself. "...Sir."

"Knew I had you pegged when I saw you walk in." Carl smiled at that. "What brings a cute thing like you in here?"

"I c-came in with some friends." Great, now he was stuttering. And the warm but hungry look on Carl's face was not helping with his erection issues. "Just looking around."

"Friends. Right." Carl just kept smiling. "Well, when you and your 'friends' are ready, we keep all the good stuff upstairs. I'm sure I'll see you up there in a bit, boy."

Cory watched as Carl walked away, still holding onto the underwear he dropped. Gathering his wits and the jockstraps, he made a beeline for the porn room. Derek was flipping through a rack of DVDs when he saw Cory walk in and waved him over.

"Find anything good?" he asked.

"A couple of things, sir." Cory handed Derek his selections. "I, uh, met Daddy Carl."

"Yeah?" Derek's eyebrows raised. "How'd that go?"

"Okay, I think?" Cory was still feeling a little flustered. "He's very … intuitive."

"Heh, knew you belonged to someone, huh?" Derek grinned.

"Yes, sir." Cory nodded. "Said he'd see us upstairs. That's apparently where they keep the 'good stuff.'"

"Then I guess we'll head up there next." Derek looked through the underwear Cory had picked out. "Not bad. Let's go see what Nic's jerking off to."

Nic was on the opposite side of the room. He was facing a wall and eagerly looking through the shelves of DVDs, a few already in his hands. Derek stalked up behind him silently, grabbing him suddenly by the shoulders to surprise him.

"HEY, WHAT'S THAT?" Derek yelled right over his shoulder, causing Nic to jump and send one of the DVD cases flying.

"Fuck you, dude!" Nic grumbled angrily. "Scared the shit out of me."

"Aww, sorry, bro. I'm sure…" Derek bent down and picked up the dropped movie, reading the title before handing it back, "*Lesbian Lick Fest 3* is a great flick."

"Two thumbs up. Like, waaaaaay up there," Cory chimed in from behind Derek, causing him to chuckle. Neither boy made any mention of the fact that Nic seemed to be *over-compensating* for some of their recent activities.

"Fuck you both." Nic grabbed the DVD from Derek before flipping them both the bird.

"No, just him." Derek pointed his thumb back at Cory. "That's why we're here, remember? So if you are done *browsing* through the ladies down here, I hear they keep the good stuff upstairs."

"Yeah, yeah." Nic put the stack down. "I'll come back for these."

"Wouldn't want to give someone the wrong impression," Derek managed to get out as he led the way out of the room.

The group walked up the stairs in the main room, leading to a second floor with a balcony wrapped around the perimeter. Tools and implements lined the walls, the kind that are a little too on the nose, furry handcuffs and riding crops like you'd see in a movie. There was an entire section devoted to *just* lube, complete with a *sampling station.* And at either end were doorways leading to more rooms with even more toys. Cory felt like a kid in a candy store.

The room closest to them was also the one they had seen Daddy Carl next to earlier. He was inside, talking to another customer while gesturing to some leather harnesses on the wall. The smell of leather was much stronger in this room than the rest of the building, with good reason—leather of all kinds was covering the walls. Derek whistled as he looked around the room while Cory and Nic were wide-eyed and silent. Harnesses, cuffs, leashes—hell, half the room was devoted to all kinds of restraints.

"You must be the boy's owner," Daddy Carl's voice boomed as he walked over to the trio, extending his hand for Derek to shake. Then he looked over to Nic, sizing him up for a moment before extending the hand to him as well and grinning cheekily. "Sorry, owners. I'm Carl, but the folks here call me Daddy. You boys looking for anything in particular, or just browsing for now?"

"We've just been looking around so far, but I think we will *definitely* be making some purchases in this room..." Derek trailed off, looking around again. "Maybe some cuffs to start?"

Carl led the boys over to one side of the room, a section seemingly dedicated to restraints for the arms or legs.

"Well, you can see we have a lot to choose from. We've got leather, nylon, neoprene… Cuffs you can padlock, cuffs that can slip right off…" Carl paused as he looked over Cory. "I'm betting you boys would do well with something like this." Carl reached out and plucked one of the leather restraints from the wall. "May I?" He directed his question to Derek and Nic.

"Please." Derek seemed to know what he was asking.

"C'mere, boy," Carl instructed Cory, who stepped forward. "Wrist out."

Cory held out his wrist for the man, who grabbed it firmly, but gently.

"These are a pretty standard set of mid-range cuffs." Carl wrapped the cuff around Cory's wrist. "They're lined with fabric so they won't irritate your sub's skin if worn for a long period, and they're sturdy enough that they won't come undone with a little tugging." He closed the cuff, flipping Cory's wrist at the same time. "And you have a D-ring here so you can easily attach them to any bondage straps or even to themselves."

Cory tried to take in all this information, but the man-handling of his wrist had him a little distracted. Between Daddy Carl's look, scent, and the way he was holding onto him, all while discussing how to restrain him, Cory could feel himself getting hard.

"How do they feel, boy?" Derek asked Cory. He was the one who would be wearing them so ultimately it was up to him.

"They feel good," Cory responded honestly as he flexed his wrist in the cuff. "Doesn't feel like it would irritate me or anything … and the other stuff sounded good too."

"I bet it did." Derek reached out to ruffle Cory's hair. "What do you think, Nic? Nic?"

Nic was distracted, staring at the opposite corner of the room. Or rather, the people in the opposite corner of the room. Two women, seemingly a couple, were examining a wooden paddle together. One of the women had a leather collar around her neck.

"Huh? Oh, uh, they sound good, dude," Nic said without bothering to look back, his walk changing to a saunter as he approached the women. "Be right back."

"*That* is Mistress Andrea and her long-time sub, Candy," Daddy Carl said to the two remaining boys. "They are going to eat him alive." He chuckled, holding out his hand to Cory to take his wrist once more, this time undoing the cuff. "Is it safe to say you boys are *new* to the scene?"

"You could say that," Derek answered for the both of them, gripping Cory's shoulder. "We have an idea of what we might like, but I'd love to get the help of a professional. Gotta make sure I'm taking care of my boy's needs properly."

"I *like* you." Carl smiled. "Tell you what: Why don't you boys just follow me and I'll give you a tour of the floor and help you get everything you need?"

"That would be awesome, Carl. Thank you." Derek wasn't going to turn down the help. He had been playing it cool so far, but the second they walked into this room, he was worried he might be in over his head.

The sudden sound of a loud SMACK followed by a YELP drew everyone's attention. Turning in that direction, the group could see Nic returning to them, hand rubbing what was apparently a sore ass. Andrea and Candy were still by the paddles, laughing to themselves.

"Aww, strike out?" Derek mock-consoled.

"Shut up. She told me if I could take a smack with that paddle silently, she'd let me fuck her girl." He was still rubbing his ass. "Fuck, that hurt."

"You're lucky she left your ass in one piece," Carl informed him. "Now then, step right over here, boy—need to find a set for your ankles now."

The group stuck together after Nic's little adventure. Carl walked them through the room, showing them more toys that Derek was happy to add to their collection. In addition to the cuffs, they also picked up a blindfold, a spreader bar, and a set of bondage restraints that would fit under a mattress (to be kept at Derek's).

"There's a couple more things I think you two would like," Carl pointed at Nic and Derek, "but they are on the other side of the floor. Follow me."

Carl led them out of the room and around the wide balcony into what could only be described as the "dildo room." Whereas walking into the other room led to more than one half-hard erection, this one made Cory want to laugh. Dildos, as far as the eye could see lined the walls. Or at least covered more than half the walls in the room. Big, small, some with extra attachments, some that vibrated, and of course a hundred different colors and shapes. It would be awe inspiring if it weren't so ... phallic.

"Uh, listen, man. Thanks for the help, but I don't think I'm gonna find anything I want in here." Nic began backing out of the room.

"What? No, not those. Although you may want to consider a plug for him. Help keep him stretched and lubed for you. No, what I wanted to show you is over here." Carl gestured to a section of the wall you couldn't see from outside. "Cock rings."

The boys stepped farther into the room. The wall Carl was gesturing to was indeed covered in cock rings.

"Oh, nice." Derek didn't hesitate, reaching and picking up one of the larger metal ones to test its weight.

The majority of the selection seemed to be made of metal, but there was also a decent amount of silicone. Nic examined one more tentatively while Cory hung back and observed. He didn't really have much use for a cock ring. Instead, he wandered off a little to the right, seeing what else the room had to offer.

More dildos were the obvious answer, but looking at some of the selection, he wouldn't know it. By far, what they had the most of were classic "realistic" looking cocks, some even modeled after porn stars. Then there were more nondescript toys, smoother and in many different colors. That led to an entire wall of vibrating "personal massagers" with enough settings and attachments to require both an instruction manual *and* a floor model to see up close. Seriously, was this place even real?

Cory recalled Daddy Carl's recommendation earlier when he came upon the butt plugs. There were dozens of different kinds to choose from. Cory looked at one made of rubber that was classified as "small" but was still thicker than the toy he had at home by a decent amount. Putting it back, he picked up another made of smooth silicone that vibrated. He tentatively pushed the button on the base of the plug, nearly dropping it in surprise at the strength of the vibration.

"Need some help there?" Daddy Carl was next to him. Cory looked over at Derek and Nic who were still looking at the cock rings and talking.

"Uh, no, sir, just looking around." Cory returned the plug to the rack.

"That's actually a pretty decent one, but the motor's a little strong for a beginner." Carl grabbed another plug, showing it to Cory. "This one is probably more your speed. Plus it has a remote, so if your sirs were ever to have you wear it out in public, well… You might end up having a lot more fun than anyone around you realizes."

"Oh, hell yeah." Nic eagerly approved of the idea as he and Derek rejoined Cory. "Def getting that one." He accepted the box from Carl.

Cory blushed at the thought of either of them having him wear the plug in public like that. The movies, a restaurant, or *oh god—school.* Nic was already looking forward to it, though Cory wasn't entirely sure if that was because Nic thought the idea was hot or just wanted to mess with him.

"Well, I think that's just about all I have to show you guys." Carl was ending their tour, but it didn't sound like he was done. "Now, if you'll follow me to the changing room…" Carl led the group out of the room to another open doorway they somehow missed, tucked just behind the staircase they walked up.

"Changing rooms? Uh, I don't think any of this is stuff you'd want someone trying on before they pay for it," Derek said as he walked through.

"Nonsense. We take customer service here at Good Vibrations very seriously." Someone new was speaking, a young man with a leather collar around his neck and cleaning supplies tucked into his belt. He turned to Carl. "Changing rooms all cleaned, boss."

"Good boy, Jonathan," Carl praised as the boy made his exit. "He's right. We take what we do here *very* seriously. Which is why I am going to sit right here while you boys go back to one of the changing booths and try these things on. Everything except the plug, at least."

Cory blushed, Nic looked confused, and Derek just smiled.

"If you insist," Derek took initiative, turning to the booths.

Before he walked away, Carl pressed a small plastic bottle into his hand. He smiled at the man, nodding as he entered a booth, only for Nic and Cory to enter booths of their own. Carl chuckled at their naïveté. He had a good feeling about these boys.

Cory was deciding which jock to try on first when Derek suddenly entered behind him.

"Cor. You were supposed to follow me," he deadpanned.

"But he's right out there!" Cory blushed again. "He'll know exactly what we are doing."

"Have you looked around?" Derek pointed to a shelf on the back wall of the booth. There was a roll of paper towels and a bottle of cleaning spray. "That's the point." He then stepped forward and pushed Cory back gently. "Now let's see you in those jocks."

"Yes, sir." Cory didn't have the energy to be embarrassed anymore and began to remove his pants.

Derek poked his head into the changing room next door, where Nic was currently fumbling with the cock ring he picked out.

"Dude!" At Derek's intrusion, he dropped the ring on the ground. "Not cool."

"We got our dicks sucked together *this morning*." Derek rolled his eyes. "Shut the fuck up and get over here, asshole."

Cory was pulling up the first jock when Nic joined them.

"Not bad." Derek gave his ass an appreciative smack. "Next."

"Glad you're having fun, boy." As Cory changed out of the first jock, Derek took notice of his growing erection. Derek began to undo his jeans, revealing a partial erection of his own. He slipped the cock ring on it and stroked himself to full hardness. "Oh yeah, that'll do. You get yours on, Nic?"

"Gimme a minute, dick." Nic's pants were still undone though he had pulled his boxers up, cock only half-inflated.

Derek rolled his eyes again and returned his attention to Cory who had the second jock on.

"Also good. Let's make sure it'll hold up though. Turn around and on your knees." Derek didn't shout, but made no attempt to keep his voice low.

Swallowing one last bundle of nerves, Cory turned around and lowered himself in front of Derek. The cock ring encircled the base of his cock, a band of metal molded just slightly to the curve of his groin. Derek stepped closer, the head of his cock brushing against Cory's mouth as he tried to capture it.

"Good boy." Derek moved his hand to the back of Cory's head, quickly pumping his cock in and out of his mouth.

Over the past few weeks, Cory had grown used to this kind of treatment. If the way his hard cock filled the pouch of his new jock meant anything, he was even starting to crave it. They were *definitely* going to have to buy these after all the precum he was about to leak into it. He was already swallowing most of Derek's cock when Nic's joined the party, sporting a black silicone cock ring. Cory gripped and stroked him with his left hand as his mouth continued to work on Derek's cock, using his right hand to play with his balls.

"Fuck yeah..." Nic muttered when Cory switched to his cock, quickly replacing the hand on Cory's head with his own.

Without missing a beat, Cory began to stroke Derek's slick cock in time with his mouth. Nic almost felt proud at seeing all their "training" pay off. Derek had no plans of ending things with a blowjob though. He pulled the small bottle Carl had handed him earlier—it was a sample bottle from the lube station they had passed on the way in here.

"You mind moving to the bench?" Derek asked Nic as he removed Cory's hand from his dick, showing Nic the bottle of lube in his other hand.

"Sure, man." Nic moved to sit on the bench, Cory crawling after him and wordlessly reinserting the cock into his mouth.

Derek kneeled down behind Cory's bent over form, the jockstrap he was wearing allowing for full access to his ass. He gave it a few appreciative smacks before popping open the cap on the lube. He applied some to his finger, which he then used to apply to Cory's hole. Cory sighed appreciatively as he felt the finger stretching him open. This was another feeling he had more than just gotten used to.

Derek worked a second finger in before slicking his cock, resting the head against Cory's hole for a moment. Then he pushed his knees forward and felt his cock slip inside. Cory moaned as he sucked down Nic. This wasn't something he saw himself doing today—both the public sex *and* taking a cock in both ends. He wasn't complaining. He loved it.

Derek slowly eased the rest of his thick cock into Cory. Their frequent couplings had really helped speed up the prep time required for fucking. Any pain Cory had felt lately was almost completely overridden by how good this felt. He subconsciously arched his back as he felt Derek bottom out behind him.

Nic tightened his grip in Cory's hair, wanting to draw his focus to the task at hand. Almost apologetically, Cory resumed his oral ministrations instantly, drawing one hand up to squeeze and tease his sack. Behind him, Nic could see as Derek squeezed Cory's ass roughly, smacking it before he started to move his hips. The three boys soon fell into a silent rhythm.

Well, nearly silent—from his spot outside Carl could hear the sounds of moans, heavy breathing, and flesh slapping against flesh. Each of the boys had a mission they were working towards and would not be deterred. While Cory focused on pleasing each of his owner's cocks with his body, Derek was worried about breeding his ass, and Nic concentrated on painting his throat.

It was only moments later when the boys reached their goals nearly in unison. When Nic grabbed his hair roughly, Cory knew what was coming, so he was prepared when Nic shoved his head down farther onto his cock and began to shoot his load down his throat. Then just as he was remembering to swallow, he felt Derek's hands on his hips tighten and his cock expand, just before he came deep inside his ass.

Cory continued to work both cocks as best he could, suckling the last drops from Nic and trying to keep Derek inside as long as possible as the two caught their breath. Then, slowly but surely, they extracted themselves and began to redress. As Derek and Nic tucked themselves away, Cory moved to grab his normal pair of underwear.

"Woah, woah, woah, you still have one more to try on." Derek stopped him as Nic exited the booth.

"Okay, sir." Cory looked puzzled, turning around to grab the third jock. It looked like a pair of briefs with a circular hole in the back and he stepped into them. "What do you think, si—"

Carl whistled from his spot behind Cory. "Very nice, boy."

Cory stared wide eyed at the man who was *not* Derek standing in the booth with him. Then he realized that Carl would have just heard *everything*, and he blushed.

"Damn, even cuter when you blush." Carl reached a hand out and placed it on the wall behind Cory, forcing the boy to sit on the bench. "Was talking with your sir. He told me I should come back here. Said you wanted to thank me yourself."

Cory didn't think his face could get redder, but hey, there's always new goals to set. His cock was also forming a very visible tent in the front of the underwear. Fuck, Derek wanted him to service this man. This *very* attractive man who was currently groping a very sizeable mound in his jeans. Cory rallied his strength.

"Yes, sir." He tentatively reached a hand out and grabbed Carl's crotch. "I *really* wanted to say thank you for all the help today. Is there anything I can do for you, *daddy*?" He looked up to see how his proposition was being received.

"Oh, I can think of a few things, boy." Carl looked down with a familiar look in his eye, hand moving to his zipper and pulling it down, fishing his already hard cock out through his fly. "But let's start here."

Cory bent forward to take Carl into his mouth, the cock nearly straining his jaw. It was about average in length, but it was thick, thicker than either Nic or Derek. That actually made it a little harder to swallow, even though it wasn't reaching the depths that either of them had. Cory was trying to be very conscious of his teeth, though it was proving difficult.

"I know I'm thick, boy." A hand pet though his hair. "You're doing a good job so far."

The praise helped Cory relax, eventually allowing him to take the thick cock deeper without thinking about it. Before he knew it, he was feeling the bear's belly pressed against his forehead, his cock nearly engulfed entirely. The rest of his pants prevented Cory from accessing everything, but he could still smell the man's musk through his open fly.

"Fuck, boy, you're good at this." Carl gripped Cory on either side of his head, gently pumping his cock in and out of Cory's mouth while the boy concentrated on minding his teeth and throat.

Much like Derek minutes before, Carl also had no intention of leaving things here. And he also retrieved that same small bottle of lube from his own pocket—Derek had slipped it back into his hand before telling him that Cory was waiting for him. So after a few more pumps into the boy's mouth, Carl pulled out and tugged him up.

He wasted no time in flipping the boy around, having him place both his hands against the wall. Cory allowed himself to be manipulated, holding the position the dom had put him in. Carl moved his hands down to Cory's ass groping and smacking it before delving his fingers into the cleft. He sought out Cory's hole, still open and slick from his previous use. The distinct smell of cum was apparent, a small trickle of Derek's load leaking out as Carl spread him wide.

"Fuck, I love a sloppy hole." Carl admired the sight before him before slicking his cock with lube. He didn't need much from the looks of it. "Ready, boy?"

Hell yeah, he was. "Yes, SIR!"

With a final spank, Carl aimed his cock forward and pushed home.

"Oh god, that's thick." Cory could feel the stretch as Carl pushed in steadily. There was a slight burn, but it was still nothing like it had been the first few times.

"Shit, boy. I may need to ask your sir if I can borrow you sometime." Carl paused when he bottomed out, enjoying the feel of the tight young ass around his cock.

Cory wouldn't be opposed to that. Though if this was any indicator, he wouldn't really have a say, would he? He breathed deeply as he got used to the feeling of being stretched this much, and once he leveled out, Daddy Carl began thrusting. *That* set Cory off as the incredibly thick cock scraped back and forth over his prostate.

"Ooooohhh fuuuucck." Cory felt like he was already close to cumming. "You're so fucking big, daddy."

Carl gave the boy a spank as he continued his fucking. He wasn't about to use a cheesy line like *"That's why they call me Big Daddy Carl,"* but ... that *was* why they called him Big Daddy Carl. He had stretched open more than just a few asses in this very changing booth. This was definitely one of the more memorable rears.

"Yeah, you like that daddy cock stretching you out, boy?" Carl punctuated his sentence with a strong thrust.

"Fuck, yes, daddy, feels so good," Cory moaned. *Oh god!* He was close to cumming, but he just couldn't push himself over the edge—until he felt Carl's hand grab his cock through his pouch. "Oh fuuuck, daddyyy..."

The orgasm tore through him as Carl's cock relentlessly pounded his ass and prostate. Carl growled low as he felt Cory's ass constrict and spasm on his cock and continued thrusting. He was close, but he was glad he pushed the boy over the edge first.

"Then fucking take my load, boy. Take daddy's cum in your hole." His thrusts turned almost volatile as his own orgasm washed over him. He felt the cum shoot from his cock as he continued trying to drive it farther into Cory. He gripped him tightly against him, not allowing the boy an inch of movement even if he wanted to take it.

As the two caught their breaths, Cory for the second time, Carl placed a hand on the wall above Cory's to brace himself. Reluctantly, he pulled himself from the boy's tight and no doubt tender ass, eliciting a sudden hiss as his head popped out. Carl chuckled as he reached for the paper towel roll and stepped back.

"Sorry about that, boy." Carl wiped his cock off before tucking it away. "You did a damn good job. Those two seem to be doing a good job with you so far."

"Thank you, sir." Cory smiled. "Sometimes I'm still not sure I believe it's happening."

"I bet you've got quite the story to tell. But your men are downstairs waiting for you." Carl looked at his watch. "Probably for a few minutes now."

"Shit, I better go." Cory finished getting dressed and made to move around the man who stopped him for a second.

"Hold on. I can tell you're all new to this, so I'm giving you the same thing I did them." Carl pulled out a business card from his pocket. "That's for the store, but it's got my cell on it too. If you ever need to talk about anything, don't hesitate to call. We look out for each other in this community."

"Thank you, sir." Cory looked over the card before pocketing it, then he leaned forward to hug the man before leaving. "See you soon?"

"Hopefully." Carl smiled as he left the booth. He had a good feeling about those boys.

# CHAPTER 5

"Seriously? You're *both* busy tonight?" Cory pouted from his seat at lunch.

"Yeah, sorry," Derek apologized. "I forgot I told Tricia we'd see that new Greta Gerwig movie tonight."

"And I *finally* got Amy Palladino to let me take her out," Nic added next. "Sorry, Cor, but there's no *way* I am passing up on a chance at that."

Tricia Helfer had been Derek's on and off girlfriend for a few years. She was tall with long, wavy black hair and was his usual date to school events and dances. They were both popular, from wealthy families, and incredibly attractive. It seemed only natural that the two of them would be together, though they were never quite serious enough to ever make it official. Amy Palladino was the blonde and well-endowed captain of the varsity cheerleading squad, and someone Nic had been trying to hook up with since she transferred sophomore year.

"It just sucks," Cory explained. "You guys both told me we were hanging out tonight." He paused and looked around to make sure no one was close enough to hear them. "It's been almost a week since we've..." He trailed off.

After their visit to Good Vibrations last week, the boys quickly found their free time eaten up. Between school work, football practice, and unexpected family obligations, the only "intimate" time any of them could find were for hurried blowjobs during or right after school. And now with girls getting in the way too, Cory was horny and frustrated.

"I know, boy. I know," Derek tried to reassure him. "We'll make it up to you. Promise."

"Okay." Cory continued pouting from his seat.

He didn't want them to make it up to him. He wanted them to spend time with him. He wanted them to *fuck him.*

"Cor, come on." Nic rolled his eyes at the dramatic display. "It's one night. Quit acting like a girl."

"Yes, *sir*," Cory forced out, his tone filled with false respect, making Nic raise his eyebrow but say nothing.

"Alright, later." Nic nodded to Derek and then left, making a beeline for where he knew Amy typically had lunch.

"You're walking a pretty thin line, Cor," Derek warned. "Careful." He took off himself, needing to hammer out the details with Tricia for their date.

Cory was left alone with his thoughts. It's not like he was jealous. He *wasn't.* He was just pissed off at them for ditching him. To what, hang out with some chicks? What could they do that he couldn't? He *knew* he was way better at suck—

"Hey, you okay, man?" The sudden question caught Cory off guard. Looking up, he came face to face with... Wait, who was this guy? Cory was pretty sure he was someone on the basketball team. He had seen him at some of the parties Nic and Derek would drag him to.

"Uh, yeah, thanks." Cory couldn't remember the guy's name. It started with a J. Jared? Jackson? Jason? "I'm fine."

"Sounded like your bros ditched you for some chicks," J-whatever opined. "Pretty shitty of them."

"It's not that big of a deal." *What's up with this guy?*

Before J had a chance to respond, the bell rang signaling the end of lunch. Seeing a chance for a quick exit, Cory grabbed his stuff, waved goodbye, and waded into the crowd of students headed to their next class. Too busy trying to get away, he didn't notice the suspicious look in J's eyes as he followed him through the crowd.

"I told you it was going to be good!"

"I never doubted that it would be." Derek smiled at Tricia from across the restaurant booth. The movie had let out a little while ago, and the two headed to the nearby burger joint for some late-night grub.

"I know. I'm just so sick of having to hear from everyone about what a 'surprise' it was that the female-directed comedy was *actually good*," Tricia groused. "Why is it still a surprise that girls are funny?"

"Yeah, that's a lot of bullshit," Derek agreed. "In a few months, it'll be some other movie, and we'll be having this conversation all over again."

He liked Tricia. The two of them always had a good time together, and she was easy to talk to. They had been "dating" on and off for most of high school. She was smart, funny, kind... They both ran in similar social circles, shared friends, and their parents even knew each other. The sex wasn't half bad either. Not that Derek was in it just for the sex. Making things between them more official had been discussed in the past, but with so much going on at school and home, they both thought it was better to keep things casual. But now that things had slowed down... Maybe it was time to revisit things.

"Then I guess in a few months, you'll have to take me out again," Tricia teased as the waiter came by to drop off their drinks and take their order.

"Yeah." Derek flashed his teeth in a smile. "Guess I will."

"Oh my *god*," Amy exclaimed from her spot on her bed, somewhat breathless. "Where did you even learn half of that stuff?"

"Can't give away all my secrets." Nic smiled to himself from his own spot next to Amy.

The two were still naked, covered in a light sheen of sweat. Nic had arrived a few hours earlier to pick Amy up, planning on taking her to dinner and then hopefully find a nice secluded spot with her somewhere to get busy. That plan went right out the window when Amy opened the door wearing nothing but a bra and underwear. Her parents were out of town, and Amy not only knew what Nic wanted from her—she wanted the same thing from him. She quickly pulled him into the house, and the two had spent the last hour and half in bed together. Nic rolled off the bed and made his way into the bathroom to clean up while Amy continued talking.

"No seriously. That was *amazing*." She stood in the doorway to the bathroom, watching Nic over the sink. "Like, I knew you football guys can get rough sometimes, but holy shit... I don't think I've ever had a guy hold me down like that. And when you started pulling my hair and spanking my ass..." She quivered for a moment. "Fuck. I didn't even know I'd like that. I owe whoever the girl is that taught you all that big time."

Nic smiled and finished washing off his dick in the sink. He'd have to pass on her praise to Cory later—and test out a few more things on him that Amy might enjoy. She wouldn't need to know about that, of course.

"Glad you had so much fun, girl." He turned and walked toward her, leaning against the doorframe. "Hopefully this wasn't just a one-time deal."

"Oh, you bet your sweet, sexy ass we are doing this again." Amy closed the distance between them, placing her hands on Nic's chest. "Like, *really* soon."

"Yeah?" Nic wrapped his arms around her body, grabbing her ass with one hand and pulling her into his chest with the other. He could feel himself getting hard again. "You up for round two right now?"

Amy grinned up at him. "Yes, *sir!*"

Cory's night was a lot less fun than either of his dom's. Resigned to spending his night alone, he kept himself busy to keep from thinking about Derek or Nic out with their girls with mixed success. He finished all his homework in barely an hour, none of his video games appealed to him, and while he debated jerking off, he knew that was still against the rules. That didn't mean he couldn't look at porn, though. He just couldn't jerk off. Easy.

No. Not easy. A single video morphed into several hours of videos, stories, and pictures. Throughout it all, Cory sat with his hands on his desk, one hand gripping the mouse tightly as if it would immediately shoot to his dick if it were free. There was a defined wet spot on the front of his briefs, cock leaking nonstop since he started. It took all of his strength not to blow his load right there. He even debated getting out his dildo, but he didn't trust himself to not cum the minute it touched his hole.

Frustrated, rock hard, and leaking, Cory fell into a restless sleep that night and woke up the next morning to a hard cock and even more sexual frustration. Cory's frustrations continued that morning as he headed to school with Derek and Nic. When Cory entered the car, the two of them were comparing notes on their respective dates.

"Duuuuuude, I told you: Amy's a freak," Nic explained excitedly.

"She seriously opened the door in her *underwear*?" Derek almost didn't believe it. "She might be hornier than *you*."

"Right?! She's perfect." Nic sounded smitten. "Seriously, dude, every trick I pulled out last night? She was into it."

Cory rolled his eyes from the backseat. Apparently being able to take a dick makes you "perfect." Where was his award?

"What about you, man?" Nic turned the conversation to Derek's date. "How'd it go with Tricia?"

"It went just fine. Good movie, grabbed a decent burger." Derek paused for a second. "Headed back to my place for the night... She left early this morning."

"Nice, man!" Nic punched him on the arm.

"Yeah... it was a good night." Derek was smiling when he looked at Cory in the rearview mirror. "How about you, Cor? Have an okay night without us?"

"It was fine. I did homework. Played some games." Cory did nothing to hide the disdain in his voice. "Woo."

Derek gave him a weird look but said nothing as they pulled into the school and parked.

"Hey, Cor—" Derek tried to talk to Cory, who was already walking away from him and Nic.

"Can't talk. Gotta get to class." He waved a hand behind him, almost dismissively.

"What the fuck is up with him?" Nic asked, just as confused as Derek.

"I don't know," Derek responded. "But I don't like where this is headed."

Spending first period away from the two of them allowed Cory to calm down some. Though he wasn't exactly smiling, he at least wasn't storming off like he did this morning. He *probably* shouldn't have done that. But when neither Derek nor Nic said anything about it in class before lunch, he relaxed a little. Maybe they knew he was just blowing off some steam. Still, he should probably apologize.

Cory approached their usual lunch table, tray in hand, intending to tell Derek and Nic he was sorry. When the three of them had a chance alone, at least. As he approached, he saw Nic talking animatedly to a few of his friends on the football team.

"...then I used my shirt to tie up her hands," Nic continued bragging. "She fucking *loved it.*"

"Are you *still* talking about last night?" Cory threw his lunch tray down on the lunch table before sitting down. "We get it. You got your dick wet. Big fucking deal."

Cory regretted the words the second they flew out of his mouth. The entire table fell silent as all eyes turned to look at him and his outburst.

"The fuck's your problem, Cor?" Derek was the first one to speak. "Might wanna try pulling the stick out of your ass.

People might start to think you're jealous or something." Derek's comment got a few of the guys at the table to laugh, diffusing the situation.

Cory sat silently, staring at his tray of food, red-faced. As he ate his lunch, he continued to listen to Nic regale his teammates with more of his evening. At one point, he dared look up and locked eyes with Derek. Shit, he was *pissed*. Cory knew he was in for it. What "it" was... That he didn't know. Still, he sought to bring no further attention to himself and kept quiet the rest of lunch. When the bell rang and the students began to disperse, Derek moved to stand behind Cory. Hand on his shoulder, he leaned down to whisper in his ear.

"Auditorium. *Now*." The order felt like fire in his ear.

"Yes, sir." He nodded, swallowed the lump in his throat, and stood up.

Dropping off his lunch tray, he made his way toward the auditorium. He entered the dark room which was once again empty. A half-built set lined the stage. Rehearsals for the school production of *Arsenic & Old Lace* were in full swing every day after school. Derek and Nic stood together at the base of the stage, talking to each other.

At the sound of Cory's entrance, both turned to look at him, distinctly less-than-pleased looks on their faces. Cory hesitated to approach them for a second, taking a deep breath before walking to stand in front of both of them. The room was once again silent.

"You want to explain to us what exactly is going on with your shitty attitude?" Derek was the one to break the silence. "You've been acting like a brat since yesterday."

"I'm sorry, sir." Cory stared at his feet. "I don't know—"

"Bullshit!" Nic jumped in. "You know *exactly* why you're acting like this. Are you seriously *that* jealous that I fucked Amy last night? Or that D was with Tricia?"

"It was *one night*, Cory. You know we can't spend *all* our time together." Derek shook his head. "Even if we *wanted* to, we have other shit to do, appearances to keep up."

"I know, but you guys said we had plans!" Cory would probably be embarrassed later by how high his voice just went. "And then you both just … ditched me!"

"I *know* what we said, Cor," Derek cut him off this time. "We didn't *ditch* you. Plans change sometimes. I told you we were sorry. I also told you we'd make it up to you. Did you not believe me?"

"I… I believed you, sir," Cory half-lied. "It just … really made me feel bad. Like you guys didn't want to hang out with me anymore."

Derek and Nic's features softened. They knew Cory had always had issues with rejection and feeling alone. It was half the reason they made a point of including him in every-thing. But still, his behavior today was unacceptable.

"Cor." Nic was grabbing his shoulder this time. "Come on, dude. You know we'd never do that to you."

Cory was too embarrassed to look up.

"I understand why you felt that way." Derek was at his other side now. "But that still doesn't excuse the way you acted. If you have a problem, you can just *talk to us*, even about this stuff. Acting like a dick just makes you a dick."

"Well, they say you are what you eat, right?" Nic quipped. Derek could only sigh at the terrible joke while Cory remained silent.

"I guess it's time for your first punishment, boy," Derek finished his thought.

"Punishment?!" Cory's head shot up.

"Yeah. When a boy misbehaves, he gets punished," Derek explained. "We've seen your porn, remember? I know you're familiar with the concept."

"But—"

"Yours is the one you should be worried about right now, boy." Nic put a stop to any further protests. "We're going to Derek's after school. We'll deal with this there."

"...Yes, sir," Cory was resigned. He knew he had this coming, but that didn't mean he wanted it to happen. Suddenly, he was pulled in by Derek for a hug.

"I'm sorry we made you feel like we were ditching you," Derek started. "I hope you'll just talk to me next time instead of acting like an asshole." He then shoved Cory toward Nic, who ruffled his hair. "Alright, we're all late for class. See you guys later."

Leaving the auditorium, the boys headed to their classes and waited for the day to finish out.

A few hours later, the three boys piled into Derek's car, headed for his house. Cory stared out the window wistfully, trying not to think about the fact that he was about to experience his first punishment. He'd already spent the last couple of hours in class doing just that. *Am I going to be spanked? Not allowed to get off? Oh god, did Derek buy that paddle at the sex toy store?!* Cory didn't want to speculate.

Once they arrived, everyone climbed out of the car and headed inside. Derek's parents were still gone, so there was no worry over having privacy. Derek didn't bother taking his stuff up to his room, opting to throw it on one of the couches in the living room.

"Alright, boy. Go get cleaned up. There's an enema kit under the sink for you. When you're finished, meet us back here, stripped." Derek made sure his instructions were very clear.

"Yes, sir." Cory put down his own bag and walked to Derek's bathroom, no questions asked. Better to just do what he was told and get this all over with.

A half hour later, a naked, freshly showered and cleaned out Cory rejoined his two doms in the living room. Both Derek and Nic were shirtless and finished the conversation they were having as he entered.

"C'mere, boy." Derek pointed to the floor next to them.

Once Cory had moved to the spot as he was directed, Derek produced a small package from his bag.

"I wasn't expecting to have to use this so soon, but now I'm glad it came in the mail a little early." It was a chastity cage. "I assume you know what this is?"

Cory nodded, his mouth suddenly drying out. He knew very well what a chastity cage was. He just wasn't sure how he felt about them. Some aspects of them turned him on—being locked up and controlled like that, having his orgasms regulated. But those same aspects worried him. Jerking off to fantasies of chastity was well and good, but after he came, he was *decidedly* less interested in remaining locked up. Also, it's not like he could jerk off *when he was locked into the thing.* But it didn't seem like he would have a choice here.

"Good. This is the first part of your punishment. This," Derek held up the cage, a small piece of black plastic, "stays on for the next week."

"Yes, sir." Cory resigned himself to his fate. "Do you know how it goes on? I've never actually worn one before."

"Uh, this one is all you, D." Nic held his hands up as if they would be filled with cocks had he left them down. "This was your idea."

"You are such a fucking baby. It's just a dick." Derek rolled his eyes. "Alright, boy, let's get this on you."

Cory spread his legs and Derek handed him the outer ring, which he fastened around his junk. Next came the sheath, which slipped easily over his shaft. Once those were in place, he did his best to remain steady while Derek attached a small padlock, locking the two together. It wasn't easy, and he could feel himself starting to grow hard for the first time since finding out he was being punished. Standing, Derek showed him the key.

"I've got one and so does Nic." Derek tossed the second key to Nic. "If it needs to come off early for some reason, we've got you covered. That means like, if it's hurting you or you're going to the doctor or something. Not because you want to jerk off."

"Yes, sir." Cory understood the concept.

"Next: a safeword," Derek continued as Cory's eyes went wide. "You're not going to enjoy what's about to happen, but it's not going to be anything *too* awful. But if for some reason it *does* get to be too much for you, I want you to be able to let us know. You say that word, everything ends, full stop."

"What's my safeword, sir?" Cory was impressed that Derek had done his research.

"Bacon-dick."

Cory snorted and immediately covered his face, trying to stifle his laughter.

"Fuck you!" Nic threw a pillow at the side of Derek's face. "Assholes!"

"Okay, okay, we'll just go with 'bacon' for now," Derek finished once he was done laughing. "Sound good?"

"Yes, sir." Cory wiped a laughter-induced tear from his eye.

"Alright." Derek's tone turned serious. "You're being punished because since yesterday you've been rude and insubordinate to both of us. You acted out, not just to us, but in front of several other people at school. Do you understand?" Derek finished listing off his charges.

"Yes, sir." Cory nodded in shame.

"I don't care how pissed off you get at us." Nic figured he should take charge at least a little. "You don't act like that. Not anymore. You have a problem? You don't throw a tantrum. You talk to us."

"Yes, sir." Cory was resigned.

"Alright, let's get this over with." Derek plopped down on the couch he was standing in front of and patted his thigh. "C'mon, over my knee."

"...What?"

"*Cor*," Derek deadpanned. "I know *damn* well you know what a spanking is *and* how it's done. So quit drawing this out and get over my lap."

Cory took a deep breath, closed his eyes for a moment, and then lowered himself over Derek. His caged cock fell between Derek's legs and his head was about halfway to the floor. He felt ridiculous.

"I feel ridiculous," he complained. A quick—though not hard—smack to his ass clammed him up.

"Well, it's not called *fun*ishment." Derek laughed at his own terrible pun before pausing. "We're going with twenty— ten from each of us. This is going to hurt. Don't worry about counting them out or anything. Make whatever noises you need to."

Cory tensed up for a moment. This suddenly was very real. He was naked over his best friend's lap about to be spanked.

"It's okay, boy." Sensing his nerves, Derek put a hand on the small of his back. "It's nothing you can't handle, and it'll be over before you know it. Promise," he soothed.

Cory took a deep breath, doing his best to relax as Derek's hand trailed down to his butt. He actually felt himself start to get hard as it rested there for a moment before it was drawn away. Before he had a chance to tense up again—*SMACK*—the first blow connected with his ass.

Cory yelped, partly in surprise but mostly in pain, as Derek administered his punishment. Before he had a chance to protest—*SMACK*—the second spank connected with his opposite cheek, causing him to yelp again. Derek gave him a chance to catch his breath before administering the next four—*SMACK SMACK SMACK SMACK*—in steady succession, alternating sides each time. After another pause—*SMACK SMACK SMACK SMACK*—Derek brought them to the halfway point.

"Fuuuuuuck," Cory yelled out after the tenth spank landed on his increasingly reddening ass. "That fucking hurts!"

"Just be glad I'm letting you curse." Derek rubbed his sore ass, half soothing and half torturing the abused flesh. "Some doms would have you counting and asking for another."

"Yes, sir. Thank you." Cory was going to be on his best behavior going forward.

The spanking fucking hurt, though it was more of just a dull, warm throbbing now. It wasn't entirely unpleasant, if he was being honest. Plus, the feeling of Derek's hand on his ass *was* kinda nice.

"Alright, my turn!" Nic said almost gleefully from the other couch. "Get over here, boy."

Cory groaned as he extracted himself from Derek's lap. He didn't miss that Derek had to adjust a tent in his pants as he switched couches. At least he wasn't the only one kind of enjoying this. Wordlessly, he resumed the position over Nic's lap. He barely had time to register that Nic was *also* hard in his jeans before the first smack landed on his rear. He groaned in pain.

The remaining nine spanks happened in near silence, only the sounds of flesh hitting flesh and Cory's whimpers of pain filling the room. Nic fell almost into a trance as he methodically finished out Cory's punishment. His breathing grew heavy. With every strike of his hand, he could feel his cock grow harder and twitch.

From where he was sitting, Derek could almost feel the air crackling, the energy between Nic and Cory passing back and forth. He groped himself through his jeans where he could feel the start of a wet spot as he leaked through his underwear and into the denim.

Even Cory could feel the change, despite feeling the pain of each smack to his ass. The dull throbbing he had felt earlier had only spread, not quite making him numb but almost sedating him. With the punishment over, he felt warm, kind of fuzzy. He was in pain. He knew his ass was sore, but he was also really, *really* turned on. He felt *owned*. Nic's hand rested on him, and all three boys were breathing heavily but remained still.

It was Nic who took charge first. Grabbing one side of Cory's waist, he maneuvered him off his lap and onto the couch, his head and chest resting on the cushions while he kneeled, ass propped up at the edge. Cory said nothing as he was moved, simply held position.

"Lube." Nic motioned to his own bag—they both had taken to carrying a small bottle on them lately. Derek fished it out and tossed it over.

Kneeling down, Nic popped the cap on the bottle, squeezing some into his hand. After running it up and down his shaft, he spread Cory's ass with his other hand, making him hiss in pain, though he did not move. Inserting one and then two fingers, Nic prepared him quickly before shuffling closer and resting his cock against his ass.

Nic looked down and grabbed Cory's ass in both hands, eliciting another hiss, and spread him. The contrast between the tan skin of his cock and the almost cherry red of Cory's ass fascinated him. He moved his hips back and forth, grinding his cock over Cory's hole, drawing out a few moans alongside his whimpering.

Cory's eyes were shut, which was just fine as the only thing he'd be able to see anyway would be the couch cushions. All he could focus on were the feelings behind him as Nic kneaded and prodded at his sore ass. It hurt, but it also felt really good being played with like that. He wasn't positive, but it sure seemed like Nic was enjoying himself too, if the hard cock grinding up and down the crack of his ass was an indicator.

One of Nic's hands returned to his cock, this time taking aim and pointing toward Cory's hole. As he pressed forward, he moved his hands again, grabbing the back of Cory's neck with one and placing the other on the small of his back, holding him down and in position.

Cory groaned into the couch, the feeling of being handled combined with the stretch in his hole mixing together. He couldn't move even if he wanted to, but *holy fuck* did he not want to. He subconsciously pressed his ass backward, spreading his thighs farther and trying to take Nic's cock deeper. As the cock buried itself completely, the hand on his neck moved to his hair, grabbing a firm handful.

"Fuck," Nic muttered to himself, eyes locked onto the sight of his cock disappearing into Cory.

With a quick spank (and a yelp), Nic pulled his hips back and snapped them forward, beginning the fuck. He ground his cock against Cory's ass and heard him moan into the couch. He could feel the heat radiating from the abused skin against his groin. Then he pulled his cock out until only the head remained before smoothly sliding all the way back inside in one stroke. He continued to long-dick Cory like this for a few minutes, each stroke in eliciting another moan from Cory.

As Nic picked up the pace of his fucking, Cory gripped onto the cushions he was laid across, holding himself steady. His mind was on autopilot, focused on keeping him in position so that he could continue getting pounded by that wonderful cock in his ass. He arched his back as best as he could, no longer registering the soreness in his ass. Even when Nic would bottom out and grind their hips together, it was the scratch of his pubes and the stretch of his cock that he was focused on.

Nic's hands moved from his head to his waist, gripping firmly as Nic stood slightly. His cock never leaving Cory's hole, Nic planted his feet on either side of Cory's knees, his form towering over Cory's. Placing his hands on the couch for leverage, he drove his cock straight down, the angle pushing deeper than before. Cory once again moaned into the cushions.

As Nic resumed fucking, his strokes were now more focused on power than speed. He allowed gravity to help him as he slammed his cock down, on each pass scraping his cock directly over Cory's prostate. Cory could only continue to whimper and moan as his body was used. After only a few moments, Nic could feel Cory's ass suddenly constrict around him.

*Am I cumming?*

Cory *was* having an orgasm. But it didn't feel like a regular orgasm. There was a pressure in his groin, a pressure that had been building since Nic started sliding his cock in and out of his ass. He'd felt this before, but it had never built up so much before. His cock couldn't even get hard in the cage, but he'd never felt hornier in his life—and then suddenly, it was like a dam broke, and all that pressure was released.

"I-I think I'm cumming," Cory announced, hoping he was correct and that he wouldn't be punished. He clearly wasn't jerking off!

And thankfully, Nic understood that. The knowledge that he just made his boy, his bitch, cum hands-free only drove him to fuck even harder and faster. As he slammed into Cory more and more, he could feel his own orgasm approaching. By the time Cory was cumming dry for the second time, he was ready to blow himself.

Nic groaned loudly as he pressed his hips forward, leaning over and covering Cory's body with his own. The feeling of his prostate being pressed and scraped against overpowered any pain in Cory's ass. He could feel Nic's cock pulse as it shot load after load of cum inside him, breeding him thoroughly. He whimpered as the feeling of being owned washed over him, and he tried to press back into Nic, wanting to feel more. He could hear Nic growling in his ear as he came, and then Nic's breath against his neck as he calmed down.

Derek had watched the entire scene play out before him, hard cock in hand. He watched Nic's balls pulsate as they shot their load deep into Cory, could see the way Cory's hole pushed and fluttered when he came. It was another moment before Nic was finally able to push himself up and off Cory, extracting himself from his hole before nearly flopping onto the couch in exhaustion. Cory remained still, only moving his head so that he could look at Nic on the couch next to him.

Derek stood and walked over to the two, kneeling behind Cory as Nic once had. He spread Cory's ass and examined the sloppy, somewhat distended hole. A trickle of Nic's cum could be seen, not quite leaking out but on the verge. Derek spit into his hand and quickly slicked his cock—he wouldn't need much more lube than that.

As Cory felt Derek move into position behind him, he spread his thighs and arched his back—with what little brain power he still had, he knew what was coming and was so incredibly fine with it. The main object of his attention right now was Nic. He watched Nic sprawled on the couch next to him. He was sitting back, eyes closed, chest slowly heaving as he cooled down from what could only be described as a power fuck. Covered in a sheen of sweat, Cory wasn't sure what came over him, but he pressed a kiss to the thick, furred thigh next to his head.

The feeling of lips against his thigh had Nic opening his eyes and looking down, meeting Cory's gaze. As he looked up, Cory did his best to convey his feelings through his eyes, before feeling Derek's cock push into him, causing him to close them and groan. He then felt Nic shifting, his thigh being lifted until it was placed back down in front of Cory, spreading his legs wide. With a smile on his face that was warmer than Cory was used to, he guided Cory's face to his cock.

Cory didn't protest as the cock that had just been inside of him was pressed into his mouth. There was no urgency in Nic, nor any intent to even get his cock hard again. Cory gently nursed on the softening cock as Nic ran his hand through his hair, tasting cum, some lube, and probably a little of himself.

Derek was steadily fucking into Cory's ass as he continued to watch everything playing out in front of him. He could still feel the energy between the two, could sense that they were having some sort of moment, and he had no intention of breaking that. He also wasn't even going to *try* to match the intensity of Nic's rutting. He was just going to give Cory a nice firm dicking and dump his load.

Derek watched Cory nurse on Nic's cock, the cock that had just been fucking him. *Another skill to add to Cory's repertoire.* He looked down to watch his cock sliding in and out, looking slick with the load that he was now churning with Cory. He squeezed Cory's ass in his hands and picked up the pace, Cory's ass rippling with each slap against him. Cory whimpered around Nic's cock. It didn't seem like he was going to cum a third time, but he was still feeling the bolts of pleasure as his prostate was once again played with.

"Fuck..." Derek pressed his cock in as deep as it would go as he started to unload.

He gritted his teeth, a low groan escaping from behind them, remaining inside of Cory as he cooled off himself. He hadn't gotten worked up nearly as much as his friends, but it was more than enough for him. Gently, he removed himself from Cory's thoroughly stretched hole, a splotch of cum escaping after his cockhead. He flopped onto the end of the couch opposite Nic, on Cory's other side. Wordlessly, Derek guided Cory's face to his own cock, and Cory cleaned it gently with his mouth while all three boys caught their breaths.

"Holy shit." Cory was the first one to say anything after releasing Derek from his mouth. "That was..."

"Incredibly fucking hot?" Nic finished his thought. "Yeah. Yeah, it was."

The three were too dumbfounded to say anything more, too worn out to move. Eventually, the sticky feeling of cum and sweat finally got to them, and they begrudgingly moved into Derek's large bathroom. Nic and Derek had to help Cory stand, his legs too shaky to make it on his own. He leaned against Nic as they walked down the hall until he was able to once again stand on his own two feet.

Derek turned on the shower, and Nic handed Cory over to him, helping him lean against the shower wall. Carefully, slowly, the boys showered, Derek exiting first, and Cory staying in the longest. Cory hissed when the warm water hit his ass, feeling much hotter than it actually was. When it came time to finish washing, Cory realized he was still in his cage.

"I've really got to wear this for a week?" He prodded the black plastic encasing his member.

"Yep, it'll come off this time next week, pending any emergencies." Derek was drying his hair as he spoke. "I don't think you'll have any problems though. You seemed to do just fine with it on earlier."

"He came twice on my cock," Nic bragged as he stepped out of the shower himself. "I think he did more than fine."

Cory blushed inside the shower, half embarrassed and half ... proud? He thought that was what the feeling was. He felt good that he gave his dom something to brag about.

"Thank you, sir." Cory turned the water off and stepped out, reaching for a towel.

Once the group had finished drying off, they returned to the living room. It wasn't a total disaster, but they still needed to clean it up before Nic or Cory headed home. As they removed the evidence of his punishment, Cory relived some of what had brought them to this point.

"Thank you for punishing me, sir. I'm sorry for acting like a jealous brat earlier," he apologized as they redressed. He meant it, and he hoped that the two of them knew that. He was really going to be on his best behavior with them from now on.

At least until the next time he got punished.

# CHAPTER 6

Five days. It had been five days since Cory had been locked into his chastity cage. Five horny days in which he was still expected to suck off and get fucked by both of his dominants whenever they requested. Cory wasn't sure if he was in heaven or hell. His dick wasn't sure either.

When Cory *wasn't* horny (however rare that was), things weren't as much of an issue. In fact, he had gotten so used to the cage that a couple of times he had spaced out and attempted to use a urinal, only to remember that due to his current predicament, sitting down to pee was his only option. Other than a couple of awkward bathroom interactions, Cory was in the clear.

But the rest of the time, when Cory *was* horny, he thought he might lose his mind. He wasn't able to get hard in the cage, but that didn't stop his dick from trying. It wasn't painful, but it was a discomfort Cory was forced to deal with on a daily basis, especially in the mornings. The fact that he found the cage *itself* arousing was beside the point.

Not that he was ever alone with his thoughts enough for it to matter. Despite both boys now being in semi-regular relationships, their need for almost daily blowjobs did not abate. Cory frequently found himself on his knees with a mouth full of cock, his own straining in its cage between his legs. At least when they fucked him, there was a chance he would still get off, but the boys also seemed to be making a point of using only his mouth, denying him any orgasms at all.

He soon learned that whining about his predicament would be no good either. He was fine the first couple of days, but during and after what felt like a *long* weekend without sex, Derek and Nic found themselves fielding many frustrated pleas and complaints. After several repeat warnings, Cory was soon on the receiving end of a dubiously helpful "reminder spanking" and had a few more days added on to his punishment. His new unlock date was now next weekend, and he decided it was best to keep his mouth shut until then—except when he was ordered to open it.

"You're halfway done." Derek's voice pulled Cory from his thoughts. "Think you're gonna make it?"

"I hardly even notice it's there anymore." Cory looked around to make sure none of the other students having lunch were listening. "Unless of course, sir, you wanted to let me out early because I've—"

"Nope." Cory knew that was a longshot.

"I think that's the closest you've come to begging since last weekend though, so congrats on that," Nic said without looking up from his phone as he texted, probably with Amy.

"Yeah, you have been pretty good this week, boy," Derek agreed with Nic's assessment. "The two of us are hanging out after school today, so let's make sure you keep that up. Not that I wouldn't be happy to assist if you need a little more correcting later." He was just teasing. *Right?*

"No, sir." Cory shook his head. "All good here."

Derek turned to look at Nic who was still giving most of his attention to his phone. Things had been going well with him and Tricia, but Nic and Amy were almost inseparable. Derek and Cory were still hanging out with him, but there were more and more nights lately where he was ducking out early or showing up late because he was squeezing in some time with Amy. Nic had plans with her tonight, but they had some things to talk about beforehand.

"You still hooking up with Amy tonight?" Derek deadpanned.

"Hell yeah, dude," Nic once again answered without looking up. "Gonna be fuckin' awesome. Taking her out for some Italian food and then back home for some fun."

Derek shook his head and looked at his watch. Lunch was almost over.

"We'll just head out after fifth period since Don Juan here has plans," he told Cory.

"Yes, sir, sounds good." Cory nodded, then grabbed his bag as the bell rang. "Have a good night, sir." Cory directed his final comment to Nic as he left. He meant it. He *wanted* to mean it at least.

Derek gathered his own things and stood up, waiting a moment to see if Nic would follow. He didn't even seem to have noticed the bell, furiously texting—or more likely sexting—something to Amy. He weighed doing the right thing for a moment, but then decided it would be funnier to let him be late for class and left without saying a word.

"Strip!" Cory had barely closed the door behind him when he heard Derek give the order. He stared blankly for a moment before registering what he needed to do, dropping his backpack to begin disrobing. He had just put his shirt in his bag and was removing his jeans when Derek pulled a jockstrap from his own bag and tossed it to him.

"Wore that for a few days." Derek had removed his own shirt and belt, but stopped short of getting naked. "Feel free to give it a whiff before you put it on."

Cory examined the jockstrap for a moment before giving it a sniff. *Oh yeah, that's the good stuff.* He finished taking off his clothes and slipped the jockstrap on.

"Go put my bag in my room, toss my shirt in the hamper, and then meet me back out here," Derek said as he moved to sit on the couch.

"Yes, sir." Cory picked up Derek's things and took them to his bedroom, putting them where he knew they belonged. When he re-entered the living room, Derek was naked on the couch, legs spread wide.

"Good boy." Derek pointed to the spot in front of him. "Now get over here and get to work on my cock." Cory silently moved into position as Derek continued speaking. "From now on, whenever you are home alone with me or Nic, you strip down to your underwear or a jock. Think of it like your uniform. I like your ass being easy to access, and it'll help remind you of who wears the pants around here."

Derek guided Cory's head toward his dick as he finished his explanation, which Cory accepted into his mouth without protest—complaining about the bad pants joke wouldn't get his cage off any sooner. Besides, it wasn't like he didn't enjoy doing this. He just wanted this attention *elsewhere*. Maybe if he did a good enough job, Derek would fuck him later.

Eyes closed, Cory moved his mouth down Derek's length, taking it about three-quarters of the way before moving back up. This was practically an old habit to him by now.

He knew this dick like the back of his own hand. Probably better, seeing as he couldn't really think of what the back of his hand actually looked like right now. But Derek's cock was a different story. He had mapped this thing out with his tongue so frequently he could probably describe it to a police sketch artist if he needed to.

As Cory bobbed his head up and down, he ran his tongue along the shaft's underside. He could feel Derek's heart pulsing through the cock in his mouth. He tightened his lips as he pulled back, leaving only the head in his mouth before swallowing back down the next few inches. He felt Derek's thighs spread a little wider as he relaxed into the couch, the hand that previously guided his head long gone.

*click*

The sound of a camera shutter, or at least an electronic one, froze Cory in his tracks. He opened his eyes and saw that Derek had his phone out, aimed at him.

*click*

Cory's brow furrowed as Derek took *another* picture, this time with him looking into camera. He tried to protest, but a hand on his head kept the cock lodged firmly in his mouth, garbling any attempt at talking.

"Don't worry, boy," Derek encouraged Cory to continue sucking as he spoke. "No one is going to see these except you, me, and Nic."

Cory made no attempt to resume sucking, attempting to give Derek a stern look, which was probably betrayed by the fact that his lips were still stretched around his dick. Raising an eyebrow at his sub's display of defiance, Derek continued his explanation.

"I thought it might be fun to tease Nic a little. Show him what he's missing," Derek reasoned, leveraging some of Cory's jealousy to make his point. "Besides, you telling me you don't wanna jerk off to this when you get that cage off?" He turned his phone around to show the screen to Cory.

Dammit. That *was* hot. Cory was looking at the first pic Derek had taken, his eyes closed, most of Derek's cock in his mouth. You could see the last few inches between his mouth and groin, disappearing in the forest of pubic hair at its base. Derek flipped to the second picture, with Cory's eyes open, and even *that* pic was hot. Cory rarely if ever thought of himself that way, and decided he was very much okay with their activities being recorded, as long as they remained private. He resumed giving Derek his blowjob, silently consenting to any further pictures.

Derek smiled. He figured Cory would fight him on the pictures at first, but the chance to make Nic jealous would be enough to get him into it. Speaking of... Derek looked at the clock—Nic was still in class for another 20 minutes. He opened his texts while Cory continued sucking, tapping Nic's name and sending him the first photo he had taken, adding the caption: "Wish you were here."

A few moments later, Nic replied with a solitary middle finger emoji. Followed by a request to "send more."

Derek snickered. He happily took a few more shots, each varying slightly by the amount of cock visible/swallowed. Then he used his hand to encourage Cory to take him even deeper into his throat, snapping a few more photos once he had swallowed him down to the base. He allowed Cory to pull back once he started to gag, taking the chance to send the new images to Nic.

[Nic: Fuck his face bro]

"Well, well, well..." Derek said as he turned his phone to show the response from Nic. "We wouldn't want to disappoint him, now would we?"

"No, thir," Cory mumbled, mouth still full of meat.

"Good boy," Derek said as he stood up with his hand still in Cory's hair, moving Cory's mouth with him. "Let's help him make it through the rest of class."

One hand holding his phone, and the other on Cory's head, Derek began to pump his cock in and out of Cory's mouth. At the same time, he was also snapping photos with his phone, using his hand to position Cory how he wanted. He started fucking in and out of Cory's mouth at a leisurely pace, making sure to capture the moment he held Cory's head all the way down.

As he picked up speed, photos became more difficult to take without being blurry. So after settling into a good rhythm, Derek did the sensible thing and switched to video. Doing his best to watch the angle from the corner of his eye, Derek took the opportunity to show off some of his "skills" for the camera. Of course, Cory was doing most of the work, but that was just semantics.

Derek began fucking Cory's mouth and throat with the full length of his cock. Cory, though gagging on occasion, did his best to take every inch without complaint. His hands held onto Derek's thighs but made no attempt to slow or push him away; he merely needed some balance. Each time Cory would reach the base of Derek's cock, Derek would hold him there for a few moments before releasing and allowing him to come up for air. Cory would cough or sputter on occasion, but Derek continued to thrust through it all.

After capturing a few minutes of their fun on film, Derek was getting close to cumming. Holding the camera directly over Cory, he looked down and renewed the grip he had on his hair. As he fucked Cory's face with purpose, Cory could only look up into the camera as he accepted the oral onslaught. As he felt his orgasm approach, Derek reluctantly tore his cock from Cory and began to swiftly stroke himself.

Aimed at Cory's face and still open mouth, Derek fired off a jettison of cum which landed directly over Cory's lips and the bridge of his nose. The following shots of cum continued to paint his face, splattering him like an abstract painting. Swallowing whatever cum had landed in his mouth, Cory leaned forward to clean off Derek's cock, sucking out any remaining cum he could find. All the while, Derek continued filming, not stopping until Cory released his now-cleaned cock with an audible *pop!*

"Fuck, boy, that was great." Derek flopped back onto the couch behind him. "Hold still a second." Derek took a few more photos of Cory's cum-covered face, his lips red and swollen from use. "Alright, go clean yourself up."

Cory stood and walked to the bathroom, returning a minute later with a freshly washed face. He took a seat on the floor in front of Derek without being told. As he did, Derek leaned forward, once again showing him the screen of his phone.

"What do ya think?" Derek swiped through the photos before landing on the video. "Pretty hot right?"

"Yes, sir. *Very* hot," Cory responded, mesmerized by the images of himself on the screen. "We should definitely do more of that. If you wanted to. Sir."

Derek smiled as he pulled his phone back, once again sending a few things to Nic. A few photos, a clip of the video, and finally a shot of Cory's messy face at the end. Class would be getting out soon, and Derek snickered at the thought of him having to walk out while trying to cover up the tent he was pitching.

"Now then, boy." Derek returned his attention to Cory. "What should we do next?"

Nic adjusted himself in his pants at dinner. He probably shouldn't have used Amy's trip to the bathroom to look through the stuff Derek had sent him earlier but... Oh, well. At least he wasn't in the middle of class this time. *Asshole.*

The pictures were hot though. And that bothered him more then he wanted to think about right now. Should he really be getting turned on looking at two guys like that? He wasn't gay. He was on a date with a girl *right now*, a girl he was going to take home and have very hot sex with. It didn't make sense.

He probably shouldn't worry about it being that deep. Derek was only doing it to fuck with him. He'd need to think of some way to get him back, though. He wondered if Amy would be up for recording anything...

"Hey." Amy had returned to their booth and smiled at him from across the table.

"Hey." Nic smiled back, the thoughts of his friends all but abandoning his mind. "Hope you're having a fun night."

"It's been *okay*, I guess," she teased him. "I think I'm ready to get out of here though."

"Yeah? You got big plans later?" he teased back.

"Well, just had this bottle of wine and a pair of handcuffs at home waiting..." She looked serious for a moment. "But, if you wanna keep hanging out in some old Italian restaurant instead..."

"CAN I GET THE CHECK?" Nic looked around for their waiter, shouting his request.

*Come on, man, I have places to go, tits to see...*

This was not how Cory thought his Wednesday night would be going. He wasn't complaining, he just really wasn't expecting ... *this*. Currently, Cory was on his back in the center of Derek's bed. He was alone, which normally wouldn't be a problem, but he was also currently tied to said bed. Maybe not tied, just ... hooked? Was that what a cara-biner did? Whatever. He was *cuffed* to the bed by his arms, both stretched above his head toward either corner.

When Derek had first sat on the bed and helped him put his cuffs on, he figured he was about to spend some time being restrained. But *then* when Derek had him lie back and showed him the new bondage straps hiding under his mattress Cory pulled on his restraints, testing them. *Fuck, this is hot.*

His ankles also had cuffs on, but Derek hadn't attached them before he left the room a minute ago. He said he had to use the bathroom... It *had* only been a minute or two, right? He didn't think this was a prank ... or part of his punishment. He could probably unhook the cuffs if he needed to—

"How are your wrists?" Cory jumped. He hadn't heard Derek walk back in the room. "Do they hurt at all?"

"No, sir." Cory reflexively pulled on his wrists, testing the bonds. "They feel fine."

"Good." Cory watched Derek move to the foot of the bed. At some point, he had put his cock ring on. "Let's get the rest of you strapped in then."

Taking a hold of Cory's right foot, he stretched it to the corner of the bed, attaching it to a strap that came up from under the mattress. Then he did the same with the left.

"How's that?" He tested the restraint on Cory's ankle before allowing him to do the same.

"Seems fine, sir." Cory wiggled his toes. "No problems so far."

"Great." Derek moved back up toward the head of the bed. "I'd ask what else you thought about it, but you look like you're enjoying yourself plenty."

At the center of the bed, Cory's cock was straining in its cage, a steady stream of precum leaking from the opening at the tip and leaving a wet spot on the front of his jock. Derek needed to make sure he checked the cage for washing later, something Carl had told him to look out for. He and the older man had kept in touch over text since meeting at the sex shop, Carl offering advice whenever Derek had a question about something involving Cory and his training. Derek had started to look to him as a sort of mentor when it came to kink.

"You can thank Daddy Carl for the bondage straps." He tugged at Cory's bound wrist. "He showed me a few places online that I could find very *specific* types of toys."

"Not bad for a test run," Derek continued, tweaking one of Cory's nipples and causing the boy to jump. "And when we aren't using them, the straps just fold under the mattress, hidden from anyone else."

"They're very ... practical, sir." Though Cory was still pretty sure he couldn't get away with hiding them at *his* house.

"We should see what Nic thinks, right boy?" Derek pulled out his phone.

"Yes. Yes, we should, sir." *For ... science?*

As he was taking a few shots of Cory on the bed, Derek groped and squeezed his cock. He was starting to get hard again, thinking about the rest of his plans for the night. He kneeled on the mattress on Cory's side, hardening cock still in hand. Then he was straddling Cory's chest, his weight pressing Cory down into the mattress. He waited a moment, making sure Cory's breathing wasn't labored, before moving up toward his face.

Cory looked up as Derek towered over him. His dick, once again fully hard, looked gigantic from this angle. Derek gripped it in his hand and brought it down, slapping him in the face a few times, leaving a smattering of precum on his cheeks. Phone still out, Derek snapped a few more photos. Almost instinctively, Cory opened his mouth, chasing Derek as best he could in an attempt to capture his cock.

Derek teased him, his dick always just out of reach, tapping or stroking it against him where he couldn't reach, streaks of precum dotting Cory's face. Eventually, he acquiesced and allowed Cory to engulf him. At first only sucking on the head, Cory swallowed as much of Derek as he could from this angle.

Derek allowed him to bob awkwardly on the first few inches of his cock for a few minutes, enjoying the look of determination on Cory's face as he dutifully attended to his dom. And capturing it on film, of course. Taking pity on the poor boy, he used his free hand to grab a handful of Cory's brown hair. Pulling his head forward allowed Cory to swallow another few inches.

Derek pulled his cock from Cory's mouth. Rather than release Cory's head, he pulled it back toward the mattress. Kneeling up and forward, Derek reinserted himself, pressing his cock down into Cory's throat. He still wouldn't be able to seat himself fully at this angle, but this way he could still get most of his dick wet. Besides, Carl had showed him other positions that were *perfect* for face fucking, and they had plenty of time tonight.

Cory was doing his best to take everything he was being given. As Derek fucked down into his mouth, Cory focused on keeping his throat relaxed and making sure to breath when he was able. He could feel the head of Derek's dick scraping against his tongue, each time basting Cory's tastebuds with his fluids. Cory moaned as he felt the grip of Derek's hand in his hair tighten, only reinforcing his feeling of being restrained.

Derek slowed the pumping of his hips, removing his cock from Cory's face. He wasn't sure how Cory was going to react to what he was about to do, but he was *pretty* sure he'd be fine. Derek unstraddled Cory's chest for only a moment, turned around, and re-straddled him in reverse. Then he moved backward, hooked his feet over Cory's arms, and lowered his ass to his face.

"Eat my ass, boy." With one hand, Derek gripped Cory's hair and pulled him up toward his ass. He sensed only a moment of hesitation before he suddenly felt a wet tongue against his hole.

"*Holy shit* does that feel good," Derek said with a groan, still holding Cory's face against his ass.

Cory was also enjoying himself. He hadn't ever done this before, of course, but he'd thought about it and thought about having it done to him. When Derek first turned around, he wasn't sure what he was doing, and he knew even less when he started backing up. But he caught on pretty quickly once, you know, his face was shoved into an ass. That first lick was very, *very* tentative, but all Cory tasted was skin and maybe soap? That must have been what Derek was doing in the bathroom.

*Thank you, sir,* Cory thought as he continued to lick across Derek's hole.

"*Fuck* boy, seriously, should have had you doing this a *long* time ago." Derek continued holding Cory by the hair as his ass was eaten, but his grip was loose enough to allow

Cory to move how he wanted for now. "Bet Nic will be too chickenshit to try it though."

*Yeah, probably.* Cory thought Nic would freak out over anything being *near* his ass. Whatever.

Derek stroked his cock as he was rimmed, slow sliding his hand up and down as he ground his ass backward into Cory's face. This seriously felt *amazing.* He absolutely understood why people did this. Fuck, he could probably cum just from jerking off to this, if he wanted. But the plan wasn't to cum yet, so he kept his stroking slow and steady, working himself up but not pushing himself to the edge.

"Fuck, boy, get your tongue in there. Fucking *eat that ass.*" Derek became forceful again with the grip on his hair, and Cory did his best to appease his sir.

Prodding gently at Derek's hole, he pushed his tongue, again tasting only skin, soap, and maybe a little musk. He could only smell sweat and well, *Derek*, a scent he had become all too familiar with. He groaned a little as he pushed his tongue farther in before pulling back a little, attempting to fuck his tongue in and out as he had seen done in porn. He heard an appreciative moan from Derek above him, so he figured he must have succeeded.

Derek continued pressing his ass back, wanting to feel more of Cory's tongue. He was becoming more and more tempted to just say fuck it and stroke his cock until he came, but he still managed to restrain himself. Allowing himself a few more minutes to enjoy Cory's tongue on his hole, Derek lifted himself up and off of Cory, hearing the boy take a deep breath he probably hadn't even realized he was holding.

"Well," he turned to look at Cory, his cock still hard and leaking in his hand, "what did you think about that?"

Cory was still catching his breath. His face felt like it was covered in his own spit, and his lips and tongue were sore from so much use. But he was so turned on, his hard cock still straining in the chastity cage. He loved it.

"That was great, sir," Cory said, his voice hoarse from disuse. "I didn't think that would be something you'd be into."

"I had it on good authority that it would feel great." Tricia, for one, seemed to love it, and Carl had also recommended it to him in passing. "They were right."

Cory pulled at his bonds without thinking. He wasn't sure what was next—Derek hadn't cum, so he knew they weren't done yet. He watched as Derek moved back to the foot of the bed. He unattached each ankle from the bed straps, tucking them under the mattress when he was done.

"Just gonna try another position, boy." Derek grabbed both of his ankles and pushed his legs back, climbing onto the bed between them as if he were going to fuck him.

Cory could feel Derek's hard cock slide against his jock-clad and caged one. But Derek kept pushing his legs back, to the point of almost lifting his ass up off the bed. He then reached for additional straps from the head of the bed, attaching each ankle and adjusting the length so that both of Cory's legs were pulled up over his head, his ass aimed at the air.

"How's that feel, boy?" Derek asked as he slid a few pillows under Cory's ass.

"Uh... Okay, I guess, sir. Strange?" Cory answered as his dom continued checking all of the restraints to make sure they were even and holding steady.

"Good." Derek nodded. "Let me know if anything starts to hurt. You remember your safe word?"

"Yes, sir. Bacon," Cory repeated.

"Good boy." Derek gave him a small slap on his ass and upper thigh before climbing off the bed once more.

From this angle, Cory couldn't easily see what he was doing, but it sounded like he was getting something from the closet. When he returned a moment later, in one hand he held a bottle of lube. So he *was* getting fucked tonight. Yay!

"Well, don't you look excited," Derek teased. "But first..."

Derek held his phone in his other hand, again taking pictures of Cory in his current predicament. Climbing on the bed again, he slapped his hard cock against Cory, the jockstrap allowing for only his hole to be on display. Derek snapped a few more photos of this, and of him teasing Cory, pressing his cock head and leaving a trail of precum in its wake.

It was this photo that greeted Nic as he exited Amy's bathroom. Taking a moment to relieve himself, he had left her with her wrists cuffed together on the bed for a few minutes. He thought she would enjoy the suspense—she certainly loved the bondage.

But, *fuck*, when did D even *get* that shit for his bed?! He watched a short clip Derek sent, slapping his cock against Cory's hole, causing the boy to jump each time. D was *definitely* going to have to show him how to use those things. And maybe where he got them. *Would they fit under Amy's bed...?*

*Fuck, Amy!* He squeezed his cock in his hand, looking once more at his phone before turning off the screen. Nothing wrong with comparing notes with a bro, right?

Setting his phone to the side, Derek reached back behind him for something Cory hadn't seen him put down. It was … a dildo. *Huh?* It was black and not too big—about the same size as the one Cory had at home.

"Don't worry, boy. You'll still get the real thing. You've just been pretty good these last few days, and I thought you earned a little something." As Derek spoke, he popped open the lid on the lube, applying it to the dildo and wiping his slick fingers across Cory's hole when he was done.

Derek positioned the head of the toy at Cory's hole. He looked up to Cory's face, meeting his eyes as he pushed the toy forward and popped the head inside, causing Cory to groan. The two kept their eyes locked as Derek continued to push the toy into Cory inch by inch. The boy squirmed against his bonds, whimpering as he felt himself stretched open for the first time in a few days. Once it was fully inside, Derek held the toy still for a moment, jostling it only slightly against Cory's walls.

Then he tapped on the base.

"*AaaaAAHhhhHHhh*" was Cory's response as he felt the toy begin to vibrate within him, and he began squirming even more than before.

The toy continued to vibrate as Derek slowly pulled it back out, leaving only a few inches, and then pushing it back in. Derek smirked as he slowly fucked Cory with the vibrator. Taking care to make sure he was aimed at the boy's prostate, he kept his movements slow at first, letting him get used to the feeling. Cory had used a toy on himself, but no one else ever had and definitely not one that vibrated.

As Cory's noises of shock died down, Derek started to fuck him faster. The shrieks of surprise had given away to the steadier low moans and groans Derek had gotten used to hearing. He meant what he said: Cory had earned this.

He had talked to Carl about ways he could "reward" Cory for good behavior, something that was just for him and not incidental to something he or Nic wanted to do. This was one of the simpler ideas they'd come up with.

Cory watched Derek's face as he fucked him with the toy. When his eyes weren't rolling in the back of his head, he looked determined. Derek's cock was still hard, and he looked like he would gladly replace the toy with himself any moment now. Cory hoped he would. He was smiling just a little, his eyes going from Cory's face to his hole as he watched his own handiwork in action.

Derek *was* determined. He was going to push Cory over the edge and make him cum at least once with only this toy. He watched as Cory's breathing became more labored, his moans louder. He made sure to angle the toy up and toward his prostate, his thrusts not too fast or too slow, scraping over it *just right* on every pass.

Cory began to pant, giving high-pitched, almost breathless moans. He could feel something building up in him; he could feel the pressure inside. He was going to cum if this kept up. *Oh.* That's what Derek meant. *This* is what he earned. Cory relaxed for the toy as best he could, not that there was much of anything he could do at this point—Derek had it under control.

Derek could see that Cory was getting close and so he kept his thrusts steady, the moans growing louder and louder. Finally, Derek heard Cory's whispered "*fuck*" under his breath and felt his hole squeeze around the toy tightly. Derek continued to push the toy against the straining muscles, fucking Cory as the prostate orgasm rolled over him. The wet spot on his jockstrap had grown even larger, and there was now a stream of precum dripping down from the fabric. Cory's eyes again rolled into the back of his head before closing, his head falling to the side as he caught his breath. Once he felt Cory relax, Derek gently removed the toy, setting it to the side.

Cory was just about to thank Derek when he felt him shift, and suddenly felt something *else* at his hole. Opening his eyes, he saw Derek was now once again kneeling over him, his cock pressed at his well-opened hole. His eyes went wide as he realized what was about to happen only moments before Derek pressed forward.

"Oooooohhh fuuuuccckk" was all he could get out as Derek pushed his cock into him deep. He had already been opened up and lubed well by the toy, which combined with the fantastic orgasm he just had meant there was very little resistance for Derek. He eased in the last few inches, stretching Cory just a little deeper than the toy had earlier.

"Fuck, boy." Derek's voice sounded rough, as though he had been holding back the floodgates. "Sorry, but I needed that."

He slapped Cory's thigh to punctuate things, making Cory jump. Placing one hand on the back of each thigh, Derek used his weight to press Cory's legs even farther back, using the leverage to begin sliding his cock in and out of Cory's ass. Cory could only groan, not having had a moment to form a coherent thought since his orgasm. It was not unlike when Derek and Nic would both take a turn with him, not even a moment between cocks to gather his wits.

Cory was okay with this, though. Derek wasn't hurting him. Hell, maybe he'd even get to cum again—he still had three more days of chastity after all. He warmed to his second fucking of the night quickly, throwing his head back and moaning as he enjoyed the sensations.

Seeing Cory relax fully was all the signal Derek needed to start fucking in earnest. He pulled his hips back until only an inch or two remained within the smaller boy, then allowed his weight to carry him back down, slapping his thighs against Cory's. Each slap of skin would be punctuated by a groan from Cory, a combination of the pressure over his prostate and some of the wind being knocked out of him. With Cory's legs held up the way they were, neither boy had to worry about holding them up or straining Cory's muscles. He'd probably still be a little sore once they were done, but at the moment, he couldn't care less.

Derek dropped his upper body, holding himself up on his hands as his hips continued to thrust down into Cory's hole. Their faces hovered only inches from each other as they fucked, breathing heavily, complexions red. Sweat dripped down Derek's nose onto Cory's cheek. Both were silent other than the animalistic grunts and groans they couldn't help but make.

A feeling of possession suddenly washed over Derek, thoughts of owning this tied boy below him permeating his mind. Cursing, he gripped Cory with one hand by the throat. He didn't squeeze, didn't cut off his airflow, simply held it there, held him in place. Cory whimpered as he felt the fingers tighten around his neck, reveling in the moment of ownership.

"Who do you belong to, boy?" Derek growled out between clenched teeth.

"YoOUu, sir," Cory managed to get out between moans.

Growling again, Derek spit onto Cory's face, making Cory moan as the spray of saliva hit him. Eyes closed, he could once again only take what his dom was giving him, and take it he did.

"Fuck, boy, I'm gonna cum," Derek breathed into his ear, his body dropping farther to cover Cory's as he started. "Gonna fucking breed this hole."

Derek continuously ground himself forward, hips shaking with each shot of cum being unloaded inside of Cory. The hand around Cory's neck had migrated to one of his wrists, and Derek's body had collapsed on top of his, his head right next to Cory's left ear. He could feel Derek's breath on his cheek as his hips finally slowed and eventually stopped, the two boys now still.

After a minute, Derek lifted himself up slightly, hovering just above Cory's face. For a moment, he looked like he was going to say something... Maybe even do something... but a moment later, it was gone, and Derek was back on his knees, gently easing his cock out of Cory's hole. He carefully undid both of the cuffs on his ankles, setting his legs down gently and allowing Cory to stretch while he did the same for his wrists.

"So, what did you think, boy?" Derek was tucking away the straps under the mattress. "Good investment?"

"*Great* investment, sir." Cory stretched his arms above his head. "And thank you, for the reward."

"Like I said, you earned it," Derek praised. "Keep up the good work and there will be more rewards in your future."

Cory made to get up on his own but quickly fell back to the bed, his legs feeling like jelly. Derek laughed and helped him up, allowing him to lean against him while his Bambi-legs got back to normal on the way to the bathroom. He even turned on the shower for him.

As the two cleaned up, Cory watched Derek silently. Something about him was different. Not bad. But something between them had changed. Something that meant they were becoming more than just best friends who fuck. Cory was starting to wonder if this was just about the sex anymore.

# CHAPTER 7

Cory was practically bouncing in his seat in the back of Derek's car. It was Friday, and school had just let out; they were headed to the cabin for the weekend. That itself would normally be something Cory would really look forward to, but what he was *really* excited about was the fact that his chastity cage was supposed to come off tomorrow. He'd been on his best behavior, especially since his night alone with Derek. The possibility of earning another reward was incentive enough.

"You doing okay back there, Cor?" Nic turned in his seat, sensing Cory's excitement.

"Yes, sir!" Cory tried to rein in his energy. "Just ... looking forward to the weekend."

Cabin weekends were always fun, but this would be the first time they would be back, almost three months since the weekend Nic and Derek had first taken ownership of Cory. Nic had even told Amy he would be in the middle of the woods all weekend and wouldn't be able to check his phone much. They'd both be all Cory's, and Cory all theirs.

"Looking forward to getting that cage off too, right?" Derek turned the car off the main road into the woods as he spoke.

"The thought may have crossed my mind, sir," Cory added nonchalantly.

"Well, careful, boy. Don't get ahead of yourself," Nic warned, smiling devilishly. "You still gotta make it through tonight."

"Yes, sir." Cory knew Nic was just teasing him... Right?

"I kinda like you like this," Nic continued. "Quiet, obedient... Might need to keep you locked up and horny more often."

Cory found it hard to agree with that. He wasn't sure he'd survive being locked up any longer. The hardest part of this week and a half had been not being such a smart-ass, and that was almost impossible hanging around these two.

"Are we doing anything special this weekend, sirs?" he asked, changing the subject.

"Ouch, Cor. I'm hurt," Derek said with feigned offense. "I thought *everything* we did together was special."

"Of *course*, sir." Cory rolled his eyes. "I treasure every moment spent with you both." He made no attempt to hide the sarcasm in his voice.

"Good because we are goddamned *delightful*," Nic insisted, turning back around as Derek drove up the path to the cabin.

Derek parked the car and the three boys spilled out of the car. Popping the trunk open, they grabbed their bags and a few supplies—Derek was usually pretty good about remembering to hit the grocery store the night before a cabin weekend. Nic had just pulled out a case of water bottles and Cory made to grab them but then Nic stopped him.

"Hold on." Nic narrowed his eyes. "Aren't you forgetting something?"

Cory looked puzzled. What was he forgetting?

"Your uniform, boy." Derek motioned to his clothing. "Lose 'em."

Cory's eyes went wide for a moment. Derek and Nic expected him to strip down right there in the open? He looked around at the trees surrounding the cabin and the cover they provided, and in all their time up there Cory couldn't recall ever having someone dropping by unexpected... So, fuck it. Looking first at Derek and then locking eyes with Nic, he took his shirt off, pulled down his shorts and underwear and stepped out of them, and held his arms out to Nic to take the case of water.

Surprised and even proud at the brazen display, Nic handed over the water, which Cory took, turned around, and walked into the cabin without complaint. Nic looked to Derek.

"This is gonna be an interesting weekend."

The car was unloaded quickly, food put away, and bags unpacked. For the first couple of hours, the boys just relaxed; it had still been a school day, and they all needed to unwind. The three hung out, same as they always had here, the only difference being what they wore.

Derek and Nic were on one of the couches, both in just a pair of shorts, same as always, and Cory was in an easy chair, having changed into one of the jockstraps Derek had bought him at Good Vibrations. He liked the way it hugged his butt, and it didn't take long for Cory to stop thinking about his state of undress. He was always a little chubbier than the other two, but had become increasingly comfortable with his own body and nudity since this had all started. No one else batted an eye either.

But as was often the case with teenage boys, especially when kept in close quarters together, hormones began pumping. One minute, they were talking about the last episode of *House of the Dragon* they had watched, and the next, Derek was rubbing himself through his shorts, his erection straining the material.

"I *know* the last show ended pretty badly, but I really think—" Cory stopped mid-sentence once he noticed Derek's cock tenting his shorts.

"See something you like, Cor?" Derek taunted.

"Yes, sir, I do." He was already stripped down. No reason to play coy now.

"Great." Derek shifted on the couch. "Why don't you get over here between my legs and warm up my cock with your mouth?"

"Yes, sir," Cory said as he slid to the floor, crawling over to the couch Derek and Nic sat on.

Derek rested his hands behind his head, laying back on the couch with his legs sprawled. His shorts were still on, his erection starting to leave a small wet spot at the apex of the tent it was pitching, precum leaking through the fabric. Rather than pull down his waistband, Cory reached his hand up the leg of Derek's shorts. They were wide, so there were no issues in pulling Derek's cock out, the fabric easily sliding up his thigh to free it.

Cory took the head into his mouth, swirling his tongue around to collect and swallow the precum that had pooled there. Then he licked his way down the shaft until he reached Derek's full, furry balls. Nuzzling his face, he inhaled the intoxicating scent of his best friend and dominant. He could feel every fold of skin as he ran his tongue along Derek's sack, feeling them tighten to his body at the initial stimulation before loosening back up under his ministrations. Derek took a deep breath before letting out a nice relaxing sigh, petting his hand through Cory's hair, and guiding him to swallow his cock.

"Good boy. Nice and slow. I don't wanna cum. Just want you to make my dick feel good," Derek said as Cory began to slowly bob up and down.

He turned to Nic, and the two continued their earlier conversation as though it hadn't ended, and like he wasn't getting his dick sucked right then. Nic could only shake his head at Derek's display ... at first. A few minutes in, and he decided that not only was it a great idea, but he also wanted a turn.

After a few more minutes, Nic paused the conversation to make his request known. But it was to Derek, not Cory.

"D, send the boy over here for a minute. My dick needs a little warming up too."

Derek smiled at his friend, happy to oblige. He tugged at Cory's hair, who was too engrossed in what he was doing to be paying attention.

"Time to switch cocks, boy." Derek nodded his head toward Nic.

Cory looked over to see Nic sitting in a similar position to Derek, though with his cock already pulled out.

"Yes, sir," he said with a smile, shuffling over to Nic's end of the couch.

He mirrored his actions on Derek, starting with the head and working his way down to Nic's heavy sack. His balls were heavier than Derek's, and his body hair much thicker, the black hair coating his entire body. Cory ran his hands up

Nic's furry, muscular thighs as he moved up to take the shaft into his mouth slowly.

Nic's hand found its way to Cory's hair, and the conversation resumed once more. The boys continued using Cory as a cock-warmer, trading him off between them every few minutes. Cory was only too happy to share, losing track of time and the rest of his surroundings...

A few hours later and Cory was outside, standing over a grill. He was happy for the apron—burger grease burns were no fun—but wearing it, a jockstrap, and nothing else outside felt a little ridiculous. He was glad it wasn't mosquito season—the idea of getting bitten on the ass made him subconsciously scratch himself.

The burgers looked good, so he walked back inside to check on the fries he had thrown in the oven. Aside from the dick being fed to him earlier, the boys hadn't eaten anything since lunch. Once Nic's stomach started rumbling mid-blowjob, the boys reluctantly pulled him up from the floor and set him about working on dinner.

Cory didn't mind cooking. It was something he actually liked doing. He had to learn how to cook for himself at a pretty young age, his mom's work schedule not allowing for many family meals together. And cooking for three people was a lot easier than cooking for himself. The fact that his inner sub warmed at the thought of doing a good job was also a nice bonus.

"Burgers should be ready in a few minutes, sirs," Cory told them as he made his way to the kitchen.

"Thanks, boy," Derek said from his spot on the couch with Nic. The two of them were nursing a couple of beers,

Derek having wrangled another 12-pack to bring with them. He turned when he heard Nic's stomach rumble again.

"Duuuude, I'm fucking starving," Nic complained. "Shouldn't have skipped lunch to hang out with Amy."

"Well, yeah, you aren't gonna be able to bulk up if all you're eating is pussy." Derek rolled his eyes.

"But it just tastes so good." Nic emphasized his statement by making a V in his fingers and flicking his tongue through.

Derek rolled his eyes, then watched as Cory exited the kitchen to walk outside again. "Bro... You ever think about how awesome this all is sometimes?"

"Actually, man, to tell you the truth," Nic started, "I try not to think about it at all."

"What do you mean?" Derek's brow furrowed.

"It's just ... so weird. It's still hard to wrap my head around this being a normal thing for us now," Nic continued, taking another swig of beer. "I never thought I'd be doing ... *that stuff* with another guy. And def not you or Cor..."

Derek could understand that. It wasn't like he'd ever pictured any of this himself. So far though, he hadn't regretted any of it. But Nic couldn't even bring himself to *name* what they were doing—sex.

"Plus ... look, I don't know what's going to happen, but I am *really* into Amy. And I'm pretty sure she's into me," Nic continued. "It's not like I'm gay. I think there could be something, like, *serious* there. I just..."

Derek watched his best friend's face as he spoke. He and Nic had been like brothers for almost as long as he could remember. He looked legitimately conflicted. Whether it was about Cory or about Amy, or maybe even something deeper, he wasn't sure. Nic didn't usually like talking about his feelings.

"I mean, what about you and Tricia, man?" As if on cue, Nic changed the subject from himself to Derek. "You guys have been seeing each other more too, right? She looks happy when she's hanging on your arm at school."

"Yeah, man, stuff with Tricia's been great." Derek and Tricia had been getting together, though not nearly as much as Nic and Amy. "I can't say we're getting up to all the shit you and Amy are, but she seems plenty satisfied."

Usually for dinner, sometimes a movie, and more often than not sex, Derek and Tricia would make plans a couple of times a week. At school, they'd walk to class together, sometimes eat lunch together, and they even went to homecoming together. They were for all intents and purposes a real couple. So why did Derek sometimes feel like he was only doing it because that's what he was *supposed* to do?

Just then, Cory walked back inside again, this time with a plate of cooked burgers.

"Fuuuuuuck, those smell so good." Nic's hungry (and slightly inebriated) caveman brain made him drop the previous subject completely. "I gotta piss. *Don't eat all the burgers*," Nic warned in a completely serious tone as he walked to the bathroom.

Derek sighed and got up to walk to the kitchen. Cory had set the burgers down and was just pulling the fries out of the oven when he entered, his ass on display as it had been all afternoon. He wolf-whistled as Cory bent over, causing the boy to chuckle.

"You're too kind, sir," Cory said over his shoulder.

Derek took a swig of his beer as he watched Cory work, pulling out the fixings for the burgers from the fridge while the fries cooled off. Cory smiled at Derek, removing his apron now that the messier parts of cooking were done. He stepped over the sink to wash his hands.

"You know, boy, I just wanted to say... Good job," Derek told him.

"Thank you, sir." Cory smiled at the praise. "But I mean, all I did was grill burgers. I've seen you do it a million times."

"No, not on dinner, Cor," Derek corrected. "But I mean, good job on that too. I meant with everything. Can't say I know too many guys who would take to being a sex slave to his two best friends as well as you have."

"Well... Thank you for that too then, sir." Cory blushed.

"Alright, I'm starving. Let me help you move some of this to the table." Derek grabbed a few of the plates Cory had set out and brought them out to the living room/dining room table.

Cory hadn't really thought about it much. Things happened so fast that it all Cory could really do was go along for the ride. He guessed that maybe it hadn't started off that great, not the way he would have wanted to go about it if he'd had a say... But it had been worth it, right? The sex was fun, and Cory was learning about himself. Hell, he might have gone to college a virgin if this hadn't happened. And besides, it wasn't like Derek and Nic didn't care about him, weren't looking out for him. They always did.

Right?

"Booooooooooooy," Nic half called/half whined from outside the kitchen. "Come on! Burger me. Daddy's hungry."

Cory snorted and almost dropped the plate at Nic referring to himself as "daddy."

*Maybe in a few years...*

"Coming, sir." Cory moved past Nic to the table, setting the food down.

After Nic took his seat, the three boys tore into the food, reaching across the table and each other to grab what they needed. Thoughts of rank and station went out the window as the hungry teens filled their bellies, the eating only slowing enough to talk once all three had already put away a single burger, each now on his second.

"Good job on the burgers, Cor," Derek complimented around a mouthful of meat.

"Therouthly," Nic said as he actively tore into his burger. "Ith great."

Cory beamed at the praise, digging into his own burger. The rest of the meal was mixture of garbled words, stifled laughter, and chewing noises. Cory was the first one finished, but Nic and Derek soon followed.

"Fuck, I'm stuffed." Nic burped, loudly, after pushing his chair away from the table. He slapped a hand over his belly, which he was intentionally pushing out. "That was great, boy."

"My pleasure, sir." Cory stood and grabbed his and the other's dirty plates, bringing them into the kitchen. He was just about to go back for when he saw Derek and Nic carrying in the rest for him, setting them down on the counter next to the sink.

"Thanks again for dinner, boy," Derek told him. "Come over to the couch when you're finished."

Cory worked quickly washing the dishes. There wasn't too much to wash. He was good about cleaning as he was going, so in a few minutes, he was drying his hands off. Derek and Nic were both standing next to the couch, which they had already pulled out into a bed. On the floor next to Derek was an open duffle bag. The two were talking but stopped at Cory's appearance.

"There he is. Get over here, boy. Got a new toy to try out." Derek nodded him over. "On the bed on your back."

Cory climbed onto the pullout, assuming the position requested.

"After our little *show* the other night, Nic's been itching for a shot at tying you up again," Derek said as he reached into the bag. "Moving and setting up all the straps up here would be a pain in the ass, so I got the next best thing."

In his hands Derek held... Well, Cory wasn't sure *what* it was. It kinda looked like a neck pillow with two straps attached, each ending in a set of rather wide cuffs. Cory was lost.

"It's not exactly the same as tying you down." Derek climbed onto the bed with Cory as he spoke, Nic standing by, watching. "But it comes pretty damn close."

Derek kneeled at Cory's side. Taking the "neck pillow" portion of the device, he had Cory lift his head and settle it behind him comfortably. Then with one strap running down each of his sides, he held down Cory's thighs like he would when he was fucking Cory on his back. Pulling one of the straps tight, Derek attached the large cuff to the bottom of Cory's thigh, just above the knee. He did the same with the other strap. Then he adjusted the length of both straps so that Cory's legs were held up evenly and still spread wide. Cory could feel his confined cock begin to harden in its cage as he was manhandled.

"It's a portable sling." Derek grinned at Cory devilishly before turning to Nic. "What do you think, bro?"

"Yeah, man. I mean it's not as great as what's at your place, but this is still pretty cool and easier for transpo." Nic stood at the side of the bed, admiring Derek's handiwork. He tugged at one of the bonds holding Cory's thighs, testing the strength. "How about you, boy? Comfortable?"

"Yes, sir," Cory answered.

It was different, but Cory could already see the benefits. He didn't have to worry about holding his own legs up, and neither of them would have to help him either. He might be immobile, but that seemed like a small price to pay for the provided ease-of-access.

"Good." Nic dropped his shorts, stroking his already growing dick. "Time to take it for a test run then."

Nic moved onto the bed, kneeling next to Cory's head. He grabbed his cock and tapped it against Cory's lips, which opened automatically in an attempt to capture it. Smirking, Nic pulled back his foreskin and allowed Cory to turn and engulf his head, swiping over the built up precum. Cory's hand came up to wrap around the base of his dick, stroking it slowly. The weight on the bed shifted as Derek moved to Cory's other side, mimicking Nic. Feeling the wet tapping of another cock against his cheek, Cory grabbed it with his remaining free hand, attempting to stroke it in time with Nic's.

After a few minutes of allowing Cory the freedom to swap back and forth between the two, Nic took charge. Grabbing Cory by the hair, he held his head in place and removed the boy's hand from his cock. Thrusting his hips quickly, Nic fucked the first few inches in and out of Cory's mouth as he held him immobile.

Cory remained still and allowed himself to be manipulated. He continued to stroke Derek's cock with his free hand, no longer attempting to keep pace with Nic's cock as it pistoned in and out. He moaned as he felt Nic tighten the grip on his hair.

Extracting his cock momentarily, Nic watched as Cory struggled in vain to recapture it, mouth agape. Smacking it down against his face with a wet *slap*, he rubbed the precum-slick head across his lips and nose. Cory groaned as the scent entered his nostrils, again attempting to once again swallow down Nic's turgid length.

"Fuck yeah, bitch," Nic sneered. "You love that dick, don't you?"

"Yes, sir," Cory said almost reverently. "I love your cock, sir."

"Beg me for it then." Nic slapped his cock down a few more times. "Beg me for my cock."

"*Please*, sir, use me, use my mouth, fuck me, sir, *please*," Cory whined as he tried in vain to reach for Nic's cock with his mouth. "I want your dick, sir. I want your cum."

"Fuck yeah you do, slut," Nic taunted as he quickly shoved his way back into Cory's oral cavity, head brushing the back of his throat. As he let Cory slobber on his knob, he reached down and smacked his exposed thigh.

"You care if I go first?" Nic lifted his head to ask his question to Derek.

"Nah, bro." Derek looked down at the way Cory was attempting to almost devour Nic. "This one's all you."

Stepping off the bed, Nic rummaged through their "toy bag" for a bottle of lube. Moving between Cory's spread and lifted legs, he popped open the cap, dripping some of the clear slick liquid onto his still hard cock. Wiping the rest against Cory's hole, he slowly inserted one and then two fingers.

Cory inhaled sharply around Derek's cock, his other dom having taken Nic's place as soon as he got off the bed. Allowing him a moment while Cory was stretched, Derek waited before thrusting his hips forward. Cory's head was once again held in place as his mouth was used, this time with his ass being stretched at the same time.

Nic scissored his fingers once they were fully embedded within Cory's hole, stretching him farther. He began to pumping them in and out, rotating his hand as he did so. Cory shuddered as he felt Nic's thick fingers open him up, knuckles dragging across his prostate. Once he felt Cory was stretched and slick, Nic removed his fingers, watching the hole as it furled closed again, as if it missed having something to grip. He'd be remedying that shortly.

"Tell me again what you want, bitch." Nic slapped his cock down against Cory's thigh, his large, almost angry looking cock completely dwarfing the small plastic cage that contained Cory's.

"Fuck me, sir. Please." Cory pulled off of Derek with an audible *pop*.

Not waiting for any further begging, Nic aimed his cock against Cory's exposed hole, the head popping in easily after Nic's stretching. Cory half-groaned, half-whined as the combination of pleasure and pain that always accompanied the start of a fuck overtook him. Turning his head back toward Derek, he sucked on the head of his cock as if it were a pacifier, distracting himself from the slow burn of Nic's thick cock pushing deeper and deeper within him.

Half-wanting to help distract Cory, half-wanting to have some fun himself, Derek grabbed Cory's hair and began to push his own cock in and out, feeling the tightness of Cory's lips as they stretched around him. Looking over, he could see Nic looking down, watching as his cock was slowly swallowed by Cory's ass, mesmerized. Derek was looking forward to his own turn.

Nic was about half way inside of Cory, happy to take his time. He hadn't realized it until just now, but he hadn't fucked Cory in almost a week. That had to be some kind of a record. For every inch of cock he pushed in, he pulled another half-inch back out, slowly easing his way in and causing Cory's hole to twitch as he rubbed against his prostate.

"Fuck, boy," Nic said as he continued to look down. "That hole is just fucking starving for some cock. Look at the way it's swallowing me up."

Cory could only moan and whine around the cock in his mouth, though were he able to talk, he would have wholeheartedly agreed. Any feelings of pain were gone, and all he could feel now was the delicious pressure of Nic's thick member pressing and squeezing his prostate. He could feel his hole subconsciously gripping tight to Nic at even the slightest hint of withdrawal.

"*Goddamn...*" Nic muttered as he watched Cory's hole twitching, his toes curling. "Your hole fucking loves this dick, boy." He punctuated the end of his sentence by flexing his fully hilted cock, forcing another moan from Cory.

With no further stretching or teasing needed, Nic pulled his cock back a few inches, seeing Cory's hole pulled along with it as it struggled in vain to hold him in place. Then he watched it give way as he pushed back in, eager to accept his length once more. He gradually picked up the pace, all while watching his cock toy with Cory's hole, listening to the boy whine and feeling him struggle to writhe in his bondage.

Soon, Cory's breathing began to pick up, Derek feeling his breath and watching his chest rising and falling quicker. Nic could see Cory's feet twitching uncontrollably before suddenly feeling him bearing down on his cock as he was fucked. Nic continued to fuck forward even as Cory's hole spasmed and attempted to force him out. A sudden scream tore through the sub as his first orgasm of the night tore through him, his caged cock twitching in vain as his hole continued to spasm.

"Fuck, yeah, cum on my cock, boy." Nic began to fuck faster and pull his cock out farther. The sight of causing that to his boy, his *property,* only served to make him feel cockier than he already was. He gave Cory a few light smacks to his thigh as he continued to fuck into the now relaxed hole.

"Poor boy, been all locked up for a week and a half," Derek mocked and soothed from his spot near Cory's head. "That was even faster than last time you got one of those fucked out of you. Probably gonna wring at least half a dozen more outta you by the end of the night." He stroked Cory's cheek gently for a moment before giving it a smack and resuming his shallow face fuck.

Cory again whined around Derek's dick at the mention of having half a dozen orgasms fucked out of him. *God* he hoped so because that felt amazing. They always did, but being locked up for this long, going over a week without a *regular* orgasm, it only made cumming dry feel so much more intense. He'd almost be willing to forgo cumming any other way if every time he came felt like that. Almost.

Nic watched Cory as he sucked on Derek, his eyes half lidded. Every so often when Nic would thrust particularly powerfully, they would open more fully, Cory looking at Nic with a mixture of surprise and awe. Suddenly seeing his face scrunch up, Nic felt him bear down again as another orgasm tore through his body, eyes rolling to the back of his head.

Kneeling upright, Nic put both his arms behind his head. Sweat dripped down his hairy body, his hips never slowing from their pace. Cory watched as this stud of a man used his body as he saw fit, more than happy to give up whatever he needed. Loving the attention, Nic put on a show for his boy, flexing his arms and chest as the sweat rippled down onto Cory's stomach and groin.

Even Derek was getting a little turned on by the display. He was hardly out of shape, but attending football practice several times a week put Nic's body in a whole different category. Even the cocky look on his face had some charm to it.

He didn't blame Cory—or Amy, for that matter—for being so enamored with him.

Nic could feel that he was getting close, but he wasn't ready yet. He wanted to make Cory cum again, one more time, before he did. Grabbing him by his bound thighs, Nic pulled Cory forward, nearly dragging Derek's dick from his mouth and seating him further on Nic's cock. Then, without warning, Nic began to piston his cock in and out of Cory's hole at a rapid-fire pace.

"Oooohhhhhffffffuuuuuuucccckkkk." A long, continuous moan followed the expletive out of Cory's mouth as he felt Nic's cock jackhammering his hole. He quickly turned his head and re-swallowed Derek, needing a distraction from the sudden and intense pleasure.

Nic just watched as Cory struggled against the *slapslapslap* of his hips. He angled his cock up, ensuring that he was rubbing against his prostate with every stroke. His breathing became heavy as he kept up his furious pace, determined to make this last one something Cory would remember. He soon felt the telltale twitching in Cory's hole, followed by the intense squeeze of pressure as the feeling built within Cory. He watched as Cory's stomach muscles tightened and his toes curled once again before releasing in a sudden scream of pleasure as the orgasm washed over him. Seeing his work done was all he needed, his thrusts becoming faster for only a few moments before changing to jagged, sharp thrusts as he felt the first shot of his load building up, ready for release.

With an animalistic *roar*, Nic sheathed his cock to the hilt inside of Cory. As he unloaded his balls, he could feel Cory's hole once again gripping him tightly, as if it were trying to ensure his load would coat its confines. Pulling back but shoving forward again almost immediately, the second shot volleyed, followed by the third and fourth. He continued to slam his cock forward with each subsequent shot of cum, animal instincts pushing him to bury himself deeper still inside of his bitch.

"FUCK," Nic shouted to the ceiling as he caught his breath.

Looking up, he could see Cory was still at work on Derek's cock with his mouth, albeit slowly. His hole was still like a vice around his cock, as if it were afraid to lose its quarry. Nic allowed himself a few minutes before pulling out, his muscles sore from holding the position for so long. He watched as a trickle of cum leaked from Cory's hole before it quickly tightened up, not wanting to release any more of its creamy reward.

"It's all yours, bro," Nic said about Cory's vacant hole as he moved back to his earlier position by Cory's head, now sitting instead of kneeling. After Derek pulled out of Cory's mouth, Nic replaced it with his own cock, presented to Cory for cleaning after his breeding.

Derek moved between Cory's legs and looked at the red, wet, and angry hole before him. Grabbing the lube from where Nic had tossed it, he slicked his own cock, using his own fingers to prod at Cory's hole. Cory whined at the intrusion, but he wasn't sure if it was in protest or desire.

"Damn, dude, you fucking wrecked him," Derek told Nic as he aimed his cock at Cory's hole. "Now, it's my turn."

Cory again groaned as he felt himself stretched wide on a cock once again. Thanks to Nic, Derek did not have to struggle or fight his way in, Cory's hole's weak attempts to keep out any further intruders in vain.

"Fuck." Derek watched much as Nic did as his cock was swallowed by Cory's ass. "I don't care if this sounds weird, but I seriously love fucking his hole when it's been stretched out like that. We've practically given poor Cory here a pussy with how bad we've wrecked his hole." Derek watched as the lips of Cory's hole followed his cock each time he pulled out, letting the filthy words fall from his mouth, knowing the effect they would have on Cory as he was talked about him like an object. As if on cue, Cory groaned at his use of the word "pussy."

"He's a real fucking cock hound when he wants to be, huh?" Nic added as Derek began to steadily fuck in an out of Cory, no longer watching his hole but instead watching the rest of him. Cory's breath was once again starting to labor, each seemingly accompanied by a small high-pitched moan. "Fuck, look he's cumming again."

Cory's muscles tightened up again for the fourth time, and then suddenly released as he came yet again on his second cock of the night. Nic's half-softened cock still in his mouth, Cory could only moan weakly in vain as Derek fucked him through it. Every time he came, it felt more intense, took more out of him. He was practically exhausted, and he was the only one currently unable to move.

"Good boy." Derek rubbed Cory's lightly fuzzy belly as he continued to fuck. "Now let's get another two of those out of you before we finish."

"Mmmmph?!" Cory whined, unsure if he could manage that. Fuck, he wasn't going to have a choice.

"Yeah, boy." Derek placed his hand near Cory's groin, above his caged cock, to help hold him in place and get some leverage. "I know you got it in you. Come on, cum for me again."

Cory cried out, mouth still full. He could already feel another building, the time between them shrinking each time he came. He squeezed his toes together as he felt the familiar muscle tightening begin.

Feeling Cory's hole squeeze him once more, Derek immediately picked up the pace. Each orgasm wasn't just happening closer together, they were also getting stronger, and Derek felt like his cock might be forced right out of Cory's hole, forcing him to fuck through the spasming muscles. By the time Cory's fifth orgasm had finished, Derek was jackhammering as fast as Nic had been when Cory was bred the first time.

"One more, boy. Come on," Derek encouraged.

Nic's cock no longer in his mouth, Cory's face was buried again his thigh, letting out short, breathy moans as he was fucked. Derek could sense Cory's exhaustion, could see how hard he and Nic had pushed him. He was proud. He just wanted to see this through to the end.

"Nnnnggh... Sir." Cory moaned weakly. He could feel it happening again. One more time, that was what Derek wanted. He could cum for his sir, one more time...

"That's it, boy. Cum on my cock. You can do it," Derek continued to speak gently to Cory, the opposite of the onslaught his cock was unleashing on his ass. As he felt the familiar twitching and squeezing around his cock, he knew he had met his goal.

"Aaahhh, sir!" Cory was cumming, like *really* cumming. He still felt like he was having one of the most intense orgasms of his life, but he felt something else, some kind of pressure in his cock. He couldn't think straight enough to make sense of it and just cried out, face still buried against Nic's leg.

As Derek fucked his way against Cory's weakly protesting walls, he watched as something shot from the head of Cory's caged cock. *Was... Was that pee? Did I just make Cory piss himself?* His stomach muscles rippled and his toes curled, weak, exhausted groans falling from his lips.

"*Holy shit, dude.* I think I just made him squirt. Like a girl. Look." Derek was in awe as he fucked forward, ignoring the fact that he was nearly ready to cum himself. Fuck what he said earlier. He needed to make *THAT* happen again.

Nic watched as Derek spoke, pointing to Cory's cock where a small pool of... well it wasn't water, lay trapped between Cory's belly and crotch.

"Ohfuckohfuckohfuck it's happening againnnn." Cory could barely control his voice, all his muscles once again tightening and making him bear down, once again losing control of his bladder.

"*Holy shit, bro!* You did." Nic was also in awe. "I didn't even think that was possible."

"Fuuuuuuck, boy, that's so fucking hot. I'm cumming. Fucking take it—" Derek spoke his words rapid-fire, emotions of lust and pride and cockiness all rushing to his head at once as he reached the precipice of his fuck, his own orgasm spilling out.

Bending over Cory's body, he suddenly grabbed him by the shoulder, pulling him back onto his cock, and he thrust his hips forward to meet them, slamming and holding his cock as deep inside Cory as possible. As he felt his cock unload, his own cum mingling with Nic's, he also felt Cory's caged cock spurt once more, the warm liquid coating both of their stomachs. He held himself there until he felt his own cock finish twitching. savoring the warmth of the body contact Cory provided.

Holy shit, how was it that every time they fucked, they somehow found ways to make it hotter? He was finding himself getting insanely turned on by things he never would have even thought about a few months ago. His cock twitched, still embedded in Cory and causing the boy to groan weakly, too exhausted to move or protest. Derek knew he needed to get up. Needed to get a towel and clean up. He just didn't fucking care. He was perfectly happy right where he was, buried to the hilt inside his boy, next to his best friend.

Right now, life was fucking good.

# CHAPTER 8

"What if it rains? You sure the lock will be okay with the water?"

"Should be," Derek reassured a questioning Cory. "I mean, you've been showering with it on, right?"

"Oh, yeah." Cory sounded a little dumbfounded.

"It's a clear day, but if it does get stuck, I'm pretty sure we've got a bolt cutter in the garage at home," Nic half-joked.

"No, thank you." Cory's hands moved to cover his junk.

It was late Saturday morning, and the boys were walking together through the woods. After their energetic post-dinner fuckfest the night before, the boys turned in early, Derek and Nic cleaning up while Cory laid on the pulled-out couch in a fucked-out daze. Too exhausted to move anywhere else, the three boys passed out in a tangled, sweaty heap.

That meant they actually woke up at a decent hour the next day instead of sleeping through the afternoon like they usually would. After spending the morning cleaning themselves up (and out, in Cory's case), the boys decided to take advantage of the day's warm weather and head to the nearby lake for the day. They weren't going to swim—even in Florida, it was too cold for that. The boys grabbed a few blankets and changed into their shorts before they made some sandwiches, threw them in a bag with some sodas, and headed out.

Located in the middle of Hartford Forest, Lake Shepard was a popular hangout spot for kids in the area to throw late night lakeside parties. Derek and Nic had been to a number of such parties, and Cory had been dragged along to a couple of them himself. It was not uncommon to see the telltale signs of empty beer cans and a burnt-out campfire when walking along the trails.

Before long, the boys arrived at their destination, a sandy shore with a nearby cliff that was perfect for jumping off of. At least that's what they always thought when they were kids. The calm waters stretched out before them. The only sounds they could hear were the birds in the trees above. They seemed to be alone with no boats on the water and all the nearby shores empty. Even though the weather was warmer than it typically was this late in the year, it was doubtful that anyone else planned a lake trip for the day.

"Water's real calm. I can't even hear anything other than the forest," Derek said as he walked toward the shore, looking out over the lake.

"Perfect. We've got the place to ourselves." Nic dropped the bag he was carrying next to a tree.

"Good. Remember last time we were here?" Cory put down his own bag, reaching in to take out the blankets they packed. "You kept hitting on those girls from the softball team until you pissed them off so much they threw your stuff in the water. I don't feel like helping you fish it out aga—"

A pair of shorts suddenly hit Cory in the back of the head mid-sentence. Turning around, Cory caught sight of Nic's tanned and furred ass as he posed naked with his foot on a large rock.

"See something you like?" Derek chuckled as he teased Cory, taking off his own shirt and shorts and tossing them to the sub. "It is a nice day, after all."

Cory was slightly red in the face as he stood there, still holding both boys' clothes. *Am I supposed to...?*

"You scared or what?" Derek challenged as he laid out one of the blankets. "It's nothing we haven't seen before."

It wasn't Nic looking that had Cory worried. It wasn't even about being naked at all—it was the cage. Being caught naked outside might be embarrassing on its own, but how in the hell would he explain the cage around his dick?

"Come on, Cor!" Nic taunted. "Unless you're really that scared..."

With a sigh, mostly to himself, Cory dropped the clothes he was holding and took off his shirt. Then, after taking a deep breath, he hooked his thumbs into his waistband and pulled his shorts down. Before he had too long to think about it, he tossed them to the side.

"Took you long enough," Nic teased as Cory took a seat on the blanket.

"Whatever, bacon-dick."

Derek only laughed as Nic threw chips at Cory in response.

The boys spent the next hour or so relaxing, talking, and goofing around. It felt like they were in middle school again. Once they started to get hungry, they figured it was time for lunch.

"Go ahead and pass out the food, Cor." Nic gave the order as he spread his legs wide. He was clearly enjoying the freedom.

Handing some food to the both of them, Cory took his own seat and tucked into his sandwich. The boys ate quietly, the sounds of their chewing barely audible over the rest of the forest's sounds. After finishing his first sandwich, Derek was the one to break the silence.

"So... Only got a few more playoff games until the regional championships, right?" Derek aimed his question at Nic, unsure of how it would be received. The loud groan in response told him all he needed to know.

"Don't remind me, dude." Nic was sitting against the base of a tree, eyes closed. "It's all my dad talks about when I'm home."

"Are you worried about losing or something?" Cory asked before starting in on his second sandwich.

"Nah, not really. We're probably gonna win." Nic shrugged. "There's even gonna be college scouts watching, as Dad likes to remind me."

"That's good though, right?" Cory knew he was going to have a hard time covering tuition. He'd love to qualify for an athletic scholarship.

"Maybe? I still don't even know if I *want* to play football in college. Dad sure has his fuckin' mind made up though. Wouldn't be surprised if he's already got *where* I'm going picked out for me too." Nic paused, no longer enjoying being the focus of his friends' attention. "What about you, Cor? You applied early to schools over the summer, didn't you?"

"Huh? Oh, yeah, a few. I haven't heard anything back, yet," Cory lied a little. He had actually heard from them, even got acceptance letters ... but he was *also* still waiting to hear from some scholarship opportunities. Until he had a better idea of what his financial situation was going to be, Cory wasn't going to be able to accept any offers. If he didn't manage to win any of them, he might be looking at a few years of community college instead.

Cory *also* lied for the same reason the three of them always avoided talking about college stuff. Any of them actually talking about where they wanted to go would confirm something they already knew—that they were going to different schools, and this would probably be the last year the three of them would be together like this. Cory wanted to ignore that information for just a little while longer.

"Any idea where you wanna go?" Derek asked exactly what Cory didn't want to answer. "You've got a *lot* of options for anything computer or engineering related..."

"There's a few places I looked at..." Cory skipped past any information about his financial limitations. "No matter where I end up going, I'm worried about how my mom is gonna be without me."

"She'll be fine," Derek reassured him. "You know she wouldn't want to do anything that would screw up school for you."

"That's what I'm worried about." Cory was starting to lose his appetite. "That something will go wrong, and she won't tell me because she doesn't want me to worry."

"Ugh, parents *suuuuck*," Nic added from his spot against the tree.

"No kidding, bro."

"How are things with *your* parents, sir?" Cory was happy to move the spotlight off of himself.

"They're *fine.*" Derek took a deep breath. "They're ... *trying,* at least."

"Are they coming back soon?"

"No, but they want to fly me out to them for Christmas at least," Derek reasoned. "Better than getting a bunch of deliveries at the house and opening them all myself."

"You know, you're always invited over to my place Christmas morning…"

"Ditto, bro," Nic concurred.

"Yeah, I know. It's still not the same." Derek appreciated his friend's offers, but what he wanted was for his *own* family to care. "I'm also pretty positive my dad's working an event Christmas Day, and Mom will just end up working too. Kind of surprised they even know I'm graduating this year."

"At least they aren't on your ass about college shit," Nic tried to relate.

"They both think I'm going to the same business school they did." Derek would kill for his parents to actually talk to him about college and the future. "Mom probably expects me to come work for her after graduation, just like Craig is going to do. I think it sounds boring as hell."

"Then what do *you* want to do?" Cory asked next.

"I dunno. I think I might wanna do something with counseling or psychology?" Derek liked figuring out what made people tick. "Seems more interesting, and at least I'd be helping people instead of trying to bring in the most money."

"I think you'd make a great psychologist, sir." Cory nodded.

"Thanks, boy." Derek smiled.

"Ugh, can we talk about something else now, guys? Over the shitty parents-and-college conversation. I get enough of that crap at home," Nic griped once more. Then a lecherous look took over his face. "Besides, I can think of *much* better uses for your mouth than all that talking, boy."

Nic's change in tone caused both Derek and Cory to look over. Nic's legs were still spread, and his cock was already half hard and growing. Cory subconsciously licked his lips.

"Get over here, boy." Nic stood up and leaned back against the tree, his cock growing to full mast. "Got a treat for ya." He punctuated his sentence by grabbing and wagging his cock in Cory's direction.

Cory made to move toward Nic before remembering where they were. Looking around, he could see that the lake was still empty, and the woods were silent. Taking only a moment to psych himself up, he made his way to Nic before dropping to his knees in front of him, using the blanket to pad his knees. Wordlessly, Nic guided his dick into Cory's mouth, letting out a small sigh of pleasure as he felt the warm mouth envelop him.

Cory closed his eyes as he began to bob up and down on Nic's cock. It was quiet outside but not completely silent, and it was as if Cory could suddenly hear every individual leaf in the trees, could feel every breeze that blew by. He did his best to not let his nerves get the best of him and drowned everything else out, using Nic's scent and taste to ground him.

The sound of crunching leaves caused Cory to open his eyes, seeing Derek as he stood up next to Nic. He slowly started stroking his growing cock as he watched Cory working on Nic. Without prompting, Cory reached one of his hands up, replacing Derek's cock as he stroked it to its full length.

Cory continued to swallow Nic's cock, taking all but the last couple of inches into his throat without issue. After a few minutes of this, Cory pulled off with a soft *pop* before moving to repeat his work on Derek. Switching hands, Cory gripped Nic's wet cock, slowly stroking it in time with his mouth.

Derek gripped Cory gently by the hair, thrusting his hips forward slightly in time with Cory's mouth. As with many of their recent adventures, the thrill of what they were doing, the idea that they could be seen, only turned Derek on more. Before long, he was holding Cory's head still, steadily fucking almost his entire length in and out of his mouth.

Cory moaned around Derek's cock, feeling the grip in his hair grow tighter, holding him still. Cory could feel his own dick attempting to grow from within its confines, to no avail. *Fuck, I can't wait to get this damn cage off and jerk off again!* Whimpering, he concentrated on keeping his throat relaxed and making sure Nic's dick didn't flag.

After a few minutes of face-fucking, the boys once again swapped places, Nic holding Cory's mouth steady as he fucked it and Derek's cock once again being stroked. Cory allowed himself to be manipulated without protest, moving his head when tugged and swallowing down whatever was put in his mouth without prompting. The rough use had him turned on like it always seemed to; his caged dick was slowly dripping precum onto the blanket on the forest floor.

After another swap, Derek was back to fucking Cory's face, this time with increasing roughness. Cory was starting to have to fight against his gag reflex as Derek's full length was pummeled in and out of his throat. Before long Cory was unable to keep up with the pace. After releasing his grip on Nic as he focused on not gagging, he placed both hands on his own thighs, helping him balance as he kneeled.

"Fuck, boy, I'm getting close," Derek warned, the volatile thrusts of his hips already giving him away. "Swallow it. Take my load."

As if Cory would do anything else. After attempting to give an affirmative around the length in his mouth, Cory readied himself to follow his owner's command. After a few more thrusts, each one burying Derek's dick to the hilt, he came.

The first shot landed directly on Cory's tongue, Derek having pulled his cock back until only the first couple of inches remained. He gripped his cock firmly, quickly stroking the inches that remained outside of Cory's mouth with his hand. The subsequent shots followed the first, coating Cory's tongue as his mouth began to fill quickly. After swallowing down the first mouthful, Cory allowed Derek to finish stroking himself, squeezing every last bit from the tip. He quickly cleaned off and swallowed whatever remained once Derek had finished.

Another hand on his head pulled Cory back toward Nic, who wasted no time inserting his hard and dripping cock back into Cory's mouth. He set a brisk pace, quickly matching Derek's. The slight increase in length tickled Cory's gag reflex, but he fought that down as he happily took the throat pounding Nic was giving to him.

"Shit, I'm getting close boy." Nic spoke through gritted teeth, his hips still rocking back and forth. "Just a few more minutes."

"Hmm..." Derek said from behind Cory. "Did you guys hear something?"

"Haha, dude," Nic snarked, eyes closed. "Shut up. I'm trying to cum."

The sound of a twig snapping in the distance had Cory's eyes open in an instant, though the only thing he could see from his current location was Nic's furry stomach as it moved with the rest of his lower body, his cock pistoning in and out of Cory's throat. *What was that?*

"Okay, I definitely heard something that time." Derek sounded worried.

Frantically, Cory tried to move from his spot in front of Nic but found himself held in place as Nic continued to fuck his face undeterred. Cory could hear sounds of rustling behind him, but he couldn't make out what it was. He hoped it wasn't someone about to catch him with eight inches of dick lodged in his throat.

"*Dude*, come on. We gotta go." That was Derek again, sounding hurried, the rustling noises seemingly coming from him. "Someone's coming."

"Yeah, dammit, *me*." Nic's hips began snapping erratically, only making it more difficult for Cory to push him away. "Fuck..."

Cory found his head held in place, pushed down onto Nic's cock completely. His gag reflex fighting against the intruder in vain, he could feel it expand as it shot directly into his throat and down into his stomach. Nic continued trying to push more of his cock into Cory, his hairy groin mashed against Cory's nose. He bit his lip to keep silent, his muscles straining as his orgasm passed.

As soon as Cory felt Nic's arms relax, he pushed himself away, the wet cock still twitching in the air. Fighting to keep himself from coughing and ignoring the burn in his throat, Cory quickly turned around to see that Derek, still naked, had already gathered up most of their belongings. Hopping to his feet as best he could, Cory made to help, picking up their clothing and the blanket. Suddenly, they heard more noises in the distance, closer this time.

"—and then, like, he didn't even *ask* me if I wanted any of his fries. What kind of guy does that?" It sounded like a girl around their age, and she wasn't alone.

"*Shit*," Derek whispered. "That's it. Let's go now. That way." Derek pointed in the direction opposite of the noises; once they made it over the hill, they'd be safe.

After making sure he didn't forget any of their clothes but leaving some of their leftovers, Cory took off in a quick but quiet sprint, passing by Nic still leaning against a tree in his post-orgasmic afterglow. From behind him, Cory heard the familiar *smack* of skin on skin as Derek knocked some sense into their friend. The two re-joined him on the other side of the hill, Nic rubbing his shoulder in annoyance. Cory wordlessly handed them both their shorts so the three of them could make it back to the cabin without causing a scene.

"Idiot, we almost got caught." Derek was still whispering though his annoyance was clear.

"Whatever. We're *fine*," Nic defended. "I knew what I was doing."

Cory nearly balked at that but remembered their need to remain silent. Suddenly, the voice from earlier spoke again, this time louder.

"Eww, is that a half-eaten sandwich on the ground?"

The three boys fought to stifle their laughter as they made their way back to the cabin.

A few hours later—and after a much-needed nap—the boys were back at the cabin, once again grouped around the television together. They were watching some action movie, though Cory was only half paying attention and couldn't remember the name. There were a lot of cars and explosions. He remembered the first fifteen minutes, but then there was a sex scene and the lead guy had a *really* nice ass and Cory was *really* hor—

"Hey." The feeling of a cold glass bottle pressed against his shoulder made him jump. It was Nic, holding a bottle of beer out for Cory. "Sorry about earlier. Didn't mean to almost get caught out there like that."

"Oh, uh." Cory accepted the beer, the apology entirely unexpected. "Thanks, sir. I appreciate that."

Nic smiled and tapped his own beer against Cory's before moving back to his spot on the couch. The three boys watched a few minutes more of the movie in a comfortable silence before Derek stood to go to the bathroom. Upon his return, Cory noticed that had brought one of his bags with him.

"Alright, boy, you've been pretty well behaved since our little confrontation last week." *Oof!* Cory didn't need to be reminded. "C'mere, time to take off your cage."

"*Oh, thank god.*" The words were out of Cory's mouth before he had even thought them. Cory clapped his hand over his mouth as Nic guffawed from the couch.

"Just get over here before I change my mind, boy," Derek said with a chuckle, fishing the keys from his bag.

Cory stood from his spot on the floor and walked to stand in front of Derek. He and Nic had on shorts, but Cory had remained naked since getting back from the lake. It felt kind of weird, standing in front of his best friend with his cock aimed out. *Weird* had become the new normal lately.

Derek took a hold of Cory's caged dick to keep it steady as he inserted the small key into the lock. Nic simply watched from his spot on the couch, as uninterested as ever in handling another man's junk. He was pressed back into the corner of the couch like it might leap out and attack him. With a *click*, Derek turned the key and removed the lock, opting to allow Cory to remove the rest of the cage himself.

"Thank you, sir," Cory said, quite appreciatively.

He reached down and began to very carefully remove the plastic from around his cock and balls, happy to let his dick once more fly free. Derek took the cage from Cory and returned it to his bag. Before Cory had a chance to move back to his spot on the floor, Derek grabbed a hold of his wrist.

"Hold on, boy. We aren't done yet," Derek said as he once again rummaged through his bag, this time pulling out a small chain.

"Oh, you wanted to do that now?" Nic took a swig of his drink before sitting up.

"Figured we might as well," Derek answered, holding one end of the chain in each hand. "Just replacing one lock with another."

Cory watched Derek curiously.

"It's been about three months now since we stepped in and took charge of your training," Derek started to explain. "And aside from a few hiccups, you've handled things pretty well. So, I think you earned this: we got you a collar, boy."

"Another one of his ideas," Nic indicated. "But I have to admit, it's kinda hot knowing you're walking around marked as being owned."

Cory was at a loss for words. *A collar? Wow. That is... That is great. Right?* He knew about collars, knew they were a big deal, something that symbolized ownership. And Nic was right. They were also pretty hot. His dick sure seemed to think so. But something also felt *off*, looking at the chain Derek held in his hands.

"I... Thank you, sirs." He didn't know what else to say.

Cory stood still as Derek leaned forward to wrap the chain around the back of his neck. Cory could feel the hot breath on his chest. Once the chain was in place, he held the two ends together, attaching a small padlock which he snapped shut.

"There we go." Derek leaned back to admire his work. "It's small enough that you should be able to tuck it into your shirt. Just like with the cage, we both have a key, so if there's an emergency, either of us can take it off."

Cory reached up to feel the chain and lock. It was heavy, but not uncomfortable. Kind of a reminder of what he was. He smiled. Whatever other weird feelings he was having, he *was* happy about this. And again, his dick sure wasn't arguing.

"Hey, D, I think he likes it." For someone so grossed out by dicks, Nic sure seemed to notice his a lot.

"Good." Derek smiled at Cory. "On your knees, boy. Let's make sure you know who owns your ass."

Cory's dick twitched as he complied with the order, lowering himself to the floor. Rather than stay seated on the couch, Derek stood up, his cock already forming a tent as it began to inflate. Following his cue, Nic stood as well, and Cory was soon face to face with both of their crotches.

"Take 'em out, boy" came the next order, which Cory followed first with Derek, then Nic, reaching in and tucking the waistband of their shorts under their balls. Without prompting, he began to stroke them to full hardness.

Derek took the lead, pulling Cory's face toward his cock, who automatically opened his mouth to take him in. Bobbing up and down on a little more than half, Cory used his hand to stroke the remaining uncovered inches of flesh. As he moved his head back and forth, he felt the lock on his collar swaying, tapping him against the chest with a steady beat. That was new.

A sudden tug on that same collar caught him off guard at first, but he complied with the wordless order, moving his mouth from Derek to Nic. Holding onto Nic's cock firmly, he watched as a bead of precum grew on the head. He leaned forward and made a show of cleaning it off, moaning as he then smoothly swallowed the length of Nic's cock nearly to the hilt.

"Fuck..." Nic cursed under his breath as his hand suddenly moved to the back of Cory's head, holding him down as well as helping to get the last inch or so into his mouth.

Pulling back, Cory once again used his hand to help stroke the dick occupying his mouth, slick with his spit. Cory hummed to himself as he began to pump his mouth up and down, the collar's lock continuing to tap against his chest. Rather than spending too much time focusing on one of them, Cory made sure to switch off every few strokes. In the months since he had sucked his first cock, he was starting to think he might actually be a little skilled with his mouth.

That sentiment seemed to be shared between Derek and Nic, who were having no problems finding their rhythm as they traded off utilizing Cory's mouth and throat. The room was starting to feel hot, and both boys broke into a light sweat. The two of them were standing side-by-side, nearly touching, to make it easier for Cory to trade off without having to move much. Each boy could barely hear the sounds of his own breath over the slurping noises occasionally escaping from Cory's mouth.

For his part, Cory was also sweating, though he wasn't paying attention enough to that to notice. It was warm, but all that meant to him was an increase in the musky scent that was currently fogging his head. The way they smelled, the way they tasted... Cory's own cock was jutting straight out, rock hard and steadily leaking from the tip. He groaned low as he continued to throat their dicks.

After wiping his forehead, Derek withdrew to rummage through his bag again, leaving Cory to focus on Nic for a few minutes. When he returned, he didn't rejoin Nic in using Cory's mouth, but instead kneeled down behind him. The *snap* of the cap on the bottle of lube confirmed to Cory what was coming next, so he was prepared when the cold lube-covered finger poked at his hole. Instinctively, he arched his back to allow Derek to find his entrance more easily.

Cory moaned as he felt the finger breach him, pausing briefly as his hole adjusted. Nic picked up the slack, continuing to feed his cock to Cory, the rumbling around him from Cory's moaning drawing out his own. He watched as his cock was pumped in and out of Cory's mouth, his lips growing puffy and red as they scraped along the sides.

A second finger soon joined the first, and Cory planted his hands on the ground in front of him, allowing both boys to manipulate him as needed. His own dick remained rock hard, a trickle of precum trailing all the way to the floor. He hadn't so much as touched himself since the cage came off, and he was starting to realize that he wasn't all that bothered when it was locked up. His body didn't seem to mind.

Cory's hole twitched as the fingers were pulled from his ass, and he let out a small whine of displeasure, still hungry to be filled. A gentle tug on his collar and him opening his eyes—Nic was pulling him to his feet, Derek already having moved over to the bed, slicking lube up and down his cock. As Cory approached the bed, his arm was grabbed and he was pushed onto the mattress, with Derek right behind to arrange him to his liking.

Face down on the bed, Cory's hips were grabbed and pulled back, raising his ass to the same level as Derek's crotch. He made to get up on his hands as well, but the hand on his back told him to stay where he was. Instead, Cory grabbed onto one of the pillows above his head, pulling it to his chest. He had a feeling he was going to be in for a rough ride.

Soon, he felt a familiar *taptaptap* against his ass as Derek lightly smacked his cock against Cory's hole. Taking a deep breath and burying his face in the pillow, Cory felt his hole stretch as Derek entered him. He moaned as his prostate was scraped over, the pillow muffling most of it. Derek didn't stop pushing until he was all the way inside and his pubic hair was scratching against Cory's ass, giving the lightly furry cheeks a couple of spanks for good measure.

Derek barely gave Cory any time to adjust before he pulled his cock back a few inches, then pushed it back in. The pace increased quickly as Derek held a tight grip on Cory's hips, only leaving to give the occasional *spank* to his ass. Before long, he was pounding his dick into Cory, using his tight grip to pull Cory's ass back every time he slammed forward.

Still moaning into the pillow, Cory turned his face to the side for some much-needed air. His cock was still hard, and now steadily smacking up into his belly as Derek drilled into his ass. He could feel the precum splatter every time his cockhead hit his belly. If he was on his back, he was sure there'd be a puddle forming on his stomach.

Opening his eyes, Cory saw Nic standing next to the bed, eyes glued to the action going on behind him. Stroking his already lubed cock, he was clearly waiting for his turn. Cory whimpered at the thought of being used like this, without a care for how he felt. A particularly strong and well angled thrust had him suddenly burying his face again, once more muffling the high-pitched whine he couldn't help making.

Maybe the boys felt the need to reinforce their ownership after the collaring. Maybe just the idea of owning someone like that did it. Whatever the reason, Derek and Nic were determined to fuck him. No nonsense, no frills, no more foreplay—just fucking. Derek looked down and watched as Cory's ass swallowed his cock with ease. Then his eyes trailed up and saw the collar. With a sudden growl,

Derek planted both his hands on Cory's shoulders, his weight pinning Cory's chest to the bed.

The sudden addition of weight on his back caught Cory by surprise, though not enough to make him struggle. He could still move his head, could still breath without issue. It actually felt *good*, being pinned like that underneath Derek. Derek started fucking him even faster now, practically looming over Cory as he slammed down into his hole. Cory heard what sounded like a growl escape from Derek, who never let up on the punishing pace of his pounding.

Cory's cock continued to leak, ensuring there would be a decent sized wet spot by the time they were finished. With each pass over his prostate, his cock would throb and leak even more precum. It had been so long that felt like he was going to cum any second now, *really* cum, and he was just bracing himself for when the dam finally broke. He didn't have to wait long, as a few moments later Derek pushed him over the edge. Using the pillow to once again muffle himself, Cory squealed as he came, his cock shooting hands free onto the mattress below and up onto his belly. His hole spasmed and twitched as Derek continued to fuck, his sensitive prostate walking the line between pleasure and torture.

"Fuck, I'm gonna cum," Derek eked out through gritted teeth.

As his cock made the final few thrusts, he practically roared out his orgasm, slamming forward as each shot was fucked deeper and deeper into Cory's ass. As he caught his breath, he continued to rock his hips back and forth, his cock slightly softer but still more than enough to leave Cory whimpering. When he was finished, Derek gingerly extracted himself, moving to the side to make room for Nic, who wasted no time in replacing Derek behind Cory. Cock already lubed, he pressed his cock against Cory's open and leaking hole, pushing in before the boy had a chance to fully recover. Cory whined, out of arousal and a little pain, burying his face once more in his pillow.

"Damn, dude," Nic commented as he started his fuck. "You really stretched him out this time. Practically feels like a pussy." He punctuated his sentence with a spank, enjoying as Cory moaned and reflexively tightened his hole.

"He may as well have one these days," Derek added offhand.

Cory couldn't really argue, what with his cock quickly filling once again as Nic's nine inches stretched him open once more. It didn't seem to make a difference whether he was caged or not—Cory loved getting fucked. He hadn't exactly had the opportunity to do any fucking of his own yet, but there was no way it could compare to this. Cory's eyes rolled back in his head as Nic re-angled his thrusts. *No way.*

Nic would have agreed with him, though from the other side of things—since fucking Cory's ass the first time, he had come to almost *prefer* it, not that he would admit that to even himself. It was tighter, warmer, and he didn't have to worry about knocking Cory up. Even getting sloppy seconds like this seemed better, the walls of Cory's well-used hole squeezing around him like a vice, but still soft enough for him to pound into with no mercy.

Looking below him, he took the scene in, Cory's ass jiggling each time his cock slammed home. Above that was Cory's back, muscles straining from exertion. And farther up then that, Nic could see the collar, the symbol of his and Derek's ownership. Cory's hands were still pressed into the mattress, as if holding on for dear life. *Well that won't do.*

With both hands, Nic grabbed Cory's wrists, pulling his arms behind him and pinning them both to the small of his back. Other than a small yelp of confusion, Cory made no attempt to protest or move from where he was being held. Nic growled. *Fuck, I love this.* His thrusts grew stronger; he was going to cum any second now. Still gripping Cory's wrists tightly, Nic followed Derek's lead and all but shouted out his orgasm, pinning Cory to the mattress by his hips. Cory's hole twitched as it was once again bred, filled to the brim with his owners' cum.

Rather than climbing off Cory, Nic allowed himself a few moments to catch his breath, sprawling himself on top of the prone boy. He smiled as he felt Cory's hole continuing to squeeze and milk his cock from inside. Hell, if he had a few minutes, he could probably go again. Yeah, fucking ass was pretty great.

The boys returned home Sunday afternoon, the rest of the trip passing with little fanfare, the remaining time at the cabin split between goofing off and fucking. After he was dropped off, Cory walked up to his apartment, his hand moving up to his new collar as he did, and he smiled. He still wasn't sure *exactly* what all of this meant for the future, but it had to be a good sign, right?

His mom was out when he walked in, and Cory was thankful to get a little alone time. He briefly thought about texting Derek or Nic to ask to jerk off but realized he didn't really want to. It was weird. He had spent so much time while locked up wanting to jerk off and now that he was free... *Meh.* It wasn't as if he really needed to with Derek and Nic around now.

Cory walked to his room and turned on his computer, deciding to goof off while he had the chance. After browsing through his usual sites, he checked his email, where he saw a reminder email sent from a college he had thought about applying to about deadlines. *Hmm, actually...* Cory pulled up a list he had made earlier in the year of colleges he, Derek, and Nic had talked about applying to. Cory thought back to what Derek and Nic had said about school over the weekend. Maybe it wouldn't hurt to put in a few more applications. Having more options wouldn't be a bad thing...

"Nic, there you are!" Nic's father greeted as soon as he walked in the door.

"Hey, dad." Nic walked past his dad, intending to head back to his room, before he noticed there were guests in the living room.

"Shit, is that little Nicky?" Luis, one of his dad's friends, stood up to greet him. "When the fuck did you get so big?"

"Nic, you remember Luis, right?" Luis was an old friend of his dad's. They used to work construction together when Raphael was still putting himself through college. Nic hadn't seen him in years and didn't even know he and his dad still talked.

"Yeah, I think so. It was a long time ago, right?" Nic remembered Luis just fine. He was just really hoping this guy wasn't expecting him to still call him "*tio*." "Gabby was still a baby."

"We ran into each other at the gym yesterday," Raphael explained. "I invited him over to watch some football today. You got home just in time."

"Oh, cool." Nic cringed inwardly as he put on a fake smile. "Let me just put my stuff away."

Turning from the room, Nic's false smile fell as soon as he was out of their line of sight. Dropping his bag, Nic flopped face first onto his bed, letting out a muffled scream into the mattress. He was so fucking sick of football.

Derek logged onto his computer when he got home, once again alone. He wasted no time, jumping straight to his email so he could fire off a message to Carl. The older man insisted on using email to talk, saying things like Facebook or texting were too informal. Derek was glad Carl couldn't see him rolling his eyes over the internet.

> *Hey! So we did what I talked to you about. You were right. The collaring went off without a hitch. As soon as I put it on him, it was like all the energy in the room shifted. We both fucked him right there, didn't even need to talk about it.*

Derek had really enjoyed talking to Carl. On top of all the great toys and gear Carl had introduced Derek to, the older man had also proved to be a valuable resource in Cory's training, giving Derek both ideas of what to do and information on proper BDSM protocol. He was a great guy to bounce things off.

> *So, we've got this big party coming up, and I was looking at these remote-control vibrators...*

Lots of very kinky ideas.

# CHAPTER 9

Nic took another bite of his burger, his second one today. He was starving. There were only a few games left before the finals, and Coach had been riding the entire team extra hard. Nic wasn't worried—he knew they'd win—but he was worn out. He was really looking forward to the season being over.

"Getting to eat this much is the only good thing about being this dead-ass exhausted." Nic popped his head up to see one of his teammates, Taylor, sitting across from him eating his own burgers.

Taylor Webb was a big guy, easily over six feet tall and pushing 220 lbs. He had dirty blonde hair and a big barrel chest, which made him perfect for his position of linebacker on the team. Nic had played with him since freshman year.

"Yeah, my mom's been making all my favorite stuff on the nights before and after a game." Nic smiled at the thought. His mom was awesome.

"Lucky. My mom can't cook for shit." Taylor tore another bite from his burger. "Uthually juth endth up ordering a couple of pithas."

"I'll be glad when it's over... But I will miss all the food," Nic said with feigned wistfulness.

Wordlessly, Taylor held out his burger to him in a "cheers" motion as he continued to eat.

"The struggles of being a high school football player," Derek teased, having watched their display silently from his own seat.

"Hey, our lives are *very* difficult," Taylor half joked. "Just because we get out of classes, get hit on by all the cheerleaders, can eat everything we want, and just overall get special treatment doesn't... Wait, what was I arguing again?"

Nic snorted, mouth full of burger.

"Harhar." Derek finished off the last of his food, standing to throw away his garbage. "Well, unfortunately some of us are going to have to rely on academics to get us into college. Got another English project Cory and I gotta work on. Later, man."

Nic waved goodbye as Derek turned to find Cory at the next table, talking animatedly to Stephanie about a new video game both had picked up.

"You gotta remember to use his gadgets," Cory explained some of the game's mechanics. "If you get surrounded, just throw down an electric web or a web bomb. It'll give you the time and space to take down a couple."

"Ugh, it's just like in the Arkham games," Stephanie grumbled. "I never remember to use those in combat."

"Hey, Cor," Derek interrupted. "Sorry, but we gotta get to the library if we're gonna finish those papers today."

"Do we have to?" Cory fake whined as he started to gather his things. "Sorry, Steph. Homework calls."

"Aww." Steph looked sad. "It feels like we haven't gotten to hang out in forever. I miss you."

"Aww." Cory hugged Stephanie. It had been a while since the two of them really had a chance to talk. Probably not since... Well, explaining all of *that* to Steph might be a bit too much. But he could tell her *something*, like maybe at least that he was gay. "Miss you too. Promise we'll talk later, okay? I'll text you after school."

"You better!" Steph shouted as Derek and Cory left the courtyard and headed to the school's library.

"I swear, dude. I just don't get it," Steve, another of Nic's teammates, spoke up, watching the exchange between Cory and Steph.

"Don't get what?" Nic wasn't following.

"Why you hang out with that loser." Steve was still looking at Stephanie as she gathered together her own things. "I mean, Derek I get, he's at least cool. But the girls that dork Cory hangs out with aren't even hot. Why do you keep him around?"

Barely managing to stop himself from slamming his burger down, Nic was about to tear Steve a new asshole when Taylor beat him to the punch.

"Shut the fuck up, Steve," Taylor said without even turning his head. "Nobody thinks any of that, except you. No one cares."

"Hey, fuck you, man." Now Steve was getting defensive. "I'm just asking why he hangs out with that runt."

"Maybe if you focused less on that runt and more on your game, you might actually get off the bench before the end of the season." Steve was third string and not a particularly good player either. He hadn't played at all the last few games.

"What the fuck ever, dick." Steve flipped Taylor the bird before leaving the table.

"Dumbass." Taylor shook his head at Steve's exit.

"No kidding." Nic returned Taylor's earlier burger salute. "Thanks, man."

Taylor nodded his head, already digging back into his food.

"This MLA format shit is melting my brain," Derek groused from his side of the library table, setting down his book. "I'm getting a soda. Want anything?"

"No thanks, sir. I'm okay." Cory had hit a stride in writing his paper and wanted to keep it going.

Derek left the table leisurely, in no rush to return after getting his soda. He and Cory had been in the library a few hours now, electing to skip their fourth period classes—gym for Derek and a programming class for Cory. Their English teacher knew they'd be in here working, as were several other students, and the boys were determined to finish this today, so they kept going even after the final bell had rung.

"They got you doing their homework, too?"

Cory looked up to see who was speaking to him. It was Jackson, that guy from the basketball team from the other day. How long had he been standing there?

"What? I'm not doing anyone's homework except my own." It wasn't the first time someone made that assumption.

"Oh, sorry then." Jackson looked around the library idly. "I thought I heard you calling him sir. Sounded like he was pushing you around or something, you know?"

Cory felt his facing burning as he immediately turned bright red. Shit. He heard them? Had anyone else???

"Uh... That's just an inside joke between us," Cory stammered as he tried to cover. "It's stupid, really. I don't even realize I'm doing it sometimes." *Real smooth, Cory.*

"Well, you know if anyone is ever picking on you, I'm happy to step in and help you out." Jackson cocked an eyebrow.

"Thanks?" Cory doubted he'd need it. What he wanted was for this conversation to be over. "I... I've gotta get back to work."

"Right." Jackson smirked. "See ya around, *boy*."

Cory's breath hitched as Jackson turned to walk away, still smirking. Cory, face still flushed, could only stare down at his paper, pencil in hand, mind blank. What the fuck was *that* about? He gripped his pencil tightly. *Does he know? Did I say something else he might have heard? Was it just a fluke? Does it mean—*

"Hey," Derek put his hand on Cory's shoulder, making him jump slightly, "you okay? Did that guy say something to you? You look like you're about to lose your shit."

"Yeah... I think... I think I just ate something funny at lunch," Cory lied. "I'm fine."

Derek's look was questioning, but he didn't press.

"Well, we're both almost done here," Derek said as he returned to his seat. "Football practice should be over soon. Wanna finish up and head over to the locker room and see if Nic wants to hang or grab dinner or something?"

"That sounds cool," Cory quickly agreed, thankful for the subject change. "I only have another page or so to go."

"Me too, I think." Derek reopened his book from earlier, setting down his soda. "Let's get to it."

It was about an hour later when Derek and Cory walked toward the locker room, happy to be done with their papers. Football practice had ended a short while ago, and Derek had texted Nic to have him wait around if he wanted to hang out. Most of the players had already gone, but Cory spotted Nic's bag on one of the benches. He and some of the other players were probably still in the showers.

"Alright, I'm just gonna run to my locker real quick." Derek started to exit the locker room, seeing that they had a bit before Nic would be out. "Don't need to carry all this around with me anymore. Be back in a few minutes."

"Sounds good. I'll be here." Cory took a seat on one of the benches and pulled out his phone, deciding to try to catch a few Pokémon while he waited.

"The hell are you doing in here, loser?"

*Ugh.* Cory recognized that voice. "I'm waiting for Nic, Steve. What do you want?"

"Of course, you are," Steve sneered. "Always following him and Derek around like a little puppy. Pathetic."

Cory ignored Steve and went back to his phone. He was just about to catch a Chikorita when the phone was knocked out of his hand.

"Hey! What the fuck is your problem?!" Cory stood up and made to pick up his phone.

"*You* are my problem," Steve said as he pushed Cory by the shoulder, knocking him against the lockers. "You don't belong here, and I'm sick of you getting some free pass outta the loser club just because of who you're friends with."

Cory rubbed his sore shoulder. He looked toward the locker room exit, wondering if he could make a break for it, but knowing that Steve would be able to catch up to him pretty easily. Hopefully Derek was on his way back already...

"What the fuck is this?" Nic came walking in from the showers, towel wrapped around his waist. Seeing Cory backed into a corner by Steve, he quickly figured it out for himself. He stormed over and was in his teammate's face in an instant. Like a knight in … a bath towel. "The fuck do you think you're doing, McMillan?"

"Get the fuck out of my face, Herrera." *Uh oh, they're last-naming each other. That can't be good.* "We were just playing around, right runt?"

"Fuck you, Steve," Cory practically spit, Nic's defense giving him a boost of courage.

"Yeah, *fuck you*, Steve." Taylor decided to pile on, having just walked in from the shower himself. He walked to stand next to Nic. "There a problem here, *buddy*?"

Steve looked back and forth between the two of them, the anger building on his face. He knew he wouldn't stand a chance against both of them.

"Nah," he said, clearly not meaning it. "We're good." He then walked over to his own locker, dressing quickly and exiting, all the while being stared down by Nic and Taylor.

"What a fucking asshole." Nic shook his head. "You okay, Cor?"

"Yeah… I'm fine." Cory rubbed his shoulder again. He'd probably have a bruise tomorrow. "Don't know what his problem is."

"Probably insecure about his dick size or something," Taylor mused.

"What about whose dick size?" Derek walked back into the locker room and the middle of the conversation.

"Steve McMillan was pushing Cory around. Walked in in the middle of it," Nic explained. "Think we probably woulda ended up fighting if Taylor hadn't walked in right after me."

"Yeah, thanks Taylor." Cory finally retrieved his phone and was thankful that it seemed to be in okay shape. *Yay for phone cases!* "I owe you one."

"Nah, it's no problem." Taylor shrugged off the praise. "Just doing what anyone should."

"Hey, what about me, Cor? Don't I get a thank you?" Nic griped.

"Sorry, yes, of course, thank you. You are my knight in shining armor, sir." Cory rolled his eyes before opening them wide as he realized what just left his mouth. What was wrong with him today? Nic's eyes also grew, staring at Cory in surprise, and Derek only looked back and forth between Cory and Taylor, trying to get a read on if he had figured them out.

"Ooooohhh, so it's like that with you guys," Taylor said, nodding slowly. "I mean, I thought it was possible but figured it was a long shot."

"What... What do you mean?" Cory tried to act nonchalant. "That was just a joke."

"Guys... It's okay." Taylor held his hands up in surrender. "Seriously. I get it."

"You get *what*, Taylor?" Derek asked, eyes narrowed.

"You guys remember Jamie Mandino?" Taylor realized he'd have to explain.

"What about him?" Derek asked.

Jamie Mandino was a former student at their school. He was a year older than they were, meaning he had already graduated. Jamie was openly gay, one of the only students at school to be so. He was fairly well liked, but he never really crossed paths with Derek, Nic, or Cory.

"Yeah, well, he was also my neighbor. Lived next door," Taylor started. "And *goddamn* could that boy suck dick."

Cory choked on air at Taylor's revelation with Nic and Derek staring, mouths half open.

"...You guys okay?" Taylor looked between the three.

"Uh, yeah." Derek was the first one to snap out of it. "Just ... really caught off guard I think."

"Yeah, if you guys are trying to keep this a secret, you might wanna work on your reactions," Taylor suggested. "They're not exactly subtle."

"So, wait, you and Jamie...?" Nic questioned, still catching up.

"Started sophomore year, at a party actually." Taylor leaned back against the wall of lockers. "Things were winding down, and he and I were sitting in the backyard, splitting a bottle of wine he swiped from inside. We were pretty hammered. I forget exactly what we were talking about, but suddenly the dude just flat out tells me that he would be more than happy to suck my dick anytime I wanted it."

"Wow, he just ... went for it like that?" Cory sat on a bench, eager to hear more.

"Like I said, we were pretty drunk," Taylor continued. "I didn't know what to do at first. I'd never had a guy hit on me like that before. I asked him if he was serious, and he said yes, that he could suck my dick way better than any girl could. And he was right. Only a few minutes later and I had my dick out, and he was in between my legs, swallowing me down like I was nothing. Probably came in less than five minutes."

"What happened then, when you sobered up?" Nic asked next.

"At first I tried not to think about it," Taylor admitted. "Told myself it was just the alcohol. Which definitely helped—but then a week later, I got a text from him, asking if I wanted some more head. Didn't take me long to say yes."

"Seems mutually beneficial," Derek agreed.

"After that, he was blowing me almost daily. It became pretty obvious that he liked stuff on the rougher side of things pretty early. Started with just blowjobs, then I was fucking his face, and then I was fucking his ass. Started getting kinky, first by calling me sir, and then even calling me *daddy*... I miss that kid. I'm sure he's having the time of his life in college." Taylor ended his story a little wistfully, clearly a little let down that he no longer had access to Jamie or his mouth and ass.

"Well, you know, Cory here has a pretty talented mouth himself." Sensing an opportunity, Derek went for it.

Cory once again choked on air. His face felt like it was on fire, but his dick was also quickly filling up, the traitor. Cory wasn't opposed. Taylor was a nice, good-looking guy and apparently more than comfortable with another guy swinging on his dick. And once again, the idea of Derek loaning him out like this brought out those same mixed feelings in Cory, a combination of being turned on and just ... weird. Cory cautiously looked up at Taylor, who was clearly considering the offer. More than just considering it—Cory could see his cock beginning to tent the front of his towel.

"Yeah... I'll give your boy a test ride." Taylor moved toward his own locker. "C'mere, you."

Cory looked to Derek, who nodded his assent, and then to the entrance of the locker room.

"Don't worry," Taylor said as he rummaged through his locker. "We're the last ones here."

Cory walked over to Taylor. Without saying anything, Taylor pressed his used jockstrap to Cory's face, which he had just pulled from his bag. Instinctively, Cory inhaled, body shuddering as he was dosed with the scent.

"Thought so," Taylor said with a chuckle. "Jamie used to love that shit too."

Taylor let his towel fall to the ground, exposing his half-hard dick as Cory inhaled his jock. Cory eyed it nervously as the jock was removed from his face before Taylor pushed him down gently by the shoulders. Understanding the silent order, he lowered himself to his knees, coming face to face with what would now be his fourth cock. It was thick, like the rest of Taylor. Dark blonde hair covered him from chest to belly with a thick trail leading down to his cock. Underneath the thick member were a massive set of balls, also covered in blonde fur.

"Don't be shy now." Taylor gently pulled Cory's head toward his crotch. "Go ahead and say hello."

Cory allowed himself to be guided toward his goal, nuzzling his face into Taylor's crotch. He inhaled his scent again, not nearly as strong as in his jock but still more than enough to get Cory's head spinning. He began to lick and suck at the heavy sack, dragging his tongue along the slightly salty skin. Taylor tightened the grip on his head, holding Cory in place against his cock.

"There ya go," he cooed. "Boys like him drop the shy act pretty fast once you get a cock in their face."

Cory and Derek watched with fascination as Taylor quickly took charge of the situation, clearly used to doing this from his time with Jamie.

"Alright, let's see what you can do with that mouth." Cory's face was pulled away, revealing the dick-drunk expression on his face. "Open up."

Cory obeyed the order as he felt Taylor's rigid length tapping against his lips. His dick was huge, bigger than any of the others he'd had experience with. He opened wide, feeling his lips stretch around the thick slab of meat as it slowly pushed forward, stopping just before it poked the back of his throat. The grip on his head encouraged him to bob up and down before loosening, letting Cory set the pace as he began trying to swallow down the thick cock.

Taylor watched as Cory slowly moved back forth on his cock. After a few false starts, Cory reached up to wrap his hand around the remaining length. Taylor only chuckled, knowing that it was no easy feat for someone to take his cock into their throat. Cory's hand barely wrapped all the way around his dick, thick as it was. Taylor soon became aware of his audience, looking over to see Derek and Nic watching intently with Nic visibly sporting an erection.

"You guys want in on this?" Taylor continued holding his hand on Cory's head as he continued dutifully sucking him off. "Not trying to hog your boy."

Looking at each other only briefly, the boys didn't take long to make a decision, Nic dropping his towel and Derek unzipping his jeans as they walked over to join Taylor. Soon they were standing on either side of Taylor, surrounding Cory with an alcove of cock. Seeing his owners' cocks bobbing out of the corner of his eye, Cory reached up to grip and stroke them both.

Or that's what he attempted to do at least. Turns out that taking care of three cocks was a lot more complicated than two—at least when he was only using his mouth and hands. The locker room was soon filled with the noises of slurping and quiet moans as Cory did his best to stroke Derek and Nic in time with the bobbing of his head, but it wasn't easy. By the time he was ready to switch to one of them, he had resigned himself to the fact that one of them was going to be rather neglected as he focused on the other two.

"Aww, looks like the boy is having some trouble handling all three of us," Derek teased as he looked down at Cory, who was now deep throating Nic's cock while he stroked Taylor. Derek gripped his own cock and gave it a few strokes while he weighed his next move. "You know, he's got more than one hole to use." Derek looked lecherously at Cory's ass to emphasize his point.

"Heh, oh yeah?" Taylor looked down at Cory, who was now back to sucking him. "Think your ass could handle taking my dick, boy?"

Cory contemplated his answer, both because his mouth was currently full and because he was feeling overwhelmed. This was all moving *really* fast; Cory never thought he'd be in the middle of what was quickly turning into a gangbang in his high school locker room. But for all his concerns, he couldn't deny that he was also really, *really* into it. Hell, he was sure he had seen nearly half a dozen videos that started *exactly* like this. *But also, fuck, that is a big cock.* Cory's lips were already sore from being stretched so far around it. *Can I even take it?*

"I... I'd like to try, at least, sir," Cory said timidly after pulling off of Taylor's cock. "But I..."

"Heh, I know, boy. It's intimidating, isn't it?" Even Derek and Nic would have to admit that Taylor's cock was huge. Derek was wondering himself how Cory would handle it. "It's okay if you're nervous. Even Jamie had trouble at first, but once he got used to it..." Taylor smiled cockily at Cory as he trailed off.

"Okay." Cory took a deep breath as he agreed.

"Thatta boy!" Taylor clapped him on the shoulder. "Don't worry. I'll let these two go first and open you up for me."

Cory whimpered at the thought of being fucked by all three of them. Part of him wasn't sure if he'd be able to handle it, but the other part was wishing he was already naked and bent over.

"Sounds like he likes that idea." Nic was quickly growing more comfortable with things after seeing the way Taylor went all in. "Strip, boy."

Cory stood from his spot on the floor, all three tops moving away to give him some space as he began removing his clothing piece by piece, setting each on the end of the bench. Nic picked up Taylor's earlier discarded jockstrap and tossed it to him.

"Put that on," he ordered.

"Yes, sir." When he was finished, Cory was standing before them in nothing but a jockstrap, awaiting his next order.

"On your back on the bench." Derek, after removing his own pants, made the call for how he would be arranged, walking around to one end. He had an idea. "Down here, head hanging over the side."

Cory obeyed, first straddling the bench then lowering his back to it. His head hung over the edge and he saw the locker room upside down before Taylor and Nic once again re-entered his view, cocks in hand. As Nic took the lead and lowered his cock into Cory's mouth, Cory heard the *snap* of a plastic cap and felt Derek's cold and lubed finger begin prodding around his ass. He moaned around Nic's cock when Derek found his hole, circling around the rim a few times with the pad of his finger.

Taylor watched as Nic began to slowly fuck his cock in and out of Cory's mouth, each time pushing a little farther into his throat. Derek sat on the bench between Cory's legs, opening him up with one, then two fingers. Cory, unable to see past Nic's hairy undercarriage, could only accept what he was given as his two owners took advantage of his body. They were enjoying showing off as much as Cory was relishing being watched.

Nic pulled back after a few minutes, stepping back to allow Taylor his own turn. Taylor smiled down at Cory before quickly replacing Nic in his mouth. He began slowly pumping, not going as deep or fast as Nic, knowing Cory would still need a chance to get used to his girth.

Feeling Cory's hole was relaxed enough, Derek lifted his legs to his shoulders, sitting on the bench. After making sure he was lubed well enough, he moved forward, pressing the slick head of his cock against Cory's hole. Cory offered little resistance, more than used to taking Derek and Nic in his ass by now. He simply moaned again, this time around Taylor's cock, as he felt Derek bottoming out, hair scratching against his ass.

"Damn, this boy can really take a dick," Taylor commented as Derek started to pump his hips back and forth. The vibration of Cory's moans around his dick had him fucking more and more of his cock into Cory's mouth.

"He's had a lot of practice the last few months," Derek said cockily. "We've been training him good."

Cory, only vaguely aware that he was being talked about at that moment, could only moan again in agreement as he was used. His own cock was straining in the pouch of the jock he was wearing, twitching every time Derek passed over his prostate. A small wet spot was beginning to form as precum dribbled from the head.

Taylor pulled back as Derek continued to fuck, Nic taking over to fuck Cory's throat once more. Derek was beginning to pick up speed, and the sound of skin slapping against skin soon echoed through the locker room. Taylor stood back and watched, fascinated, when soon enough, Derek and Nic were both fucking the full lengths of their cock into Cory at each end.

"I'm starting to get close," Derek announced, standing slightly to give him more leverage.

He grabbed the backs of Cory's thighs from against his chest and pushed them back, bending Cory and exposing his hole farther. With his access made easier, Derek began to pound his cock in and out of Cory's twitching hole.

The sudden increase in speed caught Cory off-guard, though he could only whimper and moan as Derek took his pleasure from his hole. Each time Derek nailed his prostate head on, he could feel his hole twitch and spasm, the pressure beginning to build.

Nic was eager for his own turn at Cory's ass once Derek was finished. Rather than replace him in Cory's mouth, Taylor continued to stand and watch, seeing the blissed-out expression on the bottom's face as he was pounded out. A litany of whimpers and moans spilled from Cory's now-free mouth, and he could only lift his head and look up at the man fucking him.

Derek was getting close, but from the way Cory's hole was periodically squeezing him, he could tell that Cory was too. Determined to make Cory cum before he did, Derek steadily drove his cock into Cory's hole, his dick massaging the small nub of pleasure within. The pitch of Cory's moans got higher and higher until he was practically squealing with each slam of Derek's dick.

"Sir… Gonna… Fuck—!" Cory managed to get out through his gritted teeth as he felt all of his muscles tense up as the orgasm overtook him. "Nnnggghh—!"

Derek felt the telltale spasming of Cory's ass that meant he was cumming, grinning down at him cockily as he continued to fuck in and out, making Cory whimper and moan even more. His goal achieved, he was now ready to breed his boy's hole.

"Fuck, here comes your first load of the day, boy," Derek announced, both for Cory's benefit as well as Nic and Taylor's. "Gonna flood your fucking ass…"

Derek slammed his cock home, as deep as he could, as it unloaded deep inside of Cory. Cory whimpered, his jock-covered cock still hard as he felt Derek's cock pulse with each shot. Derek continued trying to pump, instincts driving him to push his cock deeper.

Finished cumming, Derek caught his breath a moment, cock still inside of Cory. Sweat bled through the shirt Derek was still wearing, and Cory's own chest and belly hair was matted to his skin. Grinning, Derek looked up to Nic before gingerly extracting himself from Cory's ass.

"You're up, bro."

"Let's get you bent over the bench now, boy." Nic walked over and stood above Cory's prone body, examining the scene. He held out his hand to Cory, helping the weak-legged boy sit up.

Cory was thankful for the position change. His neck may have been in a good position for a throat fuck, but it was starting to get sore. He lowered himself once more to the floor, this time turning around and leaning over the bench. As he heard the cap on the bottle of lube pop open once again, Taylor came back into view. Without needing an order, Cory once again began to suck on the massively thick cock when it was presented to him.

"Here comes cock number two." Nic settled in behind Cory, slapping his hard cock against Cory's hole and making him shudder.

Cory moaned softly as he was stretched again, Nic's cock finding little resistance in Cory's cum-sloppy hole. Nic gripped him by the ass tightly, pulling him back as he pushed forward. He groaned as he felt the warm wetness engulf him fully.

As Nic began to pump his cock in and out of Cory's ass, Taylor followed suit with his mouth. From this position, Cory was at least able to meet him halfway, bobbing up and down in time with Taylor's thrusts. For his part, Taylor was doing his best to match Nic's timing, never leaving Cory without at least a few inches of dick inside him.

Nic spanked Cory's ass as he fucked, watching the generous flesh jiggle, still framed by Taylor's jockstrap. Cory whimpered with each smack of his ass. Nic began to long stroke his cock in and out of Cory, Derek having loosened him up sufficiently. He watched, fascinated as his cock was swallowed effortlessly by Cory's ass, over and over.

Interested in seeing just what else Cory could handle, Taylor began to fuck more and more of his cock into Cory's mouth, steadying his head to hold it in place. As the cock drew nearer and nearer to the back of his throat, Cory could only look up at Taylor, mouth stretched wide, a look of hunger in his eyes. Taylor smirked, and pushed farther in, finally entering Cory's throat.

Cory did his best to fight his gag reflex as Taylor began pushing into his throat. His mouth was so full; there was no way he'd be able to take the entire thing, but he was damn sure going to try. Taylor continued to fuck just the first few inches of his cock into Cory's mouth, sucking a breath in when he felt Cory do his best to swallow around him. He knew his cock wasn't easy for anyone to take, so he appreciated the effort.

Derek watched the scene in front of him, his best friend in their boy's ass and a massive cock lodged in his throat. His squeezed his now softened cock, almost wishing he was hard again already so he could jump back into the group. As it was, he was content to watch as the two football players see-sawed Cory between them.

From his vantage point, Nic could only see the back of Cory's head as Taylor fucked his mouth. He wasn't able to view the action, but he could certainly hear it. Every slurp, every swallow, every gag. That combined with the whimpers and moans the fucking was drawing out was really revving Nic's engine.

"Fuck, that sounds hot," Nic said aloud as he gave Cory another slap on the ass.

"Yeah, he's an eager one for sure," Taylor added, watching as Cory did his best to take even more of his cock.

Cory could only whimper in response. His jaw was getting tired, but fuck, he was so turned on right now. Taylor's massive cock was stretching his jaw to the limit, but he was determined to take as much of it as he could. On top of that, Nic was really starting to pound him good, hitting all the right spots inside him. The front of the jock he wore was soaked with precum.

Both tops continued their assault on Cory's orifices as Derek looked on in aroused silence. While Taylor kept pumping his cock in and out of Cory's mouth steadily, Nic began to gradually pick up speed the closer he got to cumming. As he continued to stroke Cory's prostate with his dick, Cory began pushing back to meet him, chasing his second orgasm of the afternoon.

"Yeah, take that dick, bitch." Nic punctuated the word "bitch" with a spank, nearly jackhammering Cory's hole with his cock. Each slam of his cock forward elicited another squeal from Cory's stuffed mouth. Feeling Cory's ass tighten as it was spanked, Nic landed a few other smacks, the snug feeling around his cock pushing him ever closer to cumming.

"Fuck yeah, boy. Tighten that hole. Milk that load out," he growled as he rode Cory's ass ever faster.

Finally, Nic slammed his hips forward, mashing Cory's face onto Taylor's cock as he bred his ass. The combination of the sudden slam forward, the cock lodged in his throat, and his vision being blocked by Taylor's stomach caught Cory off guard, hands flying out to grab Taylor's thighs and steady himself. Nic continued to pump into his ass as he deposited his thick load, pulling his cock out with an audible *pop* as the excessive amount of cum in Cory's ass began to spill out.

Taylor extracted Cory's face from his crotch, honestly impressed at the lack of teeth he felt when Cory's mouth was forced all the way to the base. He peered over Cory's back at his cream-stuffed ass, Nic kneeling behind him and catching his breath.

"Fuck, that hole is *sloppy*." Taylor whistled, running a finger down Cory's back and ass, feeling for the sloppy entrance. "Opened him up good, though." He pulled back and peered down at Cory, who was still catching his breath. "Think you're ready, boy?"

Cory looked up at Taylor and then down at his dick. It was really, *really* thick. *How did Jamie take that? How do girls or anyone else?* He swallowed nervously.

"Yes... Yes, sir," Cory croaked, voice hoarse from the oral assault. "I think so?"

"Don't sound very sure of yourself there, Cory." Taylor chuckled as he walked around the bench, taking the bottle of lube from Nic when offered.

Seeing Taylor move behind him, Cory remained where he was. He felt Taylor move into position behind him and turned to watch as he dribbled the lube along his dick, stroking his hand up and down to spread it from tip to base. Cory whimpered at the thick rod jutting out at him. *So big... So hot...*

"He's already hungry for it." Derek watched Cory's face as he moved closer to the pair to watch the action. "I wanna get a good view of this."

"Hold on." Taylor gripped the waistband of Cory's jock, pulling it back and down his legs. Taylor again pushed the jock into Cory's face. "You might want that to bite down on, boy. Just try to keep your ass relaxed. Once I'm in there, it's going to feel amazing."

Cory took a deep breath and settled his chest on the bench in front of him, inhaling more of Taylor's musk now mixed with his own scent. He took Taylor's advice and held it in his mouth, if nothing more than to make sure he didn't bite his tongue or something.

"Hey," Taylor spoke softly, stroking a hand up and down Cory's back, "you gotta relax. Your muscles are tensed to all hell. I know you're nervous. Just breathe and let me do the rest, okay?"

Cory did his best, the stroking of his back helping to calm him down some. Once Taylor sensed that Cory had calmed enough, he rubbed the blunt head of his dick up and down Cory's slick hole. Taylor waited patiently, waiting until he felt the ring of muscle flutter open. Then he pushed in, watching as cum leaked out around his head.

Cory inhaled sharply, the sudden pain shooting through his lower half. His mouth was flooded with the taste of sweat and precum as he fought the urge to move forward, off what felt like a baseball bat being shoved up his ass. Taylor's hand returned to his back, once more stroking to help calm the boy about to be buggered.

"Jesus, you got the head in," Derek commented. "You doing okay, boy?"

Cory said nothing but tried to nod his head as he fought to relax. Taylor continued to very slowly push his cock into Cory, stopping often to allow Cory time to adjust. After what had felt like twenty minutes but was really only five, Cory couldn't believe there was still any cock left to push in.

"How... How big are you?" he gritted, removing the jock from his mouth briefly. "You're ... almost all the way in, right?"

"We're a little over halfway there, boy," Taylor told him with a chuckle while giving him a little smack on the butt. "You're doing great though."

Cory groaned into the jock once more stuffing his mouth. He was already so full, stretched so much. He was *really* glad he decided to douche this morning.

Another few minutes passed, quicker than they had before, as Taylor fed the remaining inches of his dick to Cory's ass. By the time he had his balls against Cory's ass, Cory was clinging to the bench in front of him, knuckles white. He was no longer feeling only pain. Now there was also an immense pressure pressing against him in all the right spots—including a few he didn't know he had. Opening his eyes, he turned to see Derek and Nic watching the action intently. He blushed, thinking about how he must look and sound at the moment.

"There you go, boy." Taylor clapped both hands against Cory's ass. "All ten inches inside of you."

Cory's ass twitched involuntarily at the commentary, eliciting a groan of pain and pleasure from Cory and a grunt from Taylor. Taking the noises as a signal, he slowly pulled his cock back, just an inch or two, looking down in fascination at the way Cory's hole clung to his shaft. His cock glistened with all the cum still inside the boy, helping to pave his way even deeper. He pushed those same inches right back in, pulling another groan from Cory.

"Fuck, dude. You're turning that hole out." Nic was watching intently, far more interested than he would let himself believe. He loved watching Cory's hole stretch and pull like that. Just like a wrecked pussy.

Taylor said nothing, just smiled and continued his steady fucking. He kept a leisurely pace, never removing more than half of his cock from Cory to ensure he would be adequately stretched. Before long, Cory was pushing back to meet his thrusts, his noises of pain replaced with whimpers and moans of pleasure. He knew he was going to be *so* sore tomorrow, but holy shit this felt so good. It was like Taylor's cock was so thick it was impossible for it to *not* hit his prostate with every thrust. His cock was leaking precum onto the locker room floor, still mostly soft as he was milked.

"There we go." Taylor looked like a wolf who had just caught his prey. "Told ya. Just needed to get used to it."

Derek and Nic continued to watch, fascinated, as Taylor fucked their best friend and boy in the middle of the locker room. Cory was enthusiastically throwing his ass back for Taylor, all the while happily sucking on the jock in his mouth. Suddenly, Cory's eyes opened wide, and one of his hands flew down to his soft but leaking cock.

"Oh, fuck." Cory turned to Derek and Nic. "Sirs… I'm gonna…"

Cory turned red, unable or unwilling to finish his sentence. It only took a second before what was happening clicked for Derek.

"Oh! He's gonna squirt again." He turned to Nic. "Like he did at that one night at the cabin."

"Oh, shit." Nic's face lit up. "You *gotta* see this."

"Wait, really?" Now Taylor had turned to talk to them, his voice both fascinated and incredulous as he continued to fuck forward. "You mean, like a girl? Is that even a thing?"

"Yes, sir, it's a thing," Cory gritted. "Oh, fuck—" Cory felt his muscles start to tense as another orgasm washed over him, still doing his best to hold back his bladder.

Taylor slowed his fucking, the look on his face telling the others that the gears were turning as he thought of something.

"Okay, boy..." He stopped fucking entirely and pulled Cory up from the bench, his back flush to Taylor's stomach. "Hold on, I've got an idea."

"Hold on to whaAHHH!" Cory yelped as Taylor wrapped his arms around Cory's chest and waist and held him tightly to his own chest and stomach before he stood up, cock still fully embedded within Cory's ass.

Cory lost hold of the jock as he scrambled to hold onto Taylor's arms as he was half-carried, half-walked across the locker room. With every step, Taylor's cock would flex inside of him, pulling even more moans and yelps from Cory. Barely coherent, Cory could see that Taylor was moving them into the showers, Derek and Nic following.

Taylor very carefully walked across to the wall of showers, finding a clear spot along the wall where he helped Cory to stand, hands against the wall to hold himself up. Then without anything further, he resumed fucking as if he hadn't just walked around with a boy impaled on his dick.

"Here we go." Taylor had his hands gripping Cory's hips, holding him in place. "Don't worry, boy. Just let it fly."

It didn't take long before Cory was once again feeling the pressure building. Thankful for the change in location, Cory leaned against the wall, biting his own wrist when he nearly screamed as another anal orgasm tore through him. Unable to hold back now even if he wanted to, Cory felt as a stream of nearly clear piss shot out of his cock against the shower wall.

"Holy fuck, you weren't lying." Taylor watched as Cory lost control. "That is one of the hottest things I've ever seen."

Taylor continued to fuck Cory there against the shower wall, forcing orgasm after orgasm out of him. Beet red, Cory could only close his eyes and focus on keeping his hole relaxed, still feeling embarrassed despite how turned on it seemed to make everyone else. Had he opened his eyes and looked behind him, he would have seen both Derek and Nic were now furiously jacking their cocks.

By the sixth time Cory squirted, he could no longer think straight. He was exhausted, both mentally and physically, and feeling more overstimulated than he thought possible. *Oh god, here comes another nnnNNGGghh—! This is it. This is how I die. They're going to put in my obituary that I was fucked to death.*

Lucky enough for Cory, Taylor was fast approaching his own orgasm. Each time he made Cory cum, his hole would squeeze and milk his cock. That, combined with the feeling of cockiness that all tops feel when they make a bottom-bitch cum, was more than enough to push him over the edge. He could feel Cory's hole begin to stir again, and Taylor wondered if he'd be able to bring him over the edge again before he was finished.

Taylor didn't announce his orgasm like the others—he thought it was pretty obvious when he was going to cum. His breathing grew heavier and his thrusts actually slowed down, returning to their earlier slow and steady pace. After only a few more moments, he pushed his cock inside of Cory to the hilt and held it there. Then he quickly pulled back a couple of inches before plunging it right back in as the second shot fired. He continued to pump like that with each of the next five shots.

"Please... Sir..." Cory felt Taylor as he started to unload, deeper than ever before. He was so close to cumming again. "Just need a little more..."

More than happy to oblige, Taylor delivered a few more shallow thrusts into Cory, feeling as even more cum—now including his own—leaked out of Cory's still-stretched hole. Cory was gripping one of his arms tightly, his other hand holding him up against the wall, a look of determination on his face. With a loud grunt, Cory's cock once again sprayed against the wall, his hole cumming as it was wrapped around Taylor's dick one final time.

"Fuck..." Cory mumbled, head flopping forward to the wall.

Too exhausted to continue holding himself up, Cory nearly lost his balance. Luckily, he was still attached to Taylor, who once again pulled him back to steady him, his large hand nearly dwarfing Cory's as they rested against the wall.

Taylor continued holding onto the exhausted boy as he caught his breath, eventually turning them both around so he could lean against the wall. He ever-tenderly pulled his cock from Cory, who despite his efforts could only hiss and whimper as all the rough fucking started catching up to him. Cory lowered himself to the floor, taking extra care with his sore and bruised ass.

"Fuck, hold still, boy."

Cory opened his eyes to see both Derek and Nic standing over him, both furiously jacking their cocks aimed at his face. Thinking they both wanted a blowjob, Cory opened his mouth to take one in but was stopped, held in place by Taylor.

"Nah, they want to mark you," the blonde informed him. "You just sit there and keep that mouth open."

Derek was the first blow, shots of cum landing across Cory's nose and cheeks with some landing in his mouth. Nic followed soon after and aimed more directly at his target, most of it landing inside and across Cory's lips. Now that they had cum again, all four boys remained where they were, eventually gathering the strength to clean themselves up.

The four returned to the locker room, freshly showered and drying off. The boys helped a sore but still mobile Cory to dress, and Derek agreed to take him home, helping the exhausted and fucked out boy to his car. Before leaving, Taylor pulled the sub into a bear hug, ruffling his hair and thanking him. The boys said their goodbyes, Nic and Taylor staying back to finish putting away their practice gear.

"That's a damn good boy you guys got there," Taylor mentioned off-handedly as he was wrapping up. "Thanks for letting me borrow him like that."

"Heh, no problem, man." Nic was still a little shocked by how easy Taylor found it to talk about these things. "Seems like you might actually have a few things you could teach us about handling him."

"Just say the word, man." Taylor adjusted himself in his pants as he spoke. "I miss having pussy like that on call. Sometimes you just need to dump a load, right?"

"Right, man." Nic chuckled. He should take a page from Taylor's book and stop overthinking things. "Sometimes you just need to dump a load."

# CHAPTER 10

oly shit. Nic stared wide-eyed at the scoreboard. Did they just win the game? Did *he* just win the game? Nic didn't have long to figure it out before the rest of his team ran in, slamming him from all sides as they jumped and hollered.

"Oh my god, babe! You did it!" Amy ran toward him as he approached the sideline, planting a big kiss on his lips. "That was amazing!"

As he ended his liplock with Amy and looked over her shoulder, Nic saw Derek, Tricia, Cory, and Stephanie on the other side of the barrier.

"Guys!" Nic walked toward them with Amy in tow. "Did you see—?"

"Yeah, man, of course we saw!" Derek practically shouted back, half-laughing at Nic's stupor. "You won the damn game, man!"

"It was awesome, Nic," Tricia added.

"We're headed to my place to get set up for the party." Derek had to yell louder over the noise of the crowd. "See you there?"

"Yeah, man, we'll be there." Nic waved them off, letting them get out before the crowd became too overwhelming. As he turned, he saw his family waiting for him as well, and he turned to Amy. "Wanna ride there together?"

"Of course!" Amy smiled. "Go talk to your parents. I'll meet you outside the locker room."

Nic walked over, barely able to hear anything his dad was trying to tell him as he approached. It was at that moment that Nic's teammates decided to grab him and hoist him in the air as they walked back to the locker room. He waved and shrugged at his family—he'd just have to talk to them later. This was going to be a fun night.

"Careful, I want this to be a fun night." Derek guided two jocks carrying a keg through the house and into the back-yard where the festivities were well underway. Kids from all over Hartford Heights, mostly seniors, had already begun flocking over in droves from the football game. Thanks to his older brother, Derek's place was known as a good party house.

"So... There's something I've been wanting to talk to you about." Cory twiddled his thumbs nervously as he spoke, mostly into his own lap. He and Stephanie were sitting in a couple of lawn chairs on the porch, watching as the rest of their class drank themselves stupid.

"Uh-oh, this sounds important." Stephanie quit leaning back in her chair and sat up, turning to Cory with her hands in her lap. "Okay, I'm ready."

"Booooo." Cory threw some chips from a nearby plate at Stephanie. "I'm being serious."

"Okay, sorry." She relaxed her posture. "What's up?"

Cory looked around, making sure they were alone. Then, he took a breath and closed his eyes. *Time to bite the bullet.*

"I'm gay."

Cory opened one eye when he didn't hear any response. Stephanie was there, still facing him, eating some chips.

"...Well?"

"...Was that it?"

"What do you mean, 'Was that it'?! I just came out to you!" Cory half-yelled, half-whispered.

"Sorry! I just didn't..." Stephanie paused and bit her lip. "I kind of already figured that out, you know?"

"What do you mean?" Cory was confused. Had he not done a good job hiding it?

"I dunno. It just seemed like the logical answer," Steph started explaining. "You've never mentioned girls, like, even once the entire time I've known you. Actually, I'm pretty sure you've talked about a guy being hot a couple of times. And it's not like I ever thought you were into me or I was into you."

"...Oh." He *hadn't* done a good job at hiding it.

"Sorry." Stephanie stood and walked around to Cory's side of the table and hugged him. "Didn't mean to steal your gay-thunder. You know I love and support you no matter what, blah, blah, blah."

"It's fine." Cory hugged her back before she took her seat again. "I think I just keep expecting this to not go well when I tell people."

"Assuming the worst?"

"And being pleasantly surprised when I'm wrong."

"Have you told anyone else?" Stephanie looked around at their classmates.

"Uh, not really." Cory wasn't sure it counted if the other person tells you they already knew. "Derek and Nic know. That's pretty much it."

"Aww, you told them before me? Lame." Stephanie pouted.

"So sorry. I'll check with you on all future life events before telling anyone else." Cory rolled his eyes.

"That's all I ask." Stephanie leaned back in her chair.

Cory snorted as the two went back to people-watching as more kids trickled in. A few minutes later, loud cheers and hollering signaled that the football team had finally arrived. Cory watched as Nic and the rest of his team clambered through the crowd, most of them with their girlfriends in tow. Soon the beer keg had been tapped and Nic and the others were in full party mode.

"Yeah, I think he's gonna be pretty busy tonight." Cory looked up to see Derek was walking over to them. "Hey, Stephanie. Having fun?"

"Great party as always, Derek." The girl nodded in his direction.

"Thanks." Derek turned back to Cory. "Can you come with me for a second, Cor? Need your help with something on my computer."

"Uh, okay, sure." Cory stood and turned to Steph. "Find you later?"

"Sounds good." Stephanie stood herself. "Think I'm gonna go find a beer and then try and convince the cheerleaders to make a drunk pyramid."

"Hope we don't miss that," Derek said to Cory as he led him back inside the house and upstairs. Once they got to Derek's bedroom, he pulled a set of keys out and unlocked the door.

"What did you need help with, sir?" Cory shut the door behind him as Derek walked over to his desk. Rather than touch his computer though, he opened a drawer, pulling out … a sex toy.

"That was just an excuse to get you up here." Derek walked toward Cory holding out the toy. "You know what this is?"

"A butt plug." Cory took the proffered black silicone object, noting that it weighed a bit more then it appeared at first glance. It was decent sized, probably a little thicker than Derek's cock was at the widest part. "Do you want me to put it in, sir?"

"Smart boy." Derek held his hand out. "But first, I need your phone."

Cory gave a quizzical look but said nothing, unlocking and handing over his phone.

"Good boy. Lube is in the night stand." Derek pointed toward his bed as he began swiping and tapping through Cory's phone, as well as his own.

Cory said nothing, trusting Derek enough to not do anything malicious. He unzipped his jeans as he walked over to the bed, pulling them down about half way before he fished through the nightstand for the lube bottle.

"Not too much," Derek said without looking up. "Trust me."

*Okay…* Cory popped the cap on the bottle, pouring a small amount onto the plug before spreading it around with his fingers. Then, bending over and bracing himself on the edge of the bed, Cory pressed the plug into his hole. He had cleaned and stretched himself earlier, per Derek's instructions, so it wasn't too difficult. At least the lube had warmed up when he spread it around. When he was finished, Cory pulled his up jockstrap—also per Derek's instruction—and jeans with one hand, looking around for something to wipe his hand off.

"Here." Derek tossed him a towel, allowing him to wipe the lube from his hand before handing him back his phone. "Thank you, boy. Notice anything special about the plug?"

"It's kind of heavy…" Cory thought about what that might mean. "Is it a vibrator, too?"

"Good guess!" Derek pulled out his own phone and made a few taps and swipes, causing Cory to almost drop his own phone in surprise when the plug suddenly began to vibrate. "It's a vibrating, *remote-controlled* butt plug."

Cory bit his lip to keep from moaning. The plug was very slowly pulsing in his hole, and it was making his cock chub up fast. Happy with the reaction, Derek used his phone once again to turn it off.

"It's got a phone app that uses Bluetooth to let me control it," Derek began explaining. "And now that the app is on your phone, too, I can control it from anywhere, as long as you keep your phone on you. And you *will* keep it on you tonight, won't you, boy?"

Cory's dick twitched at the implication. Derek was going to keep him plugged all night at the party, randomly turning the vibrator on and off, driving him crazy. Hell, if he wasn't careful, someone might even be able to figure out what was happening.

"Yes, sir." Cory hated that he loved the idea.

"It's gonna be a pretty busy night, and we probably won't see much of each other," Derek reasoned, as he turned the toy back on. "This way you won't feel so neglected when we can't be with you. See? I'm always looking after my boy."

"Thank you, sir," Cory managed to get out between gritted teeth as he rode the plug's pulses. "Very thoughtful of you."

"You're welcome, boy." Derek grinned lecherously, turning it off once more. "Now then, ready to head back downstairs?"

Cory thought for a moment. He briefly considered asking for the cock cage, knowing the plug would have him boning up in no time but decided against it … for now. "No, sir. All good here."

"Good." Derek smiled and turned off the plug again before leading Cory out of the room.

"Why are you locking the door, sir?" Cory asked as Derek reinserted the key to his bedroom door.

"You think I trust those animals downstairs with any of the stuff up here? Fuck, no."

"You think she knows root beer is non-alcoholic?" Stephanie and Cory were people-watching again, this time focused on a girl who was acting *way* too drunk for someone who had only downed several glasses of soda.

"Not if we don't tell her." Cory sipped his own beer, watching as the girl "stumbled" about, enjoying the attention.

"So…" Stephanie turned in her seat. "Do you have a boyfriend?"

"What?!" Cory choked on his beer, looking around to make sure no one was listening.

"Oh, relax. No one heard me." Stephanie rolled her eyes.

"Why are you asking?" Cory tried to relax.

"You've been really busy lately. I haven't even seen you online much," Steph pointed out. "Thought maybe that could be what's been taking up all your time lately."

"Oh. Well, no. Not exactly…" Cory told her, speaking the last bit into his beer bottle.

"Huh?"

"Nothing. No boyfriends to speak of. So—AAH!" Cory jumped as he felt the plug turn on once more, nearly spilling more of his poor beer.

"You okay?" Stephanie raised an eyebrow at Cory.

"Yeah, sorry." Cory did his best to hold his voice steady as the plug buzzed incessantly against his prostate. "Beer went down the wrong pipe."

Stephanie narrowed her eyes but said nothing, taking a sip of her own. Cory looked around the backyard, seeing if he could locate his tormentor. He spotted Derek a few feet away, standing with Tricia and Taylor. He smiled and waved at Cory, phone in hand. *Bastard.*

"Oh my god, she's taking her clothes off." Stephanie stared, wide-eyed, at root beer girl attempting to remove her shirt as two of her friends struggled beside her to hold it down.

"Oh, god." Cory watched as well, or at least attempted to before feeling the vibrations of the plug pulse even faster.

"I know, right? We should be filming this." Steph finished her beer and pulled out her phone. "Hold on, I'm gonna get some close-ups."

"Have ... fun..." Cory was gripping his knee tightly as he rode the waves of pleasure coming from his prostate. "I know I am..."

"You doin' alright there, Cor?" Cory looked up to see Taylor smirking as he sipped his beer. "Face is kinda red."

"Yeah, I'm fiiiiiii—" As Cory opened his mouth to respond, the plug suddenly began to move faster. Did he know? "Nnngghh. Fine."

"Yeah? That's weird." Taylor took another sip. "Derek said he heard some kind of strange buzzing noise over here. Not sure I hear anything though. You?"

"Nnnnnnnnope." Well, that answered that. He knew and was now helping to torment Cory. *Stupid hot jerk.* "All good."

"That's too bad." Another sip. "Came over to help you out, but if nothing's bothering you…"

"How would you help me?" Cory asked Taylor. He was listening. "*Sir?*"

"Why don't you come with me and we'll find out, *boy*." Taylor stepped back as he spoke, turning around and walking toward the house.

Cory stood to follow, doing his best to not look like he was walking with a vibrator in his ass. It wasn't easy, so he was thankful that as he stepped inside the plug once again stopped. Maybe Derek saw him following Taylor?

Taylor strode through the house, weaving in and out of the gathering of drunk students as Cory trailed him. He did his best to keep up with his eyes locked on Taylor when he nearly knocked someone over because he wasn't paying attention.

"Careful." It was Jackson… Why did he always seem to be running into Cory like this? "Could get a drink spilled on you or something." He had his hand on Cory's shoulder as if to steady him.

"Uh, yeah. Thanks…" Cory looked for Taylor in the crowd.

"Having fun?" Jackson took a sip of his beer.

"I guess…" Cory really wasn't sure what this guy's deal was. "Sorry, I gotta find someone…" Cory spotted Taylor's blonde hair across the room. Dude was practically a giant.

"Yeah, I'm sure you got places to be, people to take care of." Jackson nodded in Taylor's direction. "Stay safe, *boy*."

Cory took off, happy to end the conversation. Something about the way Jackson said *boy* made his skin crawl. He caught up to Taylor and let the larger boy lead him upstairs. He must have been here before because he had no problem finding his way to Derek's bedroom. When he got to the door, he pulled a key from his pocket, the same one Derek had used earlier, and unlocked the door.

"Always make friends with the dude throwing the party," he explained as he held the door open for Cory. "Gets you access to all sorts of useful things."

Taylor set his glass of beer on Derek's desk. After turning back to Cory, he moved his hands to his belt, unbuckling it and opening his fly. Then he sat on the edge of Derek's bed, legs spread wide.

"Why don't you get over here and on your knees, boy?"

Cory didn't need to be asked twice, kneeling between Taylor's legs. He looked at the bulge sticking out from his jeans and still growing and tentatively ran his hand over it.

"No need to be shy now." Cory looked up to see Taylor's smiling, slightly-tipsy face looking down at him. "You and lil' Taylor already met. Take him out and say hello."

Cory stifled a chuckle at Taylor's drunken yet sweet explanation, instead reaching forward to grip his boxer-covered cock more firmly. Taylor reflexively ground up into Cory's hand in response. Seeing no point in wasting any more time, Cory reached for the waistband on Taylor's underwear and pulled it down under his heavy balls.

*Release the kraken!* Cory thought with an inward giggle.

"Mmm... Good boy," Taylor praised as Cory lowered his mouth over his dick. He petted Cory's head as about half of his cock was swallowed down.

Cory's mouth strained over the thick shaft, using his hands to hold it steady as he did his best to bob up and down the length of cock he was able to actually fit in his mouth. He had somehow forgotten just how massive Taylor was. The struggle was reeAALLL—! The goddamned plug suddenly kicked into gear again, pulling a yelp from Cory that was only muffled by Taylor's cock. *Fuuuuuuck.*

"Hehehe, the plug start up again?" Taylor giggled at Cory's reaction. "Sounds like it. Derek is something else. I'm sure you're loving it."

Groaning, Cory wasn't so sure. Not that it didn't feel amazing, but it had barely been an hour, and it was already driving him crazy. How was he going to make it through the whole night with Derek teasing him like this? His cock was once again tenting the front of his pants, though Cory wasn't sure how much of that was the plug's doing and how much was Taylor's dick. He felt his own hard cock through his pants, moaning around Taylor as he squeezed.

"Heheheh, aww, is the poor boy horny?" Taylor was still watching for Cory's reactions. "Go ahead and pull your cock out. Jamie used to love jerking off while he blew me."

Once again, Cory didn't need to be told twice, hands shooting to his crotch to undo his fly and pull out his cock, groaning again as he felt himself up. Soon he was stroking himself with one hand while he held and stroked Taylor's cock with the other, all the while sucking down as much of the huge cock as he could. Taylor was silent as Cory worked, muttering only the occasional "fuck, yeah" and "good boy" under his breath. Other than that, the only other sounds in the room came from Cory's mouth.

Taylor's hand in Cory's hair tightened as he drew close to cumming. He made no attempt to take over Cory's movements, just an indicator that he was close as Cory continued to work. With a final muttered "*fuck*" Taylor came, his cock blowing his load directly across Cory's tongue. Swallowing down what cum had quickly filled his mouth, Cory prepared himself for the next few shots, still stroking his own cock as Taylor unloaded in his mouth.

Taylor kept his cock in Cory's mouth when he was done, allowing the boy to suckle on the softening meat as he continued to stroke himself. With the taste of Taylor still fresh on his tongue, Cory shot his own load, remembering at the last minute not to shoot it on the carpet and catch it in his hand. He released Taylor's cock and caught his breath, leaning his head against Taylor's knee for a minute. The plug was still buzzing away, less arousing now that Cory had shot his wad.

"Good boy." Taylor was enjoying the post-orgasmic high and after a few moments gave Cory a pat on the head. "Come on. We should get back to the party."

Cory sat up and allowed Taylor to stand, tucking away his cock and re-buttoning his jeans. He held out a hand to Cory to help him up, but when Cory went to take it, he remembered it was still covered in cum.

"Lemme get you a towel first."

"Okay, okay... Never have I ever ... been naked outside."

Cory took a drink as the junior on the other side of the circle finished her statement. Couldn't exactly claim he hadn't done that after that weekend at the cabin.

"When were *you* naked outside?" Stephanie inquired as she gave Cory some side-eye.

"...It was on a dare with the guys up at the cabin." That wasn't a *total* lie.

"Straight guys are so weird." Now *that* was something Cory could agree with.

He and Stephanie were sitting as part of a larger group in a circle playing a drinking game. Cory had a nice buzz going, and this time it wasn't coming from his ass. He looked around the circle and saw Nic happily chatting away with Amy next to him. That made Cory smile. He saw Tricia, but not Derek—he was nowhere to be found. He saw Steve, mentally rolling his eyes as he turned away, and Taylor was there too, sitting next to Nic and talking with another teammate.

*What was that guy's name again?* Cory was seriously the worst with names. The teammate was tall, almost as tall as Taylor, but leaner. Cory thought he might have been a running back, but he also wasn't sure if those were even the right words. He was hot, too: smooth dark skin, short cropped hair, and he already had a full beard. And that was on top of the physique that came with playing football for three or four years. *Fuck, what is his name?*

The nameless player suddenly turned his head and locked eyes with Cory, who turned away immediately, though it was too late. He felt his face turning red and hoped that maybe he could blame it on the alcohol. He nervously looked back, letting out a sigh of relief when he saw the guy no longer staring at him. Taylor, though, gave Cory a curious glance from across the circle before going back to talking with his friend.

"Never have I ever ... had sex on school campus!" Cory took a drink as the next person announced.

"*Cory,*" Stephanie stage-whispered at him, "*when did you have sex at school!?*"

"Uh... I..." Cory's eyes went wide when he realized what he had done.

Never before in his life had Cory actually been happy to hear the noises of someone violently throwing up, but there was a first time for everything. Before he had a chance to finish his explanation, the girl on Stephanie's other side suddenly became aggressively ill, throwing up all over the lawn in front of them. Several of the people in the surrounding area, Stephanie included, took off in a panic, trying to avoid the backsplash. Cory breathed another sigh of relief; he really had to be more careful. And now he was going to have to think of *something* to tell Steph...

"Hey, Cory, c'mere." Nic slurred his words as he walked over to Cory, the beer he had in hand working its magic. Amy was currently helping the girl who lost her lunch on the lawn, walking her inside with another cheerleader, and there was no sign of Stephanie. "I got something to show you. C'mon over here."

Nic walked past Cory and around the side of the house, heading toward a side door that connected to the garage. Derek had locked the door leading in from the house, but the side door was locked with an electronic lock—one that Nic and Cory both knew the code for. Nic approached the keypad and carefully entered the four-digit code, his beer-buzz affecting his hand-eye coordination. He looked back to Cory to make sure he was still behind him, giving him a smile that fell somewhere between goofy and horny.

"What did you wanna show me, sir?" Cory walked past Nic as he held the door, turning to face him, knowing full well why they were here. The garage was dark, light from the streetlights filtering in from the windows above the garage door.

"I just hadn't been able to see much of you tonight." Nic closed the door behind him, other hand already on his crotch. "It's a big night for me. Thought my boy would want a chance to show appreciation to his sir."

Cory chuckled. The beer and winning the game had definitely gone to Nic's head, but he liked it. It was just the right amount of cocky, a smirk that said, "We both know you want this," paired with just enough sweetness to make him smile. Cory was down to play this game.

"Yes, sir, thank you. You were amazing to watch out there." Cory met Nic in the middle, reaching out and grabbing his cock through his shorts. "I'd love a chance to show you just how amazing."

"Fuck, yeah, boy." Nic smiled at Cory's response. He leaned back against the door, closing his eyes as he felt Cory feel him up. "Show me how much you want to serve me."

"Yes, sir." Cory dropped to his knees as he spoke, hand still groping Nic through his pants. "Watching you play always gets me hot. You are such a fucking stud."

Cory ran his other hand up Nic's shirt and across his hard and hairy stomach. He loved Nic's body. He released Nic's cock and reached for his zipper, happily pulling out the quarterback's growing length.

"Seeing you on the field, getting all sweaty and worked up..." Cory stroked Nic slowly with his hand. "I see the way girls fall all over you, sir. Thank you for letting me worship your body and cock, sir."

The alcohol was making Cory feel bold, moving his face toward Nic's belly and nuzzling it gently. If Nic wanted to see just how much Cory wanted him, he was happy to show him. Cory kissed Nic's stomach lightly, continuing to stroke him at the same time.

"Fuck..." Nic looked down at Cory, not quite prepared for Cory's affections. "Good boy."

Cory smiled against Nic's skin, making his way back down to his cock. He nuzzled his face against its base, inhaling some of the musk that had collected over the course of the evening. Freshly showered after the game, a combination of being outside and drinking had left Nic with just the right amount of sweat for Cory to get buzzed on. He lapped at the precum beading at his foreskin before sucking along Nic's shaft, moving underneath to his hairy nuts and stopping again to first inhale, then taste his heady scent.

Nic watched as Cory moved his mouth along his stomach and crotch, breath hitching as Cory dragged his tongue along the sensitive skin. He finished off his beer, setting it down on a nearby shelf to free his hands. He pulled the front of his shirt up, tucking it behind his head without fully removing it, revealing the hairy, muscled torso underneath.

Cory took the change in dress as an invitation, allowing his hands to travel up across Nic's body before following with his mouth. He stood once he had almost reached Nic's chest, slowly snaking his tongue across the salty skin as he inched toward Nic's nipple. He returned one hand to Nic's crotch, slowly stroking while he swiped across his nipple. Cory made a mental note as Nic moaned to try this again when they were sober. He was sure the beer was letting him get away with a lot more than Nic normally would allow, but he wasn't about to stop now.

Nic closed his eyes as he felt Cory latch onto his right nipple. He was using both hands, stroking and squeezing Nic's dick with one and massaging and feeling up Nic's pec with the other. When Cory switched sides a few moments later, Nic's hand instinctively went to Cory's head, holding him in place against his chest. *Fuck... This feels good...*

"Gotta let you do this more often, boy," Nic said without opening his eyes.

Cory was more than happy with what was going on. He spent a few minutes on Nic's chest, alternating which side he used his mouth and hand on. Nic allowed him to move back and forth, though the hand on his head remained, not allowing him to pull away. Cory was fine staying where he was, but Nic's continued reactions were only pushing him to go further.

"Oh, *fuck*." Nic's hand instinctively tightened in Cory's hair when he suddenly felt the boy dive face-first into his armpit.

His mouth hung open as he was inundated with a dozen different feelings at once. He felt Cory's tongue as he lapped at his underarm skin. It felt good. Almost too good, nearly ticklish. He was slightly grossed out, but even more turned on at the fact that Cory had willingly done it. He knew the boy was into musk, but shit, he was practically devouring him.

Happy that Nic was letting him get away with this, Cory took his time cleaning Nic's pit with his tongue. Nic hadn't put on any deodorant after showering after the game, and to Cory he smelled and tasted so good. The only thing that was able to tear him away from one side was knowing that there was another fresh pocket of musk waiting for him on the other. Nic allowed him to move, still gripping him by the hair, but remaining silent other than the occasional moan or muttered curse. Cory really hoped he could convince Nic to let him do this again when they had more time. And a bed.

Suddenly, Cory *yelped* directly into Nic's underarm and grabbed his shoulders like he might fall over. Nic looked down at Cory curiously but couldn't exactly make out what was on his face. Then he noticed what sounded like a really faint buzzing noise coming from Cory, and something Derek had said to him earlier clicked.

"Oh, shit, is that the plug?" Nic pet the back of Cory's hair as he laughed. "Derek told me he had you wear that tonight."

Cory only whined as he felt the toy buzzing against his prostate. He had almost forgotten it was there—but clearly Derek hadn't. He braced himself against Nic as he tried to find his balance. Sensing an opportunity, Nic chuckled again as he helped guide him to once again kneel on the floor.

Cory was once more eye level with Nic's cock, inhaling him again as the plug forced him to steady his breathing.

"Open up, boy." Nic tapped his cock against Cory's lips. "This'll help you focus on something else."

Cory opened his mouth from instinct when he felt Nic looking for entrance. The plug was pulsing at an erratic rate, making it impossible to judge when the next pulse was going to come, which was probably what Derek intended. Since there was nothing he could do about it, Cory focused on what he could control—sucking Nic off. Breathing as best as he could through his nose, he lowered his mouth down Nic's eager cock.

"Good boy," Nic said as he relaxed against the door.

Unable to help himself, Nic moved the hand that wasn't on Cory's head up his chest, feeling up his own chest. He smirked to himself—he *was* a fucking stud. With the sudden burst of cockiness, he started pumping his hips forward into Cory's mouth, taking what he felt was already his.

Cory was actually happy when Nic started to fuck his face. The erratic pattern of the vibrator was making it almost impossible to concentrate. This way, all Cory had to do was keep his teeth out of the way and his gag reflex suppressed. The plug was also making his cock start to chub up again, though Cory doubted Nic would afford him the same courtesy as Taylor.

"Open up that throat for me, boy," Nic commanded as he plunged his cock in and out of Cory's gullet, wanting him to take even more. "Wanna feel my balls against that chin."

Cory tried to hum an affirmative, though he wasn't sure Nic even heard it. His thrusts were quickly picking up speed, already immensely turned on from the body worship Cory did earlier. Soon his balls were slapping against Cory's chin, just like he asked. Cory didn't expect to be waiting much longer, and sure enough, he soon felt the tell-tale swelling of Nic's cock as he prepared to fire his load. The first shot fired directly into the back of Cory's throat and almost made him gag. That at least prepared him for the next shots, filling his mouth rapidly and forcing him to swallow, lest he lose some.

"Swallow that load, bitch." Nic continued to pump his hips in and out of Cory's face as he came. "Take it all."

Cory hummed his approval around Nic's cock, happy to oblige his dom's request. Once the thrusting had stopped, Cory took a few moments to clean it off with his mouth, licking up any stray shots of cum he may have somehow missed. Then with a final kiss to the head, he tucked Nic's spent cock back into his jeans and zipped him back up. Nic held his hand out to Cory to help him up, something Cory was very grateful for, given that the plug was still making his movements somewhat stilted.

"Good job, boy." Nic smiled, still obviously tipsy. "That was really fuckin' hot, the way you got on my chest and pits…"

"Glad you thought so, sir." Cory beamed inwardly. "Was my pleasure."

"Let's get back. Amy is probably wondering where I went." Nic opened the door behind him, once again holding it for Cory.

The two boys walked back around the house to the back-yard, happy to rejoin the party and their friends. Neither of them noticed Steve standing on the other side of the door, watching as the boy and one of his owners walked out of the dark garage, alone, together.

"So, you *are* seeing someone?"

"Not exactly. It's ... really complicated right now," Cory did his best to explain to Stephanie.

The party was winding down, kids getting ready to leave, some already on their rideshare apps. Cory already knew he'd be crashing here. He found Stephanie in the backyard, sitting at the same table from before, looking at her phone, and he was finally ready to answer some of her questions.

"I guess that explains why you've been so busy lately." Stephanie's sad tone broke Cory's heart.

"I swear, Steph. I wanna tell you so much more..." Cory started. "Just ... give me a little more time to figure some things out. It's just..."

"Really complicated," Stephanie finished Cory's sentence. "Right. Well, whatever is going on, I hope it works out." Steph paused to look at her phone. "My ride's here. Gotta get going."

"Oh, right." Cory felt like the biggest asshole in the world as Stephanie came in for a hug.

"I promise, whatever it is you think I'm gonna freak out about, I won't," she told him as she squeezed Cory tightly. "See you on Monday!"

"See you!" Cory waved as she walked away.

He really did want to tell her everything... He was just pretty sure she was wrong about not freaking out. Cory himself was still freaking out about it. He looked around the backyard for Derek or Nic, but the only familiar face he saw was Jackson's, who only gave him another one of those weird looks he'd been throwing Cory's way. Ignoring him, he headed toward the house to continue his search. He was just rounding the corner into the kitchen when he found Derek engrossed in a conversation with Tricia.

"...and I barely saw you tonight." *Uh-oh, Tricia does not sound happy.* "Hell, this is the most we've talked all week."

"I know. I'm sorry. I've just been so—"

"Busy, yeah. That's what you've said every time you've canceled our plans the last couple of weeks." Tricia crossed her arms. "I figured that at least tonight we'd be together, but you spent the entire party on your fucking phone. Or apparently talking to anybody who isn't me."

"Trish, I'm sorry. I swear—"

"Save it, Derek. *You* were the one who asked *me* to get more serious," Trica punctuated her words with a poke to Derek's chest. "Thanks for wasting my time." She walked out of the kitchen, giving Cory an awkward smile as she passed.

Derek stood in the kitchen leaning over the counter, back to Cory. He knew Trish was right. He had been a really shitty boyfriend lately. He thought he was balancing everything he had going on pretty well, but instead it seemed like a lot of his new *interests* were monopolizing his time. He hadn't expected to be *so* into them though...

"Hey," Cory finally announced his presence as he approached Derek. "You okay?"

"Yeah, I'm fine." Derek turned and gave him an awkward smile. "I deserved that."

Cory walked over to Derek and gave him an awkward side hug.

"C'mon, let's go make sure everyone made it home or to bed safely." Derek responded by ruffling Cory's hair. "Seen Nic lately?"

"Not for about an hour," Cory recounted when he and Nic had spent some time in the garage. "Maybe he went home with Amy?"

"Nah, she left a little while ago to help get one of her friends home safe. He's around here somewhere." Derek started walking back toward the living room. "Come on. We can get this place cleaned up a little while we look."

Cory and Derek walked through the house, cleaning up as they went and making sure everyone was able to get home okay. Other than a few people passed out on couches, the place wasn't too much of a disaster. Still no sign of Nic, though.

With the inside secure, the two boys walked into the backyard to check on any remaining stragglers. There were a few kids hanging around (and a puddle of vomit), but the backyard had also avoided resembling a warzone. Derek again made sure everyone had a way to get home, but Nic was *still* nowhere to be found.

"Hmm... We should check the garage," Cory suggested, remembering how Nic pulled him in there earlier. "We were in there earlier."

"Is that where he took you?" Derek smiled before he started walking to the garage side door. "Sounds like you had a busy night."

"Something like that, sir." Cory rolled his eyes behind Derek's back as he entered the door code.

"Oh, hey," a still tipsy Nic greeted them as they opened the door. "There you guys are."

Standing next to him in the garage were Taylor and the hot, nameless football player Cory was staring at earlier. Cory flushed a little as he remembered being caught.

"Hey." Derek chuckled at Nic's demeanor. "What's up, guys? Have fun tonight?"

"Yeah, it was a great party, man," Taylor answered. "Me and Julian here were just telling Nic about some of the stuff we used to get up to with Jamie." Taylor finished his sentence with a knowing look toward Cory, currently stuck between feeling mortified and intrigued. Julian, the extremely hot football player *also* used to fool around with Jamie?

"This the boy you were mentioning earlier?" Julian looked Cory up and down, causing him to blush further.

"Yeah, that's him," Nic jumped in. "Sucks dick like a champ. Want a go?"

"*Nic.*" Derek found himself surprised at Nic's forwardness; that was usually his thing. He looked to Cory. "Well, cat's outta the bag now... What do you say, boy?"

Despite Julian's attractiveness, Cory did find himself hesitating. This would be the fifth guy Cory had fucked around with, and the third guy that Derek and Nic had "loaned" him out to. As hot as it was, Cory was starting to feel worried about things going too far or the wrong person finding out. He was gonna need to talk to Derek and Nic about this...

...after he finished sucking Julian's cock.

"Yeah, I'm in," Cory said with feigned bravado.

"Great, been trying to find some pussy all night." Julian immediately began to grope his crotch. "I hope you can suck dick half as good as Jamie did."

"Oh, he can," Taylor assured him. "Trust me."

No one else moved to pull out their cocks, so Cory walked toward Julian and kneeled in front of him, face to face with his crotch as he continued to grope it with his hand. He saw as Julian's snake of a cock began to expand down one of his pant legs. Julian slowly unzipped his jeans, reaching his hand down to free his dick from its confines.

*Holy shit.* Cory was once again face to face with *another* massive dick. Was there something in their town's water or something? It was easily as long as Taylor's, if not a bit longer, though thankfully not nearly as thick. The long dark shaft ended in a set of nicely trimmed pubes, Julian apparently being one for manscaping. His heavy, hairy balls hung underneath, and Cory could almost hear them slowly churning Julian's load. Cory's dick twitched to life as he knelt.

"Damn, he's at least as eager as Jamie was." Julian smirked as he looked down at Cory on his knees, slowly stroking his cock to its full length before pointing it in Cory's direction. "Open wide!"

Cory did as he was told and Julian's cock quickly filled his mouth. As he slowly bobbed his mouth up and down, he used one of his hands to cover the rest of Julian's shaft, using his other hand to reach down to squeeze and fondle his nuts. Unlike the others, Julian seemed perfectly content to let Cory do all the work, making no attempt to start fucking Cory's face. Once Cory felt comfortable enough in his rhythm, he started to deep throat more and more of Julian's cock. With its much more reasonable thickness, Cory was having no issues deepthroating about three quarters of the dick.

"Shit, you were right." Julian watched, fascinated as Cory slurped up and down his length. "He *is* good."

Cory looked up, mouth still full, in an attempt to convey a thank you when he felt the sudden *jolt* of the plug still in his ass coming to life once more. The sudden vibration in his hole caused Cory to jump forward, inadvertently burying the rest of Julian's dick in his throat with a muffled yelp, arms clinging to the hunky footballer's legs for support. As Cory unblocked his airflow by pulling his face away from Julian's crotch, he heard the sound of Derek chuckling behind him. *Asshole.*

"You doing okay there, boy?" Derek asked the question he already knew the answer to.

"*Goddammit, sir, you have been torturing me with that thing all night,*" Cory growled through gritted teeth as he rode out the vibrations from the plug. "*Either fuck me or take it out before I scream.*"

There was a beat of silence, in which Cory suddenly became *very* aware of how he just spoke to Derek. Then Nic burst into laughter.

"Damn, D!" Nic managed to get out. "I think you broke him." That was a good sign, though Cory was still waiting to hear what Derek was going to say.

"...Well, shit, boy. Sorry." Cory breathed a sigh of relief into Julian's crotch. "I have been playing with you all night. Only right I take care of you now."

*Yesssssss.* Cory heard the sound of a belt buckle being undone and happily went back to sucking on Julian's cock as he moved his legs back for Derek.

"I thought you were supposed to be the one in charge here?" Julian teased, looking down and giving Cory a wink. "This boy got you whipped."

"I don't know about whipped." Cory felt Derek settle in behind him as he spoke, plug slowing to a stop. He felt Derek's hands working to pull Cory's pants down past his ass. "But he's a good boy ... usually. I *did* tease him all night with this." Derek tapped against the plug before taking a hold of the base, sliding it from Cory's hole and holding it up for Julian to see. "Can't blame the boy for needing his hole filled."

Cory blushed as he was talked about and his body manipulated as if he wasn't there. He looked up at Julian somewhat nervously, but he received only a smile and a pat on the head in exchange. Shaking off his doubts, Cory resumed sucking and throating Julian's cock as he felt Derek's fingers pressing into his ass.

"Good. Wearing this all night has you nice and opened up," Derek said as he drove two fingers in and out of Cory's hole, causing him to buck and moan around Julian's dick. "Won't even have to use much lube."

The snap of a cap indicated that at least *some* lube was being used, as Derek spread it up and down his cock before moving closer to Cory, placing his feet on the outside of Cory's legs. With his jeans bunched up near his knees, he was unable to spread his legs. Cory felt Derek lowering himself, squatting on his spread legs as the head of Derek's thick cock pressed between his cheeks.

Cory mentally braced himself as he felt Derek's cock pressing forward, slipping in with ease. Derek was right, the plug had really opened him up. Might be worth wearing them more often when Cory knew he was going to spend the evening getting fucked. Cory started moaning as Derek's cock glided across his prostate, already more than halfway buried inside of him.

"There we go." Derek gave Cory's ass a smack as he bottomed out. "That better, boy?"

"Mmmhmmm," Cory moaned around Julian's meat, unable to do much else in his current position.

He continued to slurp happily away at Julian as Derek pulled his hips back and began to fuck. The next few minutes progressed in relative silence other than the occasional slurp from Cory or spank from Derek. Taylor and Nic watched the scene entranced, Nic unable to help himself from pulling his cock out and playing with it once more.

Julian had lowered to his own knees, which made it easier for Cory to not have to lean up so high. The new angle also allowed for Derek to penetrate Cory's hole even deeper, forcing more muffled moans and groans from him as he began to really slam his force forward.

"Damn, dude, he's definitely noisier than Jamie was." Julian was loving the way Cory reacted, both to his dick and the one in his ass. "I'm getting close but ... I might need to try that ass out one day."

"Heh, well I don't think our boy here would mind that much at all." Derek spanked Cory, who moaned in the affirmative.

Hearing that Julian was getting close motivated Cory, daring him to deepthroat even more of his length without fear of gagging. He wanted that load. Hard to believe only a few months ago he would have been gagging and choking all over it. He felt Julian move both of his hands into Cory's hair, gripping gently as he started tugging Cory's face forward as he sucked and slurped away, balls slapping against his chin with every thrust.

"Fuck, man." Julian was the one gritting his teeth now. "Gonna nut. Swallow it, boy!"

Cory felt Julian's cock expand in his mouth before it fired off the first volley of cum, splattering the roof of Cory's mouth. Rather than continuing to fuck his cock in and out, he pulled back, leaving barely more than the head in, gripping his cock with his hand and milking out the remaining shots. Cory moaned as he felt the remaining shots land directly on his tongue, happily swallowing Julian's salty snack as his mouth filled.

"Fuck." Julian looked down and released his cock, which was then grabbed by Cory, who made sure to squeeze every last drop out before releasing his now-cleaned cock.

"Right?" Derek gave Cory another smack as he continued fucking him. "Trained this boy good."

Cory couldn't argue with that. So he wouldn't. Instead, he closed his eyes and focused on Derek's cock in his hole as it poked and prodded his prostate. He bit his lip as he felt the pressure growing. He hoped Derek would be able to fuck at least one orgasm out of him before he came.

"Open up." The tapping of a wet cockhead against his lips had Cory opening his eyes, seeing Nic now towering over him, jerking his cock. He opened his mouth and went to take him inside, but Nic held his head in place. "No. Just open your mouth."

Cory did as he was told, holding his mouth open for Nic, who picked up the pace of his jerking. At the same time, Cory felt Derek shift as well, setting down one knee to give him more leverage. The pace and strength of his fucking picked up rapidly, and soon Cory was looking up to Nic as moans and squeals were forced from him, mouth agape.

"Fuck, move over, dude." It was Taylor, who was now standing next to Nic and also furiously stroking his cock. Oh god, they were *both* gonna paint his face. Cory felt his dick twitch and his hole squeeze tightly around Derek as he groaned loudly.

"Fuck, here it comes!" Nic was the first one to lose his load with three or four volleys of cum splattering across Cory's face and mouth. He milked his cock good, ensuring every drop landed on Cory's face or in his mouth. Cory happily licked his lips clean and swallowed, eager for Taylor to finish next. He didn't have to wait long, as he soon found Taylor's free hand in his hair, pulling his head back to hold him in place as Taylor added his own cum to the canvas of Cory's face.

"That was fucking hot." Derek's hands were now digging into Cory's hips as he held onto him tightly, slamming forward with full force. "Not much longer now, boy."

Cory only whined in response, eager to chase his own orgasm now that he had finished servicing everyone else. Or at least that's what he thought before he felt the tapping of a cock against his lips once again—Taylor and Nic expected to be cleaned off, naturally. Cory suckled on the head of Taylor's cock, ensuring that every last ounce of cum was in his belly before switching to Nic. As he worked on cleaning Nic, he felt his own orgasm begin to wash over him, letting loose a high-pitched whine as he released Nic's mostly cleaned dick. He bit his lip as he felt his hole spasming around Derek, who continued to fuck him all the way through it without stopping.

It seemed that Derek was also waiting for Cory to cum because once he felt Cory's hole relax once more, he really picked up the speed of his fuck, slamming his hips into Cory's ass at an almost punishing pace. Cory braced himself against the floor, knowing that they were in the home stretch.

"Alright, boy," Derek said to Cory as he felt the cum in his balls begin to boil. "Everyone else in here has gotten off tonight, including you. So now, it's my turn." Derek ended his statement with another smack, never slowing the speed of his thrusts.

Cory moaned again, his prostate still being manipulated with every move of Derek's dick. He felt Derek's cock as it began to swell as it prepared to fire off its own load. Cory tightened his hole, milking Derek's cock for all he was worth before he felt Derek pull his hips backward to meet his own, slamming and holding them together. Derek growled as he bred Cory deeply, unable to form any coherent words. He continued to try and push deeper with each subsequent shot, coating Cory's walls from top to bottom.

"Goddamn, guys." Julian whistled as he watched Derek and Cory coming down from their euphoria. Derek could only give him a thumbs up, still catching his breath. Cory made no attempt to move at all, instead savoring the pleasant feelings of soreness in his ass as Derek continued to occupy it. He needed to wash his face, and he definitely still had to talk to Derek and Nic about some of this stuff, but...

...if he could have spoken, he would have agreed with Julian. *Goddamn.*

# CHAPTER 11

"So, I heard you got up to some interesting stuff this weekend."

Nic closed his locker door and turned to look at Tim, another one of his teammates.

"What? The party?" Nic figured that was what he had to be talking about. It was Monday morning, the first day back at school since the game. After his victory, his family, particularly his father, had made a big deal out of celebrating nearly all weekend, and Nic was exhausted. As a result, Nic ended up driving himself to school, trying to squeeze in a few more precious minutes of sleep. "Yeah, it was a kickass night. Weren't you there?"

"That's not *exactly* what I'm talking about." Tim paused as he looked around to see if anyone was watching. "People are saying some stuff about you."

"What are you talking about? What kind of stuff?" The way the guy looked around made Nic nervous.

"Well... Someone said they saw you fucking that Cory kid at the party. People are saying you're ga—"

"*What the fuck!?*" Nic grabbed Tim by the shirt and slammed him into the locker behind him. "Who the fuck is saying that shit about me!?"

"Hey, man, chill!" Tim put hands up in surrender. "I'm just telling you what I heard. I thought you'd wanna know."

"Well, it's a fucking lie! Who the fuck is saying that?" Nic was really freaking out. Had somebody caught them at the party? They were totally alone in that garage, weren't they?

"I heard it from some of the cheerleaders." Nic's heart sank as he suddenly thought of Amy. Did she already know? "I don't know where they got it fro—"

Nic released his hold on Tim wordlessly and stormed off down the hall. He was going to get to the bottom of this. Now.

"I don't even know where to start."

"The beginning, Cor."

Cory gave Stephanie his best bitch face. The two of them had skipped their first period together at Stephanie's insistence and took off for the auditorium, a quiet place to talk. She wanted to know everything Cory had been keeping from her. And Cory wanted to tell her... He was just trying to figure out *how*. Funnily enough, they were in the same auditorium where he and Derek... *Anyway*...

"You know this isn't easy for me, right?" Cory was so nervous he was almost shaking. This was worse than coming out.

"I'm sorry." Stephanie pulled Cory in for a hug. "Start wherever you want."

"Okay." Cory took a deep breath. "So, I guess first thing is: I don't have a boyfriend. At least, that's not what ... this thing we've been doing is."

"Okay." Stephanie nodded. "So you've just been hooking up with someone?"

"Kinda… It's not exactly a relationship, but it is *something*." Cory buried his face in his hands before he continued. "I call them *sir*."

"Oh. Wow. Okay." Stephanie sat up straight as she took in the info. "So it's a … kinky thing?"

"Yeah… It's a kinky thing." Stephanie was hardly a prude, but Cory wasn't sure how well she was going to react to the full details of what exactly he had been getting up to. "Part of why it's so hard for me to talk about it to you is that I don't even know what any of it really is. What it means. It all started so suddenly and so weirdly. I don't even think they consider themselves gay or even bi…"

"Wait, *them*? They?" Stephanie clung to his choice of words. "Are we talking a pronoun kinda sitch?"

"No." *Well, here goes nothing.* "There's … two of them. Two guys. Two sirs."

"*Holy shit*, Cory." Stephanie's eyes were wide. "How did you land *two* guys—two kinky, apparently *straight* guys—at our high school!?"

"I don't know. I didn't see it coming, didn't expect them to figure that out about me…" Cory watched as the wheels seemed to be turning in Steph's head.

"Oh fuck, Cory…" She turned to him in realization. "It's Derek and Nic, isn't it?"

"I, uh, no, it's not—" Cory's eyes went wide as soon as the names left her mouth.

"Cory." He was caught.

"Please, Steph." Cory's voice was low and shaky. "Please don't say anything to anyone. If someone found out, they cou—"

"Cory, I promise." Stephanie drew him into another hug. "I won't say a word to anybody. I swear."

Cory held onto Stephanie until he felt his heart stop racing, letting go when he felt calm enough.

"So... Tell me how it started."

"It was up at the cabin," Cory explained. "Started like a normal weekend, playing video games and hanging out. Derek's brother got him a case of beer as a gift, and we were drinking those."

"Uh-oh."

"We started playing a drinking game," Cory pressed on. "But by the time I was on my third beer, it changed from a drinking game to something like strip poker. Not long after *that*, I was the first one naked. That's when they ... talked to me. They told me they knew I was gay. I let them borrow my laptop one night, and well, they found some of my porn. A *lot* of my porn. All the kinky shit."

"That's kinda fucked up," Stephanie said defensively.

"Yeah, but they didn't do it on purpose, I don't think," Cory tried to reassure her. "I wasn't exactly worried about being stealthy on my own computer. It was my own fault for lending it to them."

"I don't think that's accurate, but we can circle back." She squeezed his arm. "What happened next?"

"I started to freak out," Cory continued. "I wasn't exactly expecting them to tell *me* I was gay. They calmed me down. Told me they didn't care. That they liked what it could mean."

"What it could mean?" Stephanie was trying really hard to hide the concern in her voice, but so much of this sounded *very* concerning.

"They wanted to ... help me out," Cory hesitated. This sounded so much worse now that he was saying it out loud.

"Train me, like the subs and doms in the porn I had been looking at."

"Jesus, Cor." Stephanie was no longer pretending to hide her shock.

"I didn't really know what they were talking about at first. I mean, they're both straight. I had never gotten even a hint that either of them was into guys. I never even thought about either of them like *that* before, not really," Cory pressed on, things were about to get graphic. "But, the beer, being naked, the shock of them outing me and then asking to basically sleep with me... It didn't end up being that difficult to say yes. And after that night, it just turned into a regular thing for us. It felt kinda ... natural. For me, at least."

"Cory, that all sounds so—"

"—Weird?"

"Rapey."

"Oh god, I know." Cory buried his face in his hands. "But... Fuck, Steph, this was like one of my biggest fantasies, ever, coming true right in front of me. And it's not like they forced me, but ... that also added to how hot the whole thing was."

"Right, but that's a fantasy, Cory," Stephanie reasoned. "They got you drunk... They took advantage of you. It sounds like they knew what they were doing. Like they *planned* it."

"I know." Cory sighed. "And even after that night, there have been other times where it didn't really feel like I had the option to say no." Cory would spare her the details of the other dudes he'd been "loaned" to over the months.

Stephanie was silent for a few moments, leaning back against the wall.

"It's a lot, isn't it?"

"That's an understatement." Stephanie sat up. "How do you feel about the whole setup now?"

"Good, for the most part," Cory said honestly. "Sometimes things are a little confusing. The line between friends and the sex stuff can get blurry. And I have no idea what happens in the future. It's not like either of them thinks of this as a relationship."

"Are you okay with that?" Stephanie watched his face for his reaction.

"I think so? I'm not exactly mad about not being a virgin anymore. And there are way worse people to lose your virginity to." Cory was blunt. "I can honestly say I have enjoyed everything we've done together, even the stuff I wasn't sure about at first."

"But you know you need to talk to them about this, right?" Steph said gently but firmly. "There's so much about this that is messed up. At the very least, you need to be able to talk to them about how it makes you feel."

"I know. I've needed to talk to them for a while now." Cory sighed again. "Thanks for not thinking I'm a kinky freak for any of this."

"Oh no, I *absolutely* think you're a kinky freak for all of this," Stephanie countered with a smile. "I just don't think there's anything wrong with being a kinky freak."

"Thanks?"

"No problem." Stephanie paused, her face sobering. "You know I'm here to help you however I can, right? Want me to come with you to talk to either of them?"

"No, that's okay," Cory reassured her. "I think this is something I need to do on my own… but can we skip second period too? I'd rather not talk to Derek *right* now…"

"Of course." Steph pulled him into a side hug. "Whatever you need."

Nic paced the hallway outside of Derek's first period class, Spanish, waiting for the bell. He had spent the last forty minutes trying to track down the source of the rumor, which turned out to be very difficult when everyone involved was in class. When the bell finally rang a few minutes later, Nic made a beeline for Derek, still standing up from his desk.

"Dude, we gotta talk, *now*." Nic looked around to see if anyone was looking at him, paranoid.

"Sure, man. Everything okay?" Derek looked Nic up and down. Something was wrong.

"Not here. Come on." Nic took off out of the class, forcing Derek to jog to catch up when he made it out of the door. He led Derek outside and around the building, a spot where normally smokers would gather to hide from administrators.

"*Leave*," Nic growled at the sole student in the area, a punky looking sophomore with pink hair. The look on Nic's face alone was enough for him to stub out his cigarette and hightail it out of there.

"What's going on, bro?" Derek asked once they were alone. "You're freaking me out."

"Someone knows." Nic paced. "Someone found out about me and Cory."

"What do you mean?" Derek was still confused.

"Someone saw us, man!" Nic almost yelled before remembering that he was trying to be discreet. "There's shit going around school today. People are saying that they saw me fucking Cory. That I'm gay."

"Oh, shit." Derek's eyes went wide. "Who's saying that? Who saw you?"

"I don't fucking know!" Nic dragged his hand through his hair in frustration. "That's why I'm talking to you. I hoped you would."

"I'm sorry, dude. I have no idea." Derek shrugged. "You know I wouldn't tell anyone."

"So what the fuck do I do, man?" Nic yell-whispered. "I need you help me find the asshole spreading this around and kick his ass."

"Nic, man… You gotta calm down," Derek tried to reason with his friend. "You're just working yourself up. Freaking out isn't exactly gonna make them seem untrue."

"Fuck you, dude!" Nic was no longer whispering. "This is all your fucking fault anyway! I wouldn't have done *any* of this shit if it wasn't for you. There wouldn't *be* rumors to spread around!"

"Nic—" It was too late. Nic had already turned away and took off.

Derek sighed. This wasn't going to end well. He spent the next couple of hours trying to figure out just what was going on and where the rumors were coming from. On top of Nic freaking out and running away, Derek also didn't see Cory in their chemistry class and also worried what that meant. If people were giving Nic shit, who knows what they were doing to Cory.

Unfortunately, it wasn't terribly easy to get information out of anyone in the middle of the school day. He did his best, but aside from some very, very light info he managed to overhear, he was forced to wait until lunch to do any real legwork. Once the bell rang, he started his search, trying to find people who had already heard the rumor without spreading it further. Derek really had to be careful about who he asked, not wanting to draw more attention to the rumors, or even worse, confirm them.

Eventually, Derek was also able to trace it back to the cheerleading team. Lunch was almost over, and he was seated, trying to figure out the best way to talk to the cheerleaders about this. The football players and cheer-leaders were naturally very close, not to mention that Nic was dating their captain. The wrong question could get back to the wrong person, and if Nic was freaking out already, he might well have an aneurysm if Derek somehow made things worse.

"Hey, there you are." Derek looked up to see Cory speaking to him, looking no worse for wear. "Been looking for you all lunch."

"Oh, yeah, sorry." Derek wasn't sure what, if any-thing, Cory knew about. "Trying to figure some stuff out. What's up?"

"Well—" Cory was cut off by the bell signaling the end of lunch. "Crap. Can we talk after school? It's important."

"Everything okay?" *Maybe he did hear about it?*

"Yeah, it's just ... not stuff to talk about at school." Cory started toward his next class. "See ya fifth period?"

"Yeah, Cor. Sure." *Maybe not.* "See you then."

As Cory turned and walked away, Derek hoped he hadn't noticed the few people who were watching them, talking to each other in hushed whispers. This was going to be a long day.

"Nic, baby, you have to calm down!"

Amy and Nic were sitting in a park not far from school. After Amy, who had heard but did not believe the rumors, saw how badly Nic was reacting to them, she took him off-campus to cool down. It didn't seem to be helping much, though.

"I can't. This is driving me nuts." Nic was pacing back and forth in front of the bench Amy was sitting on.

"They're just rumors, babe," Amy reassured him. "You know I don't believe them. In a week or two, no one will even remember this."

"That's easy for you to say!" Nic exclaimed. "It's not your reputation on the line."

"Why do you care so much about this?" Amy sighed. "It's just a stupid rumor. They go around school all the time!"

"Yeah because *your* teammates spread them around!" Nic accused.

"Hey, that's not fair; they don't *start* them!" Amy defended. "No one else on the team believes it either. I even told Jenna that Steve was probably just saying it because he was still pissed off at you over something stupid."

"Steve? *Steve!?*" Nic stopped dead in his tracks at the mention of that name, fuming. "I'm going to kick his fucking ass!"

"I didn't want to tell you because I knew you'd do *this*." Amy sighed again. "Will you just sit down and chill out for a second?"

"No, fuck that." Nic was already making his way back toward the high school. "He's fucking *dead*."

"So what did you want to talk about?" Derek asked as he and Cory walked toward his car from their fifth period chemistry class. The rest of the day had been surprisingly quiet, though that probably had something to do with there being no sign of Nic anywhere since that morning.

"Well, it's about the stuff between you, me, and Nic." Cory was understandably nervous to bring things up.

"Damn, I guess you *did* hear the rumors going around then," Derek said as he unlocked his car, throwing his backpack in the backseat. "Sorry, boy. They'll blow over soon enough though. Just stupid high school bullshit."

"Uh, what rumors?" Cory had no idea what Derek was talking about as he climbed into the passenger seat. "What's going on with Nic? I didn't see him all day."

"Shit," Derek cursed and started the car. "Okay, keep in mind that dumb stuff like this gets said all the time, and it always fizzles out, but ... someone is saying they saw you and Nic having sex at the party after the game last weekend."

"What!?" Cory squawked. "Who's saying that!?"

"Don't know yet. That's what I was trying to figure out at lunch." Derek pulled out of the school parking lot and headed toward home. "It came from the cheerleaders, like it usually does, but because it's about Nic..."

"Asking them about it might make things worse," Cory finished Derek's thought.

"Right," Derek confirmed. "Nic found me after first period this morning, totally freaking out, but I haven't seen him since. He wasn't at lunch or in gym."

"I didn't see him at all. I skipped first and second period, but he wasn't in biology." Cory hadn't thought much of it at the time. "I hope he's okay."

"I think he will be; he just needs to calm down." Derek stopped the car at a red light and turned to Cory. "You seem to be taking it rather well, though."

"Enh. It's not like any of those people are my friends, and we've got what, a few months of school left?" Cory shrugged. "After you and Nic found out, and after telling Steph, it doesn't feel as scary."

"You came out to Stephanie?" Derek looked over in surprise.

"That's sorta what I wanted to talk to you about." Cory took a breath. "I talked to Stephanie this morning. She found out at the party that I had been fucking around with someone, and without meaning to, I kind of let it slip that it was you and Nic."

"Cory, you *what*!?" Derek's tone grew angry. "Fuck, that's probably where the rumor came from!"

"What? No. That's impossible," Cory reasoned. "I literally told her in the middle of first period *today*. She was with me through second. If Nic was already freaking out by then—"

"Okay, okay, it couldn't have been her." Now Derek sounded more annoyed then angry. "But you still shouldn't have told her."

"I didn't *tell* her," Cory continued defending himself. "She guessed after I told her that I had been messing around with two straight guys."

"Fuck, Cory! Why not just show her a picture of my dick in your mouth? You didn't think to lie *a little* to cover our tracks?" Derek groused as he pulled away from the now-green light. "Why were you even talking to her about it anyway? You should have just told her to mind her own business."

"Because I needed to talk to someone! A friend—someone who isn't you or Nic!" Now Cory was getting annoyed. "Not that either of you talk to me much these days anyways."

"What was that?" Derek's voice was icy.

"You and Nic never actually *talk* to me about any of this stuff!" Cory had started, and he wasn't going to stop until he got everything out. "You don't even really give me the option to say no to anything! You just tell me what I'm going to do or put me in a position where it would be hard or weird for me to not go along with it."

"What the fuck are you talking about?" Derek gripped the steering wheel tightly. He did *not* like where this was heading.

"Everything! Blowing you guys at school, loaning me out to the daddy at the porn store, blowing Taylor, and now Julian! All of it!" Cory started listing his grievances. "Even how you started this. You guys got together and planned to get me drunk and then basically made me your sex slave! And you just assumed I'd be cool with all of it!"

"Well, you were, weren't you?" Derek was trying (and failing) to not raise his voice. "Or are you trying to tell me you haven't loved every second of this? That you haven't been having some of the best sex of your life?"

"That's not the point!" Cory was frustrated that Derek seemed to be completely ignoring what he was actually saying. "I hadn't had *any* kind of sex until you decided to change that *for me!*"

"Decided for you? You mean *forced* you, right?" Derek practically snarled. "Just say it, Cory. You're saying we *raped* you."

"What!?" Cory practically choked on air at the "r" word. "No, Derek, that's not what I mean—"

It was too late—Derek was already slowing the car down, pulling over to the side of the road.

"Get out of the car." He was not about to sit here in his own car and let someone accuse him of ... *that*.

"Derek—"

"*Get out of my fucking car, Cory.*" Derek wouldn't even look at him, the anger radiating in waves.

"...Fine." Cory opened the door and stepped out, slamming it behind him. He heard the passenger window lower and turned to face it. Derek had made his point, hadn't he?

"Wouldn't want to force you to have to ride around in a car with your *rapist*." As soon as he spat the last word out at Cory, Derek peeled off, leaving Cory on the sidewalk, mouth agape as he watched the car fade away down the road.

Nearly shaking with anger, Cory forced himself to turn again and start walking toward the Burger King. His hands shook as he reached for his phone, eventually managing to pull up his mother's info and call her.

"Hey, mom." Cory did his best to hide the emotion in his voice. "Can you come pick me up? I'm at the Burger King on Middleton."

"Sure, honey. Is everything okay?"

"Yeah, everything's fine," Cory lied. "I was hanging out with Derek, but he had an emergency and had to leave before he could bring me home."

"Okay, I'll see you in a few minutes."

"Thanks, Mom. Love you."

Cory ended the call and sat on a bench outside of the restaurant. He felt like crying or screaming or even laughing at the ridiculousness of the situation. Instead, he stood up and walked inside. French fries helped everything.

"Where is he?" Nic stormed into the locker room, a man on a mission.

"Uh ... who?" The poor confused JV football player looked around nervously.

"Steve," Nic spat out. "Where is that son of a bitch?"

"Aww, what's wrong Nicky? Your boyfriend too busy?" Steve taunted as he walked in from the showers. "Sorry, man. Not into dudes."

"Shut the fuck up, you lying sack of shit." Nic tore across the locker room and grabbed Steve by the shoulders, slamming him into the lockers behind him.

"Woah, man, relax." Steve held his hands up in feigned innocence. "I don't know what you're talking about."

"I'm going to knock your fucking teeth in."

"But Nic," Steve whispered low enough so that only Nic could hear him. "We both know I'm not lying. I saw you and that fag walking out of the garage together looking very, very cozy."

Nic's face paled slightly, though the look of rage never left it. Fuck. He *did* see them.

"Yeah, thought so," Steve sneered, still whispering. "Go ahead and kick my ass, Herrera. Really makes it look like you got nothing to hide."

"Dude." Nic felt a hand on his shoulder.

It was Taylor. He said nothing else, but that was enough. Nic looked around the locker room. Everyone was staring at him and Steve. *Fuck.* Nic let go of Steve and punched the locker behind him in anger before storming back out of the locker room wordlessly.

"What the fuck was his problem?" Steve asked no one in particular, not even bothering to hide the smirk on his face.

Cory couldn't stop checking his phone. He wasn't sure why—even if Derek *had* texted him, he didn't want to talk to him. He was still too angry. And hurt. And sad. *Ugh.* After his mom had picked him up, she had to head to work, having picked up a night shift at the warehouse. Not long after she left, it started raining—a storm off the coast would be sending them bands of rain all night. That left Cory alone with just the rain and his thoughts to keep him company. And the TV.

After setting his phone down for what felt like the hundredth time, Cory went to the kitchen to rustle up something for dinner. Cory eyed the leftovers in the fridge—cold spaghetti and meatballs—before deciding the day's events called for something a little more comforting. *Mac and cheese it is!*

After setting a pot of water to boil, Cory walked out to the living room and turned on the TV, flipping through the streaming apps until he found something funny and mindless to watch while he waited. *Schitt's Creek* re-runs seemed like just the thing he needed. Anything to take his mind off of the bullshit that was his day.

Eventually, Cory returned to the kitchen to add noodles to the now boiling water. Without the TV to distract him, his mind began to wander, always bringing him back to Derek. He kept replaying the conversation in the car over and over in his head. It just turned so quickly—Cory knew it wasn't going to be an easy talk, but when he was actually saying those things out loud, when he actually thought about the way things had gone, it just made him *angry*. And it was like Derek wasn't even listening to him. He just immediately got defensive. *Was I too harsh?*

Cory sighed as he drained the pasta. No. He said what needed to be said. It wasn't his fault that Derek didn't like hearing it. Hadn't he always told Cory he needed to stand up for himself more? Shaking the thoughts from his head, Cory finished making his dinner, mixing in the orange cheese powder as he walked back out to the living room. No one said comfort food had to be good for you.

For the next half-hour, it was just Cory, his food, and the TV. Cory finished eating just as an episode ended and went to the kitchen to throw his bowl in the sink before the next one started. He was just about to sit back down when someone knocked on the door. That was strange. Cory moved to the door and peered through the peephole. It was Nic.

"Nic?" Cory questioned as he opened the door. The football player looked like a drowned rat, like he'd been walking around in the rain all night. "What are you doing here?"

"Cory!" Nic offered a big smile. "I knew you'd answer for me!"

Nic stumbled in the doorway past Cory, who had an inkling of what was going on. Nic was drunk. *Very* drunk. And wet. But why? And why was he here?

"Are you okay?" Cory followed as Nic moved into the living room, almost tripping over himself as he tried to sit on the couch. "You are very drunk."

"Yes. No. Maybe." Nic stared at his feet. "I dunno."

"Yes, you're okay, or yes, you're drunk?" Cory wasn't sure why he asked. He knew the answer to both.

"Yes 'mdrunk. No 'mnot okay." Nic looked at, then cradled, his right hand for a moment. "Oww."

"What's wrong with your hand?" Cory held the offending limb gently. The skin was broken in a few places, and it looked bruised.

"Got angry. Punched a locker." Nic wiggled his fingers slightly. "Hurts. But the rum helped."

"Yeah, I hear it can do that." Cory chuckled at Nic's demeanor but noted that he could move all his fingers, so at least nothing was broken. "Come on. Let's clean this up."

"Okay." Nic allowed Cory to guide him from the couch to his bathroom, sitting on the toilet while Cory grabbed a towel and some bandages and peroxide.

"So what happened?" Cory knelt in front of Nic, holding his hand steady as he cleaned the injury.

"Steve saw us," Nic said plainly. "Friday, in the garage. He told people at school."

"Oh." Cory stopped what he was doing for a moment. "I'm sorry."

"'Sokay. Not your fault. Shoulda been more careful." Nic gave Cory a small smile. "Not like you get much of a say in it anyway."

"So, what happened next?" Cory chuckled again as he finished cleaning Nic's hand with the peroxide. If he only knew the headache he had from saying that earlier...

"Spent all day trying to find out who it was. Asked Derek, Amy..." Nic looked at his lap. "Amy told me it was Steve. Went to kick his ass. Didn't think. Everyone saw me freaking out."

"Shit." Cory wasn't sure what to say. "Maybe it'll all blow over?"

"Should've just ignored him. Did exactly what he wanted me to do," Nic mumbled into his lap. "Went straight home after. Stole Dad's rum, got drunk..."

"And then came here," Cory finished and started wrapping a bandage over the deep abrasions.

"No. Tried to go see Amy first." Nic got very quiet. "She won't talk to me."

"Oh." Cory tried not to feel slighted. "Sorry."

"*Then* I came here," Nic explained. "Knew *you* would help me."

"Yeah." Cory sighed. "That's what I'm here for, right?"

"Yeah, you're Cory." Nic used his uninjured hand to tilt Cory's head up toward him and smiled. "You're the best. You're always there for me."

Cory's face flushed at the tender praise and attempted to pull his head away.

"You always take care of me..." Nic held him in place gently, looking softly into the smaller boy's eyes. Then, wordlessly, he lowered his head, drawing Cory's closer to his, until finally, their lips were touching.

*Oh. Oh wow. This is… This is nice.* Nic slowly moved his lips against Cory's, finishing with a small *smack* before capturing his mouth again. Cory did his best to match what Nic was doing, never having actually kissed someone before. He suddenly understood why he was forced to watch so many horny straight couples sucking face at school. Kissing was *great.*

Some water dripped from Nic's hair onto Cory and suddenly his eyes flew open. Nic was kissing him. *Nic was kissing him.* Why was Nic kissing him?! Cory didn't have long to contemplate before he felt Nic's tongue gently swiping at his lips. Instinctively, Cory opened his mouth, allowing Nic to dip his tongue in and rub it against Cory's, who again did his best to follow Nic's lead. Cory moaned lightly as he closed his eyes again, tasting the spice of the rum on Nic's breath as he probed further.

The two boys continued to lock lips in the bathroom for a few minutes longer before Nic pulled away, drawing out an involuntary whine from Cory who tried to chase his mouth. Still smiling, he stood and helped the boy to his feet, leading him by the hand to Cory's bedroom. Once inside, he pulled Cory toward him before pushing him onto his back on the bed and climbing on after him.

Cory watched as Nic climbed over him, settling between his spread legs. He held himself up with his arms, looking down into Cory's face, still smiling that same soft smile. Cory's face felt so hot, all the blood rushing between there and his crotch. Nic wasn't saying anything, and Cory didn't want to either out of fear of breaking whatever spell he was under, even if the wet clothes did feel cold against him.

Nic lowered himself atop Cory, his weight pressing them both down into the mattress. He again captured Cory's mouth with his own, this time grinding his rapidly growing cock against Cory's thigh. Cory groaned into Nic's open mouth as they kissed, the feeling of Nic against his own hard cock leaving him gasping. He felt the stubble on Nic's face scrape against his own, the hint of roughness pushing Cory further into his headspace.

All of Cory's moans and whines beneath him drove Nic to go farther, to get rougher. He began to push more into Cory's mouth, dominating his tongue as they battled, mapping out the interior of Cory's mouth. The aggression only turned Cory on more as he worked to move his tongue against Nic's without ever trying to take charge of the kiss. Nic drew his good hand up and cupped Cory's face, holding him in place and making Cory whimper as his mouth was plundered.

Spurred on by Cory's submission, Nic started using his teeth, biting at Cory's lips as they kissed. He growled, holding them between his teeth before driving his tongue deep into Cory's mouth. Cory could only moan and do his best to keep up.

As their kissing grew rougher, so did their dry humping. Nic ground his hips down, pressing Cory deep into the mattress. Cory whimpered with each scrape of Nic's hips, the rough denim of his jeans easily overtaking the thin cotton of his shorts.

After pulling back for a moment, Nic kneeled up, towering over Cory. He pulled his wet t-shirt up and over his head, revealing a damp furry chest and stomach. Smirking as Cory ogled him, he tugged on Cory's own shirt, silently instructing him to take it off. As Cory fumbled to pull it up, Nic undid the fly on his jeans, shucking them and his underwear down in one smooth motion. Cory threw his shirt from the bed just as Nic was leaning back down to kiss him again, somewhat awkwardly shuffling his jeans the rest of the way down his legs, kicking them off to join his shirt.

Nic and Cory quickly returned to making out. The rough hair on Nic's chest rubbed against Cory's own light fuzz. The skin-on-skin contact had Cory shivering, and he wrapped his arms around Nic's back to pull him closer. Reaching up into Cory's hair, Nic tugged his face to the side as he began moving his mouth toward his ears, making Cory buck and shudder as he sucked and nibbled along the ridge.

Tightening his grip to hold Cory in place, Nic moved from the ear down Cory's neck. At first leaving only a trail of light, wet kisses, he gradually began to scrape his teeth over his sub's skin. As Cory continued to moan, he tightened his arms and scraped his nails down Nic's back, all while Nic sucked on Cory's neck, worrying the skin between his teeth.

"Oh, fuck, sir," Cory exclaimed as he grabbed Nic's back more tightly. He was probably going to have a hickey, but he really didn't care anymore. He turned his head even farther to the side to give Nic better access to his neck.

Nic growled when Cory moved, seeing his canvas expand. He bit into Cory's skin, leaving marks up and down from his neck to his collarbone. He removed the hand from Cory's hair and brought it down to the waistband of Cory's shorts and tugged, attempting to pull them down under Cory's ass. When Cory felt what he was trying to do, he lifted his ass, allowing them to be pulled down to his legs, where he somewhat awkwardly attempted to help with their removal.

"Fuck it," Nic growled as he tore himself away from Cory's neck, lifting and then ripping Cory's shorts from his legs. "Lube."

Cory nodded his head in understanding, scooting himself farther up the bed so that he could reach his nightstand. He opened the top drawer and fumbled blindly inside for the tube. Once he had it, he moved back to his previous position, handing it to Nic before lying back beneath him.

Nic popped the cap on the tube, squirting a small amount of the clear slick liquid onto his fingers. Then he dropped back down onto the bed, this time next to rather than on top of Cory. He snaked his injured arm under Cory's neck, pulling him back in for another kiss while his lube-covered fingers dove between Cory's legs, behind his balls.

Cory still couldn't entirely believe this was happening. He whimpered in Nic's mouth as he felt a slippery finger rubbing against his hole. He spread his legs farther, silently urging Nic to do more. He smiled as he felt a second finger join the first before they began to slowly prod at his entrance.

As the whimpers grew louder, Nic grew bolder and continued to slowly stretch Cory's hole with his fingers as they made out. Soon Nic was pumping three of his fingers in and out of Cory's hole, nearly down to the last knuckle. Cory continued to moan and groan into Nic's mouth as they kissed, attempting to lift his hips to meet Nic's fingers. Cory felt Nic's mouth twist into a grin against his own, Cory's movements telling him that he was ready for the real thing.

Nic pulled his hand from Cory's hole, moving to kneel between his spread legs. He grabbed the lube bottle, popping the cap and applying it up and down his shaft as he tossed the bottle to the side, close enough to reach if they needed it later. Nic grabbed Cory's legs and lifted them to his shoulders, shuffling forward until his cock met Cory. He rubbed the slick length up and down his boy's ass, swiping repeatedly over the hole and making it twitch and furl.

Nic locked eyes with Cory as he pressed forward, the head of his cock easily popping into the well-prepped hole. Once inside, he grabbed Cory's legs, moving them from his shoulders to his elbows. That meant he was able to bend

Cory's body—and his own—enough for their mouths to meet. Nic eagerly kissed Cory again as he felt inch after inch of his cock slowly sinking into Cory's hole. Cory whimpered around Nic's tongue as his hole was stretched, sucking on the rum-flavored appendage from instinct.

Nic growled as he felt Cory's ass swallow the last few inches of his cock. He ground their hips together, flexing his cock and forcing more noises from the beleaguered boy. Without ever disconnecting their mouths, Nic pulled his cock back slowly, pushing it back once only the head remained inside. He kept up this languid pace as he continued to kiss Cory slowly and deeply.

If Cory's eyes were open, he was sure they'd be rolling to the back of his head. The kissing, the rough feel of Nic's stubble and teeth, the heat of their bodies and breaths, the fact that *he was getting fucked...* It was true sensory overload for the poor boy. He scraped his nails along Nic's back as the pace of the fucking picked up. He never wanted it to stop.

Eventually, Nic had to come up for air, and he tore himself away from Cory. Moving back to a kneeling position, he let Cory's legs drop to the bed as both boys caught their breath. He looked down at Cory's body hungrily, flushed and covered in sweat. He reached down and gave his cock a few squeezes, then once again grabbed Cory's legs, this time by the backs of his thighs. He pushed them back and down, as best he could with his injured hand, and spread Cory's ass to reveal his slightly gaping entrance. He shuffled forward, using his hips to guide his cock once more toward Cory's hole, resting the head against the ring of muscle.

"Oh, fuck," Cory whispered as he looked down, nearly able to see his hole as Nic's cock prepared to spear it open again.

The exclamation had Nic's eyes flashing up to meet Cory's, still wearing the same hungry expression he had most of the night. Gripping Cory's thighs tightly, he pushed forward, reentering Cory's ass with little resistance. He wasted no time, pulling back as soon as he was fully seated. He continued to pump Cory's hole at a languid pace, looking down at the boy as he moaned and groaned as his hole was used.

"Oh, fuuuuuuck," Cory repeated, biting into his wrist as he felt as his prostate was slammed.

Nic saw Cory's toes begin to curl, felt the way his hole was starting to spasm and grip him tightly—Cory was going to cum. He tightened his grip on Cory's thighs, pushing them even farther back as he sped up the pace of his thrusts. He made sure to angle his cock, grazing over the fun-button inside Cory's ass with each pass. He could feel his heavy nuts swinging, slapping into Cory's ass with each slam home.

Cory let out a high-pitched yelp as he felt Nic increase the intensity of the fuck. He could feel his muscles tightening and spasming without his control as Nic pushed him closer and closer to orgasm. His legs struggled futilely against Nic's solid grip as he gripped the bed tightly with his free hand when it finally washed over him, muffling a low moan with his wrist still in his mouth.

Nic growled as he felt Cory milking him as he came. His pace never let up as he continued to force his thick cock into a hole that was squeezing him tightly. He watched as Cory's body relaxed after he came, though only for a moment. Soon enough the signs of another approaching orgasm became apparent, and Cory was once again gripping the bed tightly. Nic fucked his cock in and out of Cory's hole as fast as he could, loving the noises Cory made as his body once again began to cum entirely by Nic's doing.

Cory felt Nic slow to a stop as he recovered from his second dry orgasm. He opened his eyes tentatively, looking up to see Nic smiling down cockily, dick still buried inside of him. Gently, Nic released Cory's legs, bending down once more to kiss him, cock fully hilted. Cory instinctively wrapped his legs around Nic's waist, pulling him in even closer. He had to tilt his hips up at this angle, but he didn't care.

Soon after they began kissing, Nic started thrusting again, though much shallower than before. The pace was more languid as they made out, Nic lazily fucking his way in and out of Cory. He grabbed onto the sub's hair, tugging it to the side and once again attacking his ears with his tongue and teeth. He slowly sucked and nibbled on the outside of his ear, hearing Cory's mouth whimper and feeling his hole spasm.

Nic continued to steadily drive his cock in and out of Cory's hole, moving from his ear once more to his neck. As Cory moaned into Nic's own neck, he gradually sped up his thrusting, though still not reaching his previous speeds. It felt less like fucking than it did a steady grind, his cock pushing and stretching the walls of Cory's hole. Cory's hands were on his back, gripping him tighter with each pass of his cock.

Cory felt Nic's breath against his neck grow heavy as he continued to bite and suck at the skin. It felt like he had planted both of his thighs against Cory's and was using his weight to keep his ass angled *just* right for his dick. He ran his hands down Nic's back, lifting himself from the bed so he could grab at Nic's ass. He felt the thick, hairy muscles flex and release as Nic thrust, and he held on tightly as they drove forward, as if attempting to pull his sir even farther into himself.

Nic rumbled happily against Cory's neck as his ass was gripped, the sudden contact making his hips stutter. That was new. He bit into Cory's shoulder as he sped up, enjoying the way Cory pulled him closer with every thrust. He felt Cory's hole spasm again, and the knowledge that the boy was once again close to cumming goaded him to start chasing his own. He released Cory's hair, placing both of his arms on either side of his head while gripping the top of the mattress tightly with his good hand. The added leverage allowed him to speed up as he ground his cock into Cory's ass, literally pulling himself up as he fucked.

No longer able to keep up with the pace or force behind the thrusts, Cory held onto Nic's back as he rode the remainder out. He could feel that he was about to cum again and braced himself as the tell-tale signs began washing over him once more. He wasn't even sure of the noises he was making. At this point, it was all he could do to hold on. As his stomach muscles tightened, he felt the explosion centered on his hole once more.

As soon as he felt Cory relax post-orgasm, Nic started slamming his cock home. It only took a few thrusts before he was pushed over the edge and buried his cock as deeply within Cory as he could. He felt the first shot of cum leave his cock and with each subsequent shot used his grip on the mattress to push farther into Cory. Six or seven blasts later, Nic collapsed on top of Cory, both of them catching their breaths as they came down from their sex high.

As his brain came back online, Cory remembered he still had no idea why this was happening and realized that it must be a fluke.

Cory bounced up and down as he rode Nic's cock. It was only a half an hour later, and the two were still in Cory's bedroom. After their first round, Nic had extracted himself and grabbed a towel from the hamper to clean the two of them up. Neither had spoken a word, a comfortable silence passing between them as Nic worked. As he wiped the cum and lube from Cory's ass, the boy whimpered, which in turn made Nic's dick twitch, the appendage already waking back up. Unable to resist, Nic continued to tease Cory's sensitive, used hole, squeezing his own cock with his free hand.

And so, only thirty minutes later, Cory was once again speared on Nic's cock, this time on top. He held onto Nic's shoulders as he rode his lap, using the larger boy's frame to keep himself steady. Nic's hands were on Cory's ass, helping to lift and lower the tight hole he was currently occupying. He squeezed and gave one of Cory's cheeks a smack as he ground his hips down onto Nic's.

Cory's eyes were closed until he felt Nic's warm mouth suddenly encase one of his nipples. Looking down, he watched as Nic licked and bit at his chest, first the left side and then the right. He sucked each of Cory's nipples into his mouth, biting gently at the pink nubs. He opened his mouth wide to take in as much of Cory's pec into his mouth as he could, growling around the flesh in his teeth as Cory continued to ride him.

Cory wasn't sure if it was the angle or the added stimulation of Nic's hands and mouth, but he felt yet another orgasm approaching. This one also felt like it might be more on the wetter side of things.

"Fuck, need a towel," Cory managed to get out. "Gonna pee."

Nic nodded but never removed his mouth, reaching blindly on the bed for the towel he had just used to clean them up. He stuffed it between their two stomachs and encased Cory's cock in the fabric. That would just have to do for now. He continued to bite and suck on Cory's chest as he was ridden, no intention of stopping regardless.

Satisfied with the towel, Cory stopped fighting his orgasm, nearly collapsing forward onto Nic's chest as he felt his cock begin to spray, soaking the towel. As the damp material grew warm, he just hoped it would be enough to prevent any leaks.

An hour later and Cory was in the bathroom, starting up the shower. Nic had fucked him for another thirty minutes before cumming and had wrung orgasm after orgasm from Cory's hole. The towel had long been soaked with Nic eventually tossing the offending material from the bed. He didn't fucking care, and if Cory had been able to think coherently, he probably wouldn't have either. Once Nic finally came, the two passed out, collapsing together in a wet, sweaty heap on the bed.

Cory had woken up after a small nap, though Nic was still snoring deeply, probably because of the alcohol. After using another towel to clean up what he could, Cory moved to the bathroom to clean himself up. As he waited for the water to turn warm, he started to replay the day's events. Or at least he tried to until the bathroom door opened behind him just as he was stepping into the shower. It was Nic.

He crossed the bathroom quickly, stepping into the shower behind Cory without saying a word. He didn't really need to—Cory could see that he was once again hard. He grabbed Cory and kissed him hard before spinning him around and pushing him against the shower wall. At least Cory hadn't had a chance to clean the cum and lube from his ass just yet.

It was well after midnight when the two boys finally slept, both passed out in Cory's bed after one last fuck session. It was 2:00 a.m. when Nic woke up, finally having sobered up from all the rum. And it was 2:15 a.m. when he quietly climbed off of Cory's bed and got dressed, leaving the house and locking the door behind him as he returned to his own.

What the fuck was he thinking?

# CHAPTER 12

Derek angrily stomped from the kitchen back to his bed-room, nearly spilling his soda when he slammed it onto his desk. It had been three hours since he kicked Cory out of his car, and he was still fuming. Cory didn't know what he was talking about. How could he accuse him of something like that?

Derek sat down for a second and then sighed before get-ting back up. He had left his food in the kitchen. This stuff with Cory had his mind all over the place. He grumbled to himself after grabbing his plate, stalking back to his room, and flopping into the chair in front of his computer.

Sure, maybe it didn't start out under the *best* circum-stances, but it wasn't like he hadn't thought things through. He planned it out because he wanted to make sure it went well, for everyone. He *knew* what Cory wanted. He just used the beer to get him to relax and open his mind to the possi-bilities Derek would bring up.

Derek picked up a slice of pizza, the last of the leftovers from the party, and scarfed it down. All that shit about him being loaned out, not being able to say no... Again, it wasn't like Derek didn't know what Cory really wanted. He was just pushing his limits. That was what a good dom was supposed to do, right? That gave Derek an idea: Who better to ask about this than another dom and one of the aforementioned people Cory was "loaned" to? Carl.

Derek wiped the pizza grease onto a napkin and reached for his phone. After the first few emails, Carl had finally relented that, despite his age, he was perfectly capable of using text to communicate. Derek scrolled his contacts to the letter C, selecting the man's name when he found it.

[Derek: Hey, you got a minute? Something on my mind.]

Derek put his phone down and grabbed a second pizza slice as he waited for a response.

His phone buzzed a few minutes later as he finished eating, once again wiping the pizza grease from his hands before picking it up.

[Carl: Hey Derek. Sure, what's up?]

Derek thought for a moment about how he wanted to go about this. He didn't want to claim he was "asking for a friend" because that was never believable. Instead, he opted to just frame his questions around some of the stuff that happened this weekend at the party.

[Derek: Had a crazy weekend. My high school won their championship game, and we threw a big party at my place afterwards. Lots of kids, lots of beer.]

[Carl: Underage drinking aside, sounds like a fun weekend.]

[Derek: It was. But all the alcohol did have me wondering. If a sub was drinking, and you knew that by drinking they would be more open to stuff, would it be wrong to make a move? Not like wasted, just kinda buzzed.]

[Carl: I think you're getting into some murky waters there. You can't expect someone drunk to have the best judgment. It might give them the courage to finally say yes to something, but you also run the risk of them regretting it when they sober up.]

Well, that wasn't exactly what Derek wanted to hear.

[Derek: But what if it was something you knew they really wanted, deep down?]

[Carl: Still dangerous. Alcohol can make a person say or do some weird stuff. I don't think it would be worth the risk, having that kind of cloud hanging over the rest of the relationship.]

[Derek: What do you mean?]

It wasn't until today that Derek felt anything was wrong between him and Cory at all.

[Carl: Well, think about it. A sub might have their inhibitions lowered, but they're also not going to be thinking straight. In the moment, especially like that, they are going to look to their dom for guidance and will probably be willing to do a whole lot more than usual just to please them. When a D/s relationship is new, you're still setting boundaries and figuring things out. A sub needs to know they can talk to their dom about how they're feeling, and not worry about what might happen if they say no.]

Which is exactly what Cory was trying to tell him in the car. *Fuck.*

[Derek: So, if someone had been drinking, best to not try to make any moves at all?]

[Carl: Some people feel that you shouldn't mix any kind of substance—alcohol, weed, or otherwise—with playtime. The idea being that when you are in a scene, the safest thing is for you both to be totally sober. But I think if you were already an established couple, you'd probably be fine if you had a couple of beers. You already know each other's limits, and you'd probably know how much alcohol you both can handle by then too. But, if you were still new to each other, you wouldn't have that info. You'd still probably be too focused on figuring each other out, testing the boundaries, to make many good judgement calls.]

As Derek read through the giant walls of text—he wouldn't question Carl's ability to text again—his heart sank. He had really fucked up. Why hadn't he seen this before?

[Derek: Thanks, man. That helps a lot.]

[Carl: No problem, Derek. Everything okay with you?]

[Derek: Yeah, all good here], he lied. [Thanks again. TTYL]

He tossed his phone onto the bed as he sat at his desk and started replaying everything that had happened since the first night of the cabin. Fuck. How could he have been so selfish? Cory was his best friend. Cory was *more* than just his best friend. He was supposed to protect him. He was a monster.

Derek had to fix this. He just needed to figure out how.

Cory awoke slowly in the morning, the familiar pinging of his phone's alarm rousing him from a deep slumber. He stretched his limbs out, running them against the cool sheets as he woke up. As his brain booted back up for the day, memories of the night before flashed into his mind. Nic.

Cory's whole body felt sore but in a good way. He stretched his legs again, reaching down to squeeze his own thighs, the pressure on his sore muscles making him groan and causing his already hard cock (thanks, morning wood!) to twitch. Tentatively, he snaked a finger between them and under his balls, rubbing his equally sore hole. Fuck. Last night was so fucking hot... The way Nic—

Cory suddenly looked to his left, though he already knew Nic was gone. The bed was cold. The sheets didn't even look used. He had been gone a while. Sitting up, the only trace Cory could see of him even being there were the towels they used the night before and some of the slightly bloodied bandage Cory had wrapped his injured hand in. It had come off at some point and Cory had to rebandage it.

Cory reached for his phone and finally turned off the alarm before checking his notifications. Nothing from Nic *or* Derek. Cory wasn't sure he even wanted to talk to Derek right now, but he knew they needed to resolve what happened yesterday. But Nic... Where did he go? He fired off a quick text—just a "hey"—and waited a few moments for a response. Receiving none and pushing aside the thoughts of anxiety that started to bubble up, Cory clambered out of bed and headed toward his bathroom to start getting ready. It seemed he was getting himself to school today.

After brushing his teeth and taking care of a few other bathroom things, Cory walked to the kitchen to grab a quick breakfast. When he passed through the living room, he saw some of his mom's things thrown over the back of the couch. She would have gotten in a couple of hours ago probably and was hopefully fast asleep. Maybe that's why Nic left? He was worried about her finding them or asking questions. After the day he had yesterday, Cory wouldn't exactly be surprised. Either way, they'd sort this out when he got to school and hopefully talk some about last night too.

Cory threw some Pop Tarts in the toaster and walked back to his room to get dressed. He made sure any offending items from last night were put away or thrown in the hamper—his mom never went snooping, but with the way things had been going lately, it was better to be safe than sorry. He changed his clothes and picked up his backpack, grabbing his breakfast on the way out the door to the bus stop.

The bus ride was normal enough, at least at first. The closer Cory got to school, the more he found himself checking his phone. It started feeling like there was a knot in his stomach. He could feel his thumb itching to send another text, but he thought better of it. He'd see Nic in person soon enough. Eventually, the bus pulled onto campus, and the students onboard made their way off to start their own school days.

Cory wandered the school's courtyard, looking for a sign of Nic or Derek anywhere. He came up empty outside, though he did notice a few strange looks from some of the students who ran in their circles—likely still whispering about the rumors that had Nic so upset. Cory was beyond caring about that right now, so he turned his search inside and headed to Nic's locker. *There he was!*

"Hey!" Cory smiled as he walked over and stood to the side of the open locker.

"Oh, hey, Cor." Nic looked over his shoulder as he greeted him before turning back to face his locker, pulling out a book. "What's up?"

"That's what I wanted to ask you." Cory gave Nic a strange look.

"What do you mean?" Nic looked puzzled.

"You know... About last night?"

"Huh? Shit, did I show up at your place last night?" Nic looked like he was struggling to remember something. "I was so hammered, everything's kinda fuzzy."

"Yeah. You did." *Is he just fucking with me?* "When I woke up, you were gone."

"Oh, man, I'm sorry." Nic gave Cory an apologetic look. "After getting drunk, I think I remember trying to talk to Amy, then wandering around for a while."

"Y-yeah." Cory's voice stumbled. *Does he really not remember?* "You showed up pretty late. Your hand was hurt so I..." Cory gestured toward Nic's freshly bandaged hand.

"Aww, that was you? Thanks, bro." Nic gave Cory an innocuous smile as he lifted his hand. "I really gotta be more careful. I owe you one. See ya later, alright?"

"Oh. Yeah... See you later." Cory did his best to stop his voice from wavering but fell short.

He turned around before Nic had a chance to see the hurt look on his face and made his way out of the hallway. He turned a corner and headed for the parking lot. His chest was pounding and his face was hot and he just needed to get out of—

"Cory!" *Fuck.* It was Derek. Nope, he was *not* doing this right now. Dealing with one selfish jerk was enough. Cory turned and started walking the other way, doing his best to wipe his face—when did he start crying?

"Hey, Cory!" Derek jogged over. "I've been looking for you."

"Go away, Derek," Cory replied coldly and continued walking. "I don't wanna talk to you right now."

"Cory, I'm really sorry about yesterday." Derek stopped in his tracks but kept speaking. "Kicking you out of the car when you were trying to talk to me about..." Derek trailed off, still uncomfortable with the subject matter.

"Yeah, let me know how that feels." Cory couldn't help rolling his eyes and kept walking.

"Cory, wait, please." Derek reached for his shoulder. "I want to talk to you. Really talk, about everything. With you *and* Nic."

Cory paused his exit at Nic's name. That might be one way to force him to talk...

"Okay."

"Thanks." Derek sighed with relief. "Actually, have you seen him?"

"He's inside by his locker." Cory felt a twinge of hurt as he tried to block out his feelings from their earlier conversation.

"Great. I'll grab him." Derek nodded. "Meet us in the auditorium in a few minutes?"

"Sure," Cory answered without looking up. Not like this morning could get much worse.

"Okay, see you there." Derek looked Cory over. His body language was telling him something was off, but he assumed it was because of what he had said yesterday. Without commenting, he left to go find Nic.

For a brief moment, Cory considered following through with his plan to ditch campus and just leave the two of them there waiting. But, somewhat begrudgingly, he slowly made his way over to the auditorium, shuffling his way through the crowd of faces waiting for classes to start, feeling more alone than ever.

He was there first because of course he was, so he took a seat and waited. That meant he was alone with his thoughts. Did Nic *really* not remember last night? He wasn't incoherent or anything. And why did he just *leave* like that? Wouldn't he have wondered what was up when he woke up? Why did Cory even care about this? It's not like Nic was his boyfrie—

The sound of the door opening signaled Derek and Nic's arrival. Cory turned to face them as they walked in, standing to meet them in front of the stage. The three awkwardly stood in a circle for a few moments before Derek finally broke the silence.

"So," he started, unsure of just what was going on with his two friends, "things have gotten a little *intense* lately."

Cory snorted at the understatement but said nothing. Nic was mostly looking at his feet, expression blank.

"I've been thinking," Derek continued, "between what went on at school yesterday, and some stuff that happened *after* school, I think it might be best if we took a break from things for a while."

Cory rolled his eyes. Of course Derek wanted out. Probably hoped it would just blow over. *Fuck that.* "So, you—"

"Yeah, man, I've been thinking the same thing," Nic jumped in. "I don't think any of this stuff has really been for me. I think it's time to end this little experiment."

"What?" Cory wasn't surprised by the words, but they still stung. "Last night you sure seem—"

"Little experiment?" Derek gave Nic side eye. "I was just saying it might be good to back off from things a little and cool—"

"And I'm saying I think you're right," Nic countered. "Stuff is getting serious with Amy. School is gonna be over soon. I've got better things to worry about than this shit. It's just giving me a headache. All this was your idea anyway, man. I was never that into it."

"That is such bull—" Cory again tried to jump in but was again cut off.

"So what, all this is my fault?" Derek sounded offended.

"I mean, I'm not trying to blame anyone for anything but..." Nic shrugged. "Yeah, kinda."

"What the fu—"

"*HEY!*" Cory shouted over the two, determined to finally speak. "Do either of you give a fuck about what I think about any of this?"

"Cory, sorry. I'm just trying to—"

"No, you're doing the exact same shit you always have," Cory said coldly. "Try to control every little thing about the situation so that it goes exactly the way *you* want. Without ever actually talking to me about it like a person. Like your *equal*. That's the way it's *always* been with both of you."

"Wow, really, Cor?" Nic practically sneered. "Don't you think you're being a little dramatic?"

"Shut the fuck up Nic, or I *won't*." When Nic didn't open his mouth to respond, Cory hoped he understood his threat. *Asshole.* "I'm done. With everything. I want out."

"Cory, wait. I didn't—" Derek tried to explain his actions but was cut off.

"I'm *done*, Derek." Cory was just staring blankly at the floor at this point. "Take off the collar."

"Cory..." Derek was actually surprised at how much it hurt to hear Cory say that.

*"Get the fucking collar off me, Derek."* Cory clenched his fists and struggled to not grit his teeth. "Take it off my fucking neck. Now."

Derek nodded but said nothing as he fumbled for his keys in his pocket. Cory lifted and turned his head away from the two, not wanting to meet either of their gazes lest he falter in his decision. Nic watched in silence as Derek grasped the lock around Cory's neck, more concerned with shielding his feelings than letting them be known. Derek held the lock steady and turned the key until it clicked before stepping away. Cory reached up, unlatched the chain from the lock, and let the collar fall to the floor.

The three boys stood there for a moment in silence, all of them feeling the weight of the moment, but none fully grasping the repercussions. They had been friends for so long...

"Just ... leave me alone. Ignore me." Cory was the first to speak, making sure his voice was steady. "Stay out of my life."

Derek and Nic both looked at the collar as it lay on the ground, neither saying a thing as Cory turned around and walked up past the rows of seats and out of the auditorium. The sound of the double doors slamming shut behind him echoed through the room.

"I gotta..." Nic struggled to find an excuse before leaving through a different exit. "I'll see you around."

Derek stood alone in the auditorium, bending over to pick up Cory's discarded collar after he heard Nic leave. He held it in his hand and contemplated how things had even gotten to this point. But as he clumsily stuffed it into his pocket, he knew he could only blame himself.

Cory cried and hugged his knees as he sat in the corner of the auditorium lobby, not having actually left the building. He felt so shitty, so stupid, so lost. He wasn't sure he'd be able to make it through the rest of the day. He should have just gone home earlier when he had the chance.

"You alright?"

Cory's head shot up, the unexpected voice having him instinctively pushing back against the wall.

Oh god. It was Jackson. The dark-haired basketball player was one of the last people Cory wanted to see right now. "Look, can you just leave me alone? I do *not* have the energy to deal with you right now."

"Ouch." Jackson feigned being hurt but stayed where he was. "Having a rough day?"

"You don't know the half of it..." Cory muttered to himself. "Seriously, can you go? I really wanna be alone right now."

"Do you, really?" Jackson took a couple of steps towards Cory. "I saw your two buddies leaving... They seemed pretty down but not as much as you."

"Are you stalking them too, now?" Cory challenged.

"I deserve that." Jackson chuckled. "Haven't meant to be so ... weird about things. Just didn't really know how to talk to you about it."

"Talk to me about what?" Cory sniffled.

"The stuff with you and Derek and Nic," Jackson answered bluntly. "How you were their boy. Like, their *boy*."

Cory tried to nonchalantly wipe his face as he eyed Jackson warily, unsure of where this conversation was going. He'd suspected for a while that the guy had figured out what was going on but didn't know what he wanted out of it. Was he just looking for a blowjob or something?

"Hey, not judging or anything, and not looking to tell anybody either." Jackson held his hands up in front of him. "The opposite. I'm into it."

"You have *got* to be kidding me." Cory couldn't help but laugh at the ridiculous circumstances he kept finding himself in. "You are the *fifth* not-exactly-straight guy I've met in four months. Was this town built on top of a gay burial ground or something? Do I just have a big neon 'use me to explore your sexuality' sign above my head?"

"Uh, nope." Jackson couldn't help laughing either. "Maybe you just have good luck?"

"*Good* luck?" Cory snorted.

"Okay, maybe bad luck," Jackson admitted. "It did seem like maybe those guys weren't treating you very well. Taking advantage."

"Yeah. I remember when you snuck up on me in the library," Cory recalled. "You thought I was doing their homework."

"Was I wrong?"

"...About the homework." Cory sighed, sounding defeated as he leaned back against the wall.

"Wanna talk about what's going on?" Taking the lack of any banishment as a sign, Jackson took a seat against the wall next to Cory.

"There's nothing to talk about anymore," Cory stated flatly. "It's *done*."

"Ah. I guess that's why they left in a hurry," Jackson reasoned. "Did they bring you here just to dump ya?"

"What makes you think they dumped me?" Cory crossed his arms and sat up, indignant. "I dropped them. Though I bet Nic would tell it differently."

"Wow, look at you." Jackson sounded impressed. "Standing up to your friends like that."

"I don't even know if we *are* friends anymore. I don't know how to talk to them. And I don't think they know how to talk to me either. Not after..." Cory gestured vaguely into the air.

"Yeah, I guess that's probably not something most friends have to deal with."

"Another understatement." Cory sighed and turned to look at Jackson. "I shouldn't be talking to you about this. Nic would have an aneurysm."

"Well, fuck Nic," Jackson groused. "Whatever you say to me stays between us. He seems like kind of an asshole if you ask me."

"He *is* an asshole. Derek too." Cory sighed again, feeling like his emotions had finally stabilized. "Fuck. The last couple of days have been so screwed up. There's no way I'm going to class today."

"Wanna get out of here?" Jackson offered. "I've got a car, and I'm not exactly wanting to go to class either. Wanna get some food or something?"

Cory contemplated the offer for a moment. He didn't know *anything* about him other than his name and the sport he played. And that he was into dudes, apparently. But he was still treating Cory like more of a friend than either Derek or Nic had been lately. "Actually, that sounds great. Thanks."

"No problem." Jackson smiled. He knew waiting around for this boy would pay off eventually. He just had to be patient.

Derek wandered aimlessly as he left the auditorium. He wasn't sure how he was feeling about what had just happened. He wasn't surprised or even angry. He was just ...

sad. Numb. He could feel the weight of Cory's collar in his pocket as he walked toward his locker. After opening it, he just stood there, staring into nothing, lost in his thoughts. This was not how today was supposed to go. This was not how any of this was supposed to go. Maybe if he'd just—

"Hey, Der." Derek's head snapped up to his left to see Tricia standing next to him. "Everything okay?"

"Oh, hey, Tricia." Derek tried to push down his thoughts. "Yeah, everything's great."

"Really?" Tricia questioned. "Because you look like someone just kicked a puppy."

"Something ... happened, between me, Cory, and Nic." Derek sighed. He wasn't great at hiding things from Tricia, not even when they were dating. "Something that is entirely my fault, and I've been trying to fix it. But I'm starting to think I just—"

"—micromanage every aspect of what you're doing, right down to trying to control other people's emotions and feelings because you assume you know them better than they do?"

"I deserve that," Derek said sadly. Tricia's scarily accurate read almost had him speechless. "I'm sorry, Trish. I know I was a shitty boyfriend. I wasn't trying to be such a control freak. I thought I was helping."

"Derek," Tricia started with a sad smile, "you're a smart guy, but you don't know and can't control *everything*. We're only eighteen. You're already practically on your own, but that doesn't mean you don't still have a lot of shit to learn, just like the rest of us."

"I... I just don't know what to do, Trish." She was right. Derek knew that. "I'm not sure I can fix this."

"Maybe you can't." Tricia was honest. "I don't know what happened, but whatever it was, it's done. You can't go back in time."

"So what do I do?" Derek asked sadly.

"Learn." Tricia gave Derek a small smile. "Learn from your fuckups so you can hopefully minimize them going forward. So that the next person you date, so your *friends*, won't feel like they're just some kind of pet project for you to work on."

"Thanks, Tricia." Derek took her words in. "Really. I'm sorry I was such a shitty boyfriend. I'm sure the next guy you date will blow me outta the water."

"Hell, yeah, he will," Tricia bragged about her future, currently non-existent boyfriend. "And you'll be okay too. Even if you *can't* fix this." She gave Derek a semi-awkward hug before leaving him at his locker to head to her next class.

Derek closed his locker, not exactly happy but feeling better about his current predicament. He needed to let Cory, and he guessed maybe Nic now too, have time to figure things out for themselves. And he needed to spend that same time working on himself. And he knew just the daddy to talk to for help.

"You sure your hand's okay, dude?" The question came from Greg, one of Nic's teammates, from the opposite end of the picnic table.

"Yeah. I'm fine." Nic held up his bandaged hand somewhat sheepishly. "Just me being a fucking idiot like usual."

"Seriously. I thought you were gonna put Steve in the hospital or something," Greg joked.

"I'm glad you're feeling a lot better today, babe." Amy squeezed Nic's thigh. "I told you they're just stupid rumors."

"I know, I know. I should have just listened to you; it was nothing," Nic lied because Amy still had no idea that those "rumors" were true. "How about I take you to a movie tonight to make up for it?"

"Ooooooo, yay!" Amy clapped to herself. "You can finally see *Wicked* with me!"

"Uhhhh. Haven't you already seen that, like, twice?" Nic questioned.

"Yep!" Amy only smiled in return. "It's *so* good."

"Great." Shit, did his voice just crack?

"You get any calls from schools yet, man?" Greg turned the conversation back to something they both knew.

"No, not yet." At least Nic didn't think so.

There was no way his dad would keep quiet about something like that. He knew colleges had sent a number of scouts to his last game. The way his dad talked about it, it was only a matter of time before they started vying for his attention.

"I can't wait." Greg was practically bouncing in his seat. "Anyone you hoping to hear from first?"

"Heh, I guess there's probably a few..." Oh good, *this* conversation again. He turned to give Amy a quick kiss on the lips. "Be right back. Gotta take a piss."

"Gross." Amy whacked him on the arm as he stood.

Nic walked into the nearby hall, nearly empty with everyone either in class or at lunch. He entered the restroom, happy to find it empty, and leisurely walked to the urinal. He was in no rush to return to the conversation waiting for him outside. But being alone also allowed his mind to wander. Wander to things he didn't want to think about. Things like what happened with Derek and Cory this morning. Things like what happened with Cory last night.

He wasn't hurt by what happened this morning. He *wasn't*. It sucked that he wasn't going to hang out with his bros anymore, but things had to change. That's all. They were still friends. He'd see them around school. They were going on winter break soon, and then they only had a few more months to go before graduation anyway. They were going to split up one way or another. Did the reason why really matter? Nic shook himself off and walked to the sink to wash his hands.

Of course, Cory very clearly *was* hurt. That look on Cory's face this morning by the lockers... He was crushed. And Nic knew it, knew it would hurt him. But he had to do it. Last night was a fluke. He was drunk. *Very* drunk. And then he went over to Cory's place, and they... He wasn't gay. He would only have been leading Cory on if he ... let things continue. It was time to put that shit behind him.

As Nic dried his hands, he looked at himself in the mirror. What he did was for the best, for all of them... Right?

"Wow, right there in the sex shop?" Jackson took another bite of his burger.

Cory and Jackson were sitting in the lobby of a Wendy's eating. Jackson nearly took them to the Burger King Derek had left Cory at the day before, but Cory steered him there instead. It was way too early for lunch, but that didn't stop either boy from getting a burger and some fries.

"Yep," Cory said after he washed down his own with some soda. "It was fun, too. The daddy we met there was sweet. And hot."

"Is that your type: older daddies?" Jackson asked pointedly before taking another bite.

"Uh…" Cory blushed, realizing how frank he was being in public, and lowered his voice. "I mean, I'm not *not* into it? I haven't exactly had experience with a lot of guys."

"I dunno. From what you've told me, sounds like you've done a lot more than most people do before finishing high school," Jackson reasoned.

Cory blushed further and dropped his eyes to the table, Jackson's words making him feel even more self-conscious.

"Hey, I didn't mean that in a bad way," Jackson backtracked. "I just meant you probably know a lot more about what you like than other people our age."

"I guess you're right," Cory muttered. Then he saw a chance to turn the questioning around. "But what about you? Seems like you know as much about this stuff as I do."

"Internet porn is a magical thing," Jackson explained. "You start off looking at pictures of naked chicks, and somehow you end up watching men being tied up and being spanked…"

Cory snorted at Jackson's frankness and kept up his questioning. "So, are you gay then?"

"I'm open-minded." Jackson shrugged. "Don't see a reason to let labels cut down my options."

"Fair enough. I'm just gay." Cory paused. "I think that's only, like, the third time I've ever said that out loud."

Jackson laughed as he finished the last of his fries before standing to throw away his trash. "Ready to head out?"

"Yeah." Cory threw his own garbage away and followed Jackson out to his car. "You sure you don't mind taking me home?"

"Nah, it's not too far, and it's not like I've got anything better to do." Jackson unlocked his car and the two boys stepped in.

Cory buckled his seatbelt when Jackson started the car and guided him out of the parking lot and toward his apartment. Cory noticed Jackson drumming his thumbs against the steering wheel and smiled. He *was* kind of cute... Not that Cory really wanted to think about *that* right now. Lucky for him, Jackson was about to pull into his complex.

"Thanks," Cory started as Jackson neared his building, "for the ride and for just hanging out with me."

"No problem, man." Jackson smiled and patted him on the leg. "You looked like you needed a friend. And it sounds like it's been kinda rough lately."

"Yeah..." Understatement. "Well... See ya tomorrow at school?"

"Yeah, of course. Oh wait!" Jackson pulled his phone out. "Gimme your number."

Jackson fired off a quick text after Cory told him, and Cory felt his phone vibrate. "That's me. Text me anytime."

"Okay. I will." Cory smiled sheepishly.

Jackson just gave him another smile and unlocked Cory's door. "See you tomorrow."

"See you tomorrow." Cory kept smiling as he stepped out of the car, waving as Jackson pulled away before turning to walk inside. Maybe today wasn't the *worst* after all...

The next few weeks were kind of weird. He rode the bus to school in the mornings, which he hadn't done regularly in years. Classes were fine, except the ones he shared with Derek. Nic seemed fine with the cold shoulder Cory was giving him, but Derek… It was like Cory could feel his eyes on the back of his head. Cory was resolute though and didn't so much as look in his direction. It was nice to be the one with the power for once. And he wasn't alone. He had Stephanie with him at lunch. And then after school there was Jackson, who had been taking him home, where he would spend most nights studying for midterms until bedtime. Cory was keeping his mind occupied.

But now they were on break from school, and Cory had nothing to do. Normally, he'd ask the guys what they were doing, hang out, play some video games… Cory's heart sank a little at the thought of playing Smash Bros. again without them. He texted Steph, but she was nose deep in a book she had to finish before classes started up again. That left Jackson.

[Cory: Hey!]

*Oof, maybe that exclamation point is too much.*

[Jackson: Hey what's up?]

Cory smiled as the words popped on his screen.

[Cory: You doing anything? Wanna hang out?]

Cory wasn't even sure what Jackson might want to do, now that he thought about it.

[Jackson: Actually, my mom needs me to run some crap to the post office. Wanna tag along?]

Post office? Not exactly Cory's idea of hanging out.

[Cory: Sure.]

But it was better than sitting home alone right now.

[Jackson: Alright, see you in a few, boy!]

*There's that word again…*
Cory blushed slightly. Then shook his head. Better get some clothes on.

Turns out "some crap" was a few *dozen* packages. Apparently, Jackson's mom recently started some kind of Etsy business out of the house and was using Jackson to ship everything out. Jackson told Cory that he'd *tried* to explain to his mom that she could get the post office to pick them up at home, but she was more than happy to have her son do it. He was thankful for Cory's help in dropping everything off.

"Thanks again." Jackson clicked his seatbelt into place. "Guess you *are* a good boy."

Cory blushed fully this time, remembering the day in the library.

"You're welcome." *Should I? I'm allowed to flirt, right?* "Sir."

Jackson said nothing, just smiled and pulled out of the parking lot.

"So…" Cory tapped his thumb on his arm rest. "What kind of stuff are you into?"

"Do you mean like, how I like to play basketball 'stuff'?" Jackson tilted his head toward the window. "Or the sir and boy kind of 'stuff' we were talking about before?" Jackson tilted back toward Cory.

"I, uh…" Cory stammered for a second. "Both?"

"Well, I like basketball, obviously." There was even a basketball in the backseat. "I'm guessing that's not exactly your thing, though," he teased.

"Nope." Cory wasn't bothered. He knew they wouldn't connect over that. "You play any video games?"

"Some sports ones. The new Halo was cool." Very … straight. "I played a lot with my older cousins growing up."

"Cool." It was certainly better than nothing. "So… What about the other stuff?"

"I dunno. Haven't really done too much." Jackson smiled coyly as he drove in no particular direction. "Not that I'm not interested in finding out. Just haven't really had a chance, you know."

"Yeah?" Cory was *pretty* sure this was flirting. "I'm surprised. Aren't guys on sports teams supposed to be 'drowning in pussy,' as Nic liked to say?"

Jackson laughed again. "I mean, I've gotten plenty of 'pussy,' sure. But high school girls aren't exactly begging to call me sir or anything else."

"Wow, being straight sounds *so* boring," Cory teased.

"Told you, *boy*, I'm not straight." Jackson smirked.

"So sorry, *sir*." Cory could play too. Flirting was fun!

"You better be."

"How ever can I make it up to you, *sir*?"

"Okay, now you're just teasing me."

"Maybe," Cory admitted coyly. "It's fun. Didn't really get to do much flirting with Derek or Nic."

"Well, they're not here now, are they?" Jackson pointed out.

"No. No, they are not."

"So then, how do you *want* to make it up to me, boy?"

Now the ball was in Cory's court. Not something he was used to. It was just harmless flirting, right? Didn't have to mean anything. Unless he wanted it to. He was the one who got to decide if he wanted to do this or not. And wouldn't it just be awesome if either of those douchebags found out that Cory had already found someone else to fuck... What did he have to lose?

"Why don't you pull into that parking lot coming up and let me show you?"

Jackson did a double-take, not sure he heard Cory correctly, but said nothing as he turned into the grocery store lot, parking under a tree toward the back and cutting off the engine. The two boys sat silently for a moment, neither quite sure about what they were going to do next. Then, still feeling bold, Cory reached across and put his hand on Jackson's crotch. Jackson's breath hitched, but he said nothing, just looked into Cory's eyes, trying to read what was behind them. Cory gently squeezed the growing mound in Jackson's pants, the heavy denim feeling rough in his hands.

"You sure about this?" Jackson asked before letting Cory go any further.

"You want me to stop?"

"No."

"Good." Cory turned in his seat toward Jackson, using his other hand to unbuckle his belt and undo his fly. Jackson's breath hitched again as his cock was squeezed once more, only the thin fabric of his boxers covering him. Once Cory had fished his cock out of his jeans, he bent over and took him into his mouth.

Jackson hissed as he felt the warm mouth engulf him. Instinctively, he put one hand on the back of Cory's head but made no attempts to move him. He felt Cory sucking on him gently as his cock continued to grow to its full length. At a respectable six inches, he wasn't huge, but he wasn't self-conscious about size by any means. If anything, it made stuff like blowjobs much easier.

Cory continued to gently suck until he felt Jackson reach full hardness in his mouth. Then he slowly pulled up before lowering his mouth all the way back down. Time to put those cock-sucking skills to use! And though he'd never say it out loud, he was actually pretty happy to see Jackson wasn't walking around with a giant log in his pants. He could actually deep-throat him without any trouble. It was like his mouth and Jackson's dick were a perfect match.

"Fuck, boy," Jackson hissed as he gripped Cory's hair gently. "You're good at that."

"Fank you, fir," Cory mumbled around the dick in his mouth and continued working.

Jackson adjusted his seat so he could lean farther back, which gave Cory a little more room to maneuver. Pulling off his cock, Cory fished back inside Jackson boxers for his balls, pulling them out as well. After licking his way down Jackson's shaft, Cory nuzzled his face against Jackson's furry sack, taking each one into his mouth and gently rolling them around with his tongue. He felt Jackson grip his hair tighter as he did, and he continued his oral ministrations, switching back and forth between his nuts.

"Careful. Keep playing with my balls, and I won't last very long," Jackson warned.

Well, now Cory *had* to keep playing with them. He quickly swallowed down his cock, getting it nice and slick for his hand, before diving back onto Jackson's nutsack. Cory stroked his cock steadily, and he licked and sucked on Jackson's balls, hearing the boy above him muttering curses under his breath as he did. Cory smiled, pleased with himself. He could feel Jackson's balls begin to tighten and knew he was getting close.

With his free hand, Jackson gripped his armrest tightly, trying to avoid making too much sound or movement. The parking lot they were in was mostly empty, but that didn't mean they were totally camouflaged. Jackson bit his tongue as he felt himself get closer and closer to cumming, glad that Cory seemed to be able to sense it on his own.

"Fuck. Hope you swallow, boy, because I don't have anything to clean this up with." Jackson gritted as he felt Cory engulf his cock once more, bobbing up and down as he pushed Jackson over the edge.

Cory moaned as he felt and tasted the first shot of cum across his tongue. He felt Jackson's cock pulse with each volley of cum, and he eagerly swallowed it all. Once it felt like Jackson had finished, Cory cleaned him up, pulling the half-hard cock from his mouth with a soft *pop* as Jackson caught his breath.

"Shit, boy," Jackson breathed. "Wasn't expecting *that*. Thank you."

"Pleasure was all mine, sir." Cory wiped the spit from his mouth on his sleeve.

"I'll take your word for it." Jackson gave Cory a smile as he tucked himself back into his pants and readjusted his seat.

"I'd say you made up for your teasing earlier." Jackson started the car. "Guess I should get you home now."

"Yeah, I guess so." Cory smiled back sheepishly as Jackson pulled out of the parking lot and headed back toward Cory's apartment.

"That was fun." Cory's smile was a little more confident now. "Maybe we can do that again sometime?"

"Oh, I definitely think we'll be doing that again, *boy*." Jackson gave Cory a wink. They were nearing his apartment. "See ya at school tomorrow?"

"See you tomorrow, sir." Cory smiled, and with a final wave goodbye, Cory turned and walked toward his door. He felt good. He felt confident. Like he was in control of his life again. He didn't need Derek or Nic in his life to feel good. Fuck those guys.

Jackson watched as Cory walked toward his door and smiled to himself. This went better than he ever could have hoped. He had known it was only a matter of time before whatever was between Cory and his former friends imploded. And Jackson knew he'd be there to pick up the pieces. He'd have to thank them somehow.

# CHAPTER 13

"Bluh." Cory pushed away his lunch tray, unsatisfied with the cafeteria's offerings for the day. "Shouldn't have forgotten to pack my lunch today."

"I mean... I got something I can feed ya if you're still hungry," Jackson flirted from across the table.

Cory rolled his eyes but smiled. It had been two months since the fallout with Derek and Nic, and in the interim, he found himself hanging out more and more with Jackson. He wasn't ready to call him his new dom just yet, but it felt like things were headed in that direction with the way they kept fooling around. As it was, Cory was enjoying having his freedom while still having Jackson there to explore the kinky stuff. He had been hornier than ever lately; it was like Derek and Nic flipped a switch that he couldn't flip back.

"Oh, yeah, sir?" Cory flirted back. He was feeling bold. "I dunno. I'm pretty hungry."

"Come with me. I'm sure we can find *something* to fill that belly." Jackson winked.

Cory wanted to snort at the ridiculous line but stopped when he locked eyes with someone else across the courtyard:

Derek, his expression unreadable. That was fine. He didn't care what Derek was thinking or feeling. If anything, he hoped Derek knew what was going on between him and Jackson, if only to rub it in his face.

"Sounds good to me, sir." Cory stood as he spoke. "Lead the way."

Derek watched Cory and Jackson get up from their table across the school courtyard. Derek had seen the two of them together more and more frequently, almost like Cory was making sure he knew. Between the flirty looks and the two of them disappearing together, it wasn't hard to figure out what was going on. Cory had looked *right at him* just now but said nothing. For a moment, Derek thought about going after him, just to talk, but he thought better of it. Cory had made it clear that he didn't want anything to do with him. Forcing a talk would only make things worse. Still, something about watching the way Cory was running around with this guy rubbed him the wrong way.

"I don't like that guy."

"What guy?" Nic was sitting nearby, engrossed in his phone and not paying attention.

"The dude Cory's running around with now. Jeremy or Jackson or something." Derek remembered vaguely seeing him talking to Cory last semester in the library. He also remembered seeing the guy at the party and a few other places around school. "Something about him just…"

"Dude, who cares?" Nic didn't bother looking up. "Cory can do whatever he wants. He's a free man."

"That's not…" Derek sighed and shook his head. Nic had been distant and aloof since things came to a head in the auditorium. It had become apparent that he was eager to put everything behind him or even pretend none of it had ever happened. It was a struggle to get the guy to talk about *anything*, let alone what happened with Cory. Derek was surprised he was even at lunch right now. "Never mind."

"Yeah." Nic rolled his eyes, which were otherwise still glued to his phone screen. "Well, I got better shit to do than sit around and talk about Cory. See ya, man." Nic pocketed his phone and grabbed his things, waving a goodbye to Derek before heading off.

"Yeah." Derek sighed again as he watched his other best friend walk away. "See ya."

Nic sighed as he pulled into his usual spot in front of his house. He had managed to beg off seeing that movie with the singing green witch with Amy, but there was almost always something new and terrible she wanted to see. With everything that had been going on, he really just wanted to go home and not think about anything the rest of the night.

"I'm home!" Nic called out as he closed the front door behind him, hanging up his keys and heading straight to his room.

"Nic, *mijo*!" His dad called out for him from his office. "Quick, come here! I have some great news!"

Nic stopped in his tracks before he entered the hall to his room and turned toward the open door of his dad's office. Now what?

"Hey, Dad," Nic greeted as he entered. "What's up?"

"You'll never believe who called earlier today!" his dad exclaimed in excitement but was clearly hoping for an answer.

"Uh... Abuelita?" Nic played dumb.

"St. Helena University!" *Fuck.* That was his dad's alma mater. "They called with an offer! They want you to play for them!"

"That's ... great, Dad." Nic tried to fake a smile. "What did they—"

"They wanna give you a full ride, mijo!" His dad was already turning around to face his desk, pulling up his web browser. "Look! The campus is still just how I remember it."

Clearly Raphael had been doing some research. Page after page about the school was already pulled up: stuff from the school's own site, news stories about the football team. It looked like he even tried to find a few old bits of info about himself. It was a lot.

"You're gonna love it, Nic," his father barreled forward. "Playing for St. Helena's were some of the best years of my life."

"Yeah, Dad, about that..." *Of course he's already made up his mind about where I'm going to go.*

"I wonder if the locker rooms are still the same," Raphael reminisced over his son's attempt to speak. "Every home game we had this ritual where we... Well, you find out in few months when you start playing!" He laughed at his own joke.

"Dad, wait—"

"They've made it into the playoffs the last twenty-three seasons!" Raphael wasn't even looking at his son anymore. "And with you on the team, they'll make it all the way to the championships. I can't wait for your first game. I gotta call all my bud—"

"DAD!" Nic shouted, finally getting his father to clam up.

"Nic, what the hell are you yelling for? I'm just—"

"I don't wanna play for your fucking school, Dad!"

"Watch your mouth!" Raph snapped. "I was just excited for you. If you don't wanna play for St. Helena's, there were other calls from—"

"*No*, Dad." Nic decided to just lay all his cards on the table. "I don't think I want to play football in college at all."

"What are you talking about?" Raphael guffawed. "You love football. You've been playing it since you were—"

"I'm *not* little anymore, Dad," Nic cut him off, knowing this was coming. "Playing football doesn't feel the same for me anymore."

"So what, you're just quitting?" Raph stood up from his seat. "After everything your mother and I have done? The way we've supported you for years!?"

"Everything *you've* done!?" Oh good, now they were *both* yelling. "Of course you somehow find a way to make this about *you*."

"Well, you're acting like an idiot! You're throwing away everything you've worked for!"

"No, Dad, I'm not!" Nic stood his ground. "Say I play football in college, then what? I go pro and destroy my body and brain? Go broke by the time I'm forty, driving around the country giving speeches for cash? That's not the kind of life I want."

"So then what the hell do you think you—"

"**Nicolas. Raphael.**" Nic and his father turn to see Nic's mother, Luciana, standing in the doorway. "What are you yelling about? I can hear you across the house."

"I was just trying to tell Dad—"

"Lucy, he's talking crazy—"

Luciana raised her hand in a silent order for both men to quiet once more. "Go to your room, Nicolas."

"But Mom—"

"*Now.*" Luciana didn't even look at Nic, only glared daggers at her husband.

"*Si, mama.*" Nic knew enough not to argue with her when she was angry.

Stopping himself before he gave his father one last look of annoyance—pissing his mom off wasn't going to do him any favors—he left the room in a huff. He stormed through the living room, ignoring his sisters who were trying very hard to look like they weren't listening to the copious amounts of muffled Spanish curses coming from Dad's office, and went to his room, slamming the door behind him as he sat on his bed. After sitting still for only a moment, the irritation of what had just happened all caught up to him at once, and Nic suddenly slammed the top half of his body face down, screaming his frustrations into his pillows.

Why did his dad have to be such an asshole?

It was maybe an hour later when Nic heard someone knocking at his bedroom door.

"Nicolas... It's your father."

Nic rolled his eyes but sat up on the edge of the bed. "Come in."

Raphael opened the door and closed it behind him before pulling out Nic's desk chair and having a seat, facing Nic on the bed.

"Your mother says she won't let me eat dinner until we talk," he attempted to joke.

Nic snorted but said nothing, continuing to stare at the floor.

"I'm sorry for yelling earlier," Raphael started to apologize. "Have you ... always hated football?"

"I don't *hate* football, Dad." Nic sighed. "I just don't think it's what I want to do for the rest of my life."

"How long have you felt this way?" he asked with concern.

"I think it really only started in the last year or two," Nic started to explain. "Once people started talking about college and going pro, I just started to think that maybe it wasn't something I really wanted to make a career of. Football is fun, but it's also exhausting and time consuming, and it *hurts*. Thinking about doing it for the next ten or twenty years just twists my stomach."

"I had no idea, mijo. I'm sorry," Raph apologized sincerely. "I was never trying to push you into something you didn't wanna do. I always thought you and I could talk about anything together."

"Well, that's kind of the problem, Dad. We don't really talk at all," Nic continued his explanation. "You were always into my little league and middle school games, but once I hit high school, it became the only thing you ever talked about. It was always about how practices were going or when the next game was or how great me winning was." Nic paused, having something of an epiphany. "I think that might actually be one of the reasons I don't really like it that much anymore."

"As you and your sisters got older, I knew less and less how to talk to you." Raphael sighed. "It was so simple when you were little. All I had to do was focus on the things I *thought* you liked, instead of trying to learn anything new." He sighed again. "I'm a shit father."

"You're not shit, Dad." It was Nic's turn to comfort his parent. "You just need to talk to us more. We're older, but we're still your kids. We just like more things than just football and shopping. I can't speak for Gabby or Dani, but you should probably talk to them too."

"I'm still sorry, Nic." Raph nodded. "I know this doesn't make up for anything, but I hope it's a start."

Nic nodded as well. This was by far the best talk he'd had with his dad in years. It *was* a start.

"So, back to college and St. Helena's..." Raph tentatively turned the conversation back to the sensitive subject that started all this. "I still think you should play football in college."

Nic cocked an eyebrow and squared his jaw. Was his dad being serious? "Dad, we *just* talk—"

"Hear me out." Raphael held his hands out in front of him to ease Nic. "Not for St. Helena's or any school you don't want to. But these schools are offering you a full ride. Tuition, room and board, everything. You don't have to go pro. You can study whatever you want, wherever you want. You've put in a lot of work the last four years on the field. You *earned* those scholarships. I don't think you should throw all of that away. At least hear what some of the schools have to offer and then make a decision. And if you *really* don't want to play ball anymore, we can still afford to send you to college. Just hear them out."

Nic sighed. That was fair. "Okay, Dad. I'll at least see what they have to offer first."

"That's all I'm asking." Raph smiled. "So, what else has been going on, with school, with your friends?"

Nic groaned mentally. He didn't feel like talking about *any* of the stuff with Cory or Derek, but he couldn't exactly lecture his dad on not opening up to his kids and not open up himself. He'd just need to leave a lot of the more intimate details out.

"School's been fine. It's my last semester so there's not much left to do except get ready for finals." Nic paused for a moment, taking care with his words for the conversation that was to follow. "Cory, Derek, and I aren't really talking anymore. We kind of had a falling out. Doesn't really matter now since school's almost over anyway."

"Oh, that's too bad." Raph looked a little disappointed. "You've been friends with those boys for a long, long time. What happened?"

"A lot of little problems that ended up leading to a big problem." Nic glossed over the whole "I've been fucking Cory" bit. "Some of it is my fault. Girls, football, a few assholes at school... They all just came to a head one day, and now none of us are really talking to each other."

"Well, I think we've seen all the good that not talking does." Raph half-chuckled. "I know it may seem trivial, but those two have been your friends longer than anyone else. A lot of your friends from the last few years will fade away, but those two have been with you through a lot."

"I know, Dad, but it's just..." Nic had to think about his words carefully. "It's like football. We've all changed a lot since we were little... Maybe we're just outgrowing each other."

"Maybe. Or maybe there's something you are avoiding dealing with because this seems easier. You *did* say some of it was your fault." *Ouch. Critical hit, Dad.*

"Some of it, yeah. I was kind of a jerk. I said and did some stuff that hurt some people." Understatement, but there wasn't really an easy way to explain just what he had done to Cory. "But... I dunno. School's over in a couple of months. We're all splitting up for college. It just seems easier to let it go and move on. Make new friends. Who stays friends with the people they knew in high school anyway?"

"You don't remember your *tios*, Javier and Carlos?" The two weren't actually related to them, just two of his dad's old friends. "I met them both in high school, played football with them, and we've stayed friends all these years. I just talked to Carlos yesterday. His daughter just got engaged." Nic remembered Carlos' daughter Ana. She used to babysit him. She was his first crush. "That's why football is such a big deal for me. It led to so many great things in my life, and I wanted you to have the same experience. I just forgot to think if that's what *you* wanted too.

"I told you. Most of your friends from high school *will* fall away," Raph continued. "Maybe you'll talk to them online or see them at a reunion, maybe you won't. But some friends are in it for life. And I think that's what you have with those two boys."

"But what am I supposed to do, Dad?" Nic knew the answer but didn't like it and was hoping for a parental reprieve.

"Talk to them. Hear them out." Raph stood from his seat. "Just like with football and college, don't let everything you've gone through the last few years be for nothing just because it seems easier. You owe it to yourself—and them."

"I'll think on it, Dad. Thanks." His dad was right, of course, but he also didn't know a lot of the unique circumstances surrounding the boys' relationship. Nic still wasn't sure what he should do.

His dad held his arms open for a hug, and Nic stood to give him one. It wasn't even one of those awkward "no homo" style hugs he was used to.

"I love you, son. I know I don't say that enough."

"I love you too, Dad." *Cue the audience going "aww."*

"Dinner should be ready in about an hour, as long as your mother is satisfied." Raph turned toward the door but didn't move just yet. "Now I'm going to try to talk to your sisters."

"Oof. Good luck." Nic would love to sit in on *that* awkward chat. "Just talk to them like you did me. You'll be fine."

"Thanks, mijo." Raph nodded to himself and then exited the room, leaving Nic to resume sitting on his bed.

So, the football/college/dad issue had largely been taken care, but Nic still had a lot to think about. He flopped back onto his bed and sighed. Being a mature adult sucked.

A few weeks later, it was Friday night, and Derek found himself driving through Lakefield. It wasn't just a random visit. He had called Carl the night before, asking if they could talk. It was the first time they had spoken in months; Derek having felt too ashamed to talk sooner. But he needed the advice, and given the seriousness of some of the issues at hand, Derek thought it would be best to talk in person.

Derek eyed the GPS on his phone as he turned into a neighborhood, making sure he didn't miss his street. Once he found the right address, he parked on the street in front of the house and got out. It was a small, nice looking, one-story house, not a giant empty monstrosity like his own. He locked his car, walked toward the door, knocked, and waited for Carl to answer.

"Derek, good to see you. Come in!" Carl smiled as he held the door open, closing it behind Derek as he entered.

"You want anything to drink? Water?" Carl asked as he led Derek to the living room.

"No, thank you. I'm okay right now." Derek was eager and anxious to get started and took a seat on the couch.

"Now, what was so important that you wanted to drive all the way out here to talk to me about?" Carl asked as he took a seat on the opposite end of the couch.

"It's a lot. It's about my friends and the sensitive stuff I was asking you about a while back." Derek was ready to just lay everything on the table.

"I thought they might be related." Carl nodded. "What's going on?"

"Cory, Nic, and I split up." Derek sighed.

"Oh. Sorry to hear that." Carl always thought the three of them together was kinda sweet.

"It happened at the end of last year. It was Cory's decision, ultimately, but it was my fault. It started the day before." Derek started mentally ordering the events leading up to the present.

"What happened the day before?"

"Two different things, actually. First, someone had seen Nic and Cory fooling around at the party I told you about a while back." Derek grimaced. "They started spreading it around school, which made Nic freak out. That one *isn't* my fault."

"Shit. Are they both okay?" Carl sat up a little. "I was outed in high school myself. It was awful."

"Cory actually didn't seem that phased." Derek hadn't thought much of it at the time. "Nic freaked out the first day, but he's fine now. And I wouldn't exactly say he was outed. He still thinks of himself as straight. He just waited for the rumors to die down and used his girlfriend to fuck the gay away."

"Come again?" Carl cocked his head like a dog.

"Yeah, that's like a whole other thing." Derek waved vaguely off to the side. "Nic has never exactly been comfortable with his sexuality. Falls into very bro-like behavior when his masculinity is questioned."

Carl sat, mouth slightly agape, at the insightful teenager on his couch. "And what about you?"

"I figured I was at least bi a while ago. Just never really came up before." Derek shrugged. "I think I still mostly lean toward girls, but I don't think you can have as much gay sex as I have without being at least a little bi. It doesn't really seem like a big deal."

"I envy you. Do you know the mental and emotional hoops people my age had to jump through to come to terms with their sexuality back then?" Kids these days really *did* have it easy.

"People are gay, Carl," Derek joked.

"What about Nic?" Carl was curious about the other boy.

"I said it wasn't a big deal for me." Derek shook his head. "Nic is another story."

"And what was the *other* thing that happened?" Carl pushed on.

"It was the end of the day, and Cory and I were in my car leaving campus. He had told me he wanted to talk." The exact thing Carl told him was important for a sub to be able to do.

"Uh huh." Carl nodded and waited for Derek to continue, already not liking the direction this seemed to be headed.

"He told me had talked to his friend about the three of us, and I ... freaked out, a little," Derek admitted. "I thought maybe she might have been the source of Nic's rumors. She wasn't, but Cory did talk to her about other things. Like parts of our *arrangement* he was having problems with, things he couldn't really talk to anyone about. The way Nic and I would keep him in the dark about a lot of things. The times we put him in a few ... compromising positions. Or, uh, the way I kinda went about starting this whole thing."

"You know, I was always curious." Carl leaned back, sure he was in for *quite* a story. "How *did* your little arrangement come together?"

"It started after me and Nic found Cory's porn. Not just vanilla stuff—full kink. We both tried to pretend like it never happened, let it fade away, but it wouldn't stop nagging at our minds. We were both way more into it than either of us wanted to admit, but we didn't know what to do about it. So we made a plan. *I* made a plan." Derek took a deep breath before continuing.

"That weekend, we took Cory up to my family's cabin, and we got him drunk. Once he was a few beers in, we went for it. We told him we found his porn. He freaked a little at first until we told him that we were more than okay with him being gay, and then we … convinced him to suck our dicks. I had done a little research on BDSM, and using *that*, we spent the rest of the weekend … training Cory." Derek looked up at Carl to see his slack-jawed, wide-eyed expression.

"Jesus titty-fucking Christ, boy." Carl sat up. "What the fuck were you thinking?"

"I know. I *know*. I'm a piece of shit who was only thinking with his dick. It gets worse." Derek took another deep breath. "He brought that night up and how we … took advantage of him. And I… I lost it. I started yelling at him, kicked him out of the car, and left him in front of a Burger King. Told him that he shouldn't be forced to ride with his … rapist." Derek couldn't bring his eyes up from the floor this time. He was thankful Carl was silent and barreled forward.

"That was the night I talked to you about the party stuff, which wasn't entirely just about the party. I wanted to find Cory the next day and apologize. He was angry but said we could talk. I grabbed Nic, and we met in one of our usual spots. I tried to apologize … for more than just the day before. I wanted to give us a chance to start over, start the *right* way.

"I don't really understand what happened next. I started talking, but then Nic jumped in and said he wanted to end the whole thing. It caught me off guard. Cory too but not nearly as much. I think something happened between them, but I don't know what. Cory was as angry with him as he was me. He said he was done too—with everything. He had me take off his collar, and he walked out." Derek thought sadly about the discarded chain sitting in one of his drawers at home. "I haven't spoken to Cory since, and Nic has been doing everything he can to keep me at arm's length too. Can't say I really blame them." Derek sniffled, not realizing his eyes had started to water. He waited a few moments before finally looking up at Carl, who was giving him a thoroughly unimpressed look.

"I don't even know where to start. I can't believe... All the times we've talked, and you never once told me *any* of this." Carl was bewildered. "My own damn fault. Should've thought to question a little more about how the three bare-ly-legal young men came to find themselves in a kink-based triad. That's what I get for thinking with my own dick," Carl mumbled to himself.

"I know but... What do I do? How do I fix this?" Derek almost whined.

"Fix this?" Carl boomed with laughter. "You *don't*. There's nothing to fix. You count yourself lucky the worst thing you lost was your friend, and you leave that boy alone."

"What? No, I *have* to fix this! Ever since that day, Cory's been hanging out with this other guy, and I *know* they're fucking, and I just have a really bad feel—"

"*Derek*." Carl steadied his gaze at the boy on the other end of the couch. "When you decided to go forward with that little plan of yours, you made every possible bad deci-sion along the way. You lied to, manipulated, and *used* one of your best friends because the thought of it made your dick hard.

"That boy has had his entire life turned upside down. You went from best friend, and by your own admission, *protector,* to his dom and owner *in a single night.* You even took away his choice to come out of the closet to you." Carl sat back on the couch. "And Derek, I remember high school. You and I both know there's no way Cory was the first virgin you've been with. You *know* what that can do to a person's emotions. You leave that boy alone and count yourself lucky that that's the end of it."

Derek was silent as he let Carl's words sink in. Carl was right. This was just Derek's incessant need to be a control freak coming up again. Still, Derek wasn't *only* concerned with Cory... "What about Nic?"

"You leave him be too. Sounds like that boy is dealing with some things about himself that he's not ready to admit," Carl said somewhat thoughtfully. "Not saying he's any less guilty of doing the same things to Cory, but I'm willing to bet that until he can come to terms with his own sexuality, the rest of this would just be lost on him."

Derek was again silent for a few minutes, mind blank. He felt numb. "I... I don't know what to do without those two. They've been my friends forever."

"You'll be okay." Carl slid over on the couch and patted Derek on the leg. "I know it seems like the end of the world right now, but you'll heal, I promise. Come on. I'm starving. Let's order a pizza."

Carl stood and walked toward the kitchen, not waiting to see if Derek was following. The sudden subject change caught Derek off guard ... but pizza *did* sound pretty good right now.

Carl smiled when he saw Derek entering the kitchen. Nothing to soothe a broken teenage heart like some pizza. He pulled the menu for his favorite local place and asked

Derek about toppings and phoned in the order. They had about a half hour to kill until it got there.

"Thanks for talking to me about all of this." Derek pulled out one of the bar stools from the kitchen counter. "And for not … thinking I'm a monster."

"Not a monster." Carl chuckled as he returned the pizza menu to the side of the fridge. "An idiot, maybe, but one I hope will use this to learn from his mistakes in the future."

"I will. I *really* will." Derek was being stoic. "I just never thought about what it would be like to lose my two best friends. I didn't expect it to hurt like this."

Carl snorted before he realized Derek was being serious. "You still think this is *just* about losing your two best friends, kid?"

"What do you mean?"

"Boy, you spent nearly every day for three or four months with these two. And you spent nearly *all* of that time together in close, intimate quarters, having what I can only assume was some of the most intense sex of your life. You took your best friend's virginity. You put a damn collar around his neck." Carl was really going to have to spell it out. Poor kid. "I think those two stopped being *just* your friends a while ago. You're heartbroken, Derek."

"Oh." Derek stared at the granite countertop, somewhat dumbfounded.

"Yeah, 'oh.'" Carl laughed again.

"I never really…" Derek trailed off. He hadn't ever thought of his relationship with Nic or Cory that way. Hadn't thought of it as a relationship at all. It wasn't like when he had girl-friends… Was it? He did miss them, a lot. Missed hanging out with them. Hated seeing Cory with someone else. And he felt like an asshole, but he'd be lying if he said he didn't *really* miss the sex, too. "Huh."

"You learn something new every day, kid." Carl opened his fridge and grabbed two cans—only soda, of course. He had a feeling they still had a lot more to talk about before the night was over. "Alright, so now why don't you tell me what exactly is going on with your parents that you can get away with even half of this shit?"

Derek groaned. The pizza could not get here fast enough.

"Shit. That does suck." Carl wiped the pizza grease from his beard with a napkin.

"They weren't always like this. They were great when I was younger." Derek took a swig of his soda. "Once my big brother moved out, I think they both just figured I'd be gone soon enough. What's another year or two of raising your youngest son?"

"Anyone ever tell you that you're kind of a spoiled brat?" Carl chuckled.

Derek almost choked on his pizza trying to defend himself, making Carl laugh harder.

"Calm down. I'm only fucking with ya. A little." Carl waited for Derek to swallow his mouthful before continuing. "I'm not saying your parents didn't drop the ball. It sounds like they got a little too preoccupied with work to think about how that felt to you... But sixteen or seventeen years of being attentive loving parents ain't nothing. And if they *weren't* gone, you wouldn't have done or learned half the stuff you have these past few months. You're kinda acting like—"

"—The world revolves around me and my problems?"

"So you *have* been called a spoiled brat before." Carl grinned to show he was still just joking.

"Maybe not in those exact words." Derek thought back to what Tricia had said to him at school. Maybe he should just crawl into a hole somewhere...

"Hey, none of that," Carl half-ordered, trying to stop Derek from overthinking things too much. "You fucked up, and you learned. You can only try to do better going forward. Beating yourself up isn't going to make anybody feel better, least of all yourself."

"Yes, sir." Carl was right. Derek tried to shake the thoughts from his head rather than let himself be pulled down. "Thanks again for listening to everything."

"Of course, kid." Carl let the "sir" Derek slipped in pass without comment. "Not sure why, but ever since the three of you walked into the store that day, I've felt a little protective of ya. When you started asking me for advice, I was more than happy to provide. I just wish I had known a little more about what was going on sooner. Might have been able to save you some hurt."

"Do you do that often? Mentor young men in the way of kink?" Derek teased before biting into another slice.

"Heh, here and there." Carl wiggled his head from side to side. "You lot are by far the youngest, but I've trained my share of boys over the years."

"How'd you get started?" Derek was genuinely curious how someone would normally get into this sort of thing.

"Not too different from you, actually. It wasn't internet porn, but it was the first time I saw any kind of kink." Carl thought back to when he was just a little gayby, still coming out of his shell. "I was out to a few people at the time, just going through my life like normal. I was in college, and one night I decided to try going to a gay bar downtown. When I got there, I found out it was actually their weekly leather night. A lot of very attractive men walking around in their leathers and gear. I didn't stay long, got too nervous, but the whole time I was there, my dick was rock hard. I went back a few weeks later, and one of the regular doms there approached. He saw me there on my first visit and spent the rest of the night talking to me, asking me things, and telling me about kink and leather. He ended up being my first dom. We were together a little over a year." Carl smiled as he reminisced.

"You were a sub?" Derek couldn't picture the burly man sitting across from him as anything other than a dom.

"Yeah," Carl answered. "I was still new and didn't quite know what I liked then. It's pretty common for doms to have been someone's sub at one point. There's a lot more switches out there than you realize, and it's a good training tool. If you're going to dominate a sub, then you should know what it's like to be on the receiving end of things."

"That makes sense." Derek took Carl's words in as he finished his third slice of pizza before speaking further. "Have you ever trained anyone as a dom before?"

"I've had a couple of boys go on to take on subs of their own." Carl nodded.

"Would you train me?"

Carl stared at Derek, pizza halfway in his mouth. Finishing what he had chewed, he put the rest of his slice down. "You don't ever slow down, do ya boy?"

"You've basically been training me already," Derek pointed out, ignoring Carl's question. "This would just be a more hands on approach."

"What makes you think I'm even looking for a sub right now?" Carl challenged.

"Maybe you aren't," Derek admitted. "You can say no. But me being into this stuff isn't going to go away, and if I'm going to do this, I want to do it the right way. Sir."

Carl stared at Derek again before laughing. "You got some balls, kid."

"Is that a yes?" Derek avoided the obvious joke.

"No. What it *is*, is 12:30 in the morning." They had been talking for a while.

"Oh shit! I better get going." Derek pushed his chair away from the table, feeling like he had definitely overstayed his welcome.

"Boy, you aren't driving *anywhere* at this hour. Unless you got somewhere to be tomorrow, you are parking your ass on that couch tonight." Carl remained in his seat.

Derek took this as a good sign and returned to his request. "Are you sure you wouldn't rather have me in your bed, sir?"

"Cut the shit, Derek." Carl weathered his gaze at the boy who was starting to push his luck. "What you're asking for is something serious."

"I *am* serious!"

"You're also only *eighteen* and spent the last three hours coming to terms with some very serious shit—shit you aren't even close to being through with yet," Carl pointed out gruffly. "What makes you think you could handle something like that now? Why the hell are you trying to jump right back into this shit anyway?"

"I don't know. I just... I don't think this is something I can make go away, and I don't know what else to do. The only other two guys I know into this stuff..." Derek trailed off.

"Come on. Let's get the couch set up." Carl sighed and closed the pizza box, getting up to slide it into the fridge. He hated feeling like an overprotective papa bear sometimes.

Carl grabbed some spare sheets and a couple of his own pillows and got Derek situated on the couch. The boy was mostly silent, probably worried that if he pushed anymore, Carl was going to kick him out or something. A far cry from the cocky teen Carl remembered walking into his store all those months ago.

"I'll think about it." Carl hoped he wasn't going to regret this. "But that means you have to, too. This isn't a game. This is something I take very, very seriously. You need to think about everything this is gonna entail, and if you're going to be able to handle that." And Carl was going to have to weigh the pros and cons of training this boy. It was going to be a late night.

"Yes, sir, I will." Derek smiled before sliding onto the couch. "Thank you, again. Even if you don't say yes. You've been really awesome about everything, Carl."

"Night, boy." Carl smiled back and sighed to himself. *Goddammit.*

"Night, sir."

Carl flicked off the living room light and walked to his bedroom, undressing and sliding into his own bed. He thought about texting some friends for advice but explaining why he had an 18-year-old asleep on his couch asking for training was probably going to take way longer than he had the energy for right now. His first instinct was to say no. From everything he learned tonight, it seemed like Derek's life was in a freefall. He had been jumping head first into situation after situation until everything blew up at once. Carl was worried that this request for training was just a reaction to the fight with his friends and that agreeing would only make Derek's life more chaotic.

But Derek had also proven to be determined to go after what he wanted. Carl wondered if his privileged upbringing had anything do with that. It wasn't necessarily a bad thing, but it meant that if he didn't get training from Carl, he might go out and try to get it from someone else. And Carl wasn't blind. Derek was hot, and the cocky little shit knew it. It wouldn't take him long to find an interested dom. Carl had friends he was sure would be interested, but given all of Derek's baggage... At least Carl already knew the score.

Derek was also only eighteen. Legal, yes, but Carl couldn't imagine his parents being thrilled if he found out who he was running around with. Not to mention agreeing to this also meant he'd be responsible for a lot of Derek's firsts when it came to gay sex. It wasn't that Carl minded teaching a virgin the ropes, but Carl knew from firsthand experience how easy attachment can come with these sorts of things, especially in a D/s relationship. Was he ready to potentially deal with that?

He also just felt for the boy. He was hurting, bad. He really was trying to take responsibility for his actions, though Carl still wasn't sure he fully understood their weight. Carl couldn't help but want to help him. He was sweet, eager, hopeful. All qualities Carl loved in a sub.

*Dammit. Fucking papa bear syndrome.*

Carl woke early the next morning, not quite remembering when he finally fell asleep the night before. Throwing on a pair of shorts, he walked toward the living room expecting to find Derek still asleep on the couch. Instead, he found the couch empty and the smell of coffee coming from the kitchen. *The hell?*

"Good morning, sir." Derek greeted Carl as he entered the kitchen. "I made coffee!"

Carl chuckled at Derek's renewed brazenness. "Blowing smoke up my ass isn't going to convince me to say yes, boy." Still, Carl poured himself a cup before sitting at his dining room table. "Sit."

Derek took the same seat across from Carl that he had the night before.

"So, *if* I agree to do this, I need to make a few things clear." Carl had actually written some of this down on his phone last night but felt like he could remember what he needed to say. "First, this is a commitment. If you want me to train you, then that means your ass is mine, figuratively and literally, for at least a few hours a week. I don't want to say yes only to have you decide you want out in a week."

"I won't. I swear," Derek blurted.

"Second, and this one is important: this training is *not* some kind of punishment for what you did to Cory." Carl left no room for argument in his voice. "This doesn't make up for any of that; I can't offer you atonement, only Cory can, and you need to accept that it may never happen."

"I understand," Derek responded more meekly.

"Finally, if I take you on as my boy, understand that extends beyond the bedroom and dungeon. It means working on more than just your kinks, like making sure you are getting your shit together, and hopefully teaching you how to be less of a cocky asshole."

"Yes, sir." Derek remained passive, but hopeful. "Does that mean you're saying yes?"

"That means yes, boy." Carl really hoped he didn't regret this.

"Thank you, sir!" Derek exclaimed. "When can we get started?"

"Slow down, boy." Carl huffed. "Let a daddy enjoy his coffee first."

"Sorry, sir." Derek bit his lip, practically vibrating in his seat.

Carl sipped his coffee and contemplated his next move.

"You know what, boy? I think we can get started." If the boy was gonna be so insistent, he might as well put him to work.

"Really, sir?"

"Really." Carl pushed his chair away from the table, turning it sideways but continuing to sit. Then he pointed to the floor in front of him. Time to get his training started. "On your knees."

Derek's eyes went wide before he scrambled into position. The full weight of what he was just about to do didn't hit him until he looked up at Carl from his spot on the floor. *Oh shit.* He was about to suck his first dick. His eyes went wide again, and he swallowed nervously.

"There's still time to back out if you want to." Carl figured this was a good test for Derek. Not only would it teach him a little humility, but it was also an act that was solely for the other person. Carl doubted Derek was used to sex where he wasn't the one getting off.

"No, sir." Derek eyed Carl's crotch nervously and swallowed again but remained on the floor. "I told you, I'm serious."

"Alright then, boy." Carl reached down and into his shorts, tucking the waistband under his growing cock and furry sack. "You are going to kneel there and suck my cock while I finish my coffee and answer some emails." Carl leaned back in his chair and picked up his phone, looking at Derek expectantly before he got started.

"I've, uh, never—" Derek stared at Carl's almost beer can-thick dick as it finished filling out.

"I know. Don't worry. I wouldn't even expect an experienced sub to have an easy time with this thing." Carl squeezed his cock for emphasis. "Just go slow and watch your teeth. You know what you like when you're getting your own dick sucked."

Derek nodded and took a deep breath before shuffling forward. Tentatively, he reached a hand out toward Carl's dick, feeling it twitch in his grip. His own cock was half-hard in his pants, though Derek wasn't sure how much of that was due to nerves.

Carl groaned but said nothing, sipping his coffee and opening his phone. Derek was going to have to choose to suck this dick all on his own.

Derek looked up at Carl for a second and then slowly moved his face toward his dick. He could see a bead of precum was beginning to well up on the head. Cum—that was something Derek would have to get used to. *Here goes nothing.*

Derek took the head of Carl's dick into his mouth, the salty taste of his skin mixing with his precum. The taste was ... exactly how it smelled. Not great. Not terrible but not great. Still, Derek heard Carl's sharp intake of breath as he was engulfed, so Derek figured he did something right.

Carl did his best to respond to his emails, but it was a little hard to ignore the fact that there was a mouth on his dick. Still, this was more about the principle than the act. It didn't matter what Carl was doing on his phone—if he wanted his sub on his knees sucking dick, then he would be on his knees sucking dick.

And suck dick he did or at least he tried. He held Carl's dick in place with his hand, feeling every twitch and pulse as he worked. It did not take long for his jaw to tire, some-thing Carl had anticipated. Derek bobbed his head up and down on Carl's dick, only managing to take in the first few inches and not even attempting to take it farther into his throat. It was no matter. In due time, Carl would be teaching

Derek to enthusiastically and willingly take his dick however Carl wanted.

Carl watched Derek out of the corner of his eye as he read through some news articles. He waited for the telltale signs of his jaw getting tired, wanting to push him just a little further than was comfortable. To his credit, Derek did not complain once, only switching his hand part way through as he adjusted his weight on his knees. Carl had to admit he was dedicated. Time to ease up.

"Good boy." Carl gently patted Derek on the head before pushing him back from his cock. Only for a second though, before Carl pulled him back into his balls. "Work those nuts."

Derek never imagined he'd be thankful to have his face shoved into a guy's balls, but here he was. Sucking dick was no joke. Derek really underestimated Cory's skills there. He was nowhere near close to getting Carl off. Derek happily lapped and sucked at Carl's full nuts, happy to let his jaw rest.

"Good boy," Carl gritted as he felt Derek's warm tongue against his balls, gripping his dick and starting to stroke.

Wouldn't take him too long now. Carl *loved* having his balls played with—all things Derek would learn in due time. He held Derek's face against his crotch by his hair, leaving him enough room to breathe but not letting him pull away.

Derek continued to lap and suck at Carl's nuts as the hand in his hair held him in place. His cock was fully hard now, whether it was from the energy or the act Derek didn't know, but he wasn't going to question it. He gripped his own cock through his shorts and squeezed, groaning against Carl's skin.

"Hands off your dick, boy," Carl growled. "I didn't tell you to touch yourself, did I?"

Derek's hand shot away from his dick at the sudden order. Okay, *that* definitely made his dick twitch. Seemed like Derek was going to learn a whole lot of new things about himself. He planted both hands on Carl's thighs as he continued to lap at the man's nuts as he steadily stroked his cock above. Suddenly, Derek's head was pushed back, Carl moving to a standing position above him. Oh fuck, he was gonna blow.

"Open your mouth, boy," Carl ordered with a grunt. "And close your eyes, or this might burn."

Derek only had a second to prepare before he was on the receiving end of his first facial. Derek felt Carl's load splash across his face, landing across the bridge of his nose and eyebrow. The second shot was lower, mostly across his lips and in his mouth. Derek nearly gagged from the abrupt and unexpected taste and texture. He didn't have a chance though, because shots three, four, and five soon followed, continuing to coat his face and fill his mouth as Carl breathed heavily above him. Eyes squeezed shut, Derek could feel Carl shake the last few drops from his cock onto Derek's face before sitting back down, finished using his new boy for the first time.

"Swallow," Carl ordered, seeing the way Derek was still holding some of his load in his mouth. "My boys don't spit."

Derek had been trying to not even breathe through his nose to avoid tasting the fresh load in his mouth. *So much for that*, Derek figured. He forced himself to swallow, the taste again a strange bitter saltiness that wasn't quite bad and wasn't quite good. He could still feel the wet cum on his face, afraid to open his eyes lest some get in.

"Good boy. Hold still." Derek felt Carl hold his face in place, using a paper towel to wipe some of his face clean. "Safe to open now."

Derek hesitantly opened his eyes, safe from any stray cum. He looked up and saw Carl smiling down at him warmly, messy paper towel still in hand. His cock was still hard, and he used the paper towel to wipe some cum still dripping from the tip.

"Not bad for your first time."

"Thank you, sir." Oof, his jaw was going to be sore later. "That was … different."

"Did you enjoy it?" Carl asked, curious.

"Yes." Derek couldn't exactly ignore the hard dick in his pants. Neither did Carl, who prodded it with his feet.

"I can see that." Carl held out a hand to help Derek to his feet. "So, still want to go through with training?"

"Yes, sir, absolutely." If anything, Derek was only more sure of himself now.

"Guess we have some work to do then, boy." Carl sighed, but smiled. "Let's get to it."

# CHAPTER 14

"You seem happier."

"I am happier," Cory told Stephanie as the two walked into the convenience store. They had been killing time until the rest of school got out.

"You're not still sad or angry about...?" Stephanie trailed off, letting the question hang in the air.

"What happened with Derek and Nic sucked. A lot." Cory did miss them, both as his best friends and in other more *intimate* ways, but with his newfound self-confidence, Cory wasn't going to second guess himself. "But I'm not gonna sit around and mope about it. I've got better things to do."

"Better *people* to do." Stephanie snickered at her own bad joke. "I'm glad you're happy. Tell me about the new guy."

"Jackson," Cory said without hesitating. When Cory asked if it was alright if he talked to Stephanie about it, Jackson had no problem. That was a nice change. "It's good. Different, but good."

"Is he like ... your boyfriend?" Stephanie asked as she flipped through a magazine rack.

"Ah, no, I don't think we're anything like that," Cory tried to sidestep the question, one he himself had thought about more than once. "I guess we're kinda just ... friends with benefits right now?"

"You okay with that?"

"Yeah." Cory shrugged. "School is literally over in like a month. I'm fine with this just being what it is." If Cory was being *totally* honest, he wouldn't have been mad if Jackson had asked him out, but he wasn't expecting it. It's not like Nic or Derek had wanted to... "What about you?" Cory was eager to change the subject. "We spend so much time talking about my love life now... Sorry."

"At least you have one. I can't wait for college. Gonna go on a slutty clothes binge as soon as I move out. Really hoe it up for the next few years." Stephanie looked wistfully off into the distance, only half-joking.

"You'll kill it, I'm sure." Cory laughed, flipping through a comic book. They still made Sonic the Hedgehog comics? "You already got accepted, right? Your first pick?"

"Virginia Tech." Stephanie nodded. "Everyone who goes to that school is so smart... I'm kinda nervous. But what about you? Did you pick a school yet?"

Dammit, Cory was trying to get the conversation *off* him. That backfired.

"Still weighing my options." He wasn't lying. He *did* have options. He just had no idea which he was going to pick. Part of him had hoped he, Derek, and Nic... "Haven't decided yet."

"Uh huh. Well you better make a decision soon. Not much longer to go." Stephanie grabbed a candy bar to pay for at the front of the store.

"Yeah, yeah." Cory rolled his eyes before checking his phone. "Hey, class is about to get out. Wanna head back?"

"So you can meet your *boyfriend* after his class?" Stephanie teased.

"He's not my boyfriend." Cory pointed out again. "But yes."

"You know, I could get used to having someone waiting for me like this." Jackson smiled at Cory as the two boys walked from the locker room to his Jeep. All the seniors needed to have theirs cleared out by the end of the month and he asked Cory to help him carry some stuff to his car before they hung out.

"Might be a little difficult considering we only have four more weeks of school left," Cory pointed out the obvious.

"I can get used to someone waiting for me like this for the next four weeks, then." Jackson threw his bag into the back of the car with Cory following suit before the two boys climbed into the car.

"So, sir, can I ask you something?" Hoping the comment might be a sign, Cory decided to ask a question he had been avoiding.

"Sure." Jackson turned to face Cory.

"Are we ... going out? Or would you like to go out?" Cory fought the urge to close his eyes. Can't hide from this.

"Oh. Uh..." Jackson stumbled over his words for a moment. "Well, no, boy. I don't think so."

"You don't think we're going out, or you don't think you want to go out?" Cory was deflated either way.

"Err..." Jackson let the question linger a little too long. "Both. Sorry, boy."

"Ah." Cory tried to hide the hurt in his voice.

"It's not that you're not great," Jackson began to back-pedal. He didn't quite see *this* coming. "It's just, I don't think that's what I'm looking for right now."

"It's okay. You don't have to explain." Cory smiled or at least attempted to. "It was a stupid question."

"No, really. It's not you. It's me." Jackson suddenly scrunched his eyes, realizing the mistake of what he was saying. "It's just that we only have a little more time together left. I don't want to get into anything serious right now. Just have some fun. Who wants to go into college in a relationship, right?" Jackson looked over and smiled after finishing his question.

"Right." Cory faked a smile. His feelings weren't *that* hurt. Jackson had a point. It just would have maybe been nice to... It didn't matter. "It's cool. I get it. Thanks for being straightforward with me."

"You sure?" Jackson smiled back. "Since we *are* on the subject of school ending, there's an end of the year party next Friday in Hartford State Park. The one the seniors always end up having next to Lake Shepard. You wanna go?"

"Hmmm..." It wasn't exactly a date, but it was something. And the party might actually be fun. Still, the last party didn't exactly go well.

"I just figured we could have some fun out there together. Get a little buzzed, run around in the woods, fool around all night." Jackson groped at his dick through his jeans. "Where anyone could catch us, but no one could see us..."

Cory snorted. Jackson had a very obvious and very strong public sex kink. Not that Cory wasn't into it himself. But still, risking getting caught at *another* party... "Last time I fooled around with someone at a party, someone spied on us and started telling the rest of the school."

"Oh. Yeah. I think I heard about that." Jackson sucked in, blew out a breath, and paused for a moment before continuing. "This would be different, though. It'd be really dark, we'd be able to sneak far enough away from everyone... and even if they did catch us, who cares? We're almost out of here. Come on. It'll be great." Jackson hit Cory on the arm and gave him a look, biting his lip. *Ugh, does that work on girls?*

"Alright. I'm in." Cory rolled his eyes. It would be a fun night, probably. Might as well end the year with a bang.

"Yessss." Jackson pumped his fist. "Gonna be a great night. I can think of a few things we can do out there alone." Jackson squeezed his slowly growing cock again, this time giving Cory an altogether different look.

Cory watched shamelessly as Jackson continued to grope himself, mouth almost watering. Damn, the "training" Derek and Nic gave him was near Pavlovian. Jackson took notice of the hunger behind Cory's eyes and decided to take advantage.

"Why don't you c'mere, boy?" Jackson reached for the adjustment lever to his seat, pushing himself away from the steering wheel. "I think we can have some fun right now."

"Right here?" Cory looked around the school parking lot. Most of the students had already left, though there were still a few unclaimed cars.

"Yeah, boy, right here." Jackson looked around himself as he undid his belt and zipper. "No one's around. You know you want to." Jackson reached into his pants and lewdly squeezed his cock again.

Cory bit his lip. He did want to. He looked around one last time, lifted the arm rest separating them, and swallowed down half of Jackson's cock.

"Fuck." Jackson hissed as he felt his dick engulfed by Cory's hot mouth. He adjusted his seat further, leaning his seat back some and giving Cory a little more room to work with.

For his part, Cory was focused on one thing: getting Jackson off before somebody caught them. He was trying to move as fast and silently as he could up and down Jackson's dick, but it was hard to fully enjoy what he was doing when in the back of his mind he was listening for anyone approaching. At the same time, he was trying to minimize any noises he was making with his mouth as he sucked. That didn't leave much room for his own enjoyment.

"Come on. Quit being so nervous." Jackson's voice rang from above him. "I can tell you're overthinking this. Just relax and trust me. If I see anyone coming, I'll pull you up, okay?"

Cory paused his movements and took Jackson's words in. He was just about to respond with a "yes sir" when he remembered he couldn't very well talk with a dick in his mouth. So instead, he took a deep breath in through his nose and put all that nervous energy into his cocksucking ability. He blocked out his surroundings and slowly eased the rest of Jackson's dick into his throat.

"There we go," Jackson praised as he pet the back of Cory's head. "Suck your sir's dick like a good boy."

Cory did as he was told, quietly beaming at the praise. He moved back up Jackson's shaft until he was at almost the head and then immediately swallowed the entire length again on his way back down. When he felt the hand in his hair tighten, Cory took it as a sign of further encouragement and began to bob faster and faster as he swallowed Jackson's dick.

"Shit, suck that dick, boy," Jackson encouraged, unable to stop thrusting up into Cory's mouth as he did. "Won't take me long if you keep that up."

Cory felt his cock begin to harden as he finally allowed himself to fully relax with what he was doing. He considered reaching a hand down to take care of himself but decided he'd rather just focus on what he was doing. Sir had his back, so he should make sure he did a good job for him. Cory moved his hand toward Jackson's crotch, figuring his hand could be put to better use playing with his balls. Just as he was about to reach his hand into the fly of his jeans—

*Thud.*

"I am so fucking glad to be done with late practices." The voice was faint, but it was distinct, a girl's. Cory's eyes flew open, though the only thing he got an eyeful of was Jackson's jeans. Cory made a muffled noise of panic and attempted to push off from Jackson's lap.

"Fuck, hold still. I'm so fucking close..." Jackson held Cory's head in place as he continued to thrust up: one, two, three times...

Another couple of thuds and then the sound of a car door being slammed. "No kidding. Won't miss it being so dark by the time we get home." The sound of footsteps on gravel became more obvious now that Cory was listening for them. Still, Cory attempted once again to extract Jackson's dick from his orifice but was again met with resistance.

"Hold on!" Jackson spoke through gritted teeth. "Here it comes—"

Cory almost gagged when the first load of cum hit his throat, though he should have been expecting it. He was still shocked, and somewhat angry, at Jackson's refusal to let him stop. Had he even really been keeping watch? What if those girls saw!? All of these thoughts pounded in Cory's head as the remaining four volleys of cum filled his mouth, the volume and fact that his mouth was still filled forcing him to swallow. Figuring he was finished with his duty, Cory for the third time tried to return to his seat and for the third time was held in place.

"Stay still. Those two girls are close." Jackson spoke in hushed tones and then reached over to fiddle with the radio that wasn't on. "Cheerleaders. They're about to leave."

Cory heard two more car doors close as Jackson said this and then an engine being turned on. When Cory heard the sound of tires over gravel fade into the distance, the hand on his head relented, finally allowing Cory to sit up.

"What the hell, man?" Cory wiped his mouth with his hand. "We almost got caught!"

"I know, I know. I'm sorry," Jackson apologized profusely. "But by the time they were close, they *definitely* would have noticed you pulling your head out of my lap. I was trying to keep us safe!"

"I thought you were keeping a lookout!" Cory let the fact that Jackson continued to fuck his mouth while they were almost being caught slip by. For now.

"I was! They snuck up on me, I swear," Jackson tried to explain. "One second we were alone, and then I looked again and two girls are loading stuff into their trunk."

Cory said nothing but rolled his eyes. *Bullshit.*

"I'm really sorry." Jackson put his hand on Cory's shoulder. "I swear it wasn't on purpose."

Cory looked at Jackson. He had such cute puppy dog eyes. *Ugh. Fine.* "It's okay."

"So does that mean you'll still come to the party next week?" Jackson gave him a hopeful smile.

"Yes. I'll still come to the party next week." Cory couldn't help but return the smile.

"If you're hoping I'm going to tell you he's unhappy, I've got bad news."

"What? No, that's... That's good." Derek sat across from Stephanie at the Bella Cafe, the local Italian and pizza place. Stephanie had agreed to meet Derek over dinner to talk about Cory. "I'm happy he's happy."

"You don't look happy." Stephanie bit into a breadstick as she watched Derek squirm.

"Well, I'm not *happy* happy, but I'm glad Cory's doing okay." Derek was being honest, not that he had anything more to lose if he was otherwise.

"Mhmm. And this has *nothing* to do with the new guy Cory's been seeing?" Stephanie crossed her arms.

"No. It's not like that," Derek defended a little too quickly.

"So then what is it like?" Stephanie was not about to blab about her friend without making sure it was safe first.

"I just want to make sure he's okay." Derek couldn't quite bring himself to meet her gaze. "I screwed up a lot. Nic and I both did. I'm not trying to get him to forgive me, or even talk to me again. I just... I want to make sure he's safe."

Stephanie silently studied Derek for a moment. "You don't trust the new guy."

"I didn't say that."

"You didn't have to." Stephanie took another bite of a breadstick. "I don't either."

"You don't?"

"No. But Cory does," Stephanie added pointedly. "I don't know anything about him. I suspect you don't either."

"I don't." Derek was again truthful. "But there's just something about him."

"Well, unless Cory says something, it's not my place—and certainly not yours—to do anything about it," Stephanie pointed out. "Why do you care so much about who Cory is seeing anyway? I know he was your best friend, but it's not like you were *together* together."

Derek let the question hang in the air, still unable to look at Stephanie directly, hoping that the silence would speak for itself. He was still trying to figure out those feelings.

"Oh my god." Stephanie narrowed an annoyed look at Derek. "I swear, you straight boys are so fucking stupid sometimes."

"Yeah, we are," Derek agreed.

"He won't stay mad at you forever, Derek." Stephanie sighed, her features softening. "But he does deserve his space for a while. He'll come around one day to talk. But even if he doesn—"

"I know," Derek half mumbled into his dinner. "It's not about that. I just want—"

"—to make sure he's happy." Stephanie gave Derek a sad smile.

"Thanks for talking to me." Derek smiled back.

Stephanie waved her half-eaten breadstick in his direction. "Thanks for dinner."

Nic dropped his duffle bag on the bench behind his locker. Like everyone else, he had to clear out his locker, including the one he used for gym and football. He had been putting it off for a while now. Something about the locker room brought back some recent bad memories. Nic looked over to still see a slight dent in the locker he had hurt his hand on. Yeah, bad memories.

They weren't all bad. Nic unzipped his bag and undid his lock, stowing that away first. As much as he was ready to quit the game, he'd had a lot of great times over the years. He'd been through a lot with his team, both in the locker room and on the field. He loved some of his teammates like family. He'd miss them. As Nic reminisced and emptied his locker, he heard someone else enter and turned to see Taylor with an empty duffle bag of his own.

"Hey." Taylor nodded in Nic's direction and set his own bag down. "Cleaning your shit out too?"

"Yeah." Nic turned back to his still half-full locker. "Kept pushing it off."

"Same here." Taylor began to load his own bag up. "The cleaning up was always the most boring part of playing."

"Yeah," Nic agreed as he packed up. "Wish we could make the waterboys or cheerleaders do this for us."

"I mean, we do both know a boy who'd *love* to handle all your sweaty jocks," Taylor teased.

"Heh, yeah…" Nic actually felt bad for having to break the news to Taylor. "I kinda ended that whole thing with Cory and Derek a while back."

"Aww, really?" Taylor sounded slightly disappointed and paused his packing. "I wondered why I didn't really see you all together much anymore. That's too bad."

"Yeah… I dunno, man. It just wasn't really working out. Wasn't *really* my thing." Nic stopped his own packing as he continued. "Plus, after the bullshit that went down last semester, I just wanna put all that shit behind me."

"Yeah, that sucked." Taylor went back to packing his bag. "But you shouldn't let some assholes decide how you're gonna live your life. Fuck 'em."

"No one is telling me how to run my life. I just got tired of dealing with a lot of the headaches and problems that were starting to come up when I was hanging out with those two." Nic continued to pack as well. "Besides, it's not like straight guys like you or me have to try hard if we wanna get laid."

"Who said I was straight?" Taylor asked, still facing his locker, a hint of cockiness in his voice.

"Oh. Uh. I didn't..." Nic stumbled. "I didn't know you were gay, man."

"Didn't say I was gay either."

"So... you're bi?"

"I'm not really worried about labels." Taylor explained. "Look, I love girls. *Love* them. But some of the hottest sex I've ever had—at least so far—has been with guys. It would be stupid to cut that out of my life just because of what someone else might think. Plus, there's the whole 'gender is a construct' thing. At the end of the day, what really makes a guy a guy and a girl a girl?"

Nic stood there and watched as Taylor packed, jaw slightly slack. Nic had been dealing with his own inner turmoil for weeks, and Taylor just came in with everything already figured out.

"You okay, man?" Taylor cocked his head when he noticed Nic staring at him.

"Yeah, sorry." Nic shook off his distracted look. "Just never knew you to be such a liberated guy."

"I read a lot." Taylor grabbed the last few things from his locker—a jersey and some socks—and tossed them in his bag, zipping it up. "We can't all fit the dumb jock stereotype." Taylor winked at Nic.

"Ha, ha." Nic rolled his eyes, finished packing his own bag, and zipped up. "You got all this shit figured out, huh?"

"I didn't always. But like I said, I couldn't pretend like the stuff I had done with guys hadn't happened. I wouldn't want to." Taylor threw his bag over his shoulder. "So the only other option was to figure out how to be okay with it."

"That's…" Nic wasn't expecting the thoughtful answer and picked up his own bag, "great, man. I wish my problems were as simple to work through."

"Dude. Seriously?" Taylor cocked his head and sighed at Nic, who was at this point being willfully obtuse. "You don't see any similarities between—"

"Hope I'm not interrupting date night."

Nic's head whipped around at the voice of a third person entering the locker room. Steve.

"Fuck off, man." Taylor beat Nic to the punch.

"No, thanks. That's more his thing." Steve walked to his own locker, here to do the same thing as everyone else. Nic should have just done this last week. Or tomorrow. Really, any time but now.

"I seriously hope someone knocks your teeth out in college." Nic could dream, right?

"Why? Your little boyfriend not sucking your dick good enough anymore?" Steve turned around to taunt. "Sure seemed like he was doing a pretty good job in the garage at our victory party."

"Shut the fuck up, you prick, or I'll knock your teeth in." Nic was across the locker room as soon as Steve finished his sentence.

"Get the fuck out of my face, Herrera." Steve fixed his gaze against Nic's. "Only saying what I saw with my own two eyes."

"You didn't see shit." Nic was beyond trying to deny anything at this point, but he genuinely didn't believe that Steve actually saw anything.

"So that *wasn't* you walking out of the garage with your boyfriend after he got done sucking your dick?" Steve added details that Nic knew he couldn't make up.

"You. Didn't. See. Shit," Nic growled through gritted teeth.

"I saw plenty. Not like it was hard to get other people to believe me. Or to get inside your head either," Steven taunted. "I really gotta thank that guy."

"What guy?" Taylor chimed in, partially to let Nic know he was still here in case he needed backup.

"I dunno. Some dude from the basketball team. Jake or something?"

"Jackson," Nic corrected him, though he hoped he was wrong.

"That's it. He found me at the party and let me know exactly where I could find you. Said I'd learn some *very* interesting info. He wasn't wrong."

"Why the fuck would he do that?" Nic was thrown. What did this Jackson guy have against him exactly?

"How the fuck should I know? I didn't ask questions." Steve scoffed. "Maybe because he hates your guts just as much as I do. Maybe because he knows you're just a stuck-up piece of shit. Maybe like me he got sick and fucking tired of seeing you run around with that fucking *faggot*—"

Nic's fist collided with Steve's face before he had even realized what happened. Steve's body was pushed back, his head slamming into the row of lockers before his body crumpled to the floor.

"Holy shit!" Taylor jumped over the bench and past Nic to Steve's prone body, checking his neck for a pulse. "Damn. He's out cold, dude."

For his part, Nic was standing wide-eyed, his hand still a fist. "I don't... I didn't... As soon as he started talking about Cory..." Nic stumbled over his words. "Fuck. I gotta go talk to Derek." This information about Jackson... Nic knew this wasn't just a coincidence.

"Go." Taylor waved him off as he propped Steve up against the lockers. "I'll stay here and make sure this asshole wakes up okay. Jesus, dude, you knocked him the fuck *out*." Taylor shook his head, half in shock, half in awe.

"Thanks, bro." Nic grabbed his bag and headed for the exit. "I owe you one!"

"You owe me like three or four for this one," Taylor said to the empty locker room and Steve's unconscious body.

"Hold on! Hold on! I'm coming," Derek called to whoever was pounding on his door. He peered out the peephole and was surprised to see it was Nic.

"Hey, what's up?" Derek opened the door and greeted his friend before moving aside to let him in.

"Hey, D." Nic walked into Derek's living room. "Sorry. It was kind of an emergency so I ran right over."

"Why didn't you text or call first?" Derek gave him a strange look.

"I ... don't know actually." Nic thought about what he was just doing. "I think it's because that's what you always see people do in movies."

"So what's up?" Derek chuckled.

"It's about Cory."

"Ah. So you wanna talk about that now?" Derek didn't bother hiding the annoyance in his voice.

"Yes, I wanna talk about that now." Nic rolled his eyes in response and sat down on the couch.

"So...?" Derek took a seat on the other couch.

"It's about that guy Cory's hanging around with," Nic continued. "Jackson."

"What about him?"

"He had something to do with spreading the rumors about me and Cory around school. He had *everything* to do with it, actually." Nic ran back through the events in his head to make sure he was getting everything right. "I was in the locker room at school, cleaning out my stuff with Taylor, when Steve McMillan walks in."

"Did you get in another fight?"

"Wasn't much of a fight." Nic could help but smirk when he thought about how he cold-cocked Steve to the floor. "But yeah, he came in, acting like the same asshole he always is. Started talking shit about me and Cory and what he saw go down at the party."

"So he *did* see you guys?" Derek was confused.

"Sort of. Steve said that when he was at the party, Jackson came up to him and told him where he could find me." Nic was still putting some of this together himself as he talked through what happened. "Told him that I was up to something he'd want to see. I don't know if he saw the actual blowjob, but he saw me and Cory leaving afterward."

"Wow. That's—"

"Really fucked up. Why would he do that?" Nic was at a total loss. "Did I do something to piss him off at some point? What would he have to gain?"

"I mean, it sounds kinda weird but ... Cory?" Derek answered though Nic was putting it together himself.

"I guess that makes sense, but that's so fucked up." Nic still couldn't quite wrap his head around it.

"I know, man, but that's really what it seems like. It's the only thing that makes sense." Derek thought back to how quickly Jackson seemed to move in on Cory. Like, literally the next day was when he first saw them together.

"We gotta tell Cory." Nic stood up.

"No." Derek remained seated.

"What?" Nic was aghast. "But we have to let him know that's the only reason this shit happened in the first place!"

"No, it's not," Derek said flatly. "A *lot* of other shit led to this. A lot of shit we're responsible for."

"But ... D," Nic tried to reason, "we can't just let Cory keep hanging out with that guy after what he did to get to him."

"Because what we did to get to him was so much better?" Derek challenged.

"That was different." Nic shook his head.

"Yeah, *we* got him drunk before we started fucking him." Derek wanted to be as blunt as possible.

Nic was silent for a moment, not expecting Derek's response to be ... this. "So, what are we supposed to do then?"

"Nothing." Derek sighed. "We need to leave Cory alone, like he asked. Everything he's pissed at us for... He's right about all of it. We completely used and took advantage of him."

"Shit, man," Nic said softly. "This was not how I expected you to respond."

"Yeah, well, I'm trying to figure some shit out so I don't keep doing stupid shit like ... this." Derek motioned between the two of them.

"I just don't feel good leaving Cory with that dick." Nic stewed in his anger. "We have to do *something*. He needs to know."

"And how exactly do we do that? 'Hey Cor, I know you want nothing to do with us and have absolutely no reason to trust us, but that guy you're hanging out with created an elaborate conspiracy to break the three of us up.' That seems like a totally normal thing to tell someone," Derek poked at the holes in Nic's plan. "I don't like it either but ... he's happy. We need to just let him live his life." Derek shared what Stephanie had told him earlier.

"But ... D... He's... He's supposed to... *We're* supposed to..." Nic could barely put his feelings to words.

"I know, man, but ... we fucked everything up. And we kept fucking it up. Cory has every right to hate us. Maybe even forever." Derek wanted to make sure he and Nic were on the same level. "So, are we gonna talk about the other stuff too?" Derek was ready to move onto another topic that had been on his mind lately.

"What other stuff?" Nic wasn't playing dumb—yet.

"The stuff where something happened between you and Cory, and that's part of the reason he wishes we were both dead at the moment," Derek answered flatly.

"I don't know what you're talking about." *Now* Nic was playing dumb.

"*Dude*." Derek was firm.

"*Fine.* The night before the split, the day I flipped out about the rumors," Nic started to share his story, mostly mumbling it into this lap, "I got really drunk that night on my dad's rum and showed up at Amy's, but she still wouldn't talk to me. So then I walked to Cory's place."

"What happened?" Derek hadn't known about any of this.

"First, he helped bandage my hand." Nic held up his now healed hand. "Then ... I kissed him."

"*DUDE!?*" Derek leapt up.

"I know!" Nic squeezed his eyes shut, trying to will himself invisible, but he continued. "We spent the rest of the night fucking. But like ... it was different. It felt different. And we ... kept making out the whole time."

"Holy shit." Derek sat back down exasperated by his friend.

"And then ... I left in the middle of the night and pretended to not remember any of it the next day at school." Nic barely finished his sentence before burying his face in his hands, ashamed of his behavior.

"Oh my god." So much more of why Cory was acting off that day was starting to click into place. "How could you do something like that?"

"I don't know! I panicked!" Nic tried to explain. "I was just so angry and sad and anxious, and I didn't have anyone to talk to... It was raining, and I showed up at Cory's place, and he took me inside and took care of me, and he was being so sweet, and he was right there in front of me, and I just..." Nic couldn't finish his statement.

"Nic ... I'm pretty sure you were Cory's first kiss." Derek stared, dumbfounded by his best friend's actions. "Like, ever."

"That... That can't be right." Nic started searching his memories.

"Can you think of a single time he's mentioned *anyone* before, even a girl? You totally broke his heart." Derek tried to imagine what Cory must have felt, being not just rejected but *forgotten* like that. "You destroyed it. *We* destroyed it."

"...I fucking suck."

"Fuck." Derek flopped back against the couch. "This fucking sucks. We fucking suck. We were both *a lot* of Cory's firsts. Maybe all of them." Derek felt like had all the answers, but none of them were to *this* specific problem.

"So what do we do, D?" Nic sounded scared, more than Derek was ever used to hearing from him.

"I dunno, man." Derek stood from his couch and moved over to sit next to Nic. "But we'll figure it out together, right?" He bumped his shoulder into Nic's.

"Right." Nic gave a small smile and bumped him back.

"Bros?"

"Bros."

# CHAPTER 15

"Do I really have to do this?"

"Yes, you do."

It was Friday, a few hours after school had ended. Derek and Nic were seated in Derek's car outside of Joe's, a local diner that was pretty popular with students from the high school. It had been the last day of classes before finals week for seniors, and the two boys had come here together for one reason: Nic needed to break up with Amy. He was just having a hard time psyching himself up to do it.

"Can't I just, like, wait until we both leave town for college?" Nic tried to weasel out of doing what he knew he needed to do. "That's only two months away, and then—"

"*Dude.*" Derek leveled his gaze with Nic. "We *both* spent the last few months cheating on our girlfriends. If Amy or Tricia knew what we had been getting up to, how do you think they'd feel? For everything we've gotten away with, this is the *least* you can do."

"Easy for you to say." Nic sighed. "You didn't do the breaking up."

"Yeah, it was really cool being dumped at my own party in front of our classmates," Derek deadpanned.

"Sorry," Nic said sheepishly.

"It's fine." Derek sighed. "I deserved it."

"Fuck, there she is." Nic watched as Amy's car pulled into the diner. "I guess it's now or never."

"It'll be fine, bro," Derek tried to reassure him. "Just let her down easy. Use the end of school as an excuse. It'll suck, but once it's over, it's over."

"I know, I know." Nic watched Amy walk into the diner, not having noticed them seated in Derek's car. "Alright. Here I go."

"I'll chill out here. Give you guys some privacy." The two boys exited the car together, though Derek stayed put, leaning against the side. "I'm right here if you need me."

Nic nodded and walked toward the diner's front doors, looking for Amy once he was inside. He spotted her at a booth in the corner and waved when she noticed him before walking over.

"Hey." Nic smiled at her but thought better of leaning over to kiss her hello, given what he was about to do.

"Hey." Amy smiled back but said nothing else.

"So…" Nic really wasn't sure how to do this. "I, uh, wanted to talk to you about some—"

"It's okay, Nic," Amy interrupted, covering one of his hands with her own. "I know what you wanted to talk about."

"You do?" Nic was a little hesitant to continue.

"Yeah." Amy gave another small smile. "You want to break up."

"Oh. Uh…" Nic stared at Amy wide eyed. *Is it that obvious?*

"It's okay, Nic." Amy squeezed his hand. "I think we should break up, too."

"You do?" Hearing that out loud stung, to Nic's surprise.

"It's been really great these last few months." Amy squeezed his hand again. "But we both know this was never about getting serious."

"Uh… Yeah, I guess you're right," Nic said with more dejection than he expected. She wasn't wrong but … he never saw himself on the opposite end of *this* particular conversation. "I didn't mean—"

"It's okay, Nic. I was doing it for the same reasons." Amy teased and gave him a wink. "Don't look so sad. A few months from now, you'll have an entire campus of girls to work your way through."

"Heh, yeah, I guess you're right." Nic chuckled. At the current moment, he wasn't quite sure what exactly was in his future.

"It's been fun, Nic." Amy stood and kissed Nic on the cheek. "You coming to the end of the year party? I'm headed there now."

"Not sure yet," Nic answered. "It's been a weird week."

"Aww. Well, I hope I see you later. Bye, Nic." Amy gave Nic one last smile before heading for the door and leaving Nic alone at the booth. A few moments later, the door opened once again, and Derek walked in, taking Amy's former seat.

"How'd it go?" Derek checked in with his bro. "She didn't look too broken up when she was leaving."

"Dude. *She* dumped *me*." And Nic was still processing it.

"Oh. That's a good thing though, right?" Derek figured he got off lucky. "No messy break up."

"Yeah, I think?" Nic sounded dumbfounded. "I just wasn't expecting it."

"That's been going around lately." Derek picked up the menu from the table. "Wanna get a burger?"

Nic looked down at his own menu. "Yeah. I could eat."

Just a few miles away, in one corner of Hartford State Park, the end of year party was kicking into gear. A few dozen soon-to-be-graduated teens had shown up in their cars, backseats filled with all sorts of snacks and supplies for one last night of high school debauchery. Cory and Jackson were there, wandering the perimeter as the festivities began.

"Having fun yet?" Jackson asked Cory as he watched two football players tap a keg.

"Oh yeah. *Loads.*" Cory took a sip of his drink—just a soda. *Why did I even come to this thing again?*

"I think I might have a load for ya." Jackson spoke loud enough for only Cory to hear.

*Oh yeah,* that's *why.* "Think you can help me out, *sir*?"

"Just follow me, boy." Jackson led Cory away from the clearing where the students had gathered and farther into the forest. The two wandered for a few minutes until any sounds or music from the other students had faded away, and they knew they were alone.

"C'mere, boy." Once he was comfortable with the distance, Jackson stopped and leaned back against a large tree, hand already rubbing at his bulge. "On your knees."

Cory eyed the growing bulge under Jackson's hand. Yeah, this is *exactly* why he came here. He obeyed the order, walking toward him and sinking to his knees. He took one last sip of his soda before putting it on the ground next to him.

"Good boy." Jackson lowered his zipper, pulling his cock out through the fly. "Now suck."

Cory grinned as he shuffled forward, placing both his hands on Jackson's thighs as he moved his mouth toward the cock before him. He moaned softly as he engulfed the head, making a show of what he was doing. Cory had come a long way from the timid boy who first learned to suck dick in a cabin not far from here. Though this wasn't necessarily what he pictured for his future either—not that he was complaining.

Jackson relaxed against the tree as he felt Cory get to work. This was a favorite of his—getting a boy or girl out here in the woods and getting them on his dick. Being out here in the open, the idea that someone could just mistakenly walk by and see what they were doing... The thrill of it drove Jackson crazy. Just thinking about it made his dick twitch as Cory worked on swallowing it down.

Jackson used his hands on Cory's head to guide him as he began to bob up and down his shaft. Cory didn't have to work at getting Jackson hard and immediately got to work deep throating him. Jackson allowed him to do most of the work but did lazily hump up into his mouth a few times. He was in no hurry, but he had planned to get more than just a blowjob while out here. When he'd had enough, Jackson tugged on Cory's hair.

"Up."

Cory let Jackson's cock slip from his mouth as he once again obeyed and stood. Jackson grabbed him by the shoulders and spun them around so that now Cory's back was to the tree.

"Strip."

Cory couldn't help looking around. Even though he knew they were alone, he felt a little nervous. It wasn't like he hadn't been naked (and almost caught) out here before. Nodding, he unbuckled his jeans and pushed them down, pulling them off his feet along with his shoes. He also removed his shirt and put it and his jeans at the base of the tree, leaving him in just his underwear (a jockstrap—one of the ones Derek had given him) and socks.

"Nice. You wore it." Jackson indicated the underwear choice. "Good boy."

"Of course, sir." Cory smiled warmly at the praise.

"Now," Jackson placed his hand against the tree over Cory's shoulder, leaning over the shorter boy, "turn around."

Cory bit his lip and turned around, bracing himself against the trunk of the tree in front of him. It was large, thick enough that Cory couldn't see around it, but that also meant it concealed their bodies from view if anyone *did* come walking this way. Cory wasn't worried. He was determined not to be nervous like the last time he was out here.

Jackson stepped up behind Cory and slapped his hard cock against Cory's ass, still sticking out through his open fly. Reaching into his pocket, he fished out a small packet of lube that he tore open with his mouth, squirting some into his hand and spreading it up and down his shaft. Squeezing out a little more, he rubbed his fingers against Cory's hole for a moment before pushing one inside and slowly fucking him with it. Once he felt Cory was lubed up enough, he stepped forward and put his wet cockhead against Cory's hole, replacing the finger with his dick.

Cory sucked in his breath and bit his lip as he felt his hole stretch around Jackson's dick. It didn't hurt, but Cory wasn't getting fucked as often these days, so it still took some getting used to. Jackson didn't rush, so Cory just closed his eyes and focused on relaxing as he felt the rest of Jackson's cock make its way into his hole. When he felt the rough denim of Jackson's jeans against his ass, he knew he was there.

"Fuck, boy," Jackson cursed as he grabbed Cory by the hips. "Nice tight hole..."

"Thank you, sir." Cory tried to give a sexy look over his shoulder, but it was more difficult than he anticipated while getting used to a dick in his ass.

Still holding Cory by the hips, Jackson pulled his cock about halfway from Cory's hole. Feeling it twitch and flutter around him, he drove back in with just a little bit of force. He continued this rhythm, slowly picking up speed as he felt Cory's hole relax more and heard light moans fall from the boy's mouth.

It didn't take too long for Cory to start enjoying himself. The boy was truly a bottom. After a few slow drags of Jackson's cock across his prostate, Cory was biting into his own wrist to drown his moans. God, he missed this. He was going to have to spend some quality time with his dildo at home after this. He started pushing his ass back to meet Jackson's thrusts, eager to have his prostate massaged more thoroughly.

"Like that dick, huh, boy?" Jackson punctuated his question with a spank.

Cory was just about to answer when someone else's voice rang through the forest.

"Jackson!" it called from a distance, coming from the direction of the party.

"Jax, yo man, where you at?" A second voice joined the first.

Jackson froze in his tracks at the sound of his name, cock still halfway inside Cory's ass. Cory was frozen himself, worried that any movement might allow some sight of him from behind the tree. What was it with his luck and these woods?

"Shit," Jackson muttered, pulling himself from Cory's hole. "Those are two of my teammates."

"Jaaacksssooonnn!" the first voice sang out. "Come on, man. We know you're out here with some chick. Just come out."

"Fuck, fuck, fuck." Jackson tucked himself back into his jeans.

"What do we do?!" Cory whisper-yelled while standing stock still, afraid that any movement might put him on display. Getting caught was *not* part of the deal.

"It's fine. It's fine. I got this." Jackson seemed like he was talking more to himself than to Cory. "I need you to wait here."

Cory gave Jackson a questioning look but let him continue.

"I'm not out to my teammates yet. Please, it's just for a few minutes. I'll lead those guys away and then meet you back at the party," Jackson finished explaining. "If those dudes caught me out here with a guy, they would never let me live it down. Please?"

"Sure." Cory did his best to hide his annoyance. He guessed he couldn't really blame Jackson for wanting to hide him. Or be surprised by yet another dude more interested in covering his own ass. "I'll see you back at the party."

"Thanks, boy." Jackson gave Cory a smile. "Promise I'll make it up to you."

Cory nodded but said nothing, leaning back against the tree as Jackson walked around to intercept his teammates. He really hoped college wasn't like this. The flakey dude part, not the kinky outdoor sex part.

"Yoooo!" Jackson called to his teammates.

"There he is!" the first guy exclaimed. "Where's the girl?"

"What girl?" Jackson played dumb, but he wasn't *technically* lying.

"Whatever poor girl you talked into letting you fuck her out here," the second guy chimed in. "Just like you did at the last three parties."

"Heh, heh." Jackson chuckled nervously. "Come on, guys. Leave her alone. She's shy."

"Alright, alright." The first guy had a thoughtful look on his face for a moment before turning back to the woods to call out, "Just so you know, you can do better!"

Cory stifled a laugh as he carefully redressed himself. He had to agree. Now to kill some time. Cory sat down and pulled out his phone. He had a couple of games on there that didn't require a connection to play and only needed a few minutes anyway.

"Why were you guys looking for me anyway?" Jackson punched his teammate on the shoulder as they walked back toward the party site together.

"Oh, dude, the party's canceled," the first teammate explained. "There's a huge storm coming in."

"Shit, really?" Jackson was bummed that it would be an early night.

"Yeah, everyone's packing up now and heading back into town," teammate #2 added. "Didn't want you getting left behind because you were getting your dick wet."

"Heh, yeah. Thanks, man." Jackson looked behind him as he walked away from the tree hiding Cory. He'd make it back in a few minutes anyway, right?

"So, you just got on your knees and...?" Nic had barely taken a bite of his burger before Derek started telling him about his recent interactions with Carl.

"That was the idea, yeah," Derek responded nonchalantly.

"Isn't that gay?" Nic seemed slower than usual on the uptake.

"Really, dude?" Derek cocked his head.

"Fine, fine," Nic conceded Derek's unspoken point. "So, you're his boy now?"

"Not exactly," Derek reasoned. "I'm more like his apprentice."

"Intern." Nic snorted.

"The pay's about the same," Derek added. "I've been with him 'training' for over a month now. It seemed weird at first, but if I'm serious about some of this stuff then—" Derek was interrupted by the ringing of his phone. He picked it up to look at the screen. "It's Cory's mom."

Nic gave a questioning look but said nothing, putting down his half-eaten burger.

"Hello? Ms. Davis?" Derek answered the call.

"Derek, hi. How are you?" Cory's mom, Julia, responded.

"I'm fine. Is everything alright?" Cory's mom didn't have much reason to call him, especially not lately.

"I'm not sure." Julia sounded worried. "I know you three had a falling out, but have you seen Cory?"

"Not since school let out earlier today," Derek answered. "Is something wrong?"

"No, I'm sure he's fine. I just can't get a hold of him." If Derek could see how Julia was pacing in her home, he'd know she was lying. "He told me he was going to a party tonight in the woods. I thought you or Nic might be there too. They just announced a thunderstorm warning for the county, and I just wanted to make sure he got home safely."

"Sorry, Ms. Davis. Nic is here with me, but neither of us went to that party." Derek was getting a little worried himself now. "We haven't seen Cory."

"Okay." Derek could feel the concern through the phone. "Well, if you do see him, can you please tell him to call me ASAP?"

"Of course. We'll both keep our eyes open for him."

"Thank you, sweetie. Try and stay dry tonight!"

"You too." Derek hung up the phone.

"Cory's missing?" Nic didn't wait for Derek to tell him about the call.

"His mom can't get a hold of him." Derek put his phone back down on the table. "He's at the end of the year party in the woods. You know phones are shit out there. She said a storm is rolling in."

"Shit. Yeah dude. Look." Nic nodded to the windows behind Derek.

The sky was a dull gray, totally overcast, but that wasn't what Nic was referring to. Large amounts of cars began pulling into the parking lot, each packed to the brim with teenagers mad that their night of partying was about to be ruined by bad weather. Most of the kids from the woods had migrated here, determined to grab one last meal with their friends and salvage the night.

"Wow." Derek turned back around. "Well, Cory will probably show up here too."

"With Jackson." Nic sneered.

"Probably." Derek sighed. "But if we see him, we need to tell him to call his mom."

"I guess." Nic sat up. "So, what else is Carl making you do?"

Derek smiled. If talking about this would help his friend get more comfortable with himself, he was happy to share.

It was the crack of thunder that eventually pulled Cory's attention away from his phone. Fuck. He had completely lost track of how long he had been out here. It was starting to get dark, and that thunder meant it was going to rain soon. Time to get a move on. He stood up and dusted himself off. Stuffing his phone in his pocket, Cory headed in the direction of the party site. Or at least what he thought was the direction.

*This is the right way, isn't it?* There were no lights, no sounds or music. Nothing. Cory could feel his chest tighten as he started to realize the predicament he might be in. Shoving down the panic that was building in his stomach, Cory took off, speeding up his search for his former classmates. He'd be fine.

That was an hour ago. About half an hour ago, it started raining. At least Cory thought it was about a half hour ago. Because about fifteen minutes ago, it started raining so hard that his phone managed to short out inside his waterlogged jeans. *Fuck.* It was raining hard now, and the sky was turning so dark Cory could barely see five feet in front of him. He was totally, completely lost.

"Fuck, fuck, fuck." With the panic now finally overtaking him, Cory collapsed against a tree, crouching down near the trunk and hugging his knees. It was getting cold. The rain showed no sign of letting up. He could barely see, couldn't use his phone, and didn't even know where he was. He didn't know what to do. He wanted to go home. He wanted his mom. He wanted his friends.

It was maybe twenty minutes after Cory's mom called when the rain finally started pouring. The diner had filled quickly and was nearly packed, almost every seat filled. Derek and Nic half expected someone to ask to share their booth, but given the subject of what they were talking about, they were glad to have some privacy.

"You're focusing too much on the sub aspect of this, man." Derek was in the middle of explaining exactly why he wanted to train under Carl. "It's not even just about the learning. He knows people, has friends. He can introduce me to other subs, boys, girls. It's like networking but for kinky sex."

"That is kinda cool," Nic agreed. The two boys had finished eating and were more or less loitering in their booth as they nursed their sodas. Derek turned to ask what he thought was the waitress for the check when he instead saw Stephanie standing next to their booth.

"Hey, guys." Stephanie had just come in, her hair and shoulders still wet from the rain. "Have you seen Cory?"

"No. Did his mom call you too?" Derek instinctively reached for his phone, but he had no new notifications.

"I got a voicemail after I got out of the woods." Stephanie slid into the seat beside Nic. "I was out there looking for Cory, but when I didn't see him, I figured he must have already left. Guess not."

"Should we be worried?" Nic asked honestly.

"I dunno. But his mom definitely is." Stephanie recalled the voicemail and Julia's attempts at seeming calm. "He told me he was going with Jackson. Have you seen *him*?"

"No, but we figured that's who he was with." Derek indicated to Nic. "Guess that's a second person to keep an eye out for."

"Done. There he is." Nic nodded his head behind Derek, who turned to see Jackson walking in with some of his basketball teammates but with no sign of Cory. "Where's Cory?"

"I dunno." Derek slid out of the booth. "Let's find out."

Stephanie scooted out to let Nic pass and followed the two over to Jackson, who was greeting some other students already sitting down. She stood a few feet back when they reached him. She wanted to watch this but from a distance.

"Hey, Jackson." Derek tapped him on the shoulder. "We need to talk."

Jackson turned around and then seemed to size Derek up. "Do we?"

Derek rolled his eyes. He did *not* have time for a dick measuring contest right now. "Where's Cory?"

"Why would I know?" Jackson responded. "It's not like I'm his *owner* or something."

"What the fu—" Derek wasn't able to finish his thought because Nic pushed past him to grab Jackson by the collar and slam him into the diner wall.

"Listen up, you piece of shit. I figure I already owe you some trouble for talking to my buddy, *Steve*." Jackson's eyes widened as he realized what Nic meant. "Yeah. Found out about that. Now, because of what *you* did, Cory went out into the woods tonight, with you. So, I will ask you this once: *where the fuck is he?*" Nic growled the question through his gritted teeth, punctuating his sentence by pushing Jackson against the wall again.

Derek almost thought he would have to separate the two, but Jackson quickly spit out an answer at Nic's implied threat.

"He was in the woods," Jackson stammered. "We were out in the trees, I went back to the campsite without him, and then everyone was packing up. I figured he'd be behind me a few minutes later. That was the last I saw of him. I swear."

"So what? He's still out there?" Derek jumped in, ignoring all the people at nearby tables who were eavesdropping. Stephanie remained silent from her perch a few feet away, though she noticed that the boys were beginning to draw a crowd. A lot of eyes were watching this "conversation" unfold.

"I dunno. Maybe. He was supposed meet me back at the campsite, but I waited for him, and then everyone started to leave..." Jackson trailed off, knowing how the end of that sentence made him look.

"Are you fucking kidding me?" Nic slammed him into the wall again.

"Nic, stop." Derek put his hand on Nic's shoulder. "He doesn't know anything else."

Nic let go of Jackson's shoulders and fought the urge to punch the wall. Didn't need to hurt his hand *again*. Especially without Cory here to...

"We gotta go find him." Nic turned to Derek, determined.

"Yeah. Let's go." Derek wasn't going to argue.

"Wait!" Stephanie finally said something. "I... I feel like I'm supposed to say something here to be responsible and stop you ... but I'm really scared for my friend."

The three stood in a small circle near the front door, formulating their plan.

"Okay, the party was at the same place it always is, right?" Derek took the lead. "Nic and I will head out and start looking there." Derek turned to Jackson who was still standing sheepishly nearby. "Hey, asshat, do you remember where in the woods you were?"

"Uhhh..." Jackson looked lost. He wasn't exactly a boy scout.

"The river," Stephanie interjected. "If you were facing the party site, where was the river?"

"To our right," Jackson responded.

"Okay, so we'll start there and head north along the river. If we can find him, we can get to my family's cabin nearby and ride out the rest of the storm," Derek planned. "Dad made sure the trees on the hill were trimmed after the last hurricane almost took out the roof."

"Okay. *Please* be safe," Stephanie pleaded. "I'll stay here and call Cory's mom. Text me your parents' numbers too. You know they are probably going to kill all of us for this, right?"

Nic nodded in agreement, but he was still determined to get out there and find Cory.

"Don't worry about calling mine. Not sure they'd even answer," Derek added. He wasn't being *entirely* cynical.

"Okay." Yeah, Stephanie was still gonna get the number from Julia and call them. "Be safe, guys." She somewhat awkwardly hugged the both of them and then returned to the booth before someone else swooped in to steal it.

"Let's go, bro." Nic opened the front door, the loud sounds of the rain hitting the pavement thundering into the diner.

"Wait, hold on." Jackson stopped them before they left and tossed them his keys. "Here, take my Jeep. It'll handle the mud a lot better than your car."

"Thanks." Derek sounded skeptical as he caught the keys. "This doesn't at all make up for—"

"I know. Just, uh, go find your boy." Jackson stepped back, wishing more than anything to just disappear.

"We will." Derek and Nic left, getting soaked as they both ran to jump in Jackson's red Jeep.

"Hey, asshole," Stephanie called to Jackson from her booth, happy to see him respond to the nickname. "You're paying for their check, too." She held the receipt for the boy's meal—a meal they just left without paying for—above her head. "And mine."

Jackson gulped and nodded, already reaching for his wallet.

Derek and Nic drove the Jeep to the edge of Hartford State Park. The rain was coming down hard and the roads were dark and muddy. Derek gripped the steering wheel tighter as they crossed the threshold. He didn't care that what he was about to do was unbelievably stupid. They had to find Cory.

Nic felt the same, attempting to peer out the windows for any sign of the boy. Turning around in his seat, he dug through Jackson's stuff and was pleased to uncover a flashlight, the heavy-duty kind used for camping.

"I think we're here." Derek could just make out the burned-out campfire in the car's headlights. "I don't see him."

"That's because fucking Jackson left him in the woods." Nic double-checked to make sure the flashlight was working. "You said north, right?"

"Right." Derek nodded in the direction they needed to start looking.

"Okay. Let's go." Nic opened his door to what seemed like a wall of rain and stepped outside.

"Cory!" Derek joined him, calling out Cory's name as the two began their search.

"Cory? Cory!" Nic manned the flashlight, moving it back and forth between the trees, hopeful that Cory might catch a glint of it.

The two boys took turns shouting Cory's name, spreading out but making sure they always stayed within each other's eye line. Didn't need to lose anyone else out here tonight. It was about ten minutes into looking that the two began to worry that they hadn't thought their plan through entirely.

"Cory!" Derek cupped his hands and called out once again.

"What if we can't find him?" Nic was starting to feel hopeless. "What if he's not even out here?"

"We *will* find him." Derek wasn't about to let any pessimistic shit deter him. "I know he's out here, and he's probably terrified."

Nic said nothing, silently continuing to use the flashlight and hoping Derek was right. A few minutes later, and just as Derek was about to suggest they start looking in another direction, Nic spotted something.

"D! There!" Nic aimed the flashlight at the mass huddled at the base of a tree. It was Cory—wet, alone, and shivering but alive.

Derek and Nic both took off toward him with Derek nearly slipping on the mud and falling on his ass in his hurry.

"Cory? Cory!" Nic lifted his head to see the boy's eyes squinting blearily.

"Nic?" Cory wasn't entirely sure what was happening. He was still outside, and it was still raining, so how was Nic here?

"Oh my god, Cory! Thank fuck." Derek joined the two boys against the base of the tree.

"'S cold." Cory was still hugging his knees, clothes soaked as he shivered.

"Come on. We gotta get him out of the storm." Derek turned Cory's head to see how responsive he was. "Cory, can you walk?"

"Dude, I think he's out of it. Grab the flashlight. I got him." Nic held Cory by the shoulders. "Cor, I need you to hang on to me, okay?"

He attempted to move Cory's arms to his shoulders and was pleased when he felt the boy tighten them around his neck. Now came the fun part—getting him up. Nic felt Cory's legs go around his waist as he was lifted and tightened his own arms under the boy's butt. Thank god for football.

The boys were closer to the cabin than the car, so Derek led the way there with Cory still clinging tightly to Nic.

Fighting against the wind and rain, the boys managed to make it up the hill with Derek fumbling through his wet pants for his keys and opening the door. Nic quickly moved toward one of the couches, Derek closing the door behind them and flipping on a lamp. Thankfully, they still had power.

"Cory?" Nic sat Cory down and saw that he was unresponsive. "Cory?!"

"I think he's in shock." Derek walked over and checked his pulse and breathing. "We need to get him dry and warm."

The two boys worked together quickly in removing Cory's soaked clothing. Derek retrieved a towel from the cabin's closet and then went back for two more when he realized how wet he and Nic were too. Once everyone was naked and dry, the two worked to pull out the couch's bed, laying Cory in the center of it.

"No signal. Probably until the storm passes." Derek looked at his phone, lips pinched in a frown. "Cory's mom is probably pulling her hair out right now."

"At least we found him." Nic sat on the side of the bed, watching as Cory slept and rubbing a hand along his arm. "Fuck, D. He's so cold." Nic sounded scared.

Derek sat on the opposite end of the bed and also felt Cory's skin. Then wordlessly, he climbed on and spooned Cory from behind. "Come on. We can help keep him warm."

"Uhh..." Nic was skeptical. "I don't really know if now is the right time to—"

"I just meant for the body heat, dumbass." Derek rolled his eyes. "He's fucking unconscious. Just get in here."

Chastised, Nic climbed onto the bed and shuffled toward Cory's front. Throwing an arm over his waist—and Derek's—he watched the sleeping boy's face. Nic wasn't sure if peaceful was the right word—he was asleep so of course he was peaceful—but he looked... Well, Nic didn't know what he looked like. He was just happy to see him. He didn't argue when Derek reached down to pull the blanket over the three of them.

The three boys laid there, one asleep as the two who were still awake listened to the storm raging outside. Neither said anything, just laid together in silence, their shared boy between them. Eventually, the two dozed off themselves, soothed by the sounds of rain against the cabin's roof.

"Mmnnggh." Cory began to stir a few hours later, waking both Derek and Nic who were still attempting to hold onto him tightly. The two moved toward either edge of the bed, giving Cory some breathing room in the center.

"Cory?" Derek watched, impatient as Cory continued to wake. "Dude, are his eyes open?"

"Cor?" It was Nic's turn. He put his hand on Cory's shoulder. "Cory, you awake?"

"Mmfff." Cory rubbed the sleep from his eyes. "Nic?"

"Yeah." Nic smiled, happy to hear Cory say his name again.

"Cory?" Derek touched him on the shoulder this time, pulling it back when he caused Cory to jump in surprise. "Sorry."

"Derek?" Cory flipped onto his back so he could see both of them. "What happened? Where are we?" Cory started running through the events of the night.

"You were lost in the woods in the middle of a storm," Nic told him.

"We found you and brought you back to the cabin," Derek explained next.

"Sounds like the storm's still going too." As Nic finished, a sudden crack of thunder rang through the cabin to prove his point.

"What do you remember?" Derek asked, watching as Cory struggled to do just that.

Cory sat up silently as he continued to process what had transpired. He remembered getting to the party. He remembered going into the woods with Jackson. Then he was still in the woods, and it was raining and—

"Where's Jackson?" Cory asked.

"Probably home in his bed," Derek said flatly. "He... We can talk about that later."

"He left me out there," Cory finished Derek's original thought.

"I'm sorry, Cor." Derek tentatively reached out to touch Cory's shoulder again.

"For Jackson?" Cory looked at Derek.

"For everything." Derek squeezed Cory's shoulder.

"Why'd you guys come looking for me?" Cory looked down at his lap sadly.

"What?" Nic moved closer to Cory. "What do you mean? You were missing. We had to look for you."

"Yeah, Cor." Derek scooted a little closer as well. "There wasn't even a question. As soon as we knew you were out here, we left. Even if you weren't talking to us, hated us, it still feels like you're..."

"Ours," Nic finished for Derek, who somehow seemed extremely eloquent with a single word.

"Yeah. Ours," Derek concurred. "You've always been ours, Cory. I'm so sorry for taking advantage of that."

Nic bumped his shoulder against Cory's, silently adding his apology to Derek's. Cory looked up, unable to stop a small smile crossing his face. But sweet words wouldn't fix everything.

"I…" Cory wasn't sure what he wanted to say. "I don't—"

"It's okay." Derek stopped him. "There's a *lot* we need to talk about. To apologize for. But I think it can wait for the morning when we can get out of here. If that's okay with you?"

Cory nodded silently.

"Good." Derek smiled. "Then for now, let's just…" Derek figured an example was better than an explanation and slid back down to lay on the bed, pulling Cory to move with him.

"Wait a sec." Nic left the bed for a minute to turn off the lamp they had left on earlier, rejoining the boys on the bed on Cory's right side.

"Why are we naked?" Cory had just noted their group nudity at Nic's brief exit.

"Your clothes were soaked. We just wanted to get you warm and dry," Derek explained before moving closer and putting an arm across Cory's chest, which Nic mirrored from his side.

Cory felt a lot of things. Happy. Confused. Worried. Safe? He didn't know what this meant, what any of it meant. *Are things just going to go back to how they were before? Can they?*

Derek saw the turmoil of emotion cross Cory's face, turmoil that would undoubtedly prevent the boy from falling back asleep. What Cory needed was a distraction. So, he leaned in, turned Cory's head by his cheek, and kissed him.

Cory's eyes were wide as he was kissed for the second time by a "straight" friend. Kissed for the second time ever. He *seriously* needed to do more of this. He allowed Derek to kiss him, opening his mouth when he felt the swipe of a tongue against his lips. He was just about to close his eyes when a cough from Nic drew his attention. Tearing himself away from Derek, he turned to look at Nic questioningly.

"Um," Nic fumbled his words, and so he followed Derek's lead and kissed the boy as well.

"I—"

"In the morning," Nic shushed Cory before he started asking too many questions and kissed him again.

In the dark of the cabin, the three boys laid in bed together, holding each other closely, hands roaming, mouths on skin, but no one made an attempt to reach for themselves. No one was trying to get off, dominate, or fuck. They were just ... being together. For comfort. Maybe for love? The morning held a lot for them to deal with.

This was enough, for now.

Derek was the first to wake, the morning light creeping in through the cabin windows. The storm had passed, and it was time to deal with the aftermath. Opening his eyes, Derek's first view was Cory's face, Nic having spooned him as they slept, all three of their limbs thrown over each other and tangled together.

Derek smiled. He didn't wanna wake them up. But he needed to be responsible. So, very reluctantly, Derek untangled his limbs from the other's, rousing them in the process.

"Morning," Derek greeted, giving them one last squeeze with his arms before releasing them and pulling himself from the bed.

"Mmmmm. Morning." Cory rubbed his eyes as he leaned up on his elbow.

Nic only grumbled to himself, flipping onto his stomach and turning his head away, determined to get more sleep.

Derek chuckled at the scene as he walked to his phone on the counter. *Perfect!* He had a signal.

"Can we go to McDonalds for breakfast?" Cory asked as he sat up. "I'm starving."

Derek cocked his head at the boy who only hours ago was half-drowned after getting lost in the woods.

"We're going to the *hospital*." Derek tossed his phone onto the bed. "Call your mom. She'll want to meet us there."

Derek got the two boys up and moving as he searched through the cabin's closet for something dry to wear. Derek had enough spare clothing that fit himself and Nic, but Cory ended up in an oversized t-shirt and some plaid pajama pants. Cory didn't have a chance to argue because as soon as he got through to his mom, she spent the next fifteen minutes making sure he was okay and telling him how worried she was. Derek used this to his advantage and got the boys dressed and out the door quickly enough.

Finding Jackson's Jeep where they had left it, the boys piled in and Derek drove them to the emergency room at the nearest hospital, Hartford General, where Cory's mom was due to meet them. They got Cory checked in, despite his protests that he was fine, and waited in his hospital room for his mom to arrive. The doctors wanted to run a few tests to make sure, but overall, Cory seemed okay other than being exhausted and slightly traumatized.

"I hate these stupid gowns." Cory sat in the hospital bed, somehow feeling like he was wearing a dress *and* was naked at the same time.

"I dunno. I kinda like that they're open back," Nic teased from his seat next to the bed.

"You would." Cory laughed before looking at both Nic and Derek. "So... Can we talk a little before my mom gets here?"

"Yeah." Derek moved from his perch against the hospital wall. "Let me start. I'm sorry, again. For everything. For the way this started, for taking advantage of you, for treating you the way I did. I know this doesn't fix anything, and there's a lot more we need to talk through, but for all of it—everything. I'm sorry."

"Me too. I'm sorry for everything he just said, and... I'm sorry for pretending to not remember the night I showed up drunk at your place." Nic stared at his lap. "I'm still ... trying to figure some stuff out, about myself, but that... That was really, *really* shitty of me."

"It was. Thanks. There... There is a lot." Cory gave a small if not sad smile to the both of them. "I don't really know where to get started but ... I'm glad we're talking again."

"I think there's something you should know about Jackson, too," Nic interjected. "About that night and the party. He's responsible for the rumor about us."

"What? What did he have to do with that?" Cory wasn't seeing the connection.

"He was basically stalking us at the party. When he saw us sneaking off to the garage together, he told Steve where he could find us," Nic clarified. "He figured that if he could cause enough of a problem for us, it might split us up." Then, he added sadly, "He wasn't wrong."

"Seriously?" Cory was dejected. He had already stopped looking at Jackson through rose-tinted glasses, but finding out how duplicitous he really was still hurt. "I'm sorry."

"Don't be. None of this is on you," Derek stated. "He's a piece of shit who left you alone in the forest last night. Fuck everything about that dude."

"Guess you should let him know where his car is..." Nic trailed off, not wanting to deal with anything Jackson related.

"That was his car, wasn't it?" Cory hadn't thought about it earlier.

"It was literally the least he could do," Derek muttered.

"So..." Cory wanted to continue this talk while they could, knowing that when his mother arrived, he'd lose all privacy while she fretted. "What about us?"

"What about us?" Derek took a seat in the other empty chair in the room. "Do you want there to be an 'us'?"

"I don't know," Cory responded. "If there was an 'us,' would we be an actual 'us'?"

"Could you guys speak English, maybe?" Nic interrupted. "Or even Spanish."

"I don't speak for Nic, Cory, but I'd still very much like for there to be ... something between us." Derek looked at Nic and then back at Cory. "For however much longer we have together this summer. Whether that's as your dom or maybe something more would be up to you. Whatever it was, it would be real. Official. However you wanna put it."

"And you?" Cory turned to Nic. He couldn't deny that at the very least, he liked being on this end of things for once.

"I..." Nic looked for the words, not nearly as great at speaking as Derek, worried he'd sound dumb. "I ... like you. I like what we have. Had. I don't... I'm still figuring stuff out, but I want to do more of that. With you. The right way."

Cory sat silently as he took in their words. It was exactly what he wanted. But did they mean it?

"There's a lot that went wrong before. A *lot*. I can't promise I won't get mad or upset when we talk through some of it. And like we keep saying, there's a lot to talk through. But ... I missed you guys. I still want to do *this* with you both." He turned to Nic. "I like you too."

Nic blushed, and Derek coughed for attention.

"Yes, I like *you* too," Cory added, before taunting, "So, you guys really missed me, huh?"

"Derek missed you so much he got himself a daddy to train him," Nic informed him with a grin.

"Dude!" Derek squawked from his seat.

"What?! Who?! Carl?!" Cory immediately pressed for answers.

Answers that sadly would have to wait, as just then, his mom burst into the room. Followed by Stephanie. Followed by Nic's parents and sisters. Derek half expected the football team to show up too. As Cory's mother rushed toward him, Cory gave Derek a look, ensuring that he would get all the details about this daddy from him later.

For now, Cory was just happy to be *theirs* again.

# CHAPTER 16

"I'm just so happy you're okay!"

"Me too, Mom."

"You are so lucky they found you out there when they did." Julia squeezed her son's hand. "How did you even get lost in the forest!?"

"I don't know, Mom. I just … got separated from everyone." Cory sighed. "I'm sorry."

Julia said nothing but bent over to kiss her son's forehead again before her attention was pulled to a nurse who had just walked in the room. She quickly stepped over and began to pepper the nurse with questions as they attempted to write something on the room's whiteboard.

"Believe it or not, she's actually calmer than she was when I was on the phone with her last night," Stephanie commented from her side of Cory's bed. "She was pretty much ready to have the army called in to go look for you."

"The forest would probably be blanketed with search parties if I hadn't called her this morning," Cory noted.

"Yeah." Stephanie slapped Cory on the arm. "Don't be such a fucking idiot next time."

"Oww." Cory rubbed his arm. "It's not like I did it on purpose."

"I know. I'm glad you're okay." She squeezed his hand. "So, other than being in the hospital, you look good. Happy, even. Something happen?" Stephanie pointedly looked between Derek and Nic sitting in opposite corners of the far side of the room.

"We talked. Worked through a few things." Cory smiled as he watched the two boys, each dealing with his own parents, one in person and one on the phone. "But we still have a ways to go before..." Cory trailed off as his mother walked back over to rejoin them, bringing the nurse with her. He gave Stephanie a look—they'd talk later, too.

As Julia oversaw the nurse examining her son, Nic was attempting to do damage control with his own very upset parents. His sisters stood off to the side together, eagerly awaiting the verbal tongue-lashing their elder brother was about to receive.

"What the hell were you thinking?" Raphael interrogated his son.

"Driving during the middle of a storm *in the dark*?" Luciana added. "*¿Eres estúpido?*"

"Cory needed help!" Nic defended. "I couldn't just leave him out there."

"You could have been killed!" Raphael fought the urge to raise his voice in the hospital room.

"Dad, if you knew one of *your* best friends was in trouble, would you just sit around doing nothing?" Nic wasn't going to feel bad about what he did.

"I would... I would..." Raphael sighed. "I'm just glad you're safe, mijo."

"Don't you *ever* do something like that again." Luciana pulled her son in for another hug.

"I won't, Mom." Nic smiled and hugged his mom before feeling his father join in from the side. "I promise."

"*What!?*" Daniela squawked, incredulous at the group hug taking place before her. "That's *it*? He's not even going to get yelled or anything!?"

"Daniela, can't you just be happy that your brother is okay?" Raphael sighed as he turned to his eldest daughter.

"We would have been grounded for a month if we did something like this!" Gabriella joined her sister in voicing her feelings about her brother getting away with what seemed like murder.

"Then I guess you better never do something like this, eh, chica?" Luciana joined her husband as the Herrera family began to argue in their corner of the room.

Nic sighed. He loved his family. Right? He looked over to see Cory's mom fussing over him and then turned to see what Derek was doing without his own parents in the room to suffocate him.

Derek wished he could say he was that lucky, but no, he was *also* dealing with his parents—just via phone call.

"How did you get lost in the woods?" Derek's mother's voice came across the line. Linda sounded far from pleased.

"No, Mom, I wasn't lost. Cory was," Derek tried explaining. "I went out to find him."

"Well, how did Cory end up lost in the woods?" Robert, Derek's father, had questions of his own. "How'd you get separated?"

"I wasn't out there with him, Dad." Derek sighed.

"Why was he alone?" Robert was used to the three boys being together.

"He wasn't alone. There was a party." Derek tried to disguise the frustration in his voice. What little information his parents gathered had all came secondhand. "I just decided not to go. Then the storm came in, and it was canceled, but Cory was still out there."

"And you took off on your own like that?" Linda chimed in. "Derek, that's so dangerous! You could have been hurt."

"I was fine, Mom," Derek half-lied. "I had Nic with me. Once we found Cory, we rode out the rest of the storm out in the cabin."

"Is the cabin okay? What about your car?" Dad questioned.

"I didn't use my own car, and the cabin's fine, Dad." Derek was starting to get whiplash being bounced between his two parents.

"I'm just glad you boys are all okay." Linda steered the conversation back to what mattered. "I don't ever want you running off like that again without telling me first."

"How was I supposed to tell you, Mom?" Derek was done hiding his annoyance. "You haven't been home in months."

"I…" Linda didn't have a response to that. "I'm sorry, Derek. Actually … your father and I are coming home a little early now, next week."

"You are?" Derek was dumbfounded. He hadn't even bothered keeping track of when they were supposed to be home.

"Yes. We've been gone longer than usual, son." Robert confirmed their plans. "Hopefully when we get home, we can talk and catch up on everything."

Derek was silent for a moment, completely caught off guard. "Yeah, Dad. Sure."

"We love you, sweetie," Linda told her son.

"Love you, too." Derek looked around the room as he spoke, watching his other two friends engrossed with their own families. Last night had led to a lot of things changing. Hopefully for the better.

It was a few hours before Cory would be released, and Julia insisted that Derek come over and spend the night at their place, not wanting him alone after everything. Derek accepted, hiding his reluctance due to not knowing how Cory felt about it, though Cory himself made no objection.

Nic went home with his parents, and Derek, after getting Jackson's number from Stephanie, texted him to let him know he was driving his Jeep back to the diner. He left the doors unlocked, tossing the keys in the glovebox when he swapped over to his own car, smirking as he imagined Jackson's stress over his car's security. He then drove to his house, changed, packed for the night, and headed to Cory's.

Things felt much weirder than it had any other time Derek had been over. After eating an oversized lunch Julia had prepared for them, the two boys went up to Cory's room alone. After a few minutes of awkward silence, both boys attempted to break the ice at the same time.

"So do you want to—"

"I think we should—"

After both stopped, Derek motioned for Cory to continue, letting him take the lead on things here.

"I know we still have a lot of things to talk about," Cory started to explain his plan for the evening. "But we need Nic here for that. He probably won't be able to come over here until tomorrow, so for tonight do you think we could … press pause on all of that stuff and just hang out? Like we used to?"

"Yeah." Derek smiled at Cory. He could do that. "Smash Bros.?"

The two spent the rest of the evening together, playing video games and watching TV, any thoughts of sex or romance buried under the mountain of pizza the two eventually ordered. Things didn't get weird again until it was time for bed. The boys had shared a bed hundreds of times in the past—hell, they cuddled in one last night—but for some reason, Derek felt like he should be sleeping on the floor. Cory had to physically pull him onto the bed, assuring him that it was fine. Before the two slept, a few texts back and forth with Nic confirmed that he'd be coming over the following day to talk.

The two boys woke late in the morning, eventually plied out of bed with the promise of breakfast, once again far larger than it needed to be. Cory and Derek then headed back to his room to kill time until Nic got there.

Just before noon, a knock on the front door signaled his arrival.

"Hey, Ms. Davis," Nic greeted Cory's mother when she opened the door.

"Nic! Good to see you, sweetie." Julia gave him a hug after letting him in. "The boys should be in Cory's room. I'm actually about to run out to the grocery store, so I'll see you when I get back."

"Thanks!" Nic headed down the hall to Cory's room, finding the door open and Cory and Derek sitting on the bed waiting for him. "Hey, guys."

"Hey." Derek smiled.

"Hey. Mind closing the door?" Cory asked. "In case Mom comes back."

Nic closed the door before sitting in Cory's empty desk chair. Once again, an awkward silence filled the room, no one quite sure how to proceed, but all of them knowing they needed to.

"So, we need to talk about stuff, right?" Nic had had enough of these difficult conversations lately and decided to bite the bullet.

"Yeah," Cory concurred. "I need... I think I need to say some stuff. Just get it out of me." He took a deep breath. "Sometimes it feels like I have all this anger and frustration that just keeps building up right—" Cory raised his hand to his chest. "Here. So let me just say everything I need to say first."

Derek turned his body to fully face Cory as both he and Nic waited for him to continue.

"A few months ago, when we all..." Cory started a thought but changed his mind. "No, when *you* both made things end the way they did. That... That fucking *sucked*. Both of you sucked.

"Derek." Cory turned toward Derek on the bed to his left. "When I tried talking to you in the car about things that we *needed* to talk about, you blew up on me. You didn't just yell at me. You kicked me out of your car." Cory hugged his knees. "I still remember what it felt like being left on that curb.

"It wasn't even you blowing up that was the problem. That wasn't great, but we've yelled at each other before. But you were mad at me for just *trying to talk to you*. It was like I had the sudden realization that I *couldn't* talk to you anymore at all. Not like my best friend, not like we used to. I felt so ... alone. Abandoned.

"Then came Nic." Cory turned to his right toward Nic's chair. "That night, the night you... The night before everything happened, when you came over. I know you were drunk, so I don't know how much you actually remember, but that night was..." Cory searched for the right word. "I don't know. Special? It felt different. What you were doing. I mean, fuck, you—" Cory cut himself off for a second to glance at Derek, caring for only a moment if any of this was new info for him before continuing. "You kissed me. A lot. We spent almost the entire night together fucking and making out and cuddling. It felt like a lot more than just sex.

"And then you were just … gone. No message, no note… The bed was cold. And when I saw you at school, you pretended like you forgot the whole thing. You looked me in the eye and told me that everything from the night before was a blank." Cory paused and sniffled, starting to lose the fight to keep his emotions in check. "You were still wearing the bandage *I* put on your hand. Your excuse didn't even make sense. How did you even get home?" Cory gave a sad chuckle. "Even after all the kinky shit we've done together, I don't think I've ever felt so used. It wasn't just sex. You took advantage of how I f-felt about you." Cory sniffled again, a tear escaping.

"Cor, I'm sor—" Nic wanted to comfort the boy but was stopped when Cory put his hand up, composing himself before continuing.

"You guys were my best friends. You were more than that. You were practically my entire world at that point. It was like you both spent all that time making sure I'd feel close to you and then did everything you could to push me as far away as possible. I didn't know what to do with myself."

Cory took a deep breath before raising his gaze to Nic's, letting him know it was okay to talk.

"Cory, I'm sorry," Nic finished his earlier apology. "For … using you the way I did. For lying about it the next day. For pretending like I didn't care about any of it. It *did* mean something to me, but I—" Nic was struggling to say the words. "I was really, really angry that day, and I used that as an excuse to get really, really drunk, and I think, maybe

... I used *that* as an excuse to do things I really wanted to do. That I was too afraid to have done otherwise.

"That's not an excuse. Everything I did still sucks, but there's something..." Nic stared at his lap, sounding lost. "Everything in my life used to make sense. Then after that night at the cabin... No, after that night with your laptop, it all changed. And ever since, things keep happening, and it... It feels like I don't know who I am anymore.

"But like I said, that's not an excuse." Nic looked up, his own eyes watering slightly. "I-I'm sorry, Cor. I'm so sorry."

"Thank you." Cory stood and hugged him. "No matter what happens, you're still Nic."

"And if we have to, we'll figure out who you are now together," Derek offered from the bed, not wanting to intrude on their moment. But now it was his turn.

"I'm sorry too, Cory," Derek began as Cory returned to his spot on the bed.

"I never meant to make you feel the way you did. I knew I was hurting you. I could see it in your eyes when I kicked you out of the car... I scared you. I never want to make you feel like that. I want you to always be able to talk to me, especially if we're..." Derek still wasn't sure what to label any of this and didn't want to push for anything now either. "I used to look out for you, protect you, even before any of this.

"I'm realizing I might have more flaws than I can admit. That maybe I'm a little cockier than I deserve to be, that I can act like a know-it-all, that I jump into things without thinking them all the way through. And then when those things go badly, I avoid taking responsibility. And because of all of that, I screwed things up with us. With all three of us. Bad. I'm sorry to you too, Nic. You wouldn't even be in this situation if it wasn't for me."

"It's okay, D." Nic was surprised that he was receiving an apology at all. "I think even if this hadn't happened now, these things would have come out for me eventually."

"I fucked up. And I know I can't take back what happened, and I'm not asking you to do anything about it now, but I hope you can forgive me and trust me again one day, Cor. I'm sorry for everything," Derek finished his apology.

"We'll get there." Cory scooted over a little and squeezed Derek's hand for a second. "But that does lead to the next thing I need to talk about.

"Throughout this whole… Throughout everything that's happened, there's always been this … weird feeling hanging over things. This anxiety. A weight that I can't shake off. It's like this nagging feeling that I still needed to keep my guard up, that I still wasn't sure what might come next. Ever since that first night when you guys…

"When you guys got me drunk so you could fuck me." Cory laid everything out on the table. However ugly it may sound, he needed to say it. "You found out I was gay and then made a plan so you could use me to get your dicks sucked. You basically date-raped me. I never… I never let myself think about it too much. There was enough going on to distract me. But fuck, guys. You completely violated my trust and used me. I'm your *best friend*. You risked our entire relationship. You took advantage of me in the worst way because you were horny.

"And it didn't stop there. Things kept happening. You started doing things to me in public. You 'loaned' me out to guys I had never met before—someone *you* hadn't even met before—without even talking to me. You guys never talked to me about any of it. I didn't know what we were. I didn't know how or even if I *could* say no. Just like that first night, I never let myself think about it too much.

"But I... I *liked* it. I *still* like it when I think about it. Even though there's some part of me that feels anger, or shame, there's another part of me that wanted all of it. Those other feelings made sense, but part of me... Part of me loved it." Cory took a deep breath. "I loved that you never gave me a choice, that you were taking advantage of me, using me. Even how you planned for the first night in the cabin. And it's confusing and feels like there's something wrong with me because why would I want *more* of that kind of treatment? It's not normal. Right?"

Derek moved closer and put his arm around Cory's back, and Nic squeezed himself onto the bed on Cory's other side.

"I understand how you feel. The ... shame, mixed with liking it," Nic said softly. "I know it's not exactly the same but I don't think any of us expected half of this stuff."

"I don't think there's anything wrong with you." Derek squeezed Cory's side. "I mean... I liked all of the same things. I got off seeing Taylor fuck you. Using you in the school bathrooms. Even seeing you tipsy that first night." Derek went quiet. "Actually, maybe there is something wrong with me."

"I guess that's all three of us, then." Nic started running through things in his head. "Making you blow me in the woods. Fuck, I got off showing off to Taylor and Julian in the garage. Even when D was the one who sent you back to Carl when we visited the sex shop, I got like a half-chub."

"When you made me wear the vibrating plug at the football party. Or that time you guys put me in a cock cage for over a week," Cory added in a few memories, subconsciously switching from accusing to reminiscing.

Now that the tears had been shed and difficult words spoken, the air in the room was starting to shift. Without thinking, Cory reached down to adjust his growing erection. His movement did not go unnoticed, and Nic reached down to grab his own half-hard cock, making sure his movements were obvious to the other two.

"It would... It would probably be pretty messed up to get off on all of this right now, wouldn't it?" Derek posed the frivolous query, the visible tent of his own erection answering an entirely different question.

"Yes, but counterpoint," Cory offered. "We are three teenagers who are pretty much constantly horny."

"I just don't want to—" Derek was cut off by Cory's lips, which were currently on his own. Near death experiences could do wonders for self-confidence, apparently.

"I just want to take a break from talking. For now," Cory explained as he pulled back. Everything was starting to feel overwhelming, and he needed a distraction. "Please?"

Derek looked to Nic, who gave a nod.

"Okay."

The three boys moved on the bed, mimicking their positions from two nights ago with Cory lying between Derek and Nic. In the light of day, after the last night they all spent together, after everything they had just talked about, this felt so different now. New.

On his side, Nic leaned over Cory on his back, tentatively planting a kiss on his lips. Cory returned the kiss, opening his mouth once he felt Nic's tongue. He moaned softly into Nic's mouth as he felt the tongue gently swiping over his own. Cory moved his mouth in tandem with Nic, following his lead as Nic walked him through what was essentially only his third lesson in kissing.

When the two came up for air for a second, Derek moved in for his turn, putting a hand on Cory's cheek to shift his head to face him. Cory moaned again as he was kissed for the second time today, reveling in the attention being paid to him. He opened his mouth instinctively for Derek's tongue, and happily made out with his other ... boyfriend? They'd figure that out later.

Cory laughed into Derek's mouth when he felt Nic's hand tapping on his chest, impatiently waiting for his turn. He released Derek's mouth and swapped back over, Nic sparing no time in deepening the kiss. The two boys traded Cory's mouth back and forth, each kiss hungrier and more urgent than the last. Laying between them, Cory basked in the attention as he was manhandled.

After a few minutes and a half dozen kisses, a horny Nic gripped Cory by the chin, nearly tearing him away from Derek's mouth as he dove in for his turn. He unconsciously growled into Cory's mouth, his hand moving from Cory's chin to his neck before he realized what he was doing. Cory felt the hand gently grabbing his neck, not tight enough to do anything, and moaned again into Nic's mouth. This caused Nic to grasp what he was ... grasping.

He pulled back but did not move his hand, searching Cory's face to see how he felt. Cory, realizing that neither of these two would feel very comfortable taking the lead right now, reached his hand up and grasped Nic's wrist, squeezing and pulling it toward his neck. He wanted this.

That was all the go-ahead Nic needed, who tightened his hand slightly around Cory's throat and bent down to resume kissing. After that, both doms grew bolder in their actions, holding Cory by the hair or biting and sucking at his neck, shoulder, and ears while the other was kissing him. Cory could only groan and shudder as the boys discovered all of the sensitive spots on his body they would now be certain to capitalize on.

All the kissing was doing was getting everyone even more worked up. Derek was the first to ditch his clothing, tearing his shirt off and tossing it to the floor, feeling too warm. Nic and Cory soon followed suit, followed by all three of them losing their shorts. They were just getting in the way.

Cory reached down and took a hold of both boys' hard cocks, each already starting to leak precum. His own erection went untouched, but Cory was alright with that. He briefly thought about the cock cage and gave each cock in his hand a gentle squeeze before releasing them. As Derek and Nic continued to kiss him, he could feel each of their shafts grinding against his thighs and leaving a sticky trail in their wake.

Not used to being the one to initiate, but knowing someone had to move things along, Cory very reluctantly tore himself away from both of their hungry mouths, moving down the bed and flipping onto his stomach. Settling between Derek's legs first, he nuzzled his face against the base of Derek's cock and breathed deeply. Fuck, he missed that scent. Once Cory had had his fill, Cory left a trail of wet, sloppy kisses up the shaft of Derek's dick, enveloping the leaking head between his lips once he reached the tip.

Derek moaned as his cock was swallowed for the first time in three weeks. He moved his hand to Cory's hair, gently gripping it as he felt Cory sink down his shaft. Cory slowly bobbed up and down, reaching over with his free hand to stroke Nic's now no-longer-ignored erection. Cory used his free hand to slowly stroke Derek's heavy sack, feeling the weight of his full nuts between his fingers.

As Cory worked his shaft, Derek looked over to Nic, who looked back. This was nice. He'd missed this. Smiling, Derek threw his arm over Nic's shoulder, pulling him closer, enjoying having the chance to bond with his bro like this again. Nic chuckled and watched as Derek got his dick swallowed, patiently waiting his turn.

After Derek's meat was sufficiently moist, Cory switched over to Nic, settling between his thick, hairy thighs. Cory wasted no time in repeating what he'd done with Derek, nuzzling into the crook of Nic's thigh and nutsack, savoring the intoxicating musk he had missed so much. Unwilling to leave the source of this scent, Cory took his time working each of Nic's balls with his lips, sucking each one into his mouth and bathing them with his tongue.

And so Cory was once again swapped back and forth between Derek and Nic, each of them taking turns plundering his very willing mouth. Just as with the kissing, the boys became bolder as time went on, gripping his hair like a handle, controlling the movements of his mouth, or just outright fucking his face. Cory happily gave up his mouth, grinding his own cock into the bed beneath him.

"Are you okay to get fucked?" Nic posed the question as Cory began to work Derek's length with his mouth once more.

Pausing, Cory thought about it for a moment before nodding his agreement. Nic smiled and rolled off the bed, reaching into Cory's nightstand for his lube. Cory shifted onto his knees with Derek following suit so that Nic had enough room to move in behind Cory.

On his knees and elbows, Cory worked Derek's cock as he felt Nic's weight shift the bed behind him. He felt Nic's hand squeeze his ass before spanking it lightly. Cory moaned and arched his back, spreading his thighs wider and showing off his hole. He deep throated Derek's cock as he heard the snap of the lube cap being opened and moaned again when he felt Nic's slick fingers moving across his hole.

Nic slowly pumped his finger in and out of Cory's hole, watching the way the rim clung to it. He felt Cory shudder as he moved across his prostate, and he repeated the action steadily, feeling the tight hole twitch each time. As Nic added a second finger, Cory tried to focus on the task before him instead of behind him, but soon he was pressing back onto Nic's hand as he worked his hole open. Derek picked up the slack, holding Cory's head in place as he fucked his cock in and out of Cory's mouth.

Cory eyes were closed as he was being penetrated at both ends. He felt each pass of Nic's fingers, the way Derek's dick was stretching his lips and throat, the smell and taste of Derek's cock, the sounds of Nic's fingers pumping in and out of his ass. Cory was in heaven. But he needed more and whined around Derek's cock.

Feeling that his hole was open enough, Nic ran his slippery hand over the thick slab of his meat, smacking it against Cory's ass a few times before running the head up and down his crack. He could feel Cory pushing back, feel the fluttering of his hole as he pushed to get the head of Nic's cock inside of him.

Nic grinned and kept up his teasing a little longer before taking pity on poor, worked-up Cory and pushing forward.

Cory whimpered as his hole was breached. It had been some time since he'd taken someone of Nic's girth. Nic went slowly, letting each inch of his cock be slowly swallowed by Cory's ass, pausing occasionally when he felt Cory tighten up. Soon enough, Cory felt the scratch of Nic's hairy lower half against his ass and thighs and knew he had taken it all. Arching his back farther, Cory settled into his position, letting Derek and Nic have at it.

Nic wasted no time in starting to pump his length in and out of Cory's hole. Looking down, he was once again mesmerized by the tight hole as it was stretched and pulled along his cock. He settled into a steady rhythm, firmly driving about half his length in and out of Cory. Cory continued to whimper and moan as the thick cock scraped over his prostate over and over, making him see stars.

Derek also looked down, watching the euphoric, almost bewildered gaze on Cory's face as he was fucked silly. Holding Cory by the back of his head, Derek fed his own dick in and out of Cory's oral cavity, eventually matching with Nic's rhythm so there was never less than a foot of dick in Cory at any given moment. Both boys, upon realizing they were in sync, met each other's gaze.

Both boys were sweating as they plunged their pricks in and out of the boy between them, something they had almost become experts at over the past year or so. Derek smiled. He was happy. Nic was too. The air in the room started to thicken as they locked eyes, slowly being drawn closer together, bending over Cory's prone form. This... This was something that was missing, and they hadn't even realized it.

If asked, either boy would probably say they kissed the other first, but it didn't really matter. As soon as their mouths met, it was like this was something they had been doing for years. There was no slowness, no sweet pecks between them, no gentle guidance like they gave Cory. Just two hungry mouths fighting for dominance. And fight they did, growling into each other and biting at lips and tongues.

Cory's eyes shot open as he heard the sound of lips smacking above him. The only thing he could see, however, was Derek's hairy crotch as it drove his dick in and out of Cory's mouth. *Fuck! Are they kissing?!* Cory wanted to watch, dammit! Not wanting to risk killing the moment, Cory could only close his eyes and try to imagine the scene above him. They were gonna have to do a repeat show for him later or something.

The three boys moved their bodies in tandem as if this were a dance they had practiced countless times. And they had, in some ways. As Derek and Nic kissed, they each held the other steady with an arm on the other's shoulders. Their other hands were each on Cory, one behind his head and one on his hip, holding him in place as they continued to pillage his orifices. Cory's own cock was half-hard, smacking up onto his stomach as his hips were pumped forward by Nic's thrusts. He could feel the familiar signs of an orgasm building behind his balls as his hole was continuously plundered.

Cory came suddenly, his hole spasming and pushing against Nic's cock as it wracked his body. As he felt Cory lose control around his dick, Nic pounded his hips forward furiously, the knowledge that he fucked Cory until he came on his dick driving him to his own. He sank his dick to the hilt as he felt the first blast of cum shoot from his cock, pulling back and driving forward again for the second shot. And watching Nic fuck Cory through his orgasm, prolonging it and drawing out an almost continuous moan from Cory was enough to send Derek over the edge as well, forcing his cock to the back of Cory's throat for the first volley of his load, pulling back and shooting the rest into his mouth.

Carefully extracting themselves and then collapsing together in the center of the bed, the three lay together in the warmth of the room. They were each covered in a thin sheen of sweat, panting as they caught their breaths. The air in the room was still heavy. Cory would need to crack the window before his mom got home.

"That was..." Derek exhaled. "That was awesome."

"Yeah," Nic responded, Cory humming his agreement.

"So, what now?" Derek sat up, looking at Cory for guidance.

"I can't promise I won't want to talk about this stuff again. And there's still stuff that confuses all three of us," Cory explained. "But we talked about a lot, and at least right now, I'm feeling pretty good about things?"

Hearing Cory say this, Derek and Nic turned and smiled at each other.

"But I think I need to talk to Jackson now."

"*What?*"

"What!" Both boys nearly shouted in unison.

"Why do you need to talk to that asshole?" Nic let the disdain he felt bleed into his voice.

"I dunno. Closure?" Cory reasoned. "It just feels weird leaving things how they are. I want to know why … why he did any of this."

The room was silent for a moment.

"Okay." Nic sputtered a protest, but Derek held his hand up. "In a public place. Where Nic and I can watch you both."

Cory thought for a moment about protesting those conditions—he had just gotten done standing up for himself. But it didn't seem like too much to ask. Jackson had hurt the two of them too, and if he was being honest, he liked the feeling of protectiveness that hearing Derek talk like that brought out.

"Okay."

Cory texted Jackson after that. When he didn't get a response, Nic sent one of his own that was a lot less … polite than Cory's. That got a response pretty quickly. Cory set up the plans—in about half an hour, they would meet up at Joe's to talk. Cory was pretty much ready to go right then, but Derek took his time because in his words, "That asshole can sit there and wait on us for a minute." Cory rolled his eyes at the obvious power play but said nothing, happy to have a ride and their support anyways.

Derek pulled into the parking lot at Joe's forty minutes later, and the boys walked in. Jackson was sitting at a booth, looking nervous as hell with a lone glass of water sitting in front of him. Cory led the group over toward his table, sliding into a seat when he was close enough. Jackson's head shot up, but he said nothing as he looked between the three boys.

"Alright, we'll be right over there, Cory." Derek pointed toward the diner's bar and started to walk over before noticing that Nic wasn't behind him, too busy giving Jackson a death stare. With a tug on his shoulder, Nic followed Derek and grabbed a stool.

"So... Hi," Cory started.

"Hi." Jackson didn't—maybe couldn't—look up from his glass on the table in front of him.

After waiting a minute to see if Jackson was going to volunteer anything, Cory said fuck it and barreled forward with what he needed to say. "So that was pretty fucked up."

"Cory... I'm so sorry. I seriously didn't expect to leave you out there like that last night. I thou—"

"I'm not just talking about last night," Cory cut him off. "I'm talking about the way you played Derek, Nic, and I against each other. Did you..." Cory tried to hide the hurt in his voice. "Did you ever even really like me at all?"

"I... Yes, Cory. I did. Do." Jackson finally met Cory's gaze. "I know you probably won't believe me, but I've actually liked you for a while."

Cory was confused but said nothing, letting Jackson continue.

"I think it was at a football game last year. Saw you hanging out with Derek. Thought you were cute." Jackson was back to staring at his still-untouched glass of water. "Didn't think much else of it until this year when I saw the three of you together again. Something seemed different. It wasn't hard to figure out what was going on."

"So, what? You were … jealous?" Cory hoped Jackson didn't expect him to feel flattered.

"No, not jealous but… I dunno. I was horny, and when I pieced together the kind of stuff you guys were doing, I wanted some too." Jackson paused then looked up at Cory. "I didn't think it would actually work, the things I was saying to cause friction."

"Well, it did." Cory turned to look at Derek and Nic, who were watching them intently. Nic was still glaring at Jackson like an over protective guard dog. "Pretty spectacularly. You basically outed me *and* Nic."

"I'm sorry," Jackson said softly.

"Been hearing that a lot lately." Cory sighed. "What's really fucked up is, I think if you had just *talked* to us? We probably would have ended up hooking up anyways, and I probably would have remembered it fondly instead of…" Cory gestured vaguely between the two of them.

"I… I'm just really sorry, Cory." Jackson didn't know what else *to* say. "I get if you don't wanna talk to me anymore after this."

"Not like I have to worry about seeing you in school much longer." Cory had gotten the answers he needed. They were done here. He slid out of the booth. "See you at the reunion or whatever."

"Yeah, see ya," Jackson said a sad goodbye to Cory's back as he made his way toward the bar and his two … men.

"Everything alright?" Derek asked as Cory approached.

"I think I got all I'm going to get out of that." Cory nodded his head.

"Ready to go home?" Nic slid off his stool.

"Yeah." Cory smiled. "Let's go home."

# CHAPTER 17

"I dunno about this, man."

"What's the problem?"

"It just feels weird."

"Well, too bad because it's too late to turn around now. We're almost there."

Derek and Nic went back and forth in the front seat of the car currently en route for a day trip to Lakefield. Cory sat in his usual spot in the back, the boys having regrouped after their afternoon chat (and sex) the day before. After they got back from Cory's meeting with Jackson, they were at something of a loss as for what to do next. They were working toward rebuilding the trust between them again, but this was Cory's first ... *anything* involving another person, let alone two, and Derek or Nic certainly didn't have relationship experience that came close to what they were dealing with now.

So, Derek suggested they do the same thing he'd done the last few times he felt lost like this: talk to Carl—or Sir as Derek was expected to call him now. Carl had also told him he could go with Daddy, but Derek wasn't quite there yet.

Cory was onboard with the idea right away, but Nic bristled, remembering Derek's description of what he did on his last visit. It took a little convincing, but eventually he agreed after reassurances that it was *just* to talk.

Derek sent a few texts, and Carl said that he was happy to talk to the trio—and that they were a trio again at all, so they met up again the next day at Cory's before hitting the road. With school almost over, none of the boys had any other obligations or much else to do at all. Nic was expecting this to be a fairly quick visit, but Derek was glad that the rest of the day was open, just in case.

Carl was out on the porch when the boys arrived. He stood as they pulled up, waving them over as they clambered out of the car. Cory and Derek walked right over, but Nic seemed to be dragging his feet.

"Boys, good to see you. Glad you got here safe." Carl moved to open his front door and lead the way inside. "Heard things have been kinda crazy for you all lately."

"Something like that, Sir," Derek answered for the group. "Thanks for agreeing to talk to us."

"Of course, boy. That's what I'm here for." Carl smiled before showing the boys to his living room, taking a seat in a large armchair while the three boys settled in on the couch. "So, catch me up."

Derek ran through a somewhat condensed version of the last few days with Cory adding the occasional detail: Cory's night in the woods, Derek and Nic running off to find him, the night in the cabin, the hospital, and finally their talks yesterday—which led Derek to what they were here to talk about today.

"So, we're okay, or at least getting there," he told his new dom. "And we wanna try doing this thing again—the right way."

"There are also a few things that are still confusing me a little. Like, with some of the things we did..." Cory trailed off, getting embarrassed. "The times when I wouldn't really get a say in what was happening, or it was a little *forced*, I ... liked it? How do we... Is that even normal? To want something like that?"

"That's perfectly normal, boy. Common even," Carl assuaged Cory's fears. "It's just another form of humiliation, and there are *plenty* of subs into that. You like the idea of being made to do something you don't wanna do, things you're maybe ashamed of liking, right?"

Cory nodded silently.

"As long as you had talked about it beforehand, set your boundaries, there's no reason you can't do things like that. It's all about trust." Carl smiled before continuing. "Cory, I want to apologize to you for my part in what happened the first time I met you. I didn't exactly have all the info at the time, but I probably could have used some better judgment in the store that day. I'm glad you boys have worked through some of your problems and figured out that you want to try things again, but..."

"But what, Sir?" Derek prodded when Carl trailed off.

"You boys have been through a lot lately. Together and on your own. And aren't you all supposed to be going off to college soon?" Carl reasoned. "I'm not so sure this is something you should be taking on right now. Maybe you need to slow down for a bit."

"Come on, Sir. You can't be serious." Derek looked like he might jump to his feet. "If you won't help us, we can find somebody else who will."

"That a threat, boy?" Carl cocked an eyebrow at Derek's brazen display.

"No, Sir, but…" Derek backed down with his tone but kept pushing. "The toothpaste is already out of the tube. We can't squeeze it back in. Plus, you already agreed to keep training me. Isn't there some kind of lesson about keeping your word?"

"Alright." Carl sighed. These boys were gonna run him ragged. "But that means things progress at my pace. If I tell you you're not ready for something, I expect you to listen to me."

"Yes, Sir." Derek nodded, as did Cory. "Thank you."

"Derek, why don't you go show Cory the training room I introduced you to after our first session?" Carl turned his focus to the silent boy on the couch. "I think Nic and I need to have a chat."

Nic's eyes grew wide, silently pleading Derek for help.

"Uh." Derek looked between Nic and Carl for a moment. "Yes, Sir. C'mon, Cory." Derek led the boy out of the room.

The room fell silent as Carl looked over the nervous boy on the couch. Nic swallowed. *What's gonna happen now?*

"Calm down, boy. It's not like I'm gonna shove a dick in your mouth." Nic coughed and sputtered in surprise, making Carl laugh as he stumbled for a retort. "I'm teasing. You need to relax."

"I'm not…" Nic huffed. "You just caught me off guard. Are you just trying to fuck with me? I'm fine."

"Yeah, well, you don't exactly look fine. Or like you wanna be here at all." Carl cut to the chase. *No sense in wasting everyone's time.* "You sure this is something you wanna do?"

"What?" Nic genuinely didn't know what Carl was getting at. "Of course I do. That's why I'm here."

"That was the first thing you've said since you sat down," Carl pointed out. "On top of everything I've seen and heard about, I'm just not sure this is really your thing."

"Look, I'm not backing out of anything," Nic said firmly. "I just didn't come over here looking to be trained like those other two."

"Well, good, cause I'm not looking to train you," Carl told him flatly. "This isn't about that. This is about you not being comfortable with gay sex. I made a joke about you sucking dick, and you choked on the *air*."

"Because I'm not—!"

"I don't care what you wanna call yourself, kid," Carl cut Nic off quickly. "But you need to get over the fact that you've been having gay sex for the past six months. Because that's what it is, Nic. You may not be gay, but the sex you've been having very much is. And if you wanna keep doing what you're doing with those two, you're gonna need to get over your hangups about it. Because I can tell you now, it's gonna get really old really fast, especially when those two start exploring their options with all the new-found freedom college is gonna bring. You won't be in high school anymore. It sounds like a cliché, but it's very easy to drift apart once you're not forced to see someone every day."

Nic was quiet for a moment as he took in Carl's words. "We only have the rest of the summer together anyway. What does it matter?"

"Ah, yes. Giving up before you even try. I remember my own football coach teaching us that one," Carl said dryly before taking a breath, his features softening. "Kid, I wish I could give you some more help here, but I'm sorry to say that I am 100% a gay man. I never questioned myself or had to deal with this sort of internal conflict. I'm not saying you gotta run home and come out of whatever closet you may be in, but you need to at least try to figure out a way to get comfortable with this. For all of your sakes."

Nic said nothing, again taking in the older man's words, before nodding slowly.

"You drove here, right?" Carl waited for Nic to respond yes before continuing. "Okay. I am going to go back to my playroom now and use Cory to teach himself and Derek about bondage and something called 'impact play.' You can either head back with me and maybe learn some things yourself, or you can head out now. I'll make sure those two get home safe. I'm sure they'd understand." He paused for a moment before standing, waiting for Nic's decision.

Nic looked up at the dom, wracking his brain over what to do. His immediate instinct was to take the out he'd been offered. Derek and Cory knew he wasn't into coming over here. He could just catch up with them later at home. On the other hand ... Carl had a point. The last time Nic had tried to avoid these feelings, they took the first drunken opportunity they could to explode all over Cory. Not to mention the "bondage" part *did* sound like it could be fun. Was he doing this? He was doing this.

"Let's do this." He stood.

"Atta boy." Carl smiled before turning and leading the way to the playroom.

The door at the end of the hall was open, a dim light spilling out onto the carpet. Carl pushed the door the rest of the way open as he walked in with Nic behind him, revealing Derek pointing out a few of the implements hanging on the wall to Cory—namely a couple of paddles. The two turned around when they heard Carl entering.

"Hey, Sir, just showing him some of the—" Derek stopped mid-sentence when he saw Nic standing there. "Oh. Hey, man." He and Cory had both figured he'd be looking for any excuse to get out of here.

Nic nodded his head in Derek's direction but said nothing. He didn't know what *to* say. He was taken back by the scope of the room. It was big. And full of ... stuff. Stuff Nic had never seen before. He looked around wide-eyed at the whips and floggers hanging from the wall, the cuffs and ropes on a table, the leather benches he could only imagine were at the perfect height to bend someone over. There was even a giant wooden cross against the far wall... Nic swallowed dryly. He suddenly didn't know what to do with his hands. Did he usually stick them in his pocket or...?

Carl, sensing that Nic was overwhelmed and figuring it was possible that he would just be watching this time around, pushed ahead with his original plan.

"Like what you see boy?" Carl directed the question at Cory.

"Yes, sir." Cory nodded. "You have a really awesome playroom." Cory was in awe of the treasure trove of toys surrounding him, things he'd only fantasized about using before.

"You tend to amass a collection over the years." Carl walked over to the pair, running his hand along a leather bench before standing next to the two boys. "Not having any children helps. A lot more disposable income. So, I know what I've got planned, but was there anything in the room that caught your eye?" He gave Cory a wink.

"Um..." Cory looked down, blushing and muttering. "Maybe the fuck machine...?"

"Oh yeah?" Carl let out a little laugh. "I don't think you're quite ready for something like that, but we'll work you up to it." He looked from Cory to Derek, then behind him at the still silent Nic. "You boys ready to start?"

Derek and Cory looked at each other before nodding.

"Alright, come on over here, boy." Carl led Cory to one of the leather benches. He reached underneath and adjusted its height until the top of it was at Cory's waist. At the opposite end were a pair of D-rings, hinting at what was to come. Carl walked over to a set of drawers against the wall, opening one and fishing out a set of cuffs identical to the pair Derek had purchased from Good Vibrations months before. He held them in front of Cory. "Remember these?"

"Yes, sir." Cory smiled. He had some fond memories of those cuffs.

"Good. Now strip," Carl ordered.

Caught off guard for only a second, Cory began removing his clothing until he was only in his jockstrap, folding them on a nearby chair and returning to Carl. Taking him by the shoulder, Carl guided Cory to face the bench, gently pressing on his back to bend him over. He whistled, taking the opportunity to give Cory's ass a squeeze before moving to the other side of the bench.

"Derek, come over here and help me tie your boy down." Carl grasped Cory's left wrist, securing one of the cuffs. As Carl stretched Cory's arm toward the D-ring on his side of the bench, Derek followed suit with his right, using the provided carabiner to hold Cory in place. Cory obliged the two doms, breathing in the scent of the leather as he laid his head to the side against the bench.

"Good boys." Carl gave Cory's ass an affectionate pat. "Now, according to what Derek's told me, the last time you were on the receiving end of a spanking, you seemed to enjoy it more than just a little. That right?"

Cory's body flushed slightly, remembering the night of his punishment in the cabin, the dual spanking he had received from Derek and Nic, and the amazing sex they had right after.

"Yes, sir." He bit his lip.

"Good." Carl gave Cory's round butt a quick smack. "In a minute, I'm going to go get some toys off the wall there and show these two how to use them on you. But before we get to that, what's your safeword, boy?"

Cory snorted loudly a moment before he and Derek cracked up. Carl looked around confused and turned to Nic, who took a second to realize what they were laughing at.

"Fuck you guys." He turned to Carl to answer his unspoken question. "It's *bacon*," he gritted.

"Ooo-kay." Carl turned back to the two laughing boys who were catching their breaths. "There's a story there I'm gonna wanna hear about later. But moving along—your safeword is 'bacon.' You say that at any time, and we stop everything. But if you just need a breather or just want to slow down for a minute, I want you to say 'yellow.' Do you understand?"

"Yes, sir." Cory nodded as best he could in his trussed-up state. "Bacon and yellow."

"Good boy." Carl walked over to the wall, retrieving a medium sized leather paddle—not quite a frat paddle but bigger than one for ping pong. He walked back to Cory and laid the cool piece of leather across his ass as he began speaking to Derek and Nic. "Now, with paddles, unless the sub is one more into pain—which I don't think Cory is—you'd generally want to save a wooden paddle for punishment. Leather is softer and has a lot of flexibility in how you use it." He grasped the paddle by the handle again and rubbed it around Cory's ass slowly before giving it a few teasing taps.

"You want to start slowly. Since we're going to be using a few different things, we're just gonna make this ass a little pinker for now." As he finished speaking, Carl drew the leather back before bringing it down smoothly onto Cory's left cheek, a light *smack* followed by a small yelp of surprise from Cory. Carl repeated the action on the right and then quickly peppered the flesh before him with four more hits.

"Derek." Carl nodded the dom-in-training over, giving Cory a chance to breathe as he showed Derek how to hold and swing the paddle. "Alright, give him a few. Spread them around. Don't focus on one area for too long." Carl stroked a hand over Cory's slightly pinkened posterior, earning him a shiver as the sensitive skin was stroked. "It's less about the pain and more about making the skin feel sensitive. Then you can have more fun with it later." He gave a not-so-gentle squeeze, eliciting a whimper. "Go ahead."

Derek was overly cautious his first few swings, the paddle landing with little more than a gentle thud. When he finally found the right amount of force to use, he was rewarded with a nice *smack* reverberating from Cory's rump and a whimper from his mouth. Smiling to himself, Derek matched what he had seen Carl do moments ago, spreading the paddle's slaps across Cory's skin.

Cory squirmed as he was paddled, each *thwack* of the leather making him jump. It stung, but only a little, and the longer it went on, the duller it felt. He could hear but couldn't stop the mewling coming from his mouth. He was thankful for the wrist cuffs because he wasn't sure he would have been able to control his hands. And he certainly wasn't able to control his cock, which he felt slowly filling up as his ass was assaulted.

"Alright, let him breathe for a second," Carl directed before gently rubbing his hand across Cory's abused butt, making him suck in his breath sharply. "See? Nice and warmed up."

Derek followed suit, smiling as he noted the heat of the flesh in his hand and eliciting further whimpers from Cory.

He ran his fingertips across Cory's flank, teasing the boy as he felt the warm throb of his ass. He stroked his fingers down the crack of Cory's ass, not quite reaching his hole, and Cory tried to push back onto them.

"Alright, he's ready for a few more." Carl chuckled.

Derek resumed striking Cory's ass with the paddle, swatting him a dozen more times before pausing to give Cory another breather. As he played with Cory's ass once more, Carl turned to Nic.

"You wanna give it a shot?" he asked, Nic looking a little less like a deer in headlights now.

"Yeah. Sure." Nic nodded his head, talking to himself more than Carl.

He stepped forward and reached for the paddle, feeling the weight of it in his hand. As he got into place, Derek stepped to the side to give him some room to work. Nic took aim, almost like he was practicing a golf swing, before he made the first *smack*.

Cory yelped softly in surprise, and Nic would be lying if he said that sound didn't make his dick twitch. Grinning, he drew the paddle back and gave him another. And another.

"Mmmf." Cory whined as his ass was once more paddled.

After a few more strikes, that dull, warm feeling started to return. His dick was still half hard, and it felt like it had been leaking. A fog started to gather in Cory's head, the rhythm of Nic's strikes causing him to zone out. He didn't even realize Nic had stopped until he felt a hand stroking his back.

"You doing alright, boy?" Carl asked gently as he brought Cory's mind back to the surface.

"Mmmm. Yes, sir," Cory answered almost sleepily. He was doing pretty good right now. His ass throbbed, but it wasn't an entirely bad feeling. Everything felt warm.

"You did good, boy," Carl praised. "Going to let you rest a minute before we try something else."

Carl returned the paddle to its spot on the wall before turning to Derek and Nic, who had taken a spot next to Cory, each with a hand on him, stroking from back to ass. Carl smiled and turned back to the wall, this time removing a short black flogger. Before walking back over, he paused, deciding to remove his shirt. No reason not to get comfortable...

"You boys ready for round two?" Carl walked back to end of the bench, flogger in hand.

Derek and Nic exchanged a glance. Yeah, they were both enjoying the hell out of this. Each boy had a sizeable lump forming in his pants. Squeezing Cory's hot ass and making the boy whimper only made them harder.

"Yes, Sir," Derek answered for the both of them. He was eager to see what, or who, would come next.

"What about you, boy?" Carl checked in with Cory one more time. "You ready for more?"

"Yes, sir." Cory sounded more clear-headed. He attempted to straighten his position out as best he could.

"Alright. Now, this," Carl dragged the flogger over Cory's ass lightly as he spoke, "is a flogger. It might look a little scary at first, but when done properly, a good flogging can feel more pleasant than that paddling you just received."

Carl motioned for Derek and Nic to move back and give him some space. He raised the flogger to just over his shoulder. Then, in a quick and steady motion, he brought the tails of the tool down, swiping them across the sensitive skin of Cory's ass.

Cory gasped, surprised at the new sensation. Like that paddling, it stung, but just barely. It was like dozens of little slaps cascading against his skin. Cory whimpered as Carl repeated the action, switching between his left and right cheek. Every time the flogger landed, his skin felt like it was getting warmer, more sensitive. The noises he was making were starting to get longer, if not louder.

"These are fun to look at and a good visual for the parts of the skin that will be more sensitive." Carl paused after the sixth strike, tracing the lines he was creating on Cory's ass with his finger and making the boy squirm. "The marks won't last too long, but I'll give you some lotion to help with the soreness when we're done," he explained before moving back into position to continue.

Cory relaxed his head against the bench, closing his eyes and letting the dull warmth overtake him. His body squirmed as the flogger rained down on his ass and thighs, and he made no attempt to control it. It was like a dance, the slap of the leather, followed by the sting of the tails, and then the heat of his ass.

Cory was soon lulled him into a warm fog. If it weren't for Carl checking in on him every few minutes, Cory was sure he would have zoned out entirely. It barely registered when Carl handed the flogger to Nic to try, only realizing that he had a different assailant when he saw Carl standing in front of him as the flogger continued to come down.

Nic adjusted himself in his pants as he gave the flogger to Derek. This was really not something he expected to get into. The rough sex, the risky public stuff—sure, that made sense. But he never saw himself with all the leather and whips and chains and stuff. He still was not sure he did. But this was hot, especially the way Cory reacted, how he was restrained, taking everything they gave him. There was no question he liked it—his cock was hard and pointing between his legs, steadily leaking.

Derek took the same position Carl and Nic had before him. He could sense they were almost done—Cory didn't have much skin left that was untouched. Paranoid over causing him any unnecessary pain, he was cautious about the force behind his swings. He took his time teasing between flogs, finding new ways to make Cory shiver.

When he felt Cory had had enough, Carl motioned for Derek to stop, taking the flogger and placing it on the bench for a moment.

"Nice work, boys." He undid Cory's wrist restraints as he spoke.

"You back with us?" Carl stroked Cory's hair. "Derek, there should be a mini fridge behind you. Grab a bottle of water for Cory."

Derek retrieved and tossed a bottle to Carl, who opened it and helped Cory lean up to drink.

"Mmmhhh." Cory's eyes fluttered open as he stretched and then relaxed his arms.

"How you feeling, boy?" Carl asked as Cory came to his senses.

"Good. Warm. Horny." Cory's relaxed state gave him no reason to answer anything but honestly.

"I bet. Did you enjoy that?" Carl asked as he walked back around to Cory's back end.

"Yes, sir," Cory said dreamily.

"Good." Carl rubbed his back. "You just relax and finish your water."

"Now boys," Carl continued his lesson with Derek and Nic. "Something I know you've not been doing any of is aftercare. Aftercare is a very important part of *every* kink scene. Whenever you finish up a scene, no matter how 'light' it may have seemed, you need to take a moment—for your sub *and* yourself—and check in with each other."

"Sometimes, when a scene gets *too* intense, it can leave a mark on you. And I'm not talking about the flogger," Carl joked, helping Cory to more water. "All the endorphins and adrenaline can mask serious injuries, not to mention that the sudden drop in both can have your body shaking with chills. And that's not even getting into the mental and emotional issues that can happen."

"Fuck, what kind of stuff do you think we're into?" Nic was offended by the implication. "It's not like we're gonna do something dangerous."

"It doesn't have to be dangerous. Think about it," Carl continued. "You spend an hour or two being degraded and abused, even if they are things you *love*, they are still going to affect you. And I'm serious about this being for the dom as much as it is the sub, because doing the degrading and abusing can be just as hazardous. You need to be just as careful with yourself."

"That's why you're always making us take those breaks during training, even when I tell you I feel fine," Derek wonders aloud.

"Exactly." Carl nods his head. "The most important thing is that you communicate. You have to be honest and tell each other how you are feeling, or else you won't be able to take care of each other properly. Understand?"

"Understood."

"Got it," both tops agreed in unison.

"Now then, how are you feeling, boy?" Carl asked Cory.

"Good, sir," Cory answered. "I think I'm ready for more."

"Perfect." Carl walked around to Cory's rear. "Now, don't move a muscle."

Carl suddenly took a kneeling position behind Cory, an action which had both Nic and Derek tilting their heads curiously. He then placed both hands on either side of

Cory's ass, spread him wide, and dove face first at his hole. Time to show these boys how it was done.

Cory yelped loudly as he felt Carl's wet tongue swipe across his hole. His hands scrabbled at the bench, unsure of whether he was trying to get away or push himself back farther. Not that it mattered because Carl's hands spreading him open were also holding him in place. Cory wasn't even able to form words. Every time he opened his mouth, he moaned.

Carl lapped his tongue over Cory's hole in slow repeated movements. He held the boy steady as he squirmed, the sensations no doubt driving him wild. Carl sensed that he hadn't been rimmed before, and he was happy to be the first. He held the boy's ass firmly, squeezing just enough to make the sting from the paddling and flogging apparent. This wasn't just for Cory's benefit—he needed to show Derek and Nic the proper way to do this. He started off nice and slow, running his tongue around the rim of Cory's hole.

Cory tried relaxing into the bench, able to do little else. It wasn't easy. Every movement of Carl's tongue felt like electricity on his hole. His cock throbbed between his legs. This felt so fucking good. Carl's beard scratched against his ass as he worked his tongue, made all the more apparent by his sore and sensitive ass. And then he felt Carl's tongue go *inside* of him.

Carl grinned as best as he could with his tongue buried in Cory's ass. The boy made a near-inhuman noise as Carl began to slowly tongue-fuck his hole. Carl slowly pumped his tongue in and out, stopping to lick across the outside here and there. Cory was practically a puddle, and with one final swipe of the tongue, Carl stood.

"You like that, boy?" he asked, wiping the spit from his beard.

"Uh-huh," Cory agreed, still splayed out across the bench.

"I'm guessing neither of you has ever done that for him?" Carl turned to Nic and Derek, who after watching Carl's "practical" display were standing slack-jawed and stiff-dicked. They hadn't even considered doing something like that to Cory before or what it might be like to see in action. Derek knew from personal experience that it felt great, and though he'd never admit it, Nic was curious about what it felt like himself.

"Uh... no," Derek answered for them both. "It's pretty much always been him on us."

"That seem very fair to you?" Carl knew they knew the answer.

"I guess not, but..." Nic was reasoning with himself more than Carl. "It just never really worked out that way. I don't exactly wanna suck a dick."

"Not talking about sucking dick." Carl cocked an eyebrow. "You've never eaten the ass of one of the girls you've fucked?"

Nic didn't have a response to that. He had, of course, on multiple occasions. He was no slouch about going down on a girl, and as long as they had showered, he only had to move a few inches lower... But this was a guy's ass, not a girl's. It wasn't the same thing. Right? It was definitely hairier. And precariously close to Cory's balls. Still, watching Carl eat him out and seeing the way he writhed and squirmed, the way he was still kind of out of it now—that was pretty hot.

Maybe he just needed to jump in the deep end.

Nodding to himself, Nic walked past Carl to Cory, kneeling in front of his ass. Wordlessly, he spread the cheeks before him, revealing Cory's furry and furled hole winking back at him. Definitely hairier.

"If it helps, just think of it like you're eating a pussy," Carl offered. "Hell, for some boys, that's exactly what they wanna hear."

Nic nodded. That could work. But for now... Nic closed his eyes, tightened his grip, and dove in. It was strange at first. Not bad. Other than the extra fuzz, it wasn't really that different from the last time he did this to Amy. Nic heard the boy sigh happily as he ran his tongue across Cory's hole. Unsurprisingly, he soon found that the more he did this, the more noise Cory would make.

Cory moaned as Nic ate him out for the first—and hopefully not last—time. His eyes were closed, and he bit his lip as he felt the wet, warm tongue slide across his hole. He couldn't believe Nic was actually doing this to him—but somehow he'd get used to the idea. They just might need to practice a lot. Cory could tell Nic was still testing the waters a little, his movements slow and tent—!

"Oh fuck," Cory muttered the curse as he felt Nic's tongue dive into his hole. Nevermind *tentative*.

"Having fun, boy?" Cory turned his head to see Carl standing on his other side, hard cock jutting from his open fly.

"Uh ... huh," Cory breathed and nodded his head in assent.

"Good. Now why don't you give me a nice thank you for that rim job?" Carl posed the rhetorical question, hand already on Cory's head and pulling him toward his cock at the bench's edge.

Cory's mouth, already half open, wrapped around the head of Carl's thick prick. With Cory able to think about little else besides his ass, Carl rocked his hips slowly back and forth, feeding Cory his dick a few inches at a time. The boy concentrated on watching his teeth, but could do nothing about the steady stream of moans and groans spilling from behind them. As he used Cory's mouth, Carl nodded Derek over to join him, the two switching between Cory's mouth and his free hand as Nic worked.

Nic kneaded Cory's ass as he fucked his tongue in and out of Cory's hole. Carl was right. It *was* just like eating pussy. Nic *loved* eating pussy—he didn't understand why some guys didn't—and what he was doing here was really no different. He was using his mouth and tongue to tease and work the hole he was soon going to fuck. Just like he always did. Nic growled and smacked Cory's ass as he dove his tongue in even farther, living for every reaction and sound he pulled from Cory. He could easily lose track of time doing this.

"Does anyone want any more of this?" Nic lifted his head, punctuating his question with a smack to Cory's ass. "Because if not, I need to know where the lube is."

Carl and Derek looked between them and shook their heads. Both were happy to see Nic getting so into things and didn't want to do anything to impede that.

"Middle drawer, right side." Carl pointed at the set of drawers he pulled the cuffs from earlier.

Nic nodded, taking off his shirt as he retrieved the lube and undoing his fly on the way back. Nic ground his shaft against Cory's ass, the heat from the abused backside warming his groin. He watched Cory do his best to swallow Carl's beer-can cock as he applied lube to his own dick, wiping his hand along the inside of Cory's ass to help lube him up. Then, he slapped his hard cock against Cory's spit-slick hole and pressed forward.

"Mmmhhh…" Cory moaned happily around Carl's dick. His hole was so relaxed from the double rimming he had received earlier, Nic encountered almost no resistance as he pushed his cock in. Arching his back as best he could, Cory sighed happily when he felt Nic bottom out, their thighs pressed together.

Nic looked down at his cock, buried deep inside a freshly paddled behind. He roughly kneaded the abused flesh, enjoying the way Cory squirmed further as his dick rubbed against Cory's prostate. He moved his hips back and watched his slick cock pull from the hole, dragging skin and fur along with it before being pushed back in to the hilt.

Nic grabbed Cory by the hips as he sped up his pace, squeezing the flesh as he held his boy steadily. With each thrust of his cock, Cory's pink ass would bounce and jiggle, occasionally enticing Nic to spank it once more. He soon found the momentum he needed and the *real* pounding of Cory's hole began.

Cory was moaning steadily as he was fucked, the slap of Nic's hips against his ass adding just a little bit of sting to each thrust. He could feel the familiar tightness start to well up in his groin and knew Nic would be fucking him through an orgasm soon. The cock in his mouth was once again swapped, and he greedily lapped up the accumulated precum from the tip before relaxing his mouth as he was fucked from both ends. He'd been in this position so often that it almost felt natural—as did the anal orgasm he started to have at the same time.

Nic was getting close himself. He felt the tight squeeze of Cory's hole as it spasmed, feeling triumphant for making his boy cum on his cock once more. As he looked down, the sweat from his forehead dripped onto Cory's back. The rest of his chest was just as sweaty. The room was filled with the musk of the four men enjoying each other's bodies. Looking up, Nic saw that Carl and Derek were now engaged in a lip lock, Carl squeezing Derek to his side tightly as Cory swapped between their cocks. That was unexpected, but it didn't matter—Nic was cumming.

"Oh, fuck. Gonna load you up, Cor." Nic grabbed Cory by the hips tightly once more as he slammed his cock in and out erratically, grinding his cock in at its deepest and blasting his load inside. He tried to push each shot farther in than the last, the scratch of his pubes irritating Cory's sore ass even more—not that he minded. Nic bent over, holding himself up with his arms as he half-draped himself over Cory. The sweat continued dripping onto the back of the thoroughly fucked-out boy beneath him, rising and falling as he caught his own breath.

Almost tripping over himself, Nic slowly pulled his cock from Cory's hole with a soft *squelch*, the hole closing tightly behind him to prevent anything inside from escaping. After looking around in a daze, Carl pointed Nic to the room's attached bathroom, chuckling as the boy stumbled away. He fucked *himself* stupid. Switching gears, Carl looked down at Cory below him, who was still slowly nursing on the head of Carl's dick.

"Alright, boy, you stay right there. You got two more loads to take," Carl said as Derek walked around to replace Nic, who easily slipped inside the cum-filled hole.

Rather than respond, Cory simply arched his back and swallowed more of Carl's cock.

He took his training very, *very* seriously.

# CHAPTER 18

For the boys, the next few weeks flew by. First, there was finals and then their actual high school graduation. Everyone's parents were there, even Derek's, watching them cross the stage in their caps and gowns. Cory almost convinced Nic to go naked under his as a dare until Derek found out and said no. It was a weird event, one purely for show. They wouldn't even get their diplomas until the week after in the mail. But tradition was tradition.

The trio made frequent trips to Carl's house, each one with new experiences. Since that first day, Cory had been flogged, paddled, switched, and spanked with all sorts of implements. Carl had tied him in all manner of positions: on his back, on his stomach, bent in two. Derek and Nic had no trouble mastering a few of the quick and simple knots he taught them. And the last time they were there, Carl finally brought out that fucking machine...

Cory blushed as he thought back to the previous weekend. It was only for twenty minutes on the lowest setting, with a dildo not even half as big as some of the real dicks he'd taken before, but fuck if that machine didn't have

Cory's hole cumming over and over. He was a twitchy mess by the time they untied him. And that was before they all took turns fucking him again.

Cory looked at the clock and debated whether or not he had enough time to ask Derek or Nic to jerk off—thanks to Carl and his training, that rule was in effect again. He sighed—Mom said dinner would be ready soon, so probably not. Sitting at his desk, Cory knew he was just looking for ways to procrastinate anyway. He stared at the acceptance letters in front of him. Three of the colleges he applied to let him in with full scholarships. It was great, but Cory figured— *hoped*—that he'd only get into one, making his decision for him. Instead, he had to decide between three schools in three very different parts of the country.

Cory was terrible at making decisions. Derek and Nic didn't even bother asking him to pick a place to eat anymore. He'd hem and haw forever otherwise. And this was a much bigger decision than Burger King or Wendy's. He also hadn't talked to his mom yet about college, or leaving, or ... anything else. He was planning on talking to her that tonight— about college, that was. He had to—deadlines were closing in. He just needed to make a decision first.

That should be easy enough, right? Except they were all great schools with excellent computer science programs. There was the San Diego Technical Institute, located on the sunny and very gay-friendly west coast; the Technology Institute of Massachusetts, a school he'd heard about since he was a kid; and then finally John Adams University in Washington D.C., a city Cory had visited a few times as a kid and loved. Cory re-read the acceptance letters half a dozen times as he clicked through each school's website, looking for anything that might affect his decision.

"Cory!" Cory suddenly heard his mom's voice echo from the hallway. "Dinner's ready!" *Crap.* Putting down the letters, he walked to the kitchen to see his mom preparing a couple of plates for the two of them and followed her to the table.

The meal began in relative silence, the sound of forks and knives scraping over plates the only thing audible. Cory stared at his plate quietly, suddenly feeling much more awkward than he ever had at dinner before. Every time he tried to open his mouth to talk about college, he found himself shoveling more food in instead. *Why is this so weird?*

"So, have you decided on a school yet?" Julia asked without lifting her gaze from her plate.

Cory spluttered for a moment before regaining his composure. "Uh, n-no. Not yet. You knew about the acceptance letters?"

"I saw a few letters from schools in the mail, but I didn't want to pry. But you've been pretty quiet about it, and I don't think you have much time left to accept," Julia pointed out the obvious. "Now, if you're nervous about leaving home, HCC is right up the road, and we—"

"I got in. To three schools. Full scholarships," Cory cut his mother off before she tried selling him on the local community college again.

"Oh, honey, that's amazing." Julia stood and walked around the table to hug her son. "I knew you'd do it." She kissed him on the forehead before taking her seat again. "Which schools?"

"Um, San Diego Tech, TIM, and John Adams," Cory found himself mumbling, once again feeling awkward. He basically just told his mother he was moving across the country one way or another.

"Oh, wow. Those are all great schools, honey. I'm so proud of you." Julia smiled at her son warmly, if not a little sadly.

"Yeah, but..." Cory knew why she had that sad look. "They're all pretty far away from home."

"Oh, honey..." Julia came back around to his side of the table, this time with her chair. "Of course, I'm going to be sad to have you leave, but I always knew that it would happen one day." Julia squeezed her son's hand. "I figured it'd be right around now. I hope that's not something stopping you from picking a school."

"No, it's not that exactly." Cory squeezed his mom's hand back. "It's just weird, thinking about leaving. Not just you, but everything. High school, the town, my friends..." His not-quite-boyfriends.

"It's natural to miss all those things, sweetie," Julia reassured him. "But you're also going to learn and see so much more out there in the world. And you can always come back and visit. You *better* come back and visit."

"College just always seemed so far away. I can't believe it's already here." Cory frowned. "Everything is happening so fast."

"That's life, honey," Julia told her son. "One minute you're raising an adorable little boy, and the next, he's nearly dying in a rainstorm before he leaves for college."

"Ha-ha, Mom." Cory tried not to roll his eyes as she teased him.

"I'm serious. If I ever find out you're lost in the woods like that again, I'm putting a GPS tracker on you." Julia stood once more and moved back to her seat, resuming her dinner. "Now why don't you tell me about each school? Let's see if I can help you make a decision."

Cory looked at his mother fondly. He was really going to miss her. "Well, San Diego Tech just finished a new computer lab..."

"It's so nice being home," Linda said from across the table.

"I forgot how much I missed sitting at the dinner table with you both," Robert added.

"Yeah... Real great having you guys back," Derek droned as he absentmindedly pushed around the food on his plate. Ever since his parents returned, it had just been business as usual. They barely even asked him about the night of the storm. *What is the point of them coming home at all?*

"So, tell us about school, Derek," Linda started. "Did you pass everything alright?"

"I mean, you guys saw me graduate. What do you think?" Derek responded wryly. He knew he was acting like an ass, but he was really beyond caring anymore.

"Derek! Don't speak to your mother like that!" Robert admonished.

"Or what? You'll leave again?" Derek rolled his eyes at his father's reprimand. "Big fucking deal."

"Language!" Linda almost shouted from her seat.

"What has gotten into you?" Robert questioned his son.

"Seriously? *Seriously?!*" Derek put down his fork and looked his father in the eye as he spoke. "I dunno. Maybe having to live alone in an empty house while my parents were gone for *half a fucking year* has something to do with it. What do you think, *Dad*?"

"Derek, I..." Robert had to turn to his wife to break the intense eye contact. "We had no idea you felt that way."

"But that's no reason to speak to us—or anyone—that way," Linda sternly corrected.

"Sorry, Mom and Dad." Derek took a deep breath.

"Derek…" Robert started. "Your mother and I, we thought you liked the level of independence we were giving you. You seemed to thrive under it."

"When your brother was your age, he couldn't wait to get as far away from us as he could," Linda continued. "You're more than capable of taking care of yourself, so we thought you'd love having the house to yourself. We hadn't planned on staying away as long as we did, but more work kept coming in, and when we spoke, you seemed to be doing alright, so we just kept extending our stay."

"Yeah, I wanted space from you guys like any kid, but I didn't want to not see you for half a year." Derek's voice was softer than before. "I didn't have anyone to talk to. Ate every dinner and breakfast alone." Derek's voice dropped even lower. "Would you have even made it to my graduation if it wasn't for the phone call in the hospital?"

Derek's parents looked at each other silently for a moment, which was all the answer Derek needed.

"I'm so sorry, sweetie." Linda stood from her chair and walked to her son, hugging him.

"You're right." Robert soon joined his wife, hugging Derek from the other side. "We weren't thinking about you when we stayed away for so long, and we weren't here when you needed us. We are so, so sorry."

"Derek, when we thought you were lost or hurt," Linda pulled back to look at Derek's face, "we were beside ourselves. I walked right out in the middle of a meeting with a client."

"We dropped everything. Found the first flight out that we could," Robert added. "We are so happy you are safe."

"I just… I know I'm growing up and stuff, but I'm always going to need my parents." *It's a start,* Derek thought as he was hugged. "There's still things I don't know how to figure out on my own."

"We're sorry, son." Robert put his hand on Derek's shoulder. "I know we've missed a lot, but I promise, we're going to be here for you when you need us."

"Thanks, Mom. Thanks, Dad." Derek watched his parents returned to their seats. He wasn't exactly sold, but it was still nice to hear his parents apologize. He hoped things would be better now.

"So, Derek, tell us about what *has* been going on." Linda wanted her son to update her as much as he was willing. "What about colleges? I know you were thinking of applying to a few schools... Did you hear back?"

"Yeah, Derek. What about University of Columbia?" Robert jumped in, bringing up his and Linda's Alma Mater. "You're a legacy. They have to let you in there."

"No, Dad. I didn't even apply there." Derek sighed. He figured this would come up.

"What! Why not!?" Robert was incredulous.

"Because I don't want to go to business school like you guys." Derek was ready to fight them on this if he had to.

"Okay, Derek." Linda fixed her flustered husband with a gaze. "What do you want to go to school for then?"

"I honestly have no idea." Derek was smiling, mostly to himself. "But I can't wait to find out. So, some of the places I did get in..."

"Okay, so we have it narrowed down to these four, right?" Raphael looked over his son's shoulder at the computer screen.

"Yeah, Dad. I think these four are good." Nic clicked through the tabs he had open, each looking at a different college he had gotten an offer from. All four had decent football teams, but what interested Nic more was that all four had great athletic training and physical therapy majors, which Nic was starting to seriously consider for his future. He could still be involved in sports, but not running himself ragged doing it. He was actually glad he and his dad had that fight weeks ago now. Unlike his friends, he was feeling a little more confident about his future, at least educationally.

"Come on. Your mother is almost done with dinner. We can set the table." Raph patted his son's shoulder and led the way out of the room.

Before long, Nic's sisters had joined them, and the four of them were seated when Luciana entered the room carrying a large serving bowl of *ropa vieja*. Knowing there was more, Nic and his sisters ducked into the kitchen quickly to retrieve the rice and other side dishes, placing them around the bowl of meat and taking their seats.

Nic's mother said grace as she always did before everyone quickly went about filling their plates and eating. Dinners in the Herrera household were a traditional affair, something that was very important to Nic's mother and father. Not that they were quiet by any means, as the argument Nic's sisters were having to his right would attest.

"I am *not* driving her to school next year!" Gabriella was incensed. "You didn't make Nic drive me!"

"I don't want to take the bus anymore!" Next year would be Daniella's first year of high school, and her parents were expecting her to ride with her sister.

"By the time I got a car, you didn't *want* to ride to school with me," Nic pointed out. "You thought I was embarrassing."

"Only because you would always *go out of your way to embarrass me*." Gabby narrowed her eyes at her older brother. "You told everyone I was *born with a tail!*"

"Enough. Gabby, you're driving your sister to school," Luciana ended the fight. "Nic, stop tormenting your sister."

"Hey, I don't even go to the same school as them anymore!" Nic held his hands up in defense.

"Thank *god*," Dani added, glad to not have to repeat her sister's high school experience.

"Did you pick out a school yet, Nic?" Gabby asked before taking another bite.

"No, but, I'm close..." Nic was. There were just a few ... extenuating factors he needed to consider. "I'm actually gonna try to talk to the guys about it tomorrow."

"Aww, wanna get your boyfriends' opinions before you make any big decisions?" Gabby teased far closer to home than Nic was comfortable with.

"Shut up." Nic threw his napkin at his sister, which he hoped seemed like the appropriate reaction to have. That was a different conversation that Nic wasn't ready to have with anyone yet. "Maybe before I leave, I'll show Dani where you *think* you hid all the embarrassing baby pictures."

"*MOM!*"

The next day, Nic and Derek headed to Cory's house to hang out. With Derek's parents home, Cory was the only one with a place where they could get any privacy for the afternoon.

"Hey, boy," Derek greeted as they walked in, Nic ruffling Cory's hair as he closed the door behind them.

"Hey, sirs." Cory instinctively led them back to his room. "Wanna play some Smash Bros.?"

"Sure, Cor. Set it up," Derek requested. As Nic took a seat on Cory's bed, Derek sat at his desk. While Cory got the Switch ready, Derek took notice of the envelopes stacked on his desk—Cory's acceptance letters. None of them wanted to think about the future, their inevitable separation, but they really needed to. Time to put on his daddy pants, as Carl would say.

"So ... colleges," Derek started.

Nic's head perked up, and Cory stopped in his tracks at Derek's words.

"Yeah..." Nic mumbled as Cory turned around sheepishly.

The three sat in an awkward silence for a moment, the background noise filled with the video game's soundtrack.

"Look guys, I know it's hard, but not talking about it isn't gonna change anything," Derek said with a sigh. "We need to figure this out or at least let each other know what we're gonna do, right?"

"Okay, well..." Cory nodded, then took a seat on the other end of the bed. "Where are you guys thinking about going? Everyone applied and got in *somewhere*, right?"

"I, uh, have it narrowed down to four schools," Nic started first. "They're all offering me a football scholarship, but outside of that, they're pretty similar. Virginia State, UConn, John Adams, and Oklahoma. All have decent athletic majors, which is what I think I wanna do."

"I have *no idea* what I'm gonna do in college," Derek confessed. "I just applied to a bunch of random schools that seemed good, really. FCU, MassU, some school in New York, and John Adams, too."

"My acceptance letters are right there on the desk." At both boy's mention of John Adams, Cory's heart skipped a beat, but he didn't want to get his hopes up.

"TIM, San Diego ... and John Adams." Derek picked up the stack of three and thumbed through it before looking back and forth between Nic and Cory. "So, we all got into John Adams?"

"I guess we did." Nic was smiling.

"Does that mean...?" Cory let the question hang, still too worried about jinxing things.

"Guys..." Derek hated being a downer, but they needed to be realistic. "It would be awesome, but maybe picking out a college just because we can all go there together isn't the smartest idea?"

"Maybe not," Nic started reasoning. "But is there any reason we *shouldn't*? Is there a school either of you really had your heart set on? 'Cause I don't."

"I mean, living in California might be cool ... but I really did like all three schools," Cory responded.

Derek watched as his two friends rationalized what he was still sure his parents or Carl would say was a bad idea. A bad idea he very much wanted to try. *Maybe we could...*

"Okay." Derek took a breath before outlining his plan. "I still think picking out a school just because we can all go together isn't a great idea." Cory opened his mouth to argue, but Derek cut him off. "*But...* What if we all drove up and checked out the campus together? Road trip?"

All three boys looked between each other carefully, smiling.

"Road trip."

"Fuck, almost there, boy. Gonna feed you another load." Nic spoke through gritted teeth in the backseat of the SUV

Derek had rented. Cory was currently on his knees with his face buried in Nic's lap while Derek sat in the front driving.

"Mmmm," Cory moaned around Nic's dick as his head bobbed up and down.

"Alright, that's your second. We're grabbing something to eat and then we switch," Derek informed Nic as he watched the action in the rearview mirror. Derek reached down a hand to squeeze himself through his jeans. The sounds and occasional glimpses of Cory sucking Nic off in the back seat for the last hour had him all worked up.

"Fuck! Swallow it, boy!" Nic suddenly forced Cory's head down farther as he unloaded in his sub's throat. After he was done shooting, he relaxed in his seat as Cory cleaned the cum from his dick. "Of course, man. You're up next," Nic told Derek with a smile and a sigh then turned back to Cory. "Good boy."

"Thank you, sir." When he was finished, Cory sat back up in his own seat, wiping his mouth.

He was more than happy to service his doms on the road, as they had worked out that morning. In order to break up the monotony of doing all the driving, Derek and Nic agreed to switch off. Cory would have also been in the rotation, but his skills would be required elsewhere: in the backseat.

All day, between the random talks on the road and the pit stops for food, Cory had been on his knees sucking cock or bent over taking them in his ass. Nic had been the one to convince Derek that they should rent an SUV, one big enough that they could fuck in the back. Derek wasn't sold—his parents were covering this trip, and he was not about to explain a cleaning fee from the rental place because of Nic's jizz—but Nic swore he would cover it if anything happened.

After the boys had left the rental place, they pulled over and figured out how to move the seats, giving the boys a lot more "floor space" to work with. Nic would not stop making Bang Bus jokes for the first hour. Cory had made sure to clean out before they picked him up that morning and brought his douche with him in case he needed to "freshen up" while traveling. He had also brought plenty of lube and a few towels. Cory was learning to always prepare when it came to getting his ass stuffed.

"Ooooh, I want a burger," Cory requested as he re-buckled his seatbelt. He had insisted on skipping breakfast *and* lunch to his doms' consternation, wanting to make sure his prep work didn't go to waste. And considering the multiple loads he currently had situated deep in his guts, it was worth it.

"Burger it is," Derek accommodated, taking the next exit on the highway that had a diner listed.

The boys were more than happy to get out and stretch their legs for a minute before piling inside one of the small diner's booths. It was late in the afternoon, so they still had some daylight left. The boys dug into their burgers quickly, Cory's stomach happy to finally have something other than cum in it. After paying their tab, they all headed back to the car.

"There's a cheap motel that didn't look too creepy on Google like two hours up the road." Derek tossed Nic the keys before turning to Cory. "Now you, boy. Get in that back seat. I have a deposit I need to make."

"Yes, sir!" Cory opened the back door on the SUV and entered, yelping when Derek smacked his ass as he climbed in. As Nic pulled out and got back on the highway, Derek pulled Cory over to him in his seat, quickly attacking Cory's mouth with his own. Cory moaned as he kissed Derek back—he was really glad kissing was a normal part of his sex life now.

Before long though, Derek's real intentions became clear, and he pulled Cory away from his mouth, moving to kneel on the floor. Understanding what Derek wanted, Cory also lowered himself to the floor, removing the basketball shorts he was wearing (for ease of removal) and bending over the back row of seats, jock-clad ass presented for use. After discussing Derek and Nic's lecherous plans, Cory dressed with comfort and ease-of-access in mind.

Derek unzipped his pants, pulling out his cock which was quickly filling out. He reached into Cory's travel bag and pulled out their bottle of lube, stroking himself to full hardness while he moved behind the boy, kneeling between his spread legs. He slapped his cock against Cory's hole a few times, making him whimper with each wet smack. His hole was still open from use that day, one load from each of them already inside. Cory's hole twitched as he thought back to his two earlier fuckings.

Derek pushed forward, easily sliding into the wet hole in front of him. Hearing only Cory's happy groan of being filled, he quickly began to fuck the boy with long deep strokes. Looking down, he could see the white sticky cum from their earlier fun shining across his cock. As hot as it was, he was paranoid something would get on the seat. He'd just have to make this quick.

Cory felt as Derek took his ass in both hands and squeezed tight before switching to fucking him with short and fast thrusts. Cory buried his face in his arms as his noises got progressively louder with each scrape of Derek's cock over his prostate. He had no idea what had gotten into the two of them today, but Derek and Nic were damn near insatiable, fucking him to hell and back. Between the cock sucking and the fucking, Cory wasn't sure how either boy even had any cum left.

Looking into the backseat, Nic watched Derek's ass rise and fall as he pounded away. The slapping of skin on skin and Cory's muffled moans were making *him* horny again, and he kicked himself for not fucking Cory again on his last turn in the back. Nic groped his dick in his jeans. He hoped this motel was getting close...

Speaking of close, Cory was already there, curling his toes involuntarily as he felt his muscle start to tighten and his hole spasm. He bit into the seat as the orgasm was fucked out of him, groaning into the fabric. Instinctively, Cory reached down to feel the jock of his pouch, happy to find it dry except for a wet spot of precum. He hoped Derek didn't fuck him for too much longer, or he wouldn't be able to help it.

Cory's hole squeezing and massaging Derek's dick only drove him to fuck faster and harder, charging toward blowing his own load. The wet slide of his cock, the slapping of Cory's ass, even the long, low, continuous moans he was letting out, all those things made him hotter. Gripping both cheeks in his hands tightly, Derek barreled his hips forward, squeezing Cory against the seat as his load shot from his cock. He ground his hips against Cory's plump ass and covered his body, biting at his neck as Derek continued to unload deep within.

The sounds of an orgasm drew Nic's eyes to the back seat once more, watching the sweaty and heaving back of his best friend rise and fall, hearing the sounds of lips on skin as he necked with their shared sub. Cory's only movements were the occasional twitch of a leg, and his only sounds a whimper each time Derek's cock shifted inside of him.

*Seriously, where the fuck is this motel?*

"Damn, you guys couldn't wait for me to get back?" Derek quickly shut the door behind him as he re-entered the motel room with a bucket of ice.

On the bed, ignoring his entrance, were Nic and Cory, *in flagrante delicto*. Fucking, that was. Cory was on his back, legs wide and pushed back by Nic as he leaned over Cory, cock planted firmly in his hole. The two were lip locked, kissing each other hungrily as Nic pounded Cory into the mattress. Cory was surprisingly flexible and seriously considering taking up yoga in the near future. Maybe he could look up the Kama Sutra later...

"Fuck! Your hole is so fucking sloppy," Nic growled into Cory's ear as his hips slammed down. "Gonna make it even *sloppier.*"

Cory's hands scratched at Nic's back when Nic started to suck and bite on his ear. *Oh, fuck, I'm gonna cum again.* As hot as it was, Cory had to admit getting fucked in a bed was better than anywhere else he'd done it so far. He was *so* happy when they made it to the motel for the night—with an actual bathroom and a shower—but Nic was even happier.

When they first entered the lobby, he was tapping his feet impatiently as he waited for Derek to finish checking them in, nearly power-walking to the room with Cory as soon as he had the key. He threw Cory on the bed once they were inside and told him to strip—an order with which Cory happily complied. Derek watched the two start to make out while he grabbed the ice bucket but was still surprised to find that things had already progressed to the "balls deep" portion of the evening.

Cory suddenly felt Nic's body seize up above him, muttering a curse into his ear. Nic slammed down with all his body weight as he blasted his cum into Cory. With each volley that followed Nic ground his hips down, trying to push more cock into Cory than even existed. He savored the warm, wet heat beneath him, striving to make sure every drop was planted as deep inside his boy as possible.

The two caught their breath as Derek undressed and joined them on the bed. Nic pulled out with a gentle *pop* and rolled over onto his back, allowing for sweat-soaked Cory to get some much-needed air. Derek smirked at the two as they caught their breaths and considered rolling Cory over for another round himself, but he wasn't sure he had anything left in him. For now, at least. Instead he just rolled onto his side and watched the two come down from their endorphin high.

Nic was the first one to get up and walk to the shower, washing himself quickly. Cory sat up a few minutes later when he walked back into the room, ready for his own turn. As he walked to his bag to grab some soap—hotel soap sucked—he walked back through the day's events and then the previous day as he walked to the shower. Then the weeks before that as he stood under the hot water. And the many months before, all leading up to this, as he washed the grime and dirt of the day from his body.

None of this, nothing that had happened to him, was even close to where Cory saw his life going a year ago. Things were up and down, fast and slow, encompassing some of the darkest moments of his life as well as the best. And he was only eighteen. Cory finished drying his hair and threw the towel over the shower rod. When he walked back in the room, he saw the boys had moved to the room's other bed— the one they were on previously had been deemed by Nic the "fuck bed"—Derek on his laptop and Nic on his phone. Throwing on a clean jock, he climbed on between the two of them. Derek was looking at Google Maps while Nic was playing some stupid game about candy.

"We should get there pretty early tomorrow," Derek informed them. "Plenty of time to wander around the campus before we take the tour my parents scheduled for us."

"Cool, cool, cool," Nic commented without looking up from his screen.

Cory chuckled. Perfect Derek and Nic. Control freak and lazy bum.

"Hey, guys?" Cory questioned the pair.

"Yeah?"

"Sup?"

"I just wanted to say... Even if this college thing doesn't work out, even if *we* don't work out ... you guys are my best friends. Even with everything that's happened, and anything that *might* happen... I'm just really glad you guys are in my life." Cory wasn't sure what brought on the sudden surge of emotion, hating that he started choking up toward the end.

"Aww, Cor." Derek closed his laptop and turned to face Cory, pulling him close. "I feel the same way. I hope that no matter what happens, we can still be there for each other. I love you guys." Cory felt himself be hugged on his left before turning to his right to look at Nic.

"Are you guys gonna make me say some sappy shit now too?" Nic mumbled sheepishly.

"Yes!" both boys said in unison.

Nic grumbled under his breath to himself before speaking to his bedmates a little louder.

"What?" Cory and Derek cocked their heads, unable to understand the mumbled speech.

"I said, I would really miss you guys if we ever had to split up, and I'm really glad we might not have to," Nic said louder and clearer, though with his eyes closed.

"Aww." Cory turned and glomped onto Nic. "You like us."

"Uuugggghhh, yes, I like you. Shut up," Nic fake-complained as he turned to hug Cory.

The three boys squeezed together in bed, forming a huggy and misshapen beast-with-three-backs. After a few more snuggles, the boys turned out the lights and settled in for bed. Tomorrow was an important day. It would be the day that could determine where they spent the next four years of their lives. The day that would determine whether or not they stayed together. None of them wanted to say it out loud, but they all knew they had a lot riding on tomorrow and John Adams University.

They had a pretty good feeling about things, though.

# CHAPTER 19

S hit. The zipper on Cory's suitcase wouldn't close. Grumbling to himself, he tried to shove the stubborn clothing down farther, just enough to shut the bag. Maybe if he sat on it... Ugh. He really should have done this last night. He was going to be late.

The sudden knocking on the front door indicated that he already was. *Dammit.* Cory continued to put the last of his things in boxes as he heard Derek's and Nic's voices greeting his mom before coming to his room.

"Shit, Cor. You're still packing?" Nic looked at the two open boxes on Cory's bed.

"I just kept remembering things I'll need, and time got away from me." Cory threw in some of the cords for his desktop computer and sealed one of the boxes. "I swear I'm almost done."

"Okay, finish up. Nic, let's get the cars loaded up." Derek grabbed one of the boxes Cory had laid on the floor and headed back out of the apartment, Nic toting a second box behind him.

Cory ran to his closet, deciding that he *did* want to bring his old video game consoles after all. He might run out of things to play, right?

The boy's college visit a month and a half earlier went well. More than well—the boys thought the school was wonderful. Cory loved the state-of-the-art computer lab and felt right at home when he had a chance to nerd out with some of the students there. Derek still had no major picked out, but the school had a ton of options, and he had been looking through the course catalog almost daily since. Even Nic was looking forward to seeing what playing on a college team would be like, impressed with the way he heard some of the other student athletes talk about their coach. The boys all sent in their acceptance letters the day after they got home.

And it wasn't just the school; the city itself was also great. After they finished touring the school, the boys wandered around downtown D.C., taking in the sights and trying not to seem like tourists—they were probably going to live here, after all. Once the boys had all made their decision, they quickly moved on to figuring out their living situation. While dorms could be an option, none of them really liked that idea. On top of the fact that one of them probably would have to have a stranger for a roomie, the general lack of privacy would get annoying pretty quickly when they wanted some alone time.

Luckily, one of the boys had a mom and dad who were currently feeling very guilty for being neglectful. With his parents' help, Derek and the boys found a nice three-bedroom apartment—one they wouldn't have been able to afford otherwise. It was a close distance to the school and had a shuttle they could take there and back, letting them save on gas money. Derek and Nic were both taking their cars with them, which is what they were loading Cory's boxes into now. The apartment was fully furnished, so they only had to bring things like clothes and electronics, nothing they needed to rent a truck for.

Cory packed the last of his things into the box and sealed it up before walking it outside to Derek and Nic. Nic took the box from him and loaded it into his backseat. Things were tight between their two cars, but they were just able to get everything in. After talking it over, Cory decided he would be riding with Derek, something Nic had groused about, not wanting to miss out on the opportunity for road head. Derek assured him that the next time they had to take two cars, Cory was all his. Cory was just hoping they could take another road trip in an SUV like last time sometime soon.

Not that the boys were planning on leaving the city any-time soon. Ever the prepared daddy, Carl had already put them in touch with a few friends of his in the area, most of whom were *more* than happy to take a trio of kinky young men under their wings. Carl knew that, with the distance, he wouldn't exactly be able to continue being hands-on with their training, so he wanted to make sure they would be well taken care of. He also gave them the names of the local dungeon and told them about some of the more kink-friendly gay bars, should they want to explore. They boys had already promised to visit when they came home next and tell him all about it.

Cory just walked back outside with another box when he saw a familiar car pulling up—Stephanie! Excited to see her, Cory put down his box to go over and hug her as soon as she was out of her car.

"Hey, nerd!" Stephanie squeezed her friend tightly.

"Says the girl who got into one of the best tech schools in the country," Cory responded. Steph would be headed to

TIM for her first semester any day now. "What are you doing here? Don't you leave, like, tomorrow?"

"I wanted to come say goodbye!" Stephanie looked over at the cars being packed. "And help pack, but darn—looks like you guys are almost done."

"Still plenty of boxes inside, Steph." Derek walked past the two to his car, loading some of Cory's clothes into the trunk next to his own.

Stephanie rolled her eyes but followed Cory inside, saying hello to Julia and grabbing a few boxes. Cory was glad he got to see her before he left. She was going to be in an entirely different state now. Who knew when he'd get to see her again? They promised to keep in touch, texting or calling whenever they could. He was really going to miss her.

Between the four of them, they finished loading Cory's stuff into the car in less than an hour just as they had planned. As they were wrapping up, two more cars pulled up to Cory's apartment—Derek's and Nic's parents. Derek's brought pizza, and Nic's brought his sisters. Everyone's parents had come out to get together and have lunch before sending their boys off.

Squeezing back into the small apartment, everyone sat around the living room together, talking, telling stories, and maybe a little crying. All five parents of course had advice for the soon-to-be college students—the best times to take classes, how to find cheap textbooks, and, of course, where to look for free food on campus. Derek's dad even gave them some info on joining a fraternity, something that at least Cory had no intention of doing. Plans were made for return visits over the holidays with Nic's mother outright making him swear that he would be back for Christmas this year. Once all the pizza was gone, it was time to go. Cory looked in his room one last time before he joined everyone walking outside to the cars.

"Alright, son. You drive safe, and you let us know as soon as you get there." Derek's father hugged him again.

"Derek, I know you're going to be far away, but your father and I want to make sure we are still there for you however we can." Derek's mother squeezed him from the other side. "Please, whatever you need—just talk to us. We'll answer in a flash."

"We're very proud of you," his father continued. "We love you, and you've shown us that you've grown up a lot, far more than we expected. We're very impressed by the man you're becoming."

"I love you guys too." Derek kissed his mother on the cheek one last time. "Promise to make you proud."

Nic's parents were currently speaking to him in rapid-fire Spanish, so fast that he only understood about half of it.

"Mama, I know, I know." Nic hugged his still-speaking mother close. "I'll call you as soon as we get there."

"And *every* Friday." She poked him in the stomach.

"And every Friday." Nic fought to not roll his eyes. He knew this was hard on her.

"Lucy, he'll be fine." Nic's father patted him on the shoulder. "We raised him well. It's time to let him grow up."

This, of course, set Luciana off on another crying fit, which her husband immediately attempted to soothe.

"Oh god, she's going to be like this for weeks," Gabriela commented, shaking her head. "This is all your fault."

"The last time she cried this much was when *Abuelo* died," Daniela added. "That lasted for almost a month."

"Okay, could we maybe not talk about me like I'm dying?" Nic requested. "You could at least *pretend* that you're gonna miss me."

Gabby sighed and crossed her arms, fixing her brother with a look before relenting and hugging him close.

"Of course, we're gonna miss you, idiot," Gabby grumbled. "Still your fault."

"I'm gonna miss you too," Dani told him when it was her turn for a hug. "But I'm not gonna miss Gabby moving into your room so I can *finally* have my own."

"I *had* my own room until *you* were born!" Gabby scoffed.

"You were *two*." Dani turned to look at her sister. "You didn't even know what a room was!"

Nic smiled. Between his parent's blubbering and consoling and his sisters' fighting, he felt right at home. He was gonna miss his family. At least a little.

"Cory, I just want you to know how proud I am of you." Julia held her son's face as she spoke to him.

"I know, Mom." Cory blushed at the praise.

"No, really." Julia's voice grew more somber. "Things haven't always been easy for us. For so long, it's just been the two of us. We've had to work hard... *You've* had to work hard to get here. And I just couldn't be prouder to have raised a son like you. You are going to do *amazing* things in college."

"Mom..." Cory wasn't sure what to say, lest he start crying himself. His mom had always put him first, always worked hard to make sure he had everything he needed. He hoped he could one day return the favor. "I love you. I promise to keep making you proud."

"I already am, Cory." Julia hugged her son again—there was never going to be enough. She released him, taking some tissues from Luciana to dry her face.

"Ugh. I don't wanna get all sappy and stuff," Stephanie said into Cory's ear as she hugged him. "It's been a really crazy year, huh?"

"Yeah, you could say that." Cory laughed, mostly to himself since none of the adults here had any idea just how crazy. "Hopefully college is a little ... less."

"I doubt that it will be." Steph gave a sad smile. "But I think we'll survive. But you better keep in touch. Not like that H.A.G.S. bullshit people wrote in our yearbooks."

"Same goes for you. I'll try and get my PC set up as soon as we get there so we can game together." Cory promised. "I wanna hear about all the hot nerds at TIM. With pictures!"

Once all the goodbyes were said and all the hugs passed out, everyone knew it was time. Derek, Nic, and Cory piled into their respective packed cars as their families stood and watched, waving them off. Before he got in his seat, Cory turned to give one last look at the apartment he had called home for the last decade and a half, thinking of all the times, good and bad, spent there. It felt like the end of an era.

Smiling, Cory wondered what the next one would hold.

# BOOK CLUB QUESTIONS

1.  Have you ever accidentally discovered someone else's porn? What did you do?

2.  Derek and Nic obviously make some very poor choices when they first learn Cory's secret. How would you have handled it in their shoes?

3.  Have you ever visited a sex store? Was it anything like Good Vibrations?

4.  Sex in public seems to be a specific kink for some of the boys. Have you ever had sex in a risky place?

5.  Carl acts as a mentor to the boys in the world of BDSM. Would you ever seek out a mentor for something like that?

6.  Nic uses being drunk as an excuse for how he treats Cory and to hide his feelings from even himself. What

is a time in your life you did something similar to avoid dealing with your issues?

7.  By the end of the story, it is apparent that someone was attempting to break up Cory, Nic, and Derek. Has anyone ever tried to split up you and a friend or a significant other?

8.  Nic has a difficult relationship with his father, which is tied heavily to the sport of football. Are there any sports or activities that have caused you problems with a friend or family member?

9.  Derek's relationship with his own parents is also strained, largely due to their absence. How would you have felt if you were left completely alone for your last year of high school?

10. Rather than call anyone for help, Derek and Nic rush into the woods during a dangerous storm to rescue Cory. How badly did you want to yell at them?

# AUTHOR BIO

Dominic N. Ashen is an author and avid reader with a heavy focus on gay BDSM-themed erotica. After spending his youth in search of books with characters who were more like himself—queer ones, specifically—he decided to start creating some of his own. His stories star queer protagonists, most often gay and bisexual men, and feature heavy themes of dominance, submission, and all sorts of kinks. Dominic loves the fantasy, sci-fi, and horror genres and has a penchant for writing longer stories in which he is able to weave in sex and kink right alongside the plot.

Website: https://www.dominicashen.com/
Patreon: https://www.patreon.com/dominicashen
Twitter/X: https://twitter.com/DomNAshen
Facebook: https://www.facebook.com/dom.n.ashen
Instagram: https://www.instagram.com/dom.n.ashen

www.ingramcontent.com/pod-product-compliance
Lightning Source LLC
Chambersburg PA
CBHW061900310726
48972CB00004B/1109